For Carmen Diestler
with my very best wishes
Abigail Mc Carthy.
September, 1986

BOOKS BY ABIGAIL MCCARTHY

*One Woman Lost* (1986)
*Circles* (1977)
*Private Faces, Public Places* (1972)

# ONE
# WOMAN
# LOST

Best wishes
Abigail McCarthy
Jane Gray Muskie
Oct. 1986

# ONE WOMAN LOST

Abigail McCarthy & Jane Gray Muskie

*New York* ATHENEUM *1986*

This novel is a work of fiction. Any references to historical events; to real people, living or dead; or to real locales are intended only to give the fiction a setting in historical reality. Other names, characters, places, and incidents either are the product of the author's imagination or are used fictitiously, and their resemblance, if any, to real-life counterparts is entirely coincidental.

Library of Congress Cataloging-in-Publication Data

McCarthy, Abigail Q. (Abigail Quigley)
   One woman lost.

   I. Muskie, Jane. II. Title.
PS3563.C336405   1986       813'.54      85–48140
ISBN 0–689–11804–X

*Published simultaneously in Canada by Collier Macmillan Canada, Inc.*
*Composition by Heritage Printers, Charlotte, North Carolina*
*Manufactured by Fairfield Graphics, Fairfield, Pennsylvania*
*Designed by Harry Ford*
*First Edition*

# ACKNOWLEDGMENTS

ALTHOUGH *many of the settings in this Washington-based novel are real places, all the characters are fictional. We want to note, however, that there are many wives of officials who do lead or take part in movements like our character Celia's Peace Work; we wish to pay tribute to them, and to hasten to add that they are much more effective than Celia and her friends and, unlike Celia, have the full support of their husbands.*

*We are indebted to the following: to the personnel of the services that guarded our families during various campaigns and assignments for information about the various protective services; to staff at the Association of Catholic Colleges and Universities for information on women's colleges; to staff at the Leadership Conference on Women Religious and to the many women religious of our acquaintance for information on religious communities; to Dr. Franklin E. Kameny for statistics on Washington's gay community; to standard reference works and to Dr. M. B. McCarthy for information on hospital procedure and the interaction of drugs; to Washington colorist Dann Hopkins and stylist Ko Kennedy for information about hairdressers to the famous; and finally, to the daily headlines and news programs that convinced us that almost anything is possible.*

# PART
# 1

# PROLOGUE

T H E vice-president's wife was deeply worried. Worse, she was beginning to be afraid. Something was very wrong. This morning, for instance. Here she was at the Capitol and she had no recollection of how she got there. Had she driven her own small car with the Secret Service men following as usual? Or had they brought her here in the official car?

She looked across the rotunda of the Old Senate Office Building at Alec McGregor, chief of the detail, for some hint, but Alec's impassive face was unchanged. His eyes were not fixed on her but went steadily from the elevator to the great curving stairway, and from there to the doorway through which the guest to be honored at the annual Senate Ladies' luncheon would soon enter. If anything was out of the ordinary— if she had acted strangely—wouldn't he be watching her? Just then, as if he sensed her looking at him, Alec's eyes met hers and a faint smile lit his face. Celia Mann felt a little better. Perhaps things had gone as usual. But why couldn't she remember?

"No time for woolgathering, Celia," said Polly Haskins at her elbow. Polly was the Democratic co-chair of the luncheon; Eleanor Parker from Iowa, the Republican.

"Hadn't you better start the line?" she went on. "The Cabinet wives will be here any minute and Her Ladyship will be right on their heels. You know how efficient and proper she is. She wouldn't like her Second Lady dithering around, would she?" The touch of cool mockery in Polly's voice bothered Celia. She and Polly had been very good friends not so long ago. But that was before Celia had had to withdraw from what had become Polly's pet project—Peace Work.

Just now Polly was right. President Lily Batchelder, America's first woman president, Mississippi born and bred, was proper as only a

3

Southern lady could be—and intolerant of delay. She prided herself
that she never kept anyone waiting and had made it silkily clear that
she in turn did not expect to be—ever. Celia Mann sighed. She hoped
that she and Polly would one day be good friends again. In the meantime she refused to acknowledge any change.

"Was I woolgathering, Polly?" she said aloud, beckoning to Sarah
Lindblad, vice-president of Ladies of the Senate, who should be next
to her in line. "I do seem to be getting more and more absentminded
lately. I keep coming to with a start and wondering what I'm doing. I
don't know why."

"Oh, we all do that," said Polly offhandedly. "That's nothing to
worry about." She turned to join Mrs. Parker at the door, where they
would greet the incoming guests and pass them on to the line of officers
constituting the welcoming committee. But her quick look at Celia had
been sharp and appraising.

It was a professional appraisal, Celia knew. Polly had been a nurse
at the Naval Hospital when she met and married Bill Haskins and she
still helped out at the hospital from time to time. Celia's worry deepened
as she remembered once again Polly's reaction of only a week ago. It
had not really been out of Celia's mind since.

I shouldn't have said anything, Celia thought—it's so easy to start
people talking. She knew she tended to let her guard down at those
weekly meetings. The only official duty actually prescribed by charter
for the vice-president's wife is presiding over the wives' organization
called Ladies of the Senate. It was a duty Celia liked. Because of her
own years as a Senate wife she felt comfortable and at home with the
other members, old and new.

Every Tuesday that she and her husband were in Washington, she
met with them without fail. She felt relaxed as she talked with those
seated near her and greeted those who came and went. They drank
coffee. They knitted and sewed, not because they thought their handiwork vital to the Red Cross—they knew better—but because it served
the purpose cooperative handiwork had always served for women: it
gave them a reason for getting together. In this case women disparate
in race and religion, in social and economic background, from all parts
of the United States and all points on the political spectrum, gathered
amicably and informally in the bare-bones room assigned to them in
the Senate Office Building. Friendships grew as they discussed the problems of political wifehood, traded experiences, sought and gave advice.

How had they gotten on the subject of pills? Oh yes, they had been talking about jet lag and their constant need to cope with its effects.

"If we're not flying home to Alaska for some fund-raiser or other, Fred comes into the house to say we're off to Singapore or Nairobi for some interparliamentary conference," said dark-haired Nora Greenfield from Juneau. "I like it—I love traveling—but my body never knows what time it is or when to go to sleep!"

Celia had mentioned the pills her doctor brother had given her to help her relax and sleep.

"I was getting headaches from all the stress of campaigning last fall, I guess," she said.

"Did I hear you say you were taking lithium to sleep, Celia Mann?" Polly broke into the conversation from the other end of the table. Celia had nodded.

"You *can't* be," Polly had continued, her voice as flat as her slow Alabama drawl would permit. "You *can't* be. You must mean Librium. Even that isn't prescribed much anymore, but it's a muscle relaxant and a tranquilizer—a lot like Valium. Lithium is strong stuff, for people in real trouble."

"I guess you're right, Polly," Celia had said peaceably, "I guess I mean Librium. It's for when I'm keyed up and can't sleep."

But it *was* lithium. She had checked the plastic container as soon as she got home. She had not taken any since.

Why had Jim prescribed it? Did her brother think she was in "real trouble," as Polly had put it? He had insisted that she was mixed up and unreasonable. And that she imagined things.

It would be no use asking him about it. Dr. James Fifield was touchy about his authority—a doctor of the old school. He persisted in treating her like his little and not too bright sister. Intuitively Celia knew that his attitude was a defense, but she knew, too, that he would insist he knew what was best. He might change the medication but he would never admit it might be wrong. Still, the side effects might be causing the memory lapses that she found so disconcerting. And sometimes she had to make an effort to speak clearly. But it might not be the tranquilizers at all. It might be the stress tablets Jim had given her to take before meals.

Her mind kept circling the subject. Surely her brother would not give her harmful pills on purpose. She veered away from the dark suspicion, but the thought did not go away. She wished desperately that she could talk it over with Polly as she might have in the old days, but now the implied appeal in the confession she had just made was as far as she could go. Polly's airy dismissal had been a door decisively closing. No, she couldn't talk to Polly, but she would have to talk to someone soon.

She realized with a start that Sarah Lindblad was talking to her.

"—not at all the way things used to be," Sarah was saying.

What was not the way things used to be? Celia wondered. With Sarah it could be anything. Sarah was the most senior of Senate wives and stubbornly resistant to change.

I must pay attention, Celia told herself. It was no wonder she couldn't remember things, letting her mind wander as she did. She must remember to concentrate. She was letting her worries about Jim—and, yes, about her husband—come between her and everything else.

Celia Mann turned her attention determinedly to the small gray woman with the petulant face. She smiled.

"Oh, I think it is remarkable how we have held on to customs and traditions, Sarah," she said soothingly and hoped the statement applied to whatever Sarah was complaining about. "We follow pretty much the same pattern the very first Senate Ladies did. We have this lunch for the First Lady every year. We have come back to the Caucus Room in this old building to have it—just like in the days when you first came. And there is the return luncheon at the White House. We still wear the Red Cross uniforms"—she looked down at her own crisp blue-and-white costume with the Red Cross patch on the pocket. I don't remember putting it on, she thought with a clutch of her earlier panic.

"That's not what I mean, Celia," said Sarah Lindblad. "We may do the same things, but *we* aren't the same. Senate wives aren't the same. They have jobs and a lot of those that don't only come to our meetings now and then. Some only come to the luncheons. And we don't even have a real First Lady," she added aggrievedly.

Well, she's right about that, thought Celia, smiling to herself. "I'll be my own First Lady," the first woman president had announced to the press shortly after her election. "You all know how important I think the woman's side of official life is. Women value tradition and tradition safeguards our values. I want to go on helping women to fulfill that role as well as the new roles we have won for ourselves." But Sarah was right. It wasn't quite the same.

The Cabinet wives were approaching. Celia turned from Mrs. Lindblad and further discussion. "Welcome to the Senate Ladies' luncheon,

Mrs. Griffin—Betty, I should say." She extended her hand to the wife of the secretary of state.

"You said it wouldn't hurt her," John Mann, the vice-president of the United States, said angrily to his brother-in-law, "but here she is—having these blackouts. She walked right out the door yesterday and was going down Massachusetts Avenue, for Christ's sake, when the Secret Service caught up with her. McGregor says she acted as if she didn't know him or who she was. She could get herself killed—or kidnapped—or something!"

They were closeted in the vice-president's inner office to which Dr. Fifield had come "on the double" at Mann's urgent summons. He studied Mann's perturbed face and spoke carefully.

"Calm down, Johnny," he said in a pacifying tone. "I said it wouldn't hurt her, but I also said it would get her to the stage where we had a reason to hospitalize her so that we could control the dosage. It looks as if she has reached that stage now. I'm sorry if things got a little out of hand but I did warn you that the drugs were hard to monitor outside the clinical environment."

The vice-president was somewhat mollified, but unwilling to share any blame. "We just substituted the cream when you told us to—and the rest were your prescriptions," he said defensively. Why do public men always say "we" when talking about themselves? Jim Fifield asked himself with irritation, but he replied in an impersonal professional tone.

"Of course, but the effect is cumulative and has to be measured accordingly. We have no way to do that as long as she is at home. Aside from the blackouts, have there been any other side effects?"

Mann's voice was uneasy. "I think she's getting worked up again. She was talking about the fourteenth of July last night—insisting that something is going to happen, that she wasn't imagining things that night."

There was a short silence. Then, "I thought we had convinced her that that was just a metaphor—Maurice being French and dramatic," said Fifield. His voice was worried. "It could be dangerous for her to say that to anyone else."

"Well, it would certainly sound crazy," said Mann uneasily. What did his brother-in-law mean?

Fifield stood up. "I'll call the hospital and make the arrangements.

Then I'll go see Celia and talk her into it. You and Sam work out the press release. And you'd better go along with her to the hospital for the look of the thing."

"I intend to, and not just for the look of the thing. Celia's my wife, for God's sake," said Mann in an offended tone.

Once again the annual event was under way. Celia Mann's worries receded, as one predictable phase followed another. The Cabinet wives were dispatched to the Caucus Room on the third floor where the other Senate wives, past and present, were waiting. The president-cum-First Lady arrived with a great flurry of attending Secret Service. Then the welcoming committee dissolved to reform again in the Caucus Room and the Cabinet wives joined them in the receiving line. And then came the patient standing, the cheerful automatic smiling as each of the hundred-odd women greeted her and President Batchelder, stepped between them and faced the cameras to have recorded once again her presence at the unique social event open only to her and those like her by reason of marriage.

Finally, the luncheon for which the committee had planned and labored for months. The theme this year was Gulf Coast—crab soup, pompano and pecan pie—and they ate under the arching fronds of potted palms before a backdrop of painted blue skies and dancing waves while a mixed chorus flown in from Biloxi sang spirituals. ("I declare," said the president–First Lady in her richest drawl. "It's just like down home.") Celia performed automatically. She introduced Polly Haskins and Eleanor Parker. Polly introduced the woman who gave the invocation. Eleanor made the Red Cross report and introduced the other members of the committee. Polly introduced the Cabinet wives and presented the gift to the First Lady. Like a ballet, Celia thought. It went like clockwork. No names omitted. No feelings hurt. President Batchelder, seemingly unhurried, was at her charming best.

She ended her speech with a gracious reference to Celia. "I can't tell you how my burden has been eased by the help of one of the best Second Ladies the nation has ever had. She is as helpful at ribbon cuttings and award ceremonies as I have heard she is to your meetings. And, like all of you, she is a real helpmate to her husband, who, in this administration, has a big job to do." Oh yes, thought Celia dully, I suit her well enough now. Then the president was off, with the men carrying walkie-talkies going ahead and the other Secret Service men closing in behind.

Celia lingered until only the committee was left in the room. Then she, too, left with her own Secret Service men in attendance. She changed from her uniform in the ground-floor dressing room adjacent to the committee room where the Tuesday meetings were held. ("No room *belongs* to us," she could hear the senior Senate wife from her own state instructing her long ago. "We're only here on sufferance because our husbands are in the Senate.") The dressing room was a compromise of sorts. No one else used it. The files of almost three-quarters of a century were there, and framed and faded news photos of some of the Senate Ladies greats. Celia hung her uniform on the rack, called a cheerful goodbye to the few who were left, and went out.

She turned toward the stairs leading to the courtyard where she always left her car.

"This way, Mrs. Mann." Alec McGregor's voice, cool and impersonal, stopped her. "We'll take the elevator. The car is waiting on the Capitol side of the building. There seemed to be too much coming in and out here."

Celia's heart seemed to stop. So she had not driven herself after all. And Alec was smoothly covering up for her forgetfulness. Her head whirled with conjecture and confusion as she let herself be led to the waiting gray limousine. She remembered to smile at the building attendants and the little knot of tourists who had gathered to see her leave, but her lips were stiff. As she sank back into the soft upholstery of the big car she could feel that she was pale. The fear had returned. What was happening to her? When had it started? Was it less than a year? Less than a year since she had first heard the name Leo . . . had begun to wonder about Maurice Chouinard . . . had known that Johnny was—it was hard to say it even in thought—that Johnny was lying to her.

Her mind darted here and there as the car threaded through the zigzag barricades in the street leading from the Capitol. Absently she noted the barriers, wishing they were not needed. Wishing that things were the way they had been when she and Johnny first came to Washington. Things had been fun then and exciting. They had enjoyed it all together. When had it begun to change? Long before that day of Johnny's speech in the Senate—the day she had begun to suspect things—the day she thought of as the beginning of her isolation.

And what was it that was going to happen? Something. Soon. Something terrible. The fourteenth of July. She had not imagined that date.

She had not. Now it was already April. She must think what to do.

She stared, unseeing, through the tinted glass as they passed through the streets of a newly fortified Washington. And the fear grew within her. Alec McGregor, watching her pale worried face in the rearview mirror, swore under his breath.

# .1.

L IFE HAD begun to change drastically for Celia Mann after the convention at which her husband, Senator John Mann of Ohio, was nominated for vice-president of the United States. It seemed to her afterwards that one blow after another fell in the political interval between the convention and the official beginning of the campaign after Labor Day. And that after his election, life was never the same for her again ...

Washington in 1992 lived with terror and terrorist incidents as facts of daily life. As a result of Soviet-American negotiations in the mid-1980s the threat of nuclear holocaust had diminished, but the world was not at peace. The arsenals were not augmented but lay dormant, dangers to planetary life. Conventional warfare seemed perpetually in progress or about to break out somewhere in the world. This state of affairs was compounded by the unremitting use of terror as a political tactic. The United States was no longer immune. A wave of bombings, almost certainly the result of organized and planned political terror, had demoralized the country.

Americans were habituated to violence. For decades they had eaten their TV dinners while watching the stunned, bleeding and dying victims of crazed gunmen run amok. They took their morning coffee as shiny black hearses crossed the screen bearing away the corpses left by massacres decreed by this Mafia clan or that. They moved through supermarket checkout lines and glanced absently at the faces of murderous ideologues and their hostages staring from the pages of the tabloids. The military strikes initiated by President Reagan to punish countries guilty of state-supported terrorism had relieved frustration but, in the end, had brought terror home. By the end of the decade bombing had followed bombing with frightening regularity. First, the Senate wing of the Capitol itself. Then the State Department, bombed

11

by fanatics probably sponsored by Arab fundamentalists. A radio station in Chicago bombed while broadcasting a panel discussion about Israel. A cruising steamboat exploding into a flaming charnel house at the dock in St. Louis. A stage blown apart at a revival meeting in Kansas City. And—less dramatic, almost casual—a bomb planted at the Washington Monument during the height of the tourist season. A woman from Gainesville, Florida, and her little boy had been killed, many more injured and a huge crater left gaping in the monument grounds.

Finally the Islamic Center, long the focus of Muslim fundamentalist demonstrations, was destroyed by a truckload of explosives driven by one of a suicide squad, leaving a gaping hole in the procession of stately buildings on Massachusetts Avenue.

But infinitely more disturbing were the steady stream of subsequent suicide attacks throughout the country. Here and there, everywhere, seemingly without pattern, small trucks, vans, sleek Porsches, small Renaults, were crashed into shopping malls, churches, bus stations, supermarkets—any place where people gathered.

The calculated and callous randomness in the choice of victims came home to the American people. Panic spread. The public cried out for vengeance. They demanded that their government do something—anything—to find and punish the shadowy enemy. Washington retreated behind barricades.

Predictably the military, always beset by inter-service rivalries, resisted efforts like those of the House Armed Services Committee and Senator William Cohen of Maine, who, in the last years of the Reagan administration, sought to place the anti-terrorist and unconventional warfare units under a central civilian authority. Instead Defense secretaries promised, once again, to devote effort to more intensive training, getting better equipment, and better preparation for putting the special forces under a single command in an emergency.

In the face of the public mood, peace movements began to founder. Their cohorts faded away. The young, especially the new breed of college student who had succeeded the 60s generation, seemed uninterested. Even the nuclear disaster at Chernobyl and the ones that followed in France and then Brazil did not seem to move them. The hardy and battle-worn among the peace people cast about for new leaders to move out front. They found them once again among women anxious for their children and eager for a public platform, especially among the wives of public officials, who, however much they insisted that they spoke for themselves, brought the power of their husbands' names into the fray.

In this way Celia Mann found her cause and her voice. With a few close friends who were glad to follow her lead, she founded Peace Work—a coalition of old groups and new. The coalition gave the movement new strength. And now in the 90s the opposition was attacking its leaders, as it had their predecessors in the 80s.


Both conventions were over and the Senate and the House of Representatives were back in special session.

Annabel Curtan was up an hour earlier than usual that early fall morning. She left her rooming house without allowing for the warm-up time it took her arthritic joints to adjust to the day. Consequently, her six-block walk to the Metro was slow and painful. She was unaccustomed to the rush-hour crowd and pressed as close as she could to the side of the escalator in real fear of being hurled down its precipitous length into the lighted depths below. Hurrying and impatient office-goers squeezed past her, almost running down the moving stairs, some muttering impatiently, others abusing her with impersonal and practiced obscenities.

She waited for a second train rather than joining the swarming surge into the first one. She was near the door this time and managed to slip into a seat before the press of people behind her could endanger her balance. She looked worriedly around the car as the train glided off. Surely all these people could not be going to the Capitol. She would never get a seat in the gallery, if they were.

Elderly Miss Curtan was one of the Senate Gallery regulars. Like most of the others she had grown old lobbying for causes and was a veteran of forgotten legislative wars. Like them, she was a connoisseur of Senate and House debate and Supreme Court decisions. The regulars carried creased permanent passes secured from the offices of senators from the states they called home but had not seen for years, or ancient press cards, often from news bureaus now defunct. In the late afternoon they could be seen in the Hill cafeterias in groups of two or three discussing the theater of the day over coffee and meager snacks before making their separate ways back to their rooms before dark. The guards knew them and were indulgent of their overlong stays in the galleries, but their lives had been made difficult by the new security regulations.

"I don't know if it's worth it," said Annabel as she finally sank into her preferred seat near the end of the top row right next to the family gallery. "They took everything out of my purse and I lost a package of mints that rolled onto the floor. And I had to go through the metal detector twice because I had two pennies in my pocket," she added fretfully to Colonel Ormhofer, U.S. Army, retired, who had got there ahead of her.

"Oh, it's worth it, I think," said the colonel judiciously. "Look, the vice-president is in the chair and the press gallery is almost full up. They say Senator Mann will be up next. We'll get a good look at him."

Johnny Mann waited impatiently in the cloakroom.

He was always called Johnny—even now, when it looked as if he would be vice-president of the United States and, very likely, president one day.

Leaning against the wall beside the double doors of the Democratic cloakroom, he looked like his name—big, earnest-looking, slightly rumpled, the muscles earned in his football days straining the fabric of his smoothly tailored suit jacket. He was preoccupied; his gray eyes roamed the familiar room without seeing.

"Hey, Johnny," said Bill Haskins, doubling the vowels in the flat drawl of rural Alabama, as he came into the cloakroom from the Senate floor. "You got to get yourself out there, boy—your lady's waiting up in the gallery with Polly and all the others. I tell you those girls are godalmighty serious about all this. I spoke my piece, I tell you—looked like it was the price of a warm bed at our house!"

Johnny Mann nodded without smiling. He was concentrating on keeping track of the proceedings as the other senators came and went. "They'll call me," he said briefly, his voice resisting the easy male camaraderie, the assumption of common plight. Haskins was offering friendship, he knew, and encouragement. He was saying, "We're with you. You're still one of us." But he knew, and he felt that Haskins knew, that he was alone and on his own.

Cheerful, undaunted by Mann's failure to respond, Haskins grinned at him, punched his arm playfully, and headed for the back of the cloakroom. He was greeted with boisterous shouts from the group engaged in the almost perpetual running card game.

"Yay, Haskins" . . . "Great speech, Bill—you certainly took care of that bastard Duckett" . . . "You didn't hear a word of it and you know it, you son of a bitch—hey, deal me in. I just got time to wipe you out . . ."

They could laugh, Johnny thought. Hearing them, he felt himself apart, distanced from his confreres of a decade. Senator John G. Mann of Ohio had been born with an intuitive grasp of political realities. He felt rather than thought, and today he felt that, whether he liked it or not, he was no longer like these others—dukes of the Senate, each with his own fiefdom, powerful in his own right. It was not just that he was set apart and hedged in by the appurtenances of national candidacy such as the Secret Service—like that blasted Manfuso standing there against the opposite wall trying to be invisible; it was that his power derived now from the president who had chosen him as running mate. He could no longer pick and choose his issues. The president's issues were his issues. He had a constituency of one, and that one was Lily Batchelder.

"I know, I know, John," the president had said that morning. "Celia has been attacked and you will look ungallant if you don't defend her. I grant that. But this has policy implications. The press—and yes, I might even say the world—is going to examine your speech for hints as to whether this administration will continue to opt for strength and safety rather than weakness. There can be no hint of weakness. I know you will give none." The blue eyes fixed on his were steady and direct. A pause. Then, "You must also change the thrust of this dialogue on peace. I count on you to do that. You will find a way. You always do." The voice was smooth, even silky, but it was an order. It was also an implied threat. John Mann felt it and knew that this was what the president wanted him to feel.

He did not like the bind he was in and he was inclined to blame his wife for his discomfort. A combination of unswerving, focused driving ambition, influence and luck had brought him within sight of the presidency. That—and hard work. Hard work on her part, too—he had always conceded that.

A wife was still part of the pattern when a man climbed this close to the presidency, and Celia had been a willing and helpful partner in his climb. "A good life partner for you, Johnny," his mother had said when he told her that he was going to ask Celia Fifield to marry him, and the old-fashioned phrase had stuck in his consciousness. At the convention only a month before when he had stood, glowing, at the podium, accepting the approving roars of the delegates while cameras turned, bands played and balloons floated into the haze of smoke under the roof, Celia had been beside him, smiling, waving—just as happy as he was, he would have sworn it. What more did she want? Why did she want to break the pattern? There seemed to be no reasoning with her. The irritation of early morning was still with him.

# . 2 .

IT WAS a bright September morning, the kind of morning that had filled him with a sense of life quickening again during all his Washington years. After months of being sealed in air-conditioned rooms, Washingtonians woke to fresh air and the sounds of morning coming through open windows. Waking, he had heard the snip-snip of clippers wielded by an early day gardener, the rat-tat of hammers and the whine of a saw in the distance and, underlying everything, the soughing whir of rush-hour traffic on Connecticut Avenue two blocks away. He had been content, sorting out the sounds.

And then he had remembered what the day was bringing—the meeting with the president and the session on the Senate floor. He sat up, swinging his feet to the floor, reaching for his bathrobe, standing up in one abrupt movement. "Jesus Christ!" he muttered in exasperation as he padded toward the shower. A quarter of an hour later, dressed, briefcase in hand, he came through the bath which joined their two rooms and stopped to look at his wife. She was balancing on one foot drawing on her pantyhose. The creamy white robe she usually wore at breakfast time was only loosely caught at the waist. He could see the mark of lingering summer tan above her breasts and the tan of her long legs. Her black hair, shining and glossy still despite its first streaks of white, had fallen over her face as she bent her head to concentrate on her task. Another man might have found the sight appealing, but he found himself irked by it.

"For God's sake, why don't you sit down to do that?" he said irritably.

Celia Mann threw back her head, tossing her hair off her face with a gesture grown familiar over the years, and looked at him. Her blue eyes were puzzled. But she backed up to the bed and sat down. "I guess it is

**16**

a dangerous way to do it," she said mildly, "but I can't ever seem to get them straight and smooth this way. Juanita's brought the coffee." She nodded toward the table near the window where two cups, a sprigged china coffee server and the morning's *Washington Post* and *New York Times* were set out. Johnny Mann poured a cup of coffee, took a sip, and picked up the *Post*. Without looking at her, he knew that his wife was casting about, searching for an opening to talk about the day's ordeal. He could feel it. Her desire to do so was palpable in the stillness of the room.

"Johnny," she began, and the tentativeness in her voice added to his mounting irritation.

"I don't want to talk about it," he said, leaving the room, carrying the cup and the papers with him.

Celia stared at the door through which he had gone and sighed. It was as if the brightness of the morning, the brightness that had made her hopeful, was blotted out. Her "balancing act," as he called it, used to amuse him, she thought sadly, and he had relished the half-hour they spent alone in her bedroom with their first cups of coffee as much as she did. He would scan the headlines, reading them aloud to her and commenting on the editorial page and the columns while she finished dressing. He had saved his really detailed reading until they were settled at the breakfast table downstairs. Now, more and more often, he was skipping the intimate start to their day.

The tension between them was growing, she thought. Johnny had always hated questions. He disliked explaining himself. To anyone. Early in their marriage she had learned that it was better not to press, to wait until he talked about things in his own good time, to question only when it was absolutely necessary. Now it was necessary. But this time everything seemed different. It wasn't quite the questions he resented so much. He seemed actually to resent *her*. This time *I'm* the problem, she acknowledged to herself ruefully. But we have to talk about what to do. No time to dress. I'll have to try again before he gets away.

Her heart lifted a little as she came into the breakfast room, a converted sun porch of their big old Chevy Chase house. Everything seemed so much as usual. The sun poured in. Juanita slapped around the table in her old slippers. Johnny was sprawled comfortably in his chair reading and eating at the same time. Near his right hand was the remote control for the television, which flickered silently in the corner. She glanced at it—a weatherman was moving from side to side, grinning, gesticulating, talking rapidly. It was a nice day everywhere in the United States of America.

But before she could sit down Johnny stood up, dropping his napkin on the table, still looking at the business section of the *Post* in his hand.

"Johnny, Johnny, please," Celia said beseechingly. "What is wrong? Why are you so irked? I only want to explain a few things before you have to speak this morning . . ."

"You know I have to be at the White House in twenty minutes," he answered. She could hear the effort at control in his voice. "I don't need anything explained. I have my speech ready." He lifted his briefcase.

"But there are some things the office doesn't know . . ." Celia knew it was wrong as soon as she said it. Her voice trailed off. She began again, abandoning any effort to conceal her hurt and desperation. "Johnny, what is wrong? You *said* the peace constituency was important. You *said* you wanted to be vice-president so you could keep the president honest on the issue. You *know* I wouldn't have taken the presidency of Peace Work if you hadn't approved of it. Now what am I to do? It isn't just me. It's all the others!"

"Don't get hysterical, Celia," Johnny Mann said coldly. "I've told you before, and I'm telling you again for the last time—things are different now. What matters now is the election—nothing else. For Christ's sake, why can't you understand that? You've been at this as long as I have! Just settle down and leave me alone!" He wheeled and left the room. She heard the Secret Service men greet him and the squawk of their walkie-talkies. The car door slammed and the car started up. He was gone.

Celia sat staring at the table. They had become so separate. In Ohio when Johnny was governor they were a team. Celia and Johnny. Johnny and Celia. They appeared together everywhere, at all the official functions and at the receptions and organizational dinners the governor and his lady were expected to grace with their presence. She had her own quasi-official duties and a place on commissions and boards where she represented Johnny. They lived in the Governor's Mansion where their official and private lives converged.

But Washington was different. The Hill was a world unto itself and she had no official place there. Oh, there were traditional concessions to the wives of the Congress. An official pass. A place in the gallery.

Admission to the Senate guest dining room—but never to the senators' own sanctum sanctorum. Except for her participation in the almost moribund Senate Ladies group, she had no more rights than one of the staff. She was no longer a partner—at best an assistant. She had gradually come to realize that.

And she was constantly torn between Johnny's life and the lives of their children. They had to have a secure, happy home. That was her responsibility. They had to have as normal a life as possible. That also was her responsibility. In the beginning she was busy with building lives for both of them—with school organizations, the games, car pools, parents' groups. And as that pressure eased when Peter, the older child, went off to prep school, she found herself in demand to serve on volunteer boards where the skills she had built working with Johnny were valued—as were, of course, her name and her access as Johnny's wife.

Some wives bridged the gap by working in the office on a volunteer basis. Others were a constant presence on the Hill, following the debate on the floor, attending hearings, lunching with press and constituents almost every day. Polly Haskins did that. But Johnny would not have liked it, Celia knew, and his staff would have thought it interference on her part. Anyway, her own pride kept her from it. She wanted work and a purpose of her own. Peace Work had been the answer. She sighed and stood up. Today she had to get to the Hill on time herself.

# . 3 .

J OHN MANN looked up from his speech. His eyes traveled the room
again, past his Secret Service agent against the opposite wall, past
Senator Hildebrand from Nebraska asleep behind his newspaper in one
of the old leather chairs, past the knot of players in back. His mind
registered only the comfortable and familiar and he felt calmed and less
irritable until his eyes lit on the new woman senator from Arkansas leaning over the news ticker, reading the tape.

Absently he felt her presence discordant. In that bright blue she did
not fit into the masculine frame of the cloakroom. He frowned. What
was her name? Balora? No. Ballow—she was slim and blond and the
soft material of her dress revealed the outline of her slender curving
haunch and the thrust of her breasts. Even as he noted this appreciatively, Senator John Mann disapproved. A woman senator should not
look like that. She should look more like Susan Clausen, the Republican,
who was always tailored and serious, nice-looking enough but not se-
ductive. He frowned and felt the irritability, born of his frustration,
returning.

A page came in from the floor. He looked anxiously about, then saw
the senator standing almost beside him.

"Oh," he said, startled and relieved. "Senator Mott just gave me the
sign. He's about to finish."

Johnny Mann straightened up. He felt his tie and, looking at his pale
reflection in the glass of the door, smoothed his hair. Agent Manfuso
moved to his side and spoke into the walkie-talkie to alert the agents
positioned in the Senate gallery.

"Snowbird coming out. Snowbird coming now." It was a muffled
mumble but as if by signal the men at the poker table began laying

down their hands. As John Mann and his agent went through the doors
to the Senate floor they began to follow one by one.

In the family gallery Celia Mann relaxed with a sigh. Beside her Polly
Haskins heard the sigh.

"Celia Mann, I declare," she exclaimed with amused disbelief. "You
were afraid he wasn't coming!" She watched the color rise in Celia's
face. I don't believe this girl, Polly thought to herself. I do love her.
She's so sweet and smart but sometimes she's too naive for words. No
way that Johnny Mann wouldn't show today with the press gallery full
and waiting for him.

"It's just that I'm so nervous, Polly," Celia Mann said without returning Polly's amused stare. Celia's eyes were on the Senate floor. She
watched with fixed attention as her husband strode to the majority
leader's desk, which had been yielded as usual by its rightful occupant,
the senior senator from Maine, to the Democratic speakers in the day's
debate. He put down his papers and shook the hand of the majority
leader, who lounged temporarily in the seat directly behind his own.
Then he stood leaning against the desk apparently listening to Senator
Vincent Mott who still held the floor.


"Which one is she?" asked the representative of *New York* magazine's
Intelligencer page. She was unfamiliar with the Senate and its world.
Her eyes darted about. She was not even sure which was the family
gallery but she didn't want to say so.

"There, in the front row," said the man from the Personalities column
of the *Washington Post*. "She's with Haskins, Powers, Tumalley—and
that last one's Prescott—all Peace Work types." He did not spend
much time on the Hill either but he knew his Washington. "See her?
The sort of pretty one in the purple or blue or whatever it is."

"Violet—they're calling it violet this year," said the woman from
*New York*, sure of herself for the moment. She regarded the wives in
the front row of the gallery with interest. "Oh, yes, I see her now. She
is nice-looking, isn't she? Who's the big blonde beside her? Haskins?
Where's *her* husband from? Are all those in that gallery members of
this Peace Work thing?"

"Hardly," said the *Post* man astringently. "That's Duckett's wife
there right behind them—the one in green with the gray curls. And
that's her daughter with her."

"Hmm," said the questioner. "That must be awkward."

"Doesn't seem to bother them," said the Personalities man. "That's Washington, you know. In politics they see their opponents all the time at parties and meetings. Belong to the same clubs. That sort of thing."

"Oh," said the woman from *New York*, but she was not impressed.

Celia willed Johnny to look up, to acknowledge her presence with a nod and a smile as he used to do whenever she was in the gallery. But he was apparently oblivious to the galleries for the moment and absorbed in his colleague's argument. Celia sighed again. He was still angry, she thought sadly. Things were so complicated between them. How could Polly understand? Polly was big, voluptuous and direct, and pleased Bill Haskins just as she was. She seemed to manage everything with competent ease—Bill's office, her varied club offices and committees, and Bill. Celia Mann and the other founders of Peace Work had been surprised when Polly Haskins consented to join them. An international women's coalition to focus attention on the need to build the arts of peace in a nuclear age—that did not, somehow, seem Polly's cup of tea. They had hesitated before asking her to join the American steering committee, but they had needed someone from the South—and another Democrat—for balance, so they had asked her to lunch and explained the plan.

"Why not?" Polly had said when they finally worked around to putting the question. "Y'all know I'm a practical person. And this idea of yours sounds to me like a practical way to get people's attention. Some way they have to be stopped from blowing us all up." She had become one of their most active members.

It was Polly who had organized the response to Senator Duckett's attack on Peace Work and its leaders—all Senate and administration wives. "No way is he going to get away with that," she had said, "attacking *Senate* wives on the *Senate* floor! Calling us Communist dupes! That's a flagrant violation of Senate courtesy, I tell you. Wives take their husband's rank, don't they? Well! One senator can't make a personal attack on another, can he, and not be called to account? It's the same thing." When it was put that way the Senate husbands had seen it Polly's way.

One by one they had taken the floor this morning to deplore or—as their temperaments varied—to view with alarm, or to denounce, the speech of their tradition-shattering colleague of the New Right. The object of their attention, relative newcomer Senator Alphonse Duckett, sat stiff and unrepentant in his assigned place in the very last row of Republican seats.

The Senate chamber is small compared to that of the House. Now, with the galleries overflowing and an unusually large complement of senators in their seats, it seemed to hum and pulsate with subdued sound and movement. "Haven't seen so many of 'em in place since the Test Ban Treaty vote of 1963," muttered the senior AP correspondent to his neighbor in the front of the press gallery.

"Looks as if Mann is going to wind it up," rejoined the man from UP. "Tough spot for him." The AP man nodded.

They studied the tall senator almost directly below them. His head was bent, his eyes fixed on the incongruous white-scrolled, powder-blue carpet of the chamber floor. He was ostensibly listening to Senator Mott with absorbed attention. But Johnny Mann was aware of every detail. In a few swift glances around on his way from the cloakroom to the place where he now stood he had taken in all he needed to know about the audience he would have as he addressed his fellow senators.

He had spotted Celia in her violet suit in the gallery. It was early on, he remembered, that Celia had learned what a political wife needed to know—to dress so as to be easily visible in a crowd. No one would miss her today. He had noted, too, the regulars in the press gallery and the faces of the columnists and TV legmen who did not usually grace the Senate with their attention. He was aware of the Eastern bloc representatives sitting impassive and intent in the diplomatic gallery and of the other Europeans scattered about in seats nearby. Three Chinese in blue suits sat high in the back row. A bespectacled Japanese in tailored gray occupied a second-row seat at a discreet remove from the other diplomatic spectators.

Johnny acknowledged with an amused smile and a slight lift of his hand a vigorous wave from a balding man in a well-tailored but bright blue suit who was situated conspicuously in the front row. Good old Bill, he thought; might have known he'd be here. His face sobered as he took note of the fact that the retiring vice-president, bluff old Clem Boise, was presiding. He was wondering now what the vice-president's appearance there meant.

Although the only duty the Constitution assigns to the vice-president is that of presiding over the Senate, a twentieth-century vice-president rarely does so, except when his presence may be required to break a tie. Was the old man there to report to the president? John Mann wondered. Or simply to take sardonic pleasure in what he must surely see as his would-be successor's discomfiture? Mann looked up briefly.

But the old vice-president was not listening to Senator Mott or, at the moment, giving much thought to Senator John Mann. He was leaning back in his chair absently fingering the gavel. His large bony frame still filled the chair which dwarfed smaller men, but the leathery skin of his face seemed to hang in multiple creases as if the flesh beneath had shrunk away. His eyes, half-hidden under beetling brows and heavy lids, roamed the chamber above the heads of the senators. Forty years, he was thinking, forty years in this room.

It was as if he had never really looked at the room in which so much of his life had passed. Hadn't the domed ceiling been white once? And the sconces beside the gallery doors bronze? When had everything been painted in this insipid, neutral way as if to wipe out the nineteenth-century flamboyance of the old chamber? He could not remember. But the effect was bland, bland like everything else these days. He sighed and roused himself to attention. Vince Mott had apparently been stimulated by the presence of so many reporters and the overflowing audience in the galleries. He was clearly not going to stop anytime soon and would probably run over the time allotted for his remarks. Well, let him, Boise thought indulgently; it wasn't often a workaday senator like Mott had a chance at this much attention. His wife was probably here, too.

All of Clem Boise's appearances in the Senate these days had a valedictory and autumnal quality. It was only a matter of four months now until he would be replaced, one way or another, either by the younger man standing there below or by his opponent.

He had known that it would come to this even before the president had summoned him in the early spring. They had been an uneasy team from the beginning but they had won the all-important election which returned their party to power. To Clem Boise that was what mattered. But to his mind the president was too quick to reverse course, too anxious to show strength. She was fond of saying that she was only following in the path of other good Democrats—of Jackson, of Moynihan, and others like them. For the sake of the party he hoped the president was right. But he did not really think so.

The debate over how to prevent and control terrorism had raged ever since—after the *Achille Lauro* hijacking in 1985 and after the horrifying events at the Rome airport—President Reagan had sought to isolate Libya and resorted to military reprisals. But terrorism had, as Boise noted often, continued and increased. Moderates like himself argued that improved and unified intelligence efforts would be more productive and more apt to enlist allies. It was the view to which Clem Boise stubbornly adhered. President Batchelder did not—could not, he admitted—appreciate or approve his stand.

Before he went to the Oval Office he had written the letter saying that, after all his years of public service, he was tired and would not run again.

"Guess this is what you want," he had said as he put the letter down before the president on the shining uncluttered desk.

The president had smiled and accepted the letter without demur. There had been no argument. Clem Boise had not expected any.

She had her offer ready. "I do understand, you know—about this." She indicated the letter. "There are some things we see differently. But," she added prettily and seriously, "I know you won't desert me, Clem, in these difficult times. I am going to make the Forecast Commission a permanent presidential commission and give the chairman Cabinet status. It's vital that we control intelligence and all its sources. It's our only chance of controlling terrorism. And I hope you will go on with it, Clem—continue as its chairman. Only someone who knows Washington as you do—someone with a long memory for connections—can make it succeed. Will you do that for me, Clem?"

The Forecast Commission. Clem Boise had entertained a hope that, if he must give up the vice-presidency, he might still end his public life as secretary of state. It was a faint hope, given his differences with the president and her advisers, but it had flickered until that moment. Still, the Forecast Commission was of his making and had an unfinished job. Cabinet status would strengthen it—and sweeten his stepping down. Lily was being both canny and generous. He acknowledged that to himself. He sighed.

"Yes, Lily," he said. "I'll stay on."

The vice-president's ruminations were halted by a sudden awareness of change in the atmosphere of the room. The flat, harsh tones of western Massachusetts assaulted his ears as Senator Mott raised his voice in what must surely be his peroration. The senator had turned to face his colleagues and the galleries. "The *idear*, the very *idear*, that these good ladies, these true American wives and mothers, can be called tools of foreign power, is an insult, ladies and gentlemen of the Senate. Yes, an insult! It is not only an insult to them, it is an insult to all Americans who hope that our children will grow up in a peaceful world. Benjamin Franklin, ladies and gentlemen, that great patriot, ladies and gentlemen, called work for peace—and I quote—'the best of all works.' That is what these ladies are about, ladies and gentlemen of the Senate, the work of peace. And I say to you, *God bless them!*" While his final shouted words were still reverberating, he wheeled around and addressed the vice-president in normal tones. "I yield to the gentleman from Ohio, Mr. President," he said.

The reporters in the press gallery seemed to jerk to attention. There was a buzz of talk in the visitors' galleries. People in the back rows stood up to see. In the front rows the spectators moved forward and leaned over the rails. Guards hurried down the steps, shepherding them back into their seats. On the floor, senators who had been signing letters or reading bills to pass the time put their work aside. In the back of the chamber, the aides and speechwriters who filled the leather chairs and sofas began to stand up. Others hurried in from the corridor. The vice-president brought the gavel down on his desk slowly and emphatically—once, twice, three times.

Gradually silence fell. John Mann let it deepen until the chamber seemed to ache for sound, any sound at all. Then he stepped into the well of the Senate.

"Mr. President," he said and turned to bow slightly to the vice president. His voice was quiet. "My colleagues of the Senate." He paused again; the listeners in the gallery strained to hear. Celia leaned forward in her seat. John Mann threw back his head and let his voice ring out.

"What are we to say, ladies and gentlemen, to those who sow suspicion among us? To those who whisper and point—to those who say to us, '*Here* is treachery'—'*There* is treason'?" He looked up at the galleries.

"Have they forgotten what it is to live in a house divided? A house divided in a dangerous world? Such a house shall not stand. Ah yes, my friends, just such a house, my friends, Scripture tells us, *shall not stand!*"

He paused again and turned toward the vice-president. "The clock ticks, Mr. President, the clock ticks through the night of our uncertainties." And again to the Senate. "Those who accuse, ladies and gentlemen, those who whisper, eat away at the strength of the nation. They are like deadly termites burrowing in the foundation, weakening the timbers until the whole grand edifice built by our forefathers—the very temple of freedom—comes crashing down!''


"Isn't he wonderful?" said the young nun in the visitors' gallery to her two companions. "It's so true—what he says." Her face was full of excitement. "Isn't he wonderful?" Sister Anne Marie appealed again to the older nun sitting beside her. Sister Margaret Rose nodded and patted the younger sister's hand. Instinctively she looked across at Sister Patricia, inviting her to share her indulgent amusement at the younger sister's enthusiasm. But Sister Patricia's narrow face was noncommittal, her eyes bleak. Sister Margaret Rose sighed. As she turned back to the floor she caught sight of Celia Mann across the way straining forward as if to catch every word uttered by her husband. Sister Margaret Rose wondered what she was thinking. She must be proud.

Celia was lost for the moment in a maze of feelings. She *was* proud. She had been surprised at the surge of pride she felt but she recognized it as pride not so much in her husband's words as in the command with which he held everyone's attention. It was a precarious hold. No one knew that better than she. One wrong word or one word too many and it would be gone. She felt all the elation and the identification of the connoisseur watching a superior performance. She was amazed at the primitive simplicity of her own emotion. He's mine, she was feeling; he has this power and he's mine! Like the wife of a tribal chieftain, she thought ruefully, but her exultation did not abate.

One part of her mind, however, was detached, taking note of Johnny's words, of her own response, of his effect on his listeners. She knew how seldom her husband allowed himself the luxury of this kind of oratory, in which the sense of his words did not matter as much as their music and rhythm playing on the emotions of his audience, evoking old loyalties and old memories. And she knew why.

She remembered the first time his clear light-timbred voice rang out like that—it was in a keynote speech at their state convention. As the state's youngest attorney general he had been the compromise choice for that difficult task. Keynote speeches were more often forgotten than remembered. They served to settle a convention down while delegates milled about finding their seats and reporters, lobbyists and staff were being urged off the floor. Many a bright young politician's promising career had foundered on a keynote speech. But not Johnny's. After his opening few sentences no one in the great, barnlike hall had moved until he finished.

"My God," said the ex-governor sitting beside her in the second row of seats on the stage, "my God, Celia honey, that boy of yours has got it! If he can just do that often enough he'll talk his way into the White House."

When she had told Johnny later, bringing the remark to him proudly like a prized trinket for his collection, he smiled but shook his head. Not these days, he had explained. Television had changed all that. You could move a crowd that way, and sometimes, like that night, it was worth doing. The crowd had been waiting for something, anything, to turn them on. And the TV stations weren't covering the state conventions. But the old-fashioned oratory, which came easily to him, which he had perfected in college debates and the mock trials of law school, was all wrong for TV. Television was one-to-one. The big speech, he had told her, was to be saved for special occasions.

She could count his "big speeches" on the fingers of one hand. The speech on civil rights. The speech on the shame of migrant labor. On Vietnam. On human rights. The speech seconding the nomination of President Lily Batchelder.

Each time, the departure from his usual quiet, reasoned manner (and the absence of the self-deprecatory humor that so endeared him to the Washington press corps) had taken the public by surprise. The speeches were analyzed endlessly by political commentators and praised in editorials.

Especially eloquent phrases became part of the national lexicon: "Oh, we mean well, my friends, we always mean well. Let us remember the fifty thousand who did not escape the hell paved with our good intentions in Vietnam!" . . . "Are we to accept the monstrous thought that the security of this mighty country is to be bought at the cost of small brown widows and wailing orphans in the tiny half-nations to the south?"

The stir over those speeches had pleased John Mann each time. "Born again, old girl," he would say to her as he watched the evening news, "and one step farther ahead." Because Johnny had always had a reason for those speeches. What was his reason now? For a moment Celia was seized with an irrational hope. Could it be that he was doing it for her? That he cared as passionately as she about building peace? How could she doubt that he feared for the future of their children just as much as she did? The images of her small daughter chewing nervously on one of her blond braids as she watched a newscast, of young Peter, half-man already, his adolescent body stretching to grow up to his large bony shoulders and big hands, came unbidden into her mind, and her eyes blurred with tears.


On the floor Senator John Mann had launched into a litany of the divisions that had rent the country "in my lifetime and yours." Mc-Carthyism. The witchhunt for anti-American activities. "Those who saw a threat in giving full citizenship to people of color—who mistrusted and abused their brothers and sisters, children of the same God." Vietnam. And now this attack on reasonable citizens, those who worked to make sure the balance of arms was verifiable—the very people who sought to assure us of a world with no war.

Over and over again, said John Mann, the naysayers, the callers of names, had kept the nation divided. In a century when we needed the strength of unity they had sapped that strength, nibbling like rodents at its foundation.

John Mann's voice became the voice of a man reasonably instructing his hearers.

"Today we hold the terrorists at bay. In a free country with thousands of miles of open borders east, west, north, south—in a free country with many great cities honeycombed with areas where they may find refuge, the dastardly men and women who would bomb and maim, kidnap and kill, to gain their aims—these dastardly men and women take pause. Why? Because we are united, ladies and gentlemen, united behind our president, whose wise and patient course has brought them to their knees. There can be, there *must not be*, a breach in that unity, my friends."

An impressive performance, the old vice-president acknowledged, but why did it make him uneasy? It lacked logic, of course, and it fudged the issues. Unity and balance of arms were not exactly what the ladies were talking about. Did they realize what Mann was actually doing? Disclaiming them at the same time he seemed to defend them? Involuntarily Boise looked up at the family gallery and his eyes fell on Celia. Usually he had difficulty sorting out one political wife from another but he had always liked Celia Mann. His liking had its roots in a dinner party long in the past. He had told one of his long Western stories. It was an anecdote slow to come to the point, as all his stories were, but replete with local color and characters. Celia, who had a strong

appreciation of good-humored nonsense, had been overcome with laughter. She had doubled over, snorting softly into her napkin. Ever since
then, he had had a warm regard for her. He looked approvingly at her
now. You could see from the way she sat there that she was a hundred
percent behind her husband. It was the way Clem Boise thought a wife
should be. He could not help wishing, though, that he thought a little
better of her husband.

John Mann ended his speech as quietly as he had begun it. "Reason
and respect. Reason and respect for each other, ladies and gentlemen.
It is only on those terms that we can be strong. My esteemed colleague
from Massachusetts has quoted Benjamin Franklin, that wise man who
guided us in the dawn of our republic. Let me also quote him." He
looked up at the galleries and let his voice ring one last time. " 'United
we stand! Divided we fall!' " He turned back and looked up at the vice
president. "Let us not forget that Benjamin Franklin also said that, Mr.
President. I thank you."

He took his seat. A spattering of applause came from the galleries
and the vice-president pounded it down with his gavel. "Any more such
behavior and the galleries will be cleared," he said perfunctorily and
unnecessarily. The spectators were already streaming out the doors and
the senators were clearing the floor. Most of them stopped to shake
Senator Mann's hand or clap him on the back. No doubt about it,
thought the vice-president a little bitterly, he's cleared one more hurdle.

"He didn't say anything about his wife, did he," remarked the *New
York* stringer.

"Policy speech—campaign speech," said the Personalities man, pock-
eting his notes. "Want some lunch?"

"Good show," said the Australian correspondent to the columnist
from *Newsweek*. "He reminds me a little of Winnie on his showier
days." His vowels were only a little uncertain. He sounded very aloof,
very British. "Oh, he does, does he?" said the *Newsweek* man irritably.
He was one of John Mann's admirers and friends in the press. He never
knew what to make of it when the sophisticated, witty man he knew
took off into flights of oratory.

"Peace and strength. Peace and strength," said Dieter Wenzel of the
West German *Abendblatt* to the woman from *Paris Soir*. "Here we go
again. Poor Europe."

"Where's the President's Room?" she asked as if she hadn't heard him. "Mann's having his press conference there."


In the diplomatic gallery Guillermo Martínez-Schwenger rose and stretched discreetly. Ex-ambassador, former director of the World Bank, international businessman, lobbyist, if you will, he was in that gallery often by courtesy. The State Department would have preferred otherwise but that worried him little. Senators on both sides of the aisle were his warm friends. They and their wives eagerly graced his sumptuous parties. "Bill" Martínez, as he was known to them, was an excellent host and very much at home in the United States. Son of a man who had been his country's consul, first in San Francisco, then in New Orleans, and of an English-born mother, and educated in American private schools, he spoke colloquial English and knew the ins and outs of American politics and business as few Americans did. Important Senate staffers were recipients of his generous hospitality at the horse farm in Virginia or the hunting lodge near the Chesapeake. They sat in his box at football games and traveled in his plane to air shows. Senate receptionists and guards looked forward to the elaborate and expensive fruit-and-wine baskets he sent at Christmastime. No, no one was apt to challenge his presence either here or in any of the Capitol dining rooms. No one ever had.

One the whole, he thought to himself, Mann had handled things well. Contained whatever damage there might have been. Senator John Mann was continuing to prove a good investment.

It was unfortunate that Mann had this little complication with his wife. A minor complication but unnecessary. "Bill" Martínez often said that he preferred women rounded, complaisant, long-legged and showy, splendid creatures on which to spend money in demonstration of his wealth and whose possession others envied. Luisa, his present wife, was like that. She might be demanding, even a bit grasping, but never drearily serious like these American wives. She knew how to make a man relaxed and happy, how to welcome him home from the daily wars and send him forth refreshed.

He turned and spied the Japanese diplomat who was making his way out of the row behind him.

"Well, my friend," he said formally, "what a pleasure it is to see you!" He bowed rather than proffering his hand, knowing that a man like Minister Osaka would find the American gesture repugnant. It was the instinctive knowledge of such things that brought "Bill" Martínez-Schwenger so much Japanese business. Osaka bowed in return, his smile wide and his eyes friendly behind shiny glasses.

Wish I could invite him to lunch, thought Martínez. But, alas, he was meeting Duckett at the Hyatt Regency. A bore. The senator would be full of resentment at the rebuke his colleagues had just administered. He would insist on talking about the international Communist conspiracy. A bloody bore. But what could one do? The Christian Worldwide Contra Movement, which Duckett had founded and for which he was able to raise such astonishing sums of money, was an excellent customer. At lunch he might very well unload a few more X-20s for his clients. They were worth $13 million a copy. A bore, yes, but worth it. He would see Osaka another day. Politely he stopped at the aisle and waved the minister up the stairs ahead of him.

# · 4 ·

CELIA MANN and Polly Haskins did not meet each other's eyes. They both knew that John Mann's speech was not an endorsement of their common effort, Peace Work. There was no need to voice the knowledge. In unspoken agreement they turned to gathering up the other members of the committee.

"We're going to meet the ladies from the Committee for Restraint Abroad—CRA—in the dining room," Polly told Sue Powers and Lena Tumalley. Celia said the same thing to Millie Prescott and they preceded the others up the gallery steps. Celia stopped suddenly at the sight of the man waiting in the last row of seats.

"Jimmy," she said, "I didn't know you were here!"

"I couldn't miss this show, could I?" he answered. "How did you like Johnny's speech? He certainly pulled your chestnuts out of the fire, didn't he?"

Celia stiffened but her voice was easy. "You know my brother, don't you, Millie? Dr. James Fifield?" She indicated the others. "I think you know everybody here, Jim—Sue, Lena, Polly . . ."

Polly Haskins, at the end of the line, looked Jim Fifield over. He resembled Celia but her fine features were blunted and broadened in his wider face. He was jowly and his black eyebrows were not straight like Celia's but arched and peaked. They gave his face an unappealing arrogance. Irish gone sour, Polly thought, that's how her Bill would put it—one of the Irish gone sour the way they so often do. That sarcastic, smart crack of his just shows it. But she was all smiling Southern effusiveness when she reached him.

"I declare," she said, "Celia's handsome brother! Did you come to take all us pretty ladies to lunch?"

Dr. James Fifield laughed and she saw that he could still be charming. "My bad luck," he said. "I've got another appointment. But you must give me a rain check."

"We'll do that, you hear?" said Polly and they went on past, leaving Celia alone with him for a minute.

"It's Tuesday night, isn't it," she asked, "that we're entertaining your Dr. Chouinard?"

"We're counting on it," he replied and she went on.

Dr. James Fifield watched the women disappear one by one through the door of the family gallery. The ingratiating smile with which he had so easily charmed them had vanished, replaced by a look of sullen discontent. He resented the need to be pleasant to women like that. They were so sure of themselves, so arrogant of place—and all because they had had the luck to marry men who rose to prominence. Celia, he thought to himself, was no better than the rest of them. Organizing, making speeches. As if people wanted to hear *her*. It was Johnny Mann's wife they came to hear—not Celia Fifield Mann. She ought to know that, for God's sake.

James Fifield had been one of those children of great promise who remain just that—of promise—all their days. Things had come too easily for him in the beginning. The Fifield parents had been delighted with their handsome sturdy son, and even as a toddler he had known how to use their pleasure to his advantage. At school he found his teachers just as easy to manage. He never had to work as hard as other boys to earn good grades. Celia, coming along four years later, adored him and followed him about as soon as she could walk. He was not inclined to share their mother and father with her but his initial resentment was somewhat assuaged by her admiration. It returned, however, whenever the admiration lessened.

If anyone had asked Jim Fifield if he loved his sister he would have said that of course he did. He could not, would not, recognize his own deep resentment of her any more than his continuing need for her. It was taken for granted that he was where he was because of Celia's steadfast devotion. She had made sure that her brother shared in her good fortune as Johnny Mann advanced steadily from attorney general to the governorship and then to the Senate. Grudgingly he would have acknowledged if questioned that Celia, through Johnny, had given him a start. But, he told himself, Johnny needed him now more than he needed Johnny. It was too bad he couldn't let Celia know just how much. But he wasn't going to let her spoil things for him. Johnny and the others must be made to see what a problem she could be. Even her husband didn't know her the way he did.


"That's all, ladies and gentlemen." Jule Andvik's voice was crisp and clear, cutting through the babble of voices in the President's room. She was acting as Senator Mann's press secretary today in place of Si Utley, who was at a briefing session at the White House preparing for the vice-presidential candidate's first campaign swing. "That's all," she said again. "We have to move the senator on now."

The television lights went out one by one. In their glare the vaulted old room, all gold, marble and frescoes, had looked garish and artificial, like an overly ornate stage set. In the light of its own huge chandelier with its multiple frosted globes and long dangling crystals, it took on gracious proportions again. The gilt frames of the windows and mirrors glowed softly and the red velvet draperies mellowed in color. John Mann stood leaning against the mahogany table topped with green baize at which Lincoln had sat to sign the bills brought out from the floor, and exchanged a few last jests with the men from AP and UP. It was usual for them to linger as if to emphasize their privileged place in every press conference. A few foreign correspondents stood behind them flinging questions over their shoulders. He nodded at them but ignored the questions. The Secret Service men moved into place and he turned quickly and made his way out between them, trailed by Jule and other members of his staff.

In the corridor a few reporters were still bunched in hope of putting a question as he went by, but the Secret Service moved him quickly past and into the elevator. He was gone.

Few of the tourists being conducted through the halls of the United States Capitol are aware of the hideaway offices off its main corridors. These offices are reached by twisting, narrow, seldom-used passages or by narrow old stairways leading down below the main floors—a few by creaking, small elevators leading to eyries overlooking the roofs and magnificent views of Washington. John Mann's was such an office. Having it meant that he had attained the rank of a select few in the Senate, those with enough seniority and committee power to rate space in the Capitol itself. The office meant a great deal to him, but he made very few welcome there. Even Celia had seen it only once or twice. It was very different from the suite of offices in the building half a block away where he received his constituents and where most of his Senate work was done.

He had been content to leave the room painted its curious, anonymous government tan and to use the ancient government-issue furniture left behind by the crusty old Southerner who had preceded him there. He liked the battered leather sofa and chairs, the oaken rolltop desk, the worn rug and the frayed curtains impregnated with the cigar smoke of decades. This was his own spot. This was where he came to plot, to plan, to consider, step by step, the rapid climb of Johnny Mann and his family—sometimes with Sam Drottman, his closest aide and oldest friend, sometimes alone.

Now Sam was waiting for him there. The aide had just put down his beeper. He stood for a moment looking out the single window, facing west down the mall to the Washington Monument and the glimpse of trees beyond that hid the White House from view. Johnny would make it to the White House yet, he thought. Just a few more steps. He turned to the senior senator from Wisconsin, who sat at Johnny's desk waiting, too.

"He's coming now," he said. "But remember, Tom," he added with the familiarity of long association, "we can't be too specific with him. There are things he can't know about now. Better for him not to know. We can trust Johnny to know what needs to be done. But keep off the details."

The older man grinned around his cigar. His fat florid face creased in real amusement. He puffed rapidly, took out his cigar, looked at its stubby length regretfully, then put it in the ashtray.

"Not a word about Mary Jane, my boy, not a word. That's what we used to call it, you know. It was the C's taught us Northern boys how to enjoy it, you know. And that's what they called it then. Bet those college kids would be surprised to know how long ago us country folk were using the stuff."

"C's?" queried Sam.

"CCCs—Civilian Conservation Corps. I keep forgetting how old I am—remembering stuff most of you guys never knew." He sighed gustily and insincerely. "We had a camp in my hometown. I was in high school then. They were mostly Okies—a pretty earthy, knowledgeable bunch. We learned a lot from them. They taught us country music and how to smoke Mary Jane. We never knew those shiny plants growing up and down every little coulee had such a mighty interesting usefulness. Who would have thought it would grow to save the economy of the farm states? Who would have thought it would be big, big business?" He guffawed heartily. Senator Larson was a cheerful man.

The door was flung open and a Secret Service man looked in. He moved aside and John Mann stepped through the door. "You see, it's all right, Joe," he said to the agent. "A mouse couldn't sneak in here without you knowing. You can wait outside." The agent nodded and closed the door.

Senator Larson stood up and indicated Johnny's chair with an expansive gesture. "The future vice-president's seat," he said and moved to the couch.

Sam could see that John Mann was still riding the high that followed a successful speech. "Great speech, Senator," he said.

"It was all right, wasn't it?" John Mann said and Sam knew the statement for what it was, at once a confirmation and a plea for reassurance. They never get enough approval, he thought—there's never enough to satisfy them.

"What the doctor ordered—and a whole lot more," he said with conviction. He was used to filling John Mann's needs. He nodded at Tom Larson, indicating that it was time to get down to business.

"Johnny," the older senator said, "they're worried out our way about the FBI nosing around. We just can't afford to have our third-largest crop endangered. There's a lot of little farmers that count on it. You know that. All up and down the whole Mississippi Valley and the Ohio Valley, too."

John Mann looked serious. "Yeah, I know," he said. "Sam's kept me up on that. Some alarmist got them going, talking about organized crime moving in. But Jim Fifield has the president's ear as science adviser. He's told her that there's nothing to worry about. A dry hole. It just helps out the hillbillies and the eighty-acre boys, as I understand it."

Joe Larson stood up. "That's all I wanted to hear. I wanted to be able to give them the word, soothe them down a bit." At the door he paused. "Fifield's in your family, isn't he?"

John Mann frowned but he nodded. "Brother-in-law," he said shortly.

Larson laughed. "Couldn't be better, could it?" He let himself out. For the moment Senator Mann's mood of ebullience was suppressed. He turned to his aide. "That's right, isn't it, Sam?" he asked. "The mob isn't moving in, is it?"

Sam hastened to reassure him once again. "No, it's like Jim says—small stuff, but darned important to the little growers."

"And the stuff doesn't do any real harm, they say. Not addictive like other things." Johnny Mann was reassuring himself.

"Hell, no, we've all had a joint now and then, haven't we?" said Sam mechanically. He wondered wearily if John Mann had any real idea what had been done to get him where he was today, of the deals that had to be cut. Of course not, he told himself, for once feeling resentful. That's for me. He gets the glory.

But Johnny's mood had returned. "All right, all ri-i-i-ght," he said. "Now I'm going to call the president and hear what a good vice-president I will make. Nobody can lay it on like that lady and I just plain like to hear it. And then you and I are going back to the office to celebrate with Jule and Si and the others." He reached for the phone.

Sam Drottman retreated to the window. With his back to John Mann he listened to the senator's easy charming voice responding to the president.

"I'm glad you were pleased, Madam President," he was saying. "You were right. It was important to strike just the right note."

Madam President! Sam heard the words with disgust. All the trouble they were facing—trouble Johnny didn't even know about yet—had begun with that woman's election. Trouble they would never have had if she hadn't become president at just the wrong time. Now Leo was pressing him hard and he would have to level with Johnny soon—before it was too late.

President Lily Batchelder had leapfrogged into her candidacy in the last election. She had entered the White House owing nothing to the complicated network of power-and-influence people who stood to benefit from the ascendancy of experienced male politicians from either party. The widow of a newspaper publisher with impressive credentials of her own in community betterment, she had been a reform candidate for governor of Mississippi and a two-term winner. Her career in the statehouse had given her an overwhelming following among women and blacks. By the time of the 1988 convention she had become one of the best-known governors in the country. The barrier to a woman as candidate for high office had been breached by Geraldine Ferraro in 1984. There was no stopping Lily Batchelder in 1988.

Once she was in office the influence peddlers and the shadowy backers of useful appointees and politicians were faced with a problem of unusual proportions. They had no way of reaching her or the people closest to her. They had not counted on her rise to power. She owed no one for past favors, nor did her people. Her old vice-president was a man of proven rectitude with little need for money. And unlike Carter

(also unbeholden) she had a subtle, sure touch with the capital's in-
siders. They had had to regroup, to rely on the men who were responsive
in the Senate and the House while they maneuvered to get someone they
considered their own into the administration. Through Sam and others
they had a stake in Johnny Mann. They were used to hedging their bets,
but this time most of them had all their eggs in one basket.

Sam turned as Senator Mann put down the phone.

"Look, Johnny," he said. "I've got to talk to you. It's serious."

John Mann waved him off. "Tomorrow, Sam, tomorrow." He was in
no mood to be serious.

President Batchelder had been more than pleased. Her clear Southern
voice had been warm. "That was a *very good* speech, John, really *very*
good. I have the video tape right here. It *was* really the right note. I knew
you could do it. I especially liked your diverting attention to Senator
Duckett's McCarthyism and away from"—she had paused delicately—
"other things. We must keep right on doing that, I think." Lily Batchelder was far too tactful to say that public attention must be diverted
from the activities of Mann's wife and the other women in Peace Work,
but John Mann knew what she meant. He agreed. In his euphoria he
had not even minded being taped. The steely hand in the velvet glove.

John Mann's reliance on Sam went back a long way—to the days
when he was the latest addition to the Lake City law firm of Addison,
Addison & Mann. It was an old Lake City firm which his older brother,
Adam, had taken over from the last surviving Addison. The old man
had been quite content to have the two young lawyers from the flats
bring the floundering, debt-ridden firm back to solvency. He left young
Adam Mann to his own devices, retreated to his club, and showed up
to be "of counsel" when they had clients they wished to impress. Adam
Mann, in his turn, a graduate of the community college and the city
law school, was glad to take advantage of Addison's connections to
build ties to the city's establishment but he also had connections of his
own. The practice prospered.

His older brother had sent the young John Mann to Lake City's one
private prep school, to the state university and finally to Yale Law
School. Then he brought Johnny home and set him to building a political base.

"You should know, Johnny," Adam had told him, "that the money to get started was lent to us—and we handle things for our backers in return. All legal. We're careful about that—but not what you should get into. You're the one who's going to give us class with your connections and get into the big time, run for office."

Sam had handled whatever had to be handled with the shadowy backers, but Johnny had a good idea who they were—men from what Adam called "the old neighborhood" who had taken a different path out of the flats. He did not let the connection worry him. He trusted his brother and Sam to protect him.

He had made good use of the threads tying him to old friends and acquaintances from prep school. He had joined the Yale Club and worked for the right civic causes. He had handled the affairs of young people on their way up and widows from good families in straitened circumstances. He had met Celia Fifield, daughter of the old mayor, through her mother, and married into one of Lake City's well-known families. In the end, it just seemed natural that he would run for office himself—and he was on his way.

John Mann had never put his own view into words for himself, but he saw the law as completely relative, something that was subject to change and capable of a multitude of interpretations. He was not too far separated from forebears for whom the law in the countries from which they had come was little protection. His early years in a section of the city where the police were as apt to be enemies as protectors had left their mark. Among the men in his law classes there had been little discussion of the philosophy of law or the concept that freedom was closely linked to a government of laws rather than men, but even if there had been, he would not have been much affected by it. To him the source of freedom was power. He was not interested in money for its own sake but because it was necessary to finance the march to power.

He was getting closer every day to the power he had dreamed of— first the vice-presidency, then the presidency. He would do what he had to to be sure of that.

The representatives of the Committee for Restraint Abroad were sitting in a solemn row in the reception room of the Senate Dining Room. Celia thought, as she spotted them, that they looked a little impressed and subdued, as so many visitors were, by their surroundings. Although the furniture was nondescript, the room had been planned and decorated at a time when a bumptious and growing America sought a kind of republican grandeur, and the effect had lingered. The walls were now a deep crimson and Brumidi's exuberant frescoes crowded the arches of the ceiling and ran down the walls. In this setting senators and guests important enough to be bidden to lunch came and went, greeting each other with practiced geniality and emanating an air of consequence.

The nuns were neat and sober in their polyester suits. No one would mistake them for anything but what they were. Celia looked at Sister Margaret Rose, whose snowy permanent was a precise frame for her rosy face, and at Sister Patricia, whose graying curls were close cropped. Sister Margaret Rose stood up.

Celia shook hands with Sister Margaret Rose, whom she knew slightly from her work at St. Simeon's Hospital, and the nun introduced the others.

"We brought Sister Anne Marie, although she isn't a member of the committee. She's a novice working in our hospice for the poor and she's so interested in what your Peace Work is doing." The young woman stood, clasping her hands before her almost as if she were praying, and smiled radiantly at Celia. Celia smiled back at her. "I'm glad to meet you, Sister Anne Marie," she said. Sister Margaret Rose went on. "You know Sister Patricia Black?"

"We were in school together," said Celia. "It's nice to see you, Pat." Sister Patricia nodded but did not extend her hand. Oh dear, thought Celia, suddenly remembering what had happened to the nun. And she never did like me very much.

"And here is Laura Sorenson." An intense-looking woman in a loose flowered skirt and peasant blouse grasped Celia's hand fervently. "We so appreciate what you are doing for the cause, Mrs. Mann," she said. The other woman stood a little aloof, waiting, Celia was sure, for a sign of special recognition. A big contributor? She certainly looked like one in that unmistakably authentic Chanel suit. The gold chains were real. "Alison Lonsdale, Celia." The woman's smile was bland and pleasant and her smooth creamy face with the pale blue eyes over broad flat cheekbones looked hauntingly familiar. Lonsdale. Of course. Celia remembered. California. A fund-raiser in a white, white house with a Giacometti in the garden and a terrace overlooking the ocean. "Alison!" Celia exclaimed. "What are you doing here?"

"Oh, didn't you know?" said Laura Sorenson importantly. "Alison *is* CRA in a manner of speaking. Without her help we would never have got the big demonstration we're planning for Peace Day off the ground."

The other Senate wives had joined them by then and Celia took over the introductions, making sure that they knew who Mrs. Lonsdale was— Mrs. Herman Lonsdale, the wife of an extremely rich West Coast capitalist whose technology and transportation conglomerates wove a complicated network around the globe. "Alison has been the greatest supporter of efforts for world peace, you know," she said. And Alison Lonsdale smiled. "I try to help where I can," she said. "I've been corresponding with Laura for some time—and I've just met the good sisters who are working with her so wonderfully. When Laura told me about this meeting with you Peace Work ladies I just thought I'd come east for it."

Once they were seated at the center table reserved for them in the dining room, Celia surveyed the group. She was amused to see Millie Prescott sandwiched between Sister Margaret Rose and Sister Anne Marie. It was unlikely that the austere Kansan had ever been this close to Catholic nuns before.

"No, we don't help the poor in the old way," the young novice was saying to her earnestly. "We feel now it is important just to be with them and learn from them what they need—to live like them and to be open." Celia felt a surge of amusement at the look of blank incomprehension on Mrs. Prescott's face but at the same time she was moved by the young nun's words and the lack of self-consciousness with which she explained herself. She's just a girl, and a lovely one, she thought, looking at the clear line of Sister Anne Marie's throat rising from her white collar, the pale chiseled lips and the clear brown eyes. She found herself envying the young nun's certainty and her evident happiness in it. It's a quality you seldom see anymore, she told herself—innocence. Then she realized that Patricia Black was watching her and the direction of her gaze and felt her own color rise as she collected herself and turned back to the business of ordering lunch.

Polly, beside her, plucked at her sleeve.

"Look to your right when you can," she said in a stage whisper, "and see who brother Jimmy's big date is."

Celia turned and saw her brother at a table for two in front of one of the long windows. Across from him, surveying their group, was a tall elderly man who seemed a study in gray. His suit was gray, his groomed, glossy hair was gray, his eyes were gray, even his smooth well-tended face had a grayish tinge. His eyes met hers; he had evidently been studying her and her companions but he showed no embarrassment. He bowed slightly and she nodded in return.

"Cromfield Haines?" Celia said uncertainly to Polly.

"The prez's special emergency adviser himself," said Polly, still half-whispering. "So we're an emergency—well, well. Or, more likely, you."

"Me?" said Celia automatically. Beside her she heard Polly's exasperated sigh. But of course Celia knew what Polly meant. Her connection to Peace Work was an emergency because of Johnny. To the president, Peace Work was an unnecessary complication in the tangle of foreign policy through which she picked her way. A complication. But it's so much more than that to me, protested Celia silently. It's my work.

As if sensing her thoughts, Alison Lonsdale picked up her water goblet, leaned forward, and raised it to Celia. Her throaty, arresting voice rode down the chatter of the others. "I want to propose a toast to our leader, Celia Mann," she said. "If she hadn't thought of Peace Work, our women would still be divided and left out of the international debate on death from the sky."

Celia winced and tried to stop them. Death in the sky, she thought. Must Alison Lonsdale be so lurid? But the others joined Mrs. Lonsdale in a ragged chorus. "To Celia . . . to Mrs. Mann . . . to our leader." The words rang around the table. Even Sister Patricia Black raised her goblet. When they were quiet again Celia said firmly, "Now listen, all of you. I may have thought of Peace Work but each of the Senate ladies here is as much its leader as I am. And you ladies from CRA have done as much to bring women together as we have." She was a little flushed and very conscious of the curious eyes of the diners at other tables.

Mrs. Lonsdale was undeterred. "I'm sure you're right in a way, Celia, but that's the way we think of you," she said smoothly. She looked at Laura Sorenson, who took the cue eagerly.

"And that's why we're here to ask all of you to sit on the platform on Peace Day. Oh"—she broke off—"it's going to be a wonderful day. Women, children, men from all over. There are ninety buses coming from the New York area alone. And even buses from places like Waco, Texas. Imagine! And two planeloads that we know of from western Canada . . . Oh, I could just go on—" She checked herself. "But what we really want very much is for you, Mrs. Mann, to introduce our special guests—to be the mistress of ceremonies."

Celia shook her head. "I couldn't do that," she said, "not now. Because of the campaign." She looked at their disappointed faces. "I could sit on the platform with the rest of you, I guess, but I couldn't be the mistress of ceremonies. You must see that."

The cacophony of argument that broke out among the others at the table made it clear they didn't see. Even the political wives disagreed.

"But Celia, we all agreed that we were doing this on our own and that our husbands were not involved," said Millie Prescott, "and whatever you say, Celia, you're the one people think of when they think of Peace Work." She thinks I'm declining the honor out of modesty, Celia thought. Millie was sometimes slow.

Alison Lonsdale's voice was grave. "I'm afraid that will make a great difference, Celia. You see, I guess I just assumed that you would continue to take the responsibility after what you have done so far. After all, the fate of millions may be affected by this year's Peace Day. And some of our most important show business celebrities accepted on the understanding that you would take part in the program. Stars who never joined the peace movement before are coming this time, stars like the great country singers. You know what their appeal is to grass-roots Americans. And they have their reputations to think of, too. I'm afraid what you do just makes a great difference." Her tone was admonishing. Was it even a little threatening? Celia wondered. She looked at Polly. Polly was canny. She would understand. But this time Polly was not on her side.

"Look here, Celia honey, this isn't some ladies aid society we're involved in. This is for real. Are we goin' to stop these people from just fryin' us all or aren't we? So the president doesn't like you standin' up in your own right. What's she goin' to do? Drop your husband because his wife is a peace leader? Come on! She knows all about the gender gap. That's what elected her last time, for God's sake. Her name would be just mud, I tell you." Her voice softened. "Celia, honey, this is for your children—everybody's children. We can't back down now."

Celia looked around the table. Their eyes met hers. Sue and Lena, anxious—Millie, too. Sister Anne Marie, close to tears. Sister Patricia, sardonic and skeptical. Sister Margaret Rose and, surprisingly, Laura Sorenson, sympathetic. Alison Lonsdale, watchful and inscrutable. Celia sighed.

"Well," she said hesitatingly, "perhaps I could just introduce the program, but I don't want to introduce all the guests. We could divide that up. I'll think about it." Laura Sorenson clapped her hands and they all followed her lead. Celia, smiling in spite of herself, raised her hand. "Now, wait, I said I'd think about it."

"Talk to Johnny, you mean," said Sue Powers teasingly. There was general laughter and the tension around the table eased. Again the talk ebbed and flowed like the table talk of women at lunch anywhere.


Across the room, Cromfield Haines turned his attention to James Fifield.

"Your sister is much more vivid as a personality than I remember her being. She seems to have a following. And I can't say that I see anything wrong with her, any signs of the—the deterioration you talk about."

"You don't know Celia," said Fifield irritably. "She's lost all sense of proportion, and it's not normal." He paused and controlled his voice before continuing earnestly. "I tell you, Haines, she is not the Celia I know. To resort to the vernacular, she's like someone on a high from time to time."

"Maybe, maybe not," replied Haines. "She could just be feeling her oats. In any case, we have to go carefully. I had no idea Mrs. Lonsdale was involved and I doubt that the president does. That's heavy guns, you know."

"Well, we've got to do something." Fifield's voice was surly.


Across the Hill, Guillermo Martínez-Schwenger came out of the Hyatt Regency and got into his car.

"*Vamos al finca, Ramón,*" he said to the driver, "Drive to the ranch," and reached for his car phone to call Luisa and ask her to meet him at their place near the Blue Ridge. He felt that he had done a good day's work and had earned the respite of a languorous evening with his wife and the pleasure of riding through the countryside in the morning.

Two more planes sold at $13 million apiece. His clients would be pleased. Never mind that Duckett was crazy. He shook his head, recalling their lunch conversation.

"We must gather together under the Christian banner to defeat these godless conspirators," Duckett had said. "That is the purpose now and forever of our international Christian Contra movement. You, Bill, are a chosen instrument to help us get the means into the hands of our allies across the borders. We must do everything we can to enable them to stem the tide."

"I am happy, of course, to be of whatever small help I can," Martínez had answered.

"These so-called refugees flooding in from Mexico and via the Canadian border are nothing more than Communist stooges. That Lamm in Colorado saw the danger and called it right, back in 1983 and '84. Even though he was a Democrat, I'll say that for him. He saw the problem. The numbers would overwhelm us, he said, and he was right. Why, you hardly hear English spoken right here on the streets of Washington. But he didn't see what was behind it. All these terrorist outbreaks are part of the Communist plot to destroy the Christian American way of life. Thank God for the Christian businessmen who saw that and began to act. They're all around us, these agents." He indicated a passing bus boy with a jerk of his head and lowered his voice to a whisper. Martínez leaned forward attentively in polite response.

"The only way, Bill," Duckett rasped in slow emphatic pronouncement, "the *only* way is to take control and close the borders. We have to help the forces in Mexico and Canada who are willing to do that. Then we can patrol the seas and protect our shores from the people who want to destroy our way of life."

"Yes, yes, I see," Martínez answered soothingly and absently. He was anxious to get to his lunch.

Well, he thought now as the car sped along the Potomac Parkway toward the Virginia countryside, business was business. A few years ago he and his associates had made a very good thing out of funneling the necessary supplies and hardware to the Salvadorans and to the contras in Nicaragua and Honduras after Congress made difficulties for the American military. The opportunity presented now was much the same but bigger, much bigger.

An instrument, Duckett had called him. Bill Martínez-Schwenger grimaced in distaste. But he was a practical man. A thought struck him and gave him a moment of sardonic amusement. Duckett would be discomfited, would he not, to know that his opponent of the morning, John Mann, was an instrument, too.

# . 5 .

CELIA pulled her car out from the space reserved beside the steps of the Senate wing of the Capitol and in the rearview mirror saw the gray sedan pull out behind her. She smiled to herself a little grimly. At least, she had won that one battle to have some life of her own. The Secret Service didn't drive her everywhere as they had at first. Now they just followed.

Wheeling down the hill toward Pennsylvania Avenue she laughed as she remembered Janie Fraser's shocked disbelief that first morning in June after the convention. The wife of the Canadian minister was one of Celia's favorite Washington companions and Janie had wanted to have lunch in the country "to hear all about it—every single thing."

"You mean they're going to drive us all the way to Middleburg?" Janie had said incredulously.

"That's what they say," Celia had said resignedly. "Isn't that so, Alec?" she addressed the back of the driver's head.

"Those are our orders, ma'am," he had answered. "But it won't be so bad. We're very good about not hearing anything we're not meant to hear."

Nevertheless, it had been bad. She and Janie had made constrained conversation on various innocuous topics during the long drive through the Virginia countryside. And even when they were seated at a table in the brick courtyard of the inn at Middleburg, the presence of the two men sitting at one remove seemed to spoil their usual easy intimacy. Celia had vowed "never again" and she had finally convinced both her husband and the head of the detail.

The maple at Sheridan Circle was red. All along Massachusetts Avenue butter-yellow chrysanthemums and varicolored zinnias and marigolds stood in stiff clumps beside embassy walks and drives or in crowded

**47**

pots beside the doorways. As she drove past the blackened ruins of the Islamic Center and started across the bridge, Celia noticed the muted colors of the trees in Rock Creek Park, their usual autumn fire dimmed by a sky in which the sun shone only fitfully between slowly moving gray clouds. From a plane, she thought, the clouds would seem to be soft, floating billows of white, bright in the sun. She had a quick intense wish to be on a plane going somewhere, anywhere. She felt betrayed by these signs of a Washington autumn less than glorious, smirched and blurred by creeping pollutants in the air. "Air quality in the moderate range—fifty-five for ozone," she said aloud, mimicking the weather recording.

Perhaps fall was never the glory she thought she remembered from year to year. Perhaps it was just that way in her mind because she had never really looked. Her feelings about the day merged with her feelings about the morning and the luncheon just over. She had not really enjoyed any of it. It had been a strain. She could not help worrying about Johnny's reaction if she agreed to appear on Peace Day. Yet how could she refuse? She'd been unable to join lightheartedly in the planning, and in her own silence she had become more aware of the interplay among the others.

She noticed how Alison Lonsdale exacted homage in her well-played role as benefactor of causes. And that Sue Powers let it be known, and not very subtly, that she, too, had money. And she had been genuinely offended by Patricia Black's persistent standoffishness. But most of all, she had been dismayed by Polly's stand. Everyone knew that Polly was the political intelligence in the Haskins family. Polly knew what was at stake if anyone did. She knew where President Batchelder stood. She could at least, Celia thought, have made it clear that they were asking a lot.

The aftertaste was unpleasant. Are we really friends after all? Celia Mann asked herself as she remembered the flurry of goodbyes when she said she must drive her daughter Susan's car pool and the way they seemed to draw together as she went ahead. All the way across Little Falls Parkway and out River Road her sense of isolation increased.

Celia Mann had come to Washington believing in friendship and loyalty, a belief she had sustained since childhood. She had discovered early the breadth and dimension given to experience by sharing and mutuality. She had rejoiced to find it given a name and a code in the books she read as a young girl. In her adolescent daydreaming she had conceived of love as the perfect form of friendship. Even now, in mid-life, when living had taught her that the bonds between human beings were often accidentally formed and only tenuously enduring, she held to her belief in friendship. True friendship was rare—she knew that—but it existed. And yet that afternoon she wondered if she had even one true friend in Washington. Ties were formed so easily here. And were so easily broken. She made a face to herself as she thought wryly of some long-ago resident's ironic description of the city, so apt that it had become an axiom: "Washington is the place where they never miss you when you're gone and are always overjoyed to see you back." Would any one of the men or women she knew here, with whom she had spent long and pleasant hours, put themselves at risk for her if she were in need of help? Well, for that matter, she asked herself sternly, would I risk anything for them? Yes, she answered herself, for anyone in real need, I do think I would. I hope I would. The driver of the car behind her tooted his horn in warning. Without realizing it, she had been driving slower and slower as she pondered.

She glanced at the mirror and saw Alec McGregor's worried face. He probably thinks he's guarding a nut, she thought as she stepped on the gas. Then another thought struck her. Why was it Alec himself who followed her when she was alone? He was the head of the detail; why wasn't he with Johnny? She must remember to ask him.

Behind her Alec McGregor was thinking about the same thing. He had fully agreed with the decision of his superiors. Ever since the Getty incident when a reluctant father had paid well for the return of a little-loved kidnapped son, the world's terrorists had favored the kidnapping of family members as a method of extortion. A government could risk the life of an official on principle, as in the case of Italy's murdered premier Aldo Moro, but the public was less likely to tolerate the sacrifice of innocent victims. A politician who clung to principle when the life of a daughter, a son, a wife, was at stake was under far greater pressure, as had been demonstrated in the Duarte affair in El Salvador among others. It had become more important to guard the families of officials and candidates than to guard the principals themselves.

It put an added burden on government resources, and especially on the Secret Service. In any campaign year they needed auxiliary forces. Ever since President Lyndon Johnson, after the death of Robert Kennedy, had ordered that all presidential candidates of both parties be protected, the service had had to borrow security men from other services and even from private agencies—like the tough, surly men from Sentry Central who had been added to McGregor's detail when he was assigned to the prospective vice-president. They were gruff and difficult to control and it was clear that Mrs. Mann found their presence distasteful, so Alec himself accompanied her whenever he could.

It was probably unprofessional even to let it enter his mind, but he preferred Mrs. Mann to her husband. The tall senator was a little too consciously affable and ingratiating for Alec's Scots taste. Mrs. Mann had an independent streak, all right, but women were independent these days, and all in all Alec thought that a good thing. In the ways that really mattered, Celia Mann was pleasant and cooperative.

He knew her well enough by now to realize that her occasional absentmindedness was just that and nothing more. But slowing down as she had done just now was dangerous. It attracted attention—might even give some maniac on the curb the idea of running out to her car and doing God knows what. So he had hit the horn.

"You're almost the *last* mother, Mommy," said Susan as she climbed into the car when Celia stopped before the weathered stone house that served as the Longworth Middle School.

"I'm sorry, dear," said Celia absently. "Traffic, traffic." Three other little girls fell over each other getting into the back seat.

"Can we hurry, Mrs. Mann?" said one breathlessly. "Me and Penny have our ballet lessons."

Her tone was self-important. And censorious. I really do dislike that child, Celia thought, and I shouldn't. "I'll drive as fast as I can, Elly," she said, forcing cheerfulness into her voice. "Would it help if I took you right to the ballet school?"

"Oh, no," said Elly. "*My* mother will be all ready."

I suppose she will, Celia thought. She doesn't worry about saving the world. Oh, stop. Everybody worries even if they carry on as usual. You *are* feeling sorry for yourself. But she was seized with a sudden fierce envy of Elly's mother, living her homey, everyday life. For some reason Celia imagined the other mother in a pretty kitchen with geraniums in the window, baking cookies for her importunate daughter.

Home at last, she shared milk and cookies with Susan and listened to her chatter about the slumber party to which she had been invited. She looked at her daughter's round unshadowed face and sighed. "For your children," Polly had said. Polly doesn't even have children. If only there were someone who would understand. Amy Quinn? The thought seemed to come unbidden out of nowhere. It would be an opening—an excuse to talk to Amy—to ask her advice. She hadn't talked to Amy since the convention. If only the Quinns had stayed on. But they had left right after Tom had taken himself out of the contest for the vice-presidency. When Susan wandered off to change and to feed her gerbil, Celia turned to the telephone.

The far-away ringing seemed to go on and on. Perhaps Amy was in Alaska, too? She had read that Tom was there—some kind of conference on state industry exchange. Then a click and someone on the line. "Yes?" The voice, terse and flat, was scarcely recognizable, but it was Amy's. Celia could almost see her sitting in her little office on the third floor of the Governor's Mansion.

"Yes, who is that?"

"Amy, it's Celia."

"Yes."

"Celia Mann." Surely Amy knew her voice, as she knew Amy's.

"Yes." The monosyllable was neither warm nor friendly.

"Amy, I've been wanting to talk to you for so long. I was so sorry when you left the convention."

A silence. Then Amy's voice, much closer. Cold and hostile. *"You're sorry!* That's really funny."

Celia felt her heart beginning to pound. She groped cautiously for words. "But Amy, of course I'm sorry. We're friends."

"Friends!" Amy's voice climbed and shook. "What kind of friend would do what your husband did to Tom? Don't say 'friend' to me—your friends aren't decent people!"

Celia felt the perspiration break out between her shoulder blades and the palm of her hand grow slippery on the phone. She was not sure her voice would work. "Amy, Amy, please," she said. "Amy, please don't say things like that. Amy, I don't understand."

Amy was clearly crying now. "It's easy to understand. Tom withdrew because he wants to stay alive, and he wants me and Jill to stay—" She could not finish. Celia could hear her sobbing breath as if she were in the same room. Then she started again. "Don't ever, ever call me again, Celia Mann!" The sound of the connection breaking was loud, but Celia sat listening without moving. She did not hear the mechanical recording—"Please hang up. If you need assistance, dial the operator"—

or the subsequent beep-beep, beep-beep, and finally the resigned hum of the defeated machine. What she heard was Sam Drottman's voice, that night in the convention headquarters . . .

"Leo's stuck it to him and he's backing off . . . Leo's stuck it to him . . . Leo's stuck it to him . . ."

Celia was still awake when Johnny came home. She heard his cheerful goodnight to the Secret Service men and knew he was still feeling the exhilaration of his speech and the way his press conference had topped the evening news. Would it be a good time to talk to him? After a moment she decided against it. He wouldn't have changed his mind about Peace Work, and he wouldn't want to talk about—other things. And, Celia thought, there are some things one is afraid to know. She lay still.

John Mann moved about his room whistling under his breath. He felt very good indeed. The president had been more than pleased. And she had gone on to say that, although it wasn't exactly according to protocol, she thought it would be a good idea to have John Mann and "dear Celia" at the dinner for the Canadian prime minister. "We'll have a little visit alone with him to talk about Moonlab. I think we can use your persuasive powers. I'll have someone come over to brief you tomorrow."

It was a breakthrough. So far, the president's emphasis had been on his skill at handling other legislators. Now he was being let in on foreign policy.

He hesitated before putting on his pajamas and looked at the door to the connecting bathroom. He was restless. Celia would like that—about the Canadian prime minister. She was big on international relations. He reached for his bathrobe, belted it around him, and went into the bathroom. It smelled of her familiar flowery scent—carnations. Little rivulets ran down the mirror—water that had very recently been steam. She must have bathed not long ago. She was probably awake although she had not called out to him as she usually did. Well, he thought, after this morning . . . He opened the other door.

"Celia?"

"Mm-hmmm."

"It was a good speech, wasn't it?"

She rolled over.

"A great speech," she said and opened her arms.

* * *

Later:

"I talked to Amy, Johnny. She was so strange. She said terrible things."

Johnny's voice, unmoved, offhand. "Yeah, well, I guess they wanted that nomination pretty badly."

"But, Johnny"—How much did she dare to say?—"she seems to blame you—us."

He flopped onto his back, the movement impatient. "She's just upset because I got it and Tom didn't."

"But, Johnny, they're our *friends* . . ." Then, slowly, "Johnny, who is Leo?"

A long silence. Then, "Leo? Oh, he's just some friend of Sam's."

# . 6 .

I T W A S four o'clock the next afternoon when Sam finally ushered the briefing trio from the State Department out of Senator Mann's office. Johnny, who had stood to shake hands with each one, sank into his chair and put his feet on the desk. He stared at the ceiling.

"Whew," he said into the air. "Looks as if we've got our work cut out for us tonight. It's not going to be easy to get the PM to cooperate, with all that Canada has against us just now."

Sam nodded. "Some of these issues have been festering a long time," he said. "Acid rain—still no progress there. The trade thing never worked out to their satisfaction. American ownership of resources. On some of these things Batchelder is just as bullheaded as any of the men before her."

"On the other hand, we'll be taking all the risks on Moonlab and putting up all the money. They just get the benefits of cosponsorship. Best to admit all the other stuff and concentrate on that, I think."

John Mann was not really talking to him, Sam knew. He was working things out, planning out loud. Sam turned toward the door. He had almost reached it when the senator stopped him.

"Sam—" He paused. His tone was tentative.

"Yes?"

"Celia asked me about Leo last night. Wanted to know who he was. Seems she had a talk with Amy Quinn, and Amy upset her."

Sam swore to himself but kept his voice casual.

"Oh, what did Mrs. Quinn tell her?"

"I don't know. Didn't ask. No need to open up that can of worms. But Sam, there wasn't anything, anything, well, *irregular*—about Leo's talk with Quinn at the convention, was there?"

54

"Hell, no," Sam answered. "Not as far as I know. Quinn owes Leo, just the way we do. Leo just made it clear that he was backing you and told Quinn to back off, that's all. Quinn didn't like it. Who would? He got sore and pulled out." That's more or less the truth, he thought, and it ought to satisfy Johnny.

"Yeah—just thought I'd double-check."

Sam smiled to himself. Johnny knew—he had always known—when to leave well enough alone.

John Mann looked at his watch. His voice was again assured. "Better tell them to bring the car around. I've got to pick up Celia and get to the White House by six-thirty. Have Jule call and tell her I'll dress here."

Back in his own office Sam slumped heavily into his chair. So the lady was snooping around, was she? That could be dangerous. She was like a wild card lately, apt to pop up anywhere. As if she'd not caused enough trouble with this peace stuff of hers. God, if it wasn't one thing, it was another. How had he gotten into this, anyway? Well, he'd better talk to somebody about it. Jim Fifield, he supposed. Not to Leo. Not yet.


Celia sat looking out the window. She wondered why she did not have the sense of expectancy she usually felt about going to the White House. No matter how often she had been there she had always felt excited and, yes, special to have been invited. But today she felt nothing.

There was a tapping at the window beside which she was sitting. She jumped, then laughed in relief as she saw the man standing there. Yanni! She had forgotten he was coming. Her spirits lifted at the sight of him, tall and brawny, dressed in a jogging suit, his brown mustachioed face and merry brown eyes gleaming at her good-naturedly. A part of her normal life. With his presence, things seemed to fall back into place.

"*El peluquero!*" announced Juanita unnecessarily as she bustled through the breakfast room to let him in the side door. Juanita loved diversions in the routine and Jan Michal, Celia's hairdresser, was a favorite of hers. Celia could hear his cheerful "*Cómo está?*" and his efforts to carry on a conversation about Juanita's health and family in his rudimentary Spanish. When they entered the room together Juanita's smiling face reflected her pleasure.

"Am I glad to see you!" Celia said. "My hair is an absolute disaster and I have to try to look smashing at the White House tonight. Coffee?" She gestured at the pot on the table.

"I brought both the electric curling iron and the blow dryer. We'll fix it up somehow," said Yanni, lifting the small canvas bag he was carrying. "I left the car in the lot at Saks and jogged over. Coffee? No coffee, thanks. I am steaming as it is. You'll probably have to hold your nose while I'm working."

Celia laughed and stood up. "That's a long way," she said, "and I suppose you're going to jog back? Won't you stiffen up while you're here? I thought it wasn't good to stop for any length of time." She was leading the way toward the stairs as she talked.

"Oh, this won't take long," said Yanni. "I'll just keep jumping up and down as I work, the way they do at street corners waiting for the light to change."

"I suppose you will," said Celia with mock resignation as she went into her room and settled before the mirror at her dressing table. She and Yanni had an easy, long-standing relationship. She had known him first when Johnny was governor and the governors' annual conference had met at a resort in the Pennsylvania mountains. Yanni worked in the hotel shop. When she came to Washington as a new Senate wife, he had written a note reminding her and sent a brochure on the shop he had opened in Georgetown. She had followed it up and become a steady client. It was an arrangement that worked out pleasantly for both of them. His business thrived, in part because of the government wives who came on her recommendation. In gratitude he did special favors for her, which made her busy life easier. He came to the house for comb-outs, as he was doing today, and occasionally went to the studio with her for last-minute touch-ups, when she had to appear on television.

I wonder why this is so comforting, thought Celia to herself, as Yanni began working on her hair. So much of what made her life possible depended on people like Yanni—and Juanita. Yanni would not appreciate my bracketing them together, she thought ruefully, watching his absorbed face in the mirror, and I don't really. He is a true professional. But they both care for me without making demands.

She admitted to herself that she was glad Johnny would not be coming home to change. She did not think Johnny realized it, but there was a patronizing tone in his voice and a faint note of disdain in his manner whenever he and Yanni met. She was sure that Yanni, whose intuitions were keen, was even more aware of it than she herself. Yet Johnny seemed to understand that Yanni filled a need in her life. She supposed it was something like the role Sam, or Jule, his secretary, played in his.

Yanni put down the brush and stood back. He looked satisfied.

"What are you wearing?" Yanni asked just as the phone rang. Celia, reaching for the phone, indicated a glittering sequined gown of deep red hanging on the closet door. Yanni made extravagant gestures of approval. Celia tried to keep the rising laughter from her voice as she watched him gather up his things, make a deep mock bow in her direction, and jog lightly around the room and out the door. Into the phone she said, "Oh, Peter, how good to hear from you!"

Her son's voice was excited. She looked at her watch. She had to give Peter time but Johnny would be in a fury of impatience if she wasn't ready on the dot. And with reason. It did not do to be late at the White House. But she put all she could into her voice as she answered.

"You made the first team! Oh, Peter, how great—and you just a sophomore! Your father will be so proud. He'll be announcing it to everyone at the White House tonight." It was important to keep assuring him of his father's interest. "Tell me all about it—how they made the pick and all that." She tucked the telephone between her chin and shoulder and reached for her dress. Maybe she could get the dress on as she listened.

But at the other end of the line her son had caught the hint of pressure in the mention of the White House. Some of the enthusiasm drained from his voice. She could almost see the closed, patient expression with which she was so familiar. She kept trying.

"Oh—after only the second scrimmage? Don't sound so offhand, Petey—you should be proud! Susie's going to a slumber party tonight and she'll be *so* important. When's the first game? And where? Here—with St. Alban's—wonderful. We—I'll be there, for sure."

When she finally hung up, she felt drained. That game would be on the first day of Johnny's campaign swing. Somehow she would have to manage.

"All right, all right, I'm coming," she almost snapped at Juanita, who had appeared and was nervously repeating that El Señor was waiting.


Peter Mann came out of the phone booth on the first floor of Seward Hall and began to climb the stairs to his room. He climbed slowly. He was, he decided, really dragging—bushed from practice. He thought he might just skip dinner at the training table and sack out. He wasn't really hungry. He could not acknowledge even to himself the depth of his disappointment.

His mother had been really glad for him—he knew that. If there was one thing Peter Mann was sure about it was that his mother was for him. But she couldn't really know what it was like—how really great it was that he had been picked for the first team in his sophomore year. Sometimes when he called at this time of the day—just before his parents went out—he would catch his father at home and get a chance to talk to him. It was better than calling the office and leaving a message. Peter Mann hated that. He had hoped against hope that his father would be home just now. His father knew what it meant to outdistance other contenders. To do your damnedest and win. And he would be proud. For once, Peter thought, he might have had his father's total attention.

In his room he collapsed on his bed but did not sleep. The excitement of his pick was still with him and the need to share his elation had not abated. He wondered vaguely about calling somebody else.

There was Allie Soames, the girl he liked best at Cleveland Day, the neighboring school for girls. He discarded the thought almost as soon as it came. She'd assume he was calling to make another date and he wasn't ready for that. He wished he could call Bill Cratte but he wasn't sure he should. It would be hard to get Bill now that he was on rotation at the hospital and, anyway, things weren't quite the same with him. Oh hell, nothing was the same anymore. He rolled over on his side and stared out the window into the gathering dusk. The unhappiness, which had been temporarily overridden by his elation, began to return . . .

Last summer, after the convention, they had gone back to the Cape, but having the Secret Service there spoiled everything. He could not work at the Surf Club the way he had every summer since he was in eighth grade. Too exposed, they said, too close to the road.

He remembered how good he had felt when Bill Cratte, the local Hartport college student who was assistant manager, had picked him over five others for the job. "You're a hard worker, Pete," he had said. "You remind me of myself at your age." His brown eyes twinkled and he grinned, his teeth very white in his tanned face. "We can only take so many members' sons and we want somebody who won't kite off every time he has something better to do. This job has got to come first, understand?"

Bill wasn't really a grownup but he was a dependable, reliable older person who was always there, always encouraging, always patient. And Bill was somebody you could trust. He wasn't like Tom Wentworth, who, with his wife Prue, managed the Surf Club. Even as a small boy Pete had noticed that Wentworth catered to the richer, more important members. He fawned over them and looked for ways to ingratiate himself by giving them special service, only to mimic them and make jokes at their expense behind their backs. Bill Cratte wasn't like that. He was always the same to everybody.

Bill taught Peter to sail and how to take care of gear and boats. He taught him lifesaving. And he taught him how to wait on tables. He taught him, by example, how to be of service without being subservient. Peter, often lonely for adult male companionship, tagged after him whenever he could. Little by little, Bill began to return his regard. A friendship sprang up between them.

"Never mind, Pete," Bill had consoled him when he heard the Secret Service decision. "We'll still get our sailing in. Even I can only work part time now that I'm in medical school. Things change."

But, thought Peter miserably, it wasn't just things that had changed. Bill Cratte himself had changed. Like always talking about being French-Canadian. He never used to do that. Why, the "e" on Cratte was the only thing French about Bill's family. They talked the way other Cape people talked. They didn't even know French. Oh, Bill's mother said she knew a little. And that stew she sometimes had when Peter was there for Sunday dinner—she said that was a recipe from her grandmother in Quebec. But that was all.

The summer before last there had been some sort of Cratte reunion in Manchester and Bill had come back talking about French-Canadian history and the oppression of the French by the Anglo-Saxons. He was still talking about it this summer.

Bill's new preoccupation had shadowed that one perfect day at Hartport in August. They had sailed together out through the cut that connected Hartport Harbor to the ocean. The air was so clear that everything shimmered in the sun—the sand, the white sails of the other boats, the bobbing orange buoys, the little floating schools of red markers for the lobster pots. A brisk steady wind slapped the waves against the sides of the boat. Perfect. Except for the Secret Service men following. And Bill's going on about being French.

"Oh, cut it, Bill," Peter had finally said. "I'm no Anglo-Saxon, you know that. Mann is short for Mancuski or something. We're Czech or Polish or something on my father's side."

"You should *know*," Bill had said seriously. "You should know your history."

"I just want to be American," Peter had said suddenly. "And I just want to sail." Bill didn't argue, but the day was not the same as others they had spent together. Nothing was the same. No, he decided, he wouldn't call Bill. He turned away from the window. It was dark outside.

# . 7 .

CLEM BOISE sat alone in his den sipping bourbon and watching the local television news.

"Now here's Sally Proctor at the White House," said the local anchorman, and the newswoman appeared on the screen in front of a glowing and lighted White House. "What's going on there, Sally?" he asked.

"It all seems festive here on the south lawn, Ben," she answered, "just the usual state dinner. You can hardly hear the demonstrators, which is probably why they're using this entrance instead of the north portico. President Batchelder is counting a lot on this visit of the Canadian prime minister. Word is that she expects Baxter to go away committed to a North American base on the moon instead of endorsing the All-Europe SuperLab as the other Commonwealth and the Common Market countries are doing. The prime minister and Mrs. Baxter should be arriving any minute now. And, after them, vice-presidential candidate John Mann and Mrs. Mann. The press office tells us the Manns have been invited for 'a private cocktail hour' but our sources believe that the president is counting on her new running mate to persuade the prime minister that an independent station will be more likely to ensure the safety of the hemisphere."

There it goes—the telegraphing of the potential threat of an independent and armed space station put in place ahead of the others, thought Boise grimly. Independence in space was dangerous these days. He had tried to convince the president of that. But she was deaf to his arguments. In a way he understood. It stood to reason that the first woman president would feel she had to show strength. And Lily Batchelder's concern was with the rising tide of terrorism. The victims of terrorism were not faceless and lost in numbers like the victims of war.

**61**

Those who mourned them cried out for justice in the headlines of morning papers from coast to coast. A woman, thought Clem Boise, might be especially vulnerable to those headlines. Hell, it would be hard enough for any president to handle. But a space station wouldn't eliminate terrorism—it was like trying to kill mosquitoes with a shotgun.

While he was lost in thought the anchorman had reappeared and run through a series of local happenings. Mangled cars and bleeding bodies at an intersection in northeast Washington. An overturned trailer truck and a pile-up on the Capital Beltway. A belligerent pusher being hustled out of a run-down apartment by the police. Now the White House correspondent was on the screen again. The vice-president came to attention.

"Prime Minister and Mrs. Baxter have just arrived at the south portico," the voice of Sally Proctor announced unnecessarily. The prime minister turned to the cameras after he had helped his wife out of the car and waved in a friendly fashion. He doesn't look like a pushover, Clem Boise acknowledged to himself. He must have been holding his own during the day-long negotiations and would probably hold up well enough in the talk with Lily and young Mann tonight.

Still, his position was certainly weakened by the way the French separatist movement was carrying its fight south of the border despite Lily's stepped-up security. It was no secret that little colonies of terrorists were holed up in the Great Lakes port cities like Buffalo, Erie, Cleveland, Detroit and Duluth and the towns near the border in New England where they were indistinguishable from Americans of French-Canadian origin. They went back and forth at will. That mass bombing in Manchester at the country market last week had been the last straw. Twenty-seven dead. A hundred more injured and a crater yards wide in a once-peaceful street.

Yes, Lily would make the most of that, the vice-president reflected. There wouldn't be much left to discuss when he had his own private chat with Baxter after the dinner at the embassy tomorrow. Well, they could always talk about hunting elk. Baxter was supposed to like that as much as he did himself.

The Baxters disappeared into the White House, where the president could be glimpsed waiting to welcome them. The Manns' car drew up and the Secret Service men got out to open the doors, one on each side. Boise caught sight of Alec McGregor. Good man, McGregor, he thought, as he sipped his drink. Wonder if he's turned up anything yet.

John Mann was tall and handsome under the lights and his wife's red dress glittered as she moved. Pretty woman, thought Boise again and

then—as the cameras closed in on Celia's practiced smile—doesn't look
as if she laughs as much as she used to. He switched off the set and
went in to his lonely dinner.


In his suite at the Madison Hotel, Dr. Maurice Chouinard, science
adviser to the prime minister, had also watched the Baxters and the
Manns arrive at the White House. So it went smoothly. He had done
what Fifield wanted—brought them together. It had not been hard to
convince the prime minister that he should let it be known he wanted to
talk to Mann. Baxter was wary of the woman president in any case. It
mattered not a bit to Chouinard whether the prime minister was persuaded to agree with the American president or not. In his own mind
he was sure that whoever possessed the controlling space station would
soon yield to another, greater force of which the world was not yet aware.
Still, if Fifield thought this meeting was necessary to solidify John
Mann's influence with the president of the United States, who was he to
argue? Chouinard also turned off his set and prepared to go down to his
dinner.

Maurice Chouinard was a man with only one passion. Like many
others of his generation, he had found the secondary position of the
French in Canada intolerable. He had been an early enlistee in the ranks
of the Parti Québecois, which sought a separate status for the Province
of Quebec, and had become one of its most able members. But he was
not content to stop there. In medical school at McGill University he
had gravitated to the other students who were, like the French Canadians, of minority status. He had come to realize that in every country—
especially in every Commonwealth country—there were people once
conquered and still civilly oppressed. The linking of these groups into
a worldwide network had become his dream. Maurice Chouinard was
the father of that shadowy entity called simply "The People."

He had worked at his chosen profession and, as his interest turned
more and more toward social and industrial medicine, he had found his
ties to the international health organizations increasingly useful. He
saw a direct connection between the encroachment of mining and oil
exploration on agricultural land and the impoverishment of his people.
He saw a connection between the profit-driven chemical industries and
the rise in cancer, blood disease and birth defects among the poor. He
saw noxious wastes polluting the earth, and the waters that had once
produced food made life-killing with acid rain, and he saw the con-

nection between that and world hunger. Seeing these things fed his rage.

As he moved from one United Nations or inter-American conference to another, comparing notes, sharing knowledge, he found allies. At the same time he found a way of financing his dream in the illegal traffic into which young professionals—lawyers, doctors, lower-echelon corporate executives and the like, who had passed their school years among marijuana users—were drawn with ease. Some of them were veterans of Vietnam who had, during that disturbing, divisive war, learned how to augment military pay by smuggling the rich and prized leaf of the Orient into the United States on their return flights into air bases from Moffatt Field to Otis on Cape Cod. A few of them dealt in heroin as well. Others, not dealers themselves, were the suddenly affluent, upwardly mobile, onetime pot smokers, who had graduated to the more chic and trendy use of cocaine. And, of course, there were the entertainers and sports figures who depended on the rush of drugs to fuel their frenetic energy. These were not people who wanted to deal with street pushers. Their dealers moved among them, a little flashy perhaps, but respectable enough in three-piece suits. It was easy enough for Maurice Chouinard to find men interested in making money that way.

It was hardly even necessary to be secretive about such transactions. Most of the men he knew professionally were interested only in dealing for their own use, but there were among them those who were venal enough to be interested in bigger deals. The narcotics boom in Canada and in the United States began in the early 1970s. By the late 1980s it was accounting for more than $80 billion a year in untaxed profits in the States and was expanding at the astonishing rate of $10 billion a year. The money laundering required to handle such great profits became a financial industry in itself. Small private banks were chartered on both sides of the Canadian border. Complicated real estate investment companies invested on both sides of the line. Some of the new breed of doctor-businessmen enriched by swollen medical fees became group investors in such operations. Doctor Elwood Grant was one of these. And Elwood Grant had led Chouinard to Doctor James Fifield and then to Senator John Mann and his useful backers. Political protection was necessary.

The money was flowing very freely now, and the forces of "The People" grew and multiplied and were stronger every day. They could use their profits for arms deals and, as the pressure increased to stem the flow of illegal aliens over the southwestern border of the United States, these profits also paid the people-smugglers who brought mafia hoods, Greek ship-jumpers, Latin-American drug traffickers, and terrorists through Montreal south into the United States. Yes, there were many sources of money now.

He left the hotel and took a cab.

"La Plaza on Columbia Road," he instructed the driver in his precise, unaccented English. "I will direct you if you do not know the way. One goes out 18th Street from here."

He was familiar with Washington cabdrivers and the hazards of dealing with them. The hack force, always heavily manned with part-time drivers, had been almost overwhelmed in recent years by numbers of foreign residents, many of them with only the sketchiest knowledge of the city. Others, better informed, came from cultures in which bargaining, getting the better of buyers and overcharging were at once legitimate sports and means of survival. They had transferred these talents to hacking with such eagerness that a trip across the city was often a chancy venture at best. But this time Chouinard had drawn a driver who was a native Washingtonian.

"Some folks would be mad, you talking like that, telling them the way to go," he said as he pulled away from the curb. "But I don't blame you, man. These Iranians and Nigerians are just plain giving us a real bad name. Gonna kill off the tourist business in this town, that's what they going to do. Half of 'em ain't got no license. And they steal honest folks' business right from under our noses . . ."

He continued the tirade as he threaded his way through the still-heavy traffic on Massachusetts Avenue and turned out 18th Street toward Washington's flourishing Adams-Morgan district. Maurice Chouinard half-listened as he looked out the window. He took pleasure in noting the polyglot character of the renewing neighborhood. An Afghan restaurant next to an Italian carry-out, a brasserie, a McDonald's, a veritable litany of Latin names—Miguel's, Churrería Madrid, El Caribe. He was jerked to attention by a jolting slamming of the brakes and the driver's outraged cursing.

"Goddamn spics!" the driver yelled out the window at a Mexican family in leisurely progress across the traffic lanes on their way to the El Caribe. "Lookit that, will ya," he appealed to Maurice. "Lookit that. Damn fools don't care if they get killed or not!"

Amused, Chouinard watched the Mexicans go. The father, stocky and macho, walked ahead. Two sons, perhaps ten and twelve, one smaller than the other but both replicas of their father in open-necked white shirts and blue trousers, followed. After them came the mother, in bright blue nylon, carrying one little girl and leading another. Both children wore ruffled pink dresses. It was plainly an occasion, this eating out—probably a name day, thought Maurice—and it was to be properly observed. They were not to be hurried.

The Spanish-speaking were very good at maintaining their own ways in an Anglo world, he thought as the cab finally went on. Here in the United States, especially in the Southwest, they had clung to their language and their customs for almost three hundred years. And they were learning to join with the newcomers. All together they were already a formidable Hispanic force. His own people had not done so well. The French had assimilated too easily. But he and his people had begun to reverse that. With the help of historians at the universities he had launched the Cause Famille. For several years now hundreds of people with the same name were gathered together in "family reunions" at which they were reminded of their heritage and the wrongs that had been done them. From the Cause Famille came the recruits who were needed to do the work that needed doing in the United States.

At La Plaza he paid off the still-muttering driver with relief. As he entered he looked about the little restaurant with approval. Fresh flowers, white linen, well-spaced tables. A good place to meet.

The maître d' led him to the alcove where his dinner companion waited. Francisco Hernández-Mateo, minister of the embassy of Mexico, rose and greeted him solemnly with an *abrazo*.

"It has been too long, *amigo*," he said.

"Too long," agreed Chouinard, taking his seat and opening his napkin. "But it is best to be careful."

"*Naturalmente*," the minister agreed. "Be assured that I have told everyone who would listen that we meet on public health matters." White teeth flashed under a brushy mustache. "See," he added as the waiter approached, "in honor of the occasion I have ordered the best French wine this house affords so that we can drink to our project." He tasted the wine and nodded to the waiter, who filled their glasses.

"To our project, *amigo*," he said significantly, raising his glass. "To the health of all the Americans!"

Maurice acknowledged the toast and drank. The wine *was* good. But he frowned a little. The Mexican was too ebullient. They still had a long way to go. But Hernández-Mateo's spirits were not to be dampened.

"When I think that I once thought you crazy, my friend," he said over dinner, "I am overcome with shame. No, it is true. I said to myself, this little Frenchman, this doctor, who has let him loose? Does he think he can overthrow the governments of two nations and bring the Colossus of the North to its knees? Incredible. Incredible! But now it is possible. It can happen. And it is you who have done it. I acknowledge it; I am your friend, your servant, forever. I am in your debt—I and those who come after me—forever."

And you would betray me as easily as you betray your superiors now, thought Maurice. But not yet. Just now you have too much at stake.

Aloud he said, "No one accomplishes anything without help. That is why I needed to confer with you once more, even though"—he paused delicately—"I have my men placed and watchful in every phase of the operation."

"Again *naturalmente*," said Francisco, "but what then can I tell you?"

"How it looks to you. Undoubtedly you perceive things from another perspective."

"Well then, this is what I see. My government suspects nothing. They protect the American presence but see it, as usual, as the result of the American preoccupation with outside influences in Latin America."

"And the Americans?"

The Mexican shrugged. "We have our friends in high places. And the others—ah, *amigo*, it is almost laughable how they, as they put it so well in English, rise to the bait. The religious fanatics—for them it is a crusade. And the money men—how happy they are at the prospect that there will be fewer of us." He paused and fixed his brown eyes, so dark that they were almost opaque, on Maurice. "We are sure that they are deceived in that?"

"Do not fear," said Maurice. "The strength of The People is in our numbers. No, my friend, we go by the book. On every staff, in every cadre, there will be a shadow man with every qualification to lead and to see that our ends, and ours only, are the ones served. The American officers and the CIA men will not survive the victory." He permitted himself to smile. "They will die mercifully, smiling in their moment of triumph."

Hernández-Mateo laughed aloud. "Another toast, then, to the health of the Americans."

Maurice Chouinard raised his glass, then paused and held up his hand. "But I forget—" His eyes were searching. "Did I also say that for every shadow man there is another, unknown to him, watching. There will be no slip-ups."

The minister blinked but his voice did not change. "*Naturalmente, amigo.* Let us drink."


No doubt about it, Celia thought, her former apathy disappearing as she took the proffered arm of the serious-faced young naval aide, it *is* heady to be here and to be one of those escorted to the private quarters. And to be one of the stars at a full-scale state dinner, white tie and all! She hoped nervously that her dress was appropriate. Lily was always perfectly dressed and expected others to be. Well, it was too late to worry now. They crossed the diplomatic reception room, where the soft colors of the antique mural-like wallpaper glowed in the soft light, and went into the hall. She could hear, floating down the stairwell, the sounds of the Marine Band, called the president's own, as the band members tuned their instruments. There was a sense of occasion pervading the mellow old mansion. Each resident of the White House, she thought, makes an imprint. President Batchelder's evidently was the mark of restored historical grandeur and dignity. The aide handed Celia into the small elevator, waited for John to follow, then joined them again.

On the third floor they went down the wide hall to the door of the private drawing room where the naval aide took his leave, wishing them a pleasant evening. The oval room was very bright and seemed a little too big for the people in it. Although the September night was warm, a small fire glowed in the fireplace. But the doors to the Truman balcony were open and the president stood there with Mr. and Mrs. Baxter, all three of them admiring the view.

The president's personal secretary, Mitzi Blanchette, came to meet them. Looking at Mitzi's small, bony, bland and concentrated face, Celia heard the echo of Lily's voice in her mind. "I feel strongly that the First Lady's chores are important and I think that with the excellent help of my dear friend and secretary, I can tend to them and give them the importance they deserve."

No matter what the malcontents like Sarah Lindblad might say, Celia thought to herself, Lily had combined the presidency and the First Lady-ship very well. The glow and polish of the White House reflected the presence of a careful chatelaine and all the ceremonial and traditional receptions, teas and dinners took place with precise and painstaking attention to detail. This dinner will be like that, too, Celia thought as Mitzi drew them toward a little group by the fire.

"Secretary and Mrs. Griffin, you know Senator and Mrs. Mann, I'm sure." While her husband shook hands with the secretary of state, Celia looked at the others and, with a little lurch of uneasiness, recognized Cromfield Haines standing with the tall, forbidding-looking woman who was his wife. They, too, murmured greetings, and Mitzi moved John and Celia on.

"Come, let me introduce you to the prime minister and Mrs. Baxter," she said.

The president turned as they approached. "Well, well, here's the man I wanted you to meet, Prime Minister," she said prettily. She kissed Celia's cheek. "And his pretty wife," she added. Her voice was indulgent. She might as well pat me on the head, Celia thought with a flash of resentment.

It was not the first time she had noticed how patronizing some women could be when they had become successful in careers of their own. And lord knows, Lily was successful—perhaps the most successful woman in the world.

Lily Batchelder was not very tall but she held herself erect. Beside the rather short, almost dumpy Canadian she looked stately. She was in the black she had affected since her husband's death, but it was relieved by broad bands of blue silk edging the floating sleeves and underlining the decolletage. The blue brought out her eyes and enhanced the chestnut sheen of her freshly coiffed hair. There was a gloss of perfection in Lily Batchelder's grooming. There always had been.

"I owe it to Chet to look my best," Celia remembered Lily saying when she had run into her as she emerged from Elizabeth Arden's on an impossibly muggy day when Celia herself had decided that she could not, would not, sit under a dryer. Celia supposed that Lily now owed it to the country.

Celia had known Lily Batchelder for a long time but had never felt that she knew her well. When Lily's husband served in Washington as one of the businessmen drafted by a previous administration as advisers, she and Lily had belonged to some of the same clubs. Lily was charming to everyone. She elicited general approval and always ended up either president of the group or heading the most important committee. She invariably executed her duties with quiet efficiency but never by herself. She had the knack of enlisting the energies of a bevy of devoted helpers. She was lavish in praise and encouragement and always made generous acknowledgment of any assistance she received. Her circle was ever-widening. But she had no intimates. Lily never exchanged confidences or took part in the gossip or the little intrigues with which such groups were rife. Her refusal to do so did not evoke resentment, however, because she was never righteous in her attitude; she listened to others with a seemingly genuine interest and joined in their laughter. She was popular with women and men alike. All those qualities now stood her in good stead.

"I know of your work on international health, of course," the prime minister was saying to Johnny, and as the three officials fell almost instantly into a technical discussion, Mrs. Baxter looked at Celia with a resigned expression.

"Shall we go sit down?" she asked. Celia followed her to a sofa. A white-jacketed waiter offered them champagne cocktails on a silver tray and Celia took one. Champagne cocktails, and champagne cocktails only, had been the hallmark of White House hospitality since Lily Batchelder took office. For the first time Celia felt the full import of that custom—this president did not allow for differences. Well, Johnny would manage in spite of that, she supposed; Johnny always did, but she wasn't sure about herself.

The president had detached herself from Johnny and the prime minister and was moving toward them. Her smile was sweet and brilliant but Celia felt a pinch of apprehension as she watched her approach. The president took the chair beside Celia but directed her remarks to Mrs. Baxter.

"We don't have a great deal of time before we go down," she said, "and your husband and Senator Mann and I would like to have a few private words, so I must take this opportunity to chat with you ladies."

"I'm looking forward to the dinner, Madam President," said Mrs. Baxter. "It's my first state dinner outside the home country and I've heard so much about your gracious entertaining."

"Aren't you sweet to say so?" said the president, sipping her cocktail, and her china-blue eyes beamed appreciatively. She eyed Celia speculatively. Celia felt uncomfortable under her gaze. What was Lily thinking?

Celia was certainly a beauty when I first knew her, the president acknowledged to herself, with those dark blue eyes, fine bones, and that crisp hair winging away from her temples. Of course, she is still good-looking—with the sure looks of maturity. The lines around her eyes and mouth are pleasant ones, showing no hint of the bitterness you sometimes see in the faces of political wives. But she should not be mixed up in Peace Work, not now. Some women were just unreasonable about that—they wouldn't face the realities. They didn't have to, she thought wearily.

The president stirred, smiled charmingly at them both, and patted Celia's knee as she stood up. "I'm going to leave Secretary and Mrs. Griffin and Mr. and Mrs. Haines here to entertain you ladies," she said, and, to Mrs. Baxter, "You know, this lady's husband is going to be president himself some day. I just know she will help him all she can. She's a pretty formidable politician in her own right, you know."

As President Batchelder moved off, Mrs. Baxter's eyes followed her. She looked puzzled. She had heard the hint of iron in that slow Southern voice, Celia thought.

A vivid picture from the past flashed into Celia's mind. She had gone to the Batchelders' to bring a gift to Lily's visiting grandson. It was a bright red ball and, as a present, a great success. The sturdy little three-year-old had grasped it in both hands and beamed.

"*My* ball," he announced with a hint of question in his voice.

"*Your* ball," Celia agreed happily.

He bounced it with more vigor than direction. It caromed off the coffee table, bounced twice on the Aubusson carpet, and rolled into the big drawing room. Instantly Lily was kneeling in front of him imprisoning both his hands in her own. Her smile was sweet, her voice was soft.

"Now, Ritchey, tell us where we play with balls at Nana's house."

The little boy squatted down and pulled in a useless effort to free his hands from their gentle but firm restraints.

"I know you know, Ritchey. You're Nana's big boy, aren't you? Tell us where we play with balls at Nana's house."

The answer was reluctant, but it came.

"Outside—out in the gar-den."

His grandmother hugged him. "That's right. That's Nana's big, smart boy. He knows. Now take your nice red ball outside. But first, what do we say to Mrs. Mann for bringing it to Ritchey?"

"Thank you," said the little boy. He trotted off after his ball but his smile was gone.

Why did I think of that? But Celia knew very well why she had thought of it. Where do we play with our peace things, Celia? Somewhere else. She turned to Mrs. Baxter, who was looking at her expectantly.

"She thinks I'm too interested in the peace movement," Celia explained. "At least, I think that's what she means."

Mrs. Baxter's expression was sympathetic, but with the wisdom of long political wifehood she made no comment.

There was a general shifting of places. Mrs. Griffin drew Mrs. Baxter away to a chair near the fireplace. Cromfield Haines, with a pro forma "May I?" sat down next to Celia. When she thought it over afterwards she decided that those few minutes with her were the reason for his presence at the dinner.

"I couldn't help overhearing you ladies in the Senate Dining Room yesterday," he said without preamble. "I thought you were wise to resist their invitation. If you did chair the program it would be sure to be misinterpreted now that your husband is on the ticket."

"I didn't exactly 'resist it' altogether," said Celia. She resented his manipulative smoothness. She could not forego a jab at it. "If you were listening, you must have heard that, too."

He ignored her remark. "I wondered if you realized how heavily Mrs. Lonsdale's husband is involved in trade with the Soviets."

Celia drew a breath. "Mr. Haines," she said, "I don't think you understand how most of us who are mothers feel about any threat to return to the manufacture of nuclear weapons. It's not just us in a race with Russia anymore. Almost any unstable, small country with a paranoiac dictator can, theoretically at least, have access to a bomb or a missile capable of annihilating millions. We really need Russia's help to prevent that. We women want to keep them assured that we care more deeply about the future of the planet than we do about a contest with them. After all, we did achieve a build-down and a new arms agreement—and the cessation of manufacture in 1986. They're cooperating with us on many levels. Trade happens to be one area that's important to them. Why start to threaten them again? Why blame them for this terrorism? That's how we feel—and the Europeans feel that way, too. Can't you see that?" Her voice was pleading in spite of herself.

"Perhaps the president knows things you do not," said Haines. "At any rate, is the politics of demonstration the right way to go about it? Especially when the demonstration is aimed at the administration of which your husband will soon be a part? The question is—isn't it—do you have a right to carry his name into that demonstration?" He got up, bowed, and left her sitting alone, his question echoing in her ears.

All through the glittering dinner that followed, the question remained in her mind. Did she have the right? Did she? And when the music stopped and quiet fell in preparation for the exchange of toasts, she could hear, faintly, the shouts of the demonstrators in Lafayette Park.

"Moonlab no! Moonlab no! Peace now! Peace now!" They seemed to mock her.

In the president's study, Senator John Mann was carrying out the task that had been the reason for *his* invitation. President Batchelder had given him his cue.

"The prime minister and I have gone over all our problems in detail today, John," she said. "But perhaps we are too close to the details. We need someone to clarify the essentials. Why don't you try to do that for us?"

John Mann did not hesitate. He leaned forward and spoke earnestly to the older man.

"Sir, as I see it, there are two points and two points only. First"—he held up his hands and indicated the first point by pressing back the tip of one forefinger with the other. They were big and forceful hands. The Canadian watched them as if fascinated—"first, there is the question of hemispheric security. Second, there is the danger your internal problems pose to our domestic peace. This is how we think our two countries can work together . . ."

President Lily Batchelder leaned back in her chair and watched the two men. She had been careful not to tell John Mann that the prime minister had let it be known through channels that he wanted a chance to talk with the vice-presidential candidate. Best to let Johnny think this meeting was her own idea. What Baxter really wanted was a chance to size up her probable successor in office, she assumed. He wanted to find out, if he could, whether Mann really shared her views, or whether he was biding his time. Well, clearly she had not made a mistake in picking Mann. He was doing a masterful job of supporting her position. If Baxter had any lingering doubts they should now be resolved.

When John Mann had finished with a deferential "I guess you would call that our case in a nutshell, sir," the prime minister nodded. He looked from Mann to Lily and spoke bluntly.

"I pretty well decided earlier today that you people are right about the moon base." He patted the pocket of his dinner jacket. "I'll be saying that indirectly but pretty clearly when I respond to the toast tonight." The president smiled. In recent years the after-dinner toasts at state dinners had become an artful means of conveying to the press the real focus of a meeting between heads of state, and whether there was any substantial agreement between them. They were studied and dissected over and over by commentators and columnists, who tended to brush aside the cautious official communiqués with their clichés about "useful" talks and "continued cooperation." If Baxter was hinting at support in his toast the president had what she wanted.

"It's just as well to look ahead," the prime minister went on. "You're right when you point out that Communism may not be monolithic, but the fact is that Russia and China are getting closer on more issues every day. If Germany or Italy goes Communist—well, there goes Europe. If we have reason to be unsure of Pakistan or Japan we can be isolated on this continent. That's your view. It could happen . . . it could happen. So I'll go along with your Moonlab. It could put the two of us years ahead in terms of space weaponry. I realize that." He paused and looked out the window. "Funny to think of us building on the moon, isn't it?" He was silent a moment, then shrugged. "I'll have a time with Parliament but I think we can win the thing. You'll have to be patient with us."

He paused. Then he went on heavily.

"On the other matter, I don't know what I can tell you. Short of closing down the border completely—and you both know that's a physical impossibility—there isn't much more we can do to keep terrorists from crossing into the States. We use the latest electronic equipment. All our agencies are cooperating with yours. They're infiltrating whenever they can. Now and then we catch an informer. But I want to make one thing clear—"

It was Baxter's turn to be forceful. "This so-called movement—if that's the name for it—is no simple outgrowth of Canadian separatism. That had a revival, sure, as a result of your Reagan recession. A recession in the States is a depression in Canada, especially in Quebec, as you well know. So there were flare-ups, but the Québecois don't live on another planet, you know. They've pretty well decided they can't go it alone. Our intelligence finds every indication that this terrorism is an effort—a pretty successful effort—to unite international terrorism under the banner of French Canada. But that won't wash. There's *no* evidence, no evidence at all, that the planning is done on our side of the border. There's a center somewhere, though. And we have to find it." His voice dropped. "Lord knows we want an end to this, even more than you do."

He sounds discouraged, thought John Mann. They must be right, then, those who say he can't handle it.

The president's face gave no sign of her thoughts. "We appreciate your frankness, Mr. Prime Minister," she said. She rose and extended her hand. "Shall we go in?"

\*   \*   \*

The state dinner was over. In the upstairs living quarters the president, Cromfield Haines and the taciturn Mrs. Haines were having a last liqueur.

"I thought it went well," the president said, looking at her hands.

"Yes," said Haines. "It's my judgment Mann had a good effect on him. Baxter will have to balk a little for political reasons but he'll pull it off."

"Well, I hope so, and if you say so, I'm pretty sure he will—you're usually right." She picked up her glass. "Now, what about the lady?"

"Again, in my judgment the lady is a problem."

"You don't think Johnny can convince her to withdraw from her chairmanship?"

"I think she's too committed and in too deep."

"That's a pity," said the president. "Well, we'll have to find a way."

"You can leave that to me," said Haines. "I think we can reach her through her brother."

The president smiled but said nothing.

Mrs. Haines said nothing either. She never did, thought the president with approval. "Goodnight, Debby dear," she said to the older woman and kissed her on the cheek.


Alone in her bedroom Lily Batchelder sat in front of her dressing table and brushed her hair. She was bone-tired, but faithful to the self-discipline of years, she would not have considered omitting this or any of her nightly grooming rituals. Her face in the mirror, innocent of make-up and shiny with cream, reflected tiredness but showed no sign of aging. Without makeup she looked even younger than she had earlier in the evening. Her appearance was a fact she accepted. It was one of her assets, as was her manner. Sometimes not entirely an asset, she thought a little bitterly, recalling Prime Minister Baxter's response to John Mann.

Despite everything, despite the fact that she was the elected leader of one of the most powerful nations on earth, a man like Baxter felt more comfortable when her position was ratified by someone as obviously masculine as her prospective vice-president. No, it wouldn't matter if I looked like Golda Meier, she corrected herself bitterly; he would have felt the same dealing with her.

For that very reason, women in power could show no weakness and could not choose paths that might be perceived as soft or weak. She was a veteran of boardroom battles; she knew what she had to do to win respect and keep it. Even with her husband. He had not intended her to become chairman of the board when he stepped down, but she had anticipated him. She had used her own money to buy enough shares to gain control. She had forced her own election by springing her surprise prettily and pretending she thought he would be delighted at her cleverness. He had not been fooled. She remembered the forced laugh with which he had said to the others, "See, gentlemen, it's true that the female is deadlier than the male." Well, we have to be, she answered him once again in her thoughts.

She put down her brush and began to wipe the cream off her face. She thought of Celia Mann. Why couldn't these peace women see how it really was? Lord knows she wanted peace. Cromfield Haines had repeated Celia's statement about mothers being the strength of the peace movement. Mothers defend their own, Lily Batchelder argued with Celia mentally. Don't you see that? You don't carry the burden. Give me time, Celia, give me time and I'll get your peace for you. Don't get in our way. Please don't get in our way now.


"I think you may be right about your sister after all," said Haines to Dr. James Fifield on the phone the next day. "She is not going to be reasonable about this."

"I told you—" began Fifield, but Haines interrupted.

"Have you thought of hospitalization for observation?"

"It's an idea," said Fifield slowly, "but she wouldn't go willingly and I don't think Johnny would consent to anything . . . you know. He hasn't been facing up to this thing."

"Well"—Haines's voice was musing—"perhaps not hospitalization. But she could be taken ill, couldn't she? Nothing serious—just something to take her out of action."

"Yeah." Fifield's voice was suddenly comprehending but doubtful. "Yeah . . . well . . . yeah, I see." Then, "I'll look into it," he said.

"I thought you might," said Haines. "We've all got a lot at stake here."

And just what does he mean by that? thought Dr. James Fifield as he hung up. What is he letting me know that he knows?

# . 8 .

THE FIRST DAY of the official campaign was a long one for Celia. The morning had been taken up with getting Johnny off. He never could pack for himself and Celia and Juanita got in each other's way seeing that he had enough shirts and shorts while he held the phone in one hand and signed letters with the other. At Celia's urging he had called young Peter to make it clear how much he hated missing the first game.

"I'll get to the others—some of them, anyway, son, you know that. Your mother will be there and your Uncle Jim. The family will be represented, rooting like hell for you. Good luck!"

Finally he was gone, with Si Utley and one of the new young volunteers—Celia could not keep them straight—in tow. Celia noted that again Alec McGregor was staying behind. Somebody, maybe Johnny, was concerned about her safety. The thought made her feel good.

Once Johnny was off and the house had quieted down she went up to her little study and dictated letters to Maura McGinnis, the part-time secretary who came out from the office. After that she had set about getting ready to entertain Maurice Chouinard.

"Why do you do it?" asked Maura as she was leaving. She and Celia had been friends and neighbors in Lake City. It had seemed natural, when Maura was widowed, that Celia and Johnny would help her out with a job in Johnny's office. Her understanding was a comfort to Celia when Johnny's staff seemed to demand too much.

"Oh, I got in the habit because Jim was alone and didn't have a place of his own," said Celia absently. "Sister stuff, I guess, and then some of the friends important to him, like Maurice, sort of became Johnny's friends, too."

"Well," said Maura before she let herself out, "I think it was one

77

thing when you were just a Senate wife, but now with a vice-presidential campaign on your hands—oh, I know it's no use talking . . ." She laughed over her shoulder.

The late afternoon was broken only by a call from Maura to say that Johnny had arrived safely in Chicago. "Fantastic reception, they say," she reported. "Much better than they expected. The senator says to tell you he'll call after the dinner in Lake City. He has a stop at Annunciation College, you know." And another call from her brother.

"All set for tonight?" he asked.

"All set," she responded cheerfully.

"Look, Sis," he said. His voice was strange and he hardly ever called her "Sis" anymore.

"Yes?"

"You're not really thinking of taking part in this Peace Day thing, are you?"

"Well, Peace Work is one of the sponsors, Jim, and I'm chairman of Peace Work. I don't see how I could pull out entirely. I don't have to take an active part, though. I said I'd let them know . . ."

He broke in savagely, "For Christ's sake, Celia—what is this chairman stuff? You're the wife of the vice-presidential candidate, for God's sake! That's real—this other stuff is just playing with reality. That thing will be a zoo—hippies, crazies, Commies. Do you want to ruin Johnny?"

"No, of course I don't, Jim." She paused wearily, tempted to tell him what he wanted to hear. "But I have to think of the people I asked to join and"—she tried to say it gently—"I have to make up my own mind. I'm a big girl now, you know."

His voice softened, she thought. "Look, Sis, I'm just asking you—please reconsider. This just isn't like you. Please?"

"We'll talk about it." It was always hard for her to resist him. "I'll see you later." She was thoughtful as she put down the telephone. The president. Cromfield Haines. Now Jim again. Perhaps she was being foolish. It was the conventional wisdom, after all. A political wife did not take independent stands. Not really. If it were anything else but nuclear war . . . She looked at the clock. Four. Johnny must be at Annunciation right now. Surely he would see there how strong the peace constituency was.


The long curving drive up to the Annunciation College administration building was lined with cheering students. They wore caps emblazoned with the campaign logo—*LB* overprinted on a large *M*—in bright orange and blue. Those near the door carried signs, "Go, Johnny, go!"—a reminder of his glory days as a state football hero—and the more sedate "Batchelder and Mann." Mann noted that they moved the signs up and down in synchronized rhythm as they cheered.

The campaign caravan moved slowly past them, following an advance man who trotted ahead to lead the way. First a car with Secret Service men, then the long black limousine with the bubble top in which Senator John Mann sat alone in the back seat smiling, waving and acknowledging old friends and acquaintances as well as he could through the protective glass. Si Utley, beside the driver, sat half-turned, facing the senator and keeping an eye on the press car behind them.

"Good advance work," he said approvingly. "The students' committee has turned them out from all the neighboring colleges. Look, there's a bunch from St. Andrew's—and they're here from Pruitt, too, and from the U."

"I don't know," said the senator, but his cheery smile did not falter. He kept on waving even as he made his demurral. "This could be a mistake. There's a hell of a lot of peace signs in the back rows out there."

"It's called meeting them head-on, Senator," said Utley. "That's why those sign-carriers are out in front. That movement with the signs is calculated to distract the eye—and the camera. We've learned a lot about crowd management since the days when LBJ couldn't go onto a campus."

"Let's hope it works," said Mann, still smiling out the window.

"It'll be even better inside," Utley went on. "Joey has a flying squad of collegians with a lot of practice with flash cards. They're planted just across from the TV types. And they're good. It will be just like the Olympics."

The senator nodded and gave one last wave as the limousine came to a halt. The cheering crowd near the entrance was clearly made up of Annunciation students, some of whom clutched thermoses in one hand and waved signs with the other. They had obviously staked out their positions hours in advance. Their signs were more amateurish and individual—their own work, Mann thought, not the work of any campaign professional. "Celia and Johnny," they read. "No nuke gap for Celia Mann!" and "Lake City—where it all started!" John Mann grinned and began to move toward them, grasping as many of the outstretched hands as he could, doing his best to reward them for their long wait.

He felt a pang of nostalgia for the early days of his political life when the cheering was spontaneous and the crowds gathered on their own.

The Secret Service men were out of their cars now and forming a phalanx around the senator, pushing him through the crowd and up the long flight of steps leading to the pillared portico of the old red brick building. Two nuns waited there to greet him just as the advance man had said—"The two Mrs. Mann suggested." They made a strange contrast, Mann noted, even as he recognized them.

Sister Helen Lincoln, Celia's best friend in college, was now president of Annunciation. She stood there, tall and smiling, waiting to greet him—every inch the correct executive, at first glance indistinguishable from any successful career woman of her generation. Only the small silver cross on the lapel of her gray suit indicated her affiliation with the Sisters of the Annunciation.

Beside her, Sister Mary Linda, Celia's favorite teacher, was a slight, almost gnomelike figure. She wore the traditional habit of the order. Her face was half-hidden by the white bonnet tied beneath her chin and she was completely covered by the short black cape and long black skirt. She gave the impression of age and agelessness at the same time.

"Welcome to Annunciation, John," said Sister Helen, grasping his hand. "You can see from the signs that we were hoping Celia would be with you."

"She had planned to be," he answered, "but Peter plays his first big game tomorrow against St. Alban's. One of us had to be there, you know—that's pretty important." He looked smilingly from her to Sister Mary Linda and was a little discomfited by the steady gaze of the latter's shrewd brown eyes. He knew, because Celia had reminded him often enough, that Sister Linda was an anthropologist of international reputation whose early studies, published under her secular name, Dr. Eva Marwood, were already classics of their kind, but it had always been hard for him to grasp it. She was so effaced by her dress and so unassuming. Now, however, under those eyes below the bonnet, he was uncomfortably aware of the truth. From the beginning Sam and his campaign managers had thought it best to leave Celia behind on this first swing. "It will muddy the picture with the peace stuff," Sam had said. Young Peter's football game had provided a happy solution to what could have been a sticky problem. Did the old nun guess that? He was relieved when the Secret Service men moved the nuns into their protective phalanx and hurried the three of them through the entrance.

*  *  *

Annunciation College is known for the avant-garde stance of its religious and lay faculty. It is in every way a contemporary Catholic women's college, to the current distress of its older alumnae and traditional donors. Annunciation students and teachers have marched in every demonstration from Selma to Seabrook and in those protesting U. S. intervention in El Salvador, aid to the contras in Nicaragua, and the deployment of missiles in Europe. They had supported the ERA without question. Peace Corps volunteers, urban activists, public defenders, lay missionaries, Christian socialists, are among its recent graduates. Feminist leaders, ecologists, critics of the multinationals, and liberation theologians from the Third World are familiar figures in its lecture halls. Like its counterparts in New Hampshire, it has become an almost obligatory campaign stop for Democratic candidates.

Walking down its corridors behind Sister Helen, John Mann had a strong sense of déjà vu. He had walked this way as a candidate for attorney general of his state, then for governor, then senator. As the student's sign said, this was where it had all started—in Lake City, Ohio. And it had been a leg up for John Mann that his wife, the daughter of the former mayor and a popular graduate of Annunciation, walked at his side. Not only here but everywhere in the state, Celia had always been an asset, a first-rate campaigner—like another self. When she stood in for him, everybody said her way with a crowd was as good as his own, and she made his case in a way that he could not—that is, without seeming boastful or arrogant.

Sister Helen stopped. They were at the door to the auditorium stage. He shook the thoughts of Celia away. This time things were different. He would be speaking not only to this crowd and this state but, via the media, to the whole country. John Mann concentrated on the task before him.

Inside the auditorium the band had been alerted and they swung into the University Rouser, his old campaign song. The students were on their feet yelling. Sister Linda stepped aside. Sister Helen led the way. They went out onto the stage and a blaze of lights and noise. Beside the podium an excited-looking young woman turned toward them. She clutched a wooden plaque in her hands. ("Presentation, one minute," the advance man's briefing sheet had read.) John Mann acknowledged the cheers with a practiced gesture, lifting both arms high. Then he stood and smiled and waved toward different quarters of the auditorium floor and the gallery as if he spotted old friends and valued supporters here and there, although he could see very little past the hot, glaring TV lights.

Sister Helen Lincoln's voice, firm and clear over the microphone, cut through the noise. "May I have your attention, please?" She repeated it quietly. "May I have your attention, please?" and the crowd began to subside. "We at Annunciation welcome you all. Let me present the president of our student government, who will introduce our honored guest today." The TV lights, John Mann noted almost subconsciously, began to die down as she spoke. They would probably not come on again unless he varied from his written script. For the media reports it was only a routine story, after all—another stop in still another campaign.

Sister Helen had drawn the student to the microphone. "Miss Elizabeth Moore," she said.

As Senator Mann finished ten minutes later, strong disciplined clapping burst from the organized students' section and was augmented, a little uncertainly, by applause from other parts of the audience. At a sign from the advance man, the band struck up again, now standing and moving into a double-file marching formation. The placards flashed orange and white—Mann—and, alternately, blue and white—Batchelder. The Secret Service men, reforming their wedge, moved Senator John Mann, candidate for vice-president, down the ramp from the stage, through the clapping, standing audience and out the doors of Annunciation auditorium. As he got into the waiting car, Mann caught a glimpse of Sister Linda, small and unobtrusive, standing near the steps.

"Whew!" said Si Utley. "Nice recovery, Senator. I bet Tim Milney is threatening to commit hara-kiri because he didn't check out that award. He must've assumed it was for you."

"Natural mistake," said John Mann. Wives were unlikely to come high in the priorities of an advance man in a national campaign. Still— he found himself wishing that Sam were along to chew the guy out. The media could have had a field day with that award if it had caught their attention. But he didn't think it had. "I don't think the TV guys picked it up at all, do you?" he said to Utley.

"Not any of the network guys anyway," replied his press man. "I was watching them. They were bored, talking and comparing notes. Maybe a local show got it. I don't know, but I don't think so. Anyway, you handled it. You didn't blink an eye," he added. The admiration in his voice was soothing to John Mann. He, too, felt that he had performed well in a sticky situation. In the unlikely event that the president saw or read about the incident, she would observe that too. But it shouldn't have happened.

He felt again the rush of anger that had come over him at the words of the student who introduced him. "Senator Mann," she had said, "we are very proud to have you here as the running mate of the president of the United States. But I think you know that we here think of you as a different kind of running mate—the lifetime running mate of Annunciation's alumna Celia Fifield Mann, class of '65." A ripple of approval ran through the audience; mostly from Annunciation students, John Mann surmised, and felt his smile grow fixed.

"We are proud of you both," the student continued, "and this year we are especially proud of Celia. By organizing and promoting the coalition Peace Work, she has advanced the cause of peace in the world. Therefore, we ask you to accept this plaque for her, Annunciation's award, voted by the students and faculty, honoring her for her work for peace." Some of the lights began to go on again. Applause started and began to grow.

John Mann had taken the plaque and leaned forward over the podium. His voice rode the applause down. "I thank you," he said. "Celia thanks you. I bring you her greetings. If she were with me today she would be joining with me in bringing you the peace message of this campaign and this president—peace through strength and that strength in space . . ." He had put the plaque down, gripped the podium with both hands, and let his resonant, insistent voice fill the auditorium. He knew he had done well under the circumstances.

Settling back in the car seat, he realized that he was still holding the plaque. He must have picked it up from the podium as he left. He glanced at it, hardly aware of his distaste. It was the unprepossessing sort of token stamped out of pressed wood by the hundreds for schools and joiners' groups and used for the periodic award ceremonies that are dear to the American heart. The gilt lettering glinted in the late afternoon sun. "Given to Celia Fifield Mann this day," etc. He put it down on the seat beside him, but he remained aware of it. It was an unwelcome reminder of an unnecessarily bumpy spot in an otherwise smooth and triumphal day. It was what came of Celia's stubbornness. Well, her brother had said he would lay it on the line with Celia tonight. John

Mann hoped to God that he would get through to her. He himself couldn't take much more of this kind of thing. It had brought forcibly home to him how real the political danger engendered by Celia and her involvement with Peace Work was. The peace people now gathering new strength in women's groups, church groups and on the campuses were on a collision course with Lily Batchelder's campaign theme— peace through strength.

Any more of this emphasis on Celia's leadership and he was going to look like a weakling—a man who wasn't in control of his own family. Never mind women's liberation—his political intuition told him that, if this went on, he would be perceived not as a broad-minded husband but as a man gone soft, a man who could not persuade his own wife that the administration's course was the right one. They had a word for a man like that, he thought grimly: they called him a wimp.

Utley's voice broke his reverie. "Well, anyway, Senator, there won't be any booby traps at the labor dinner tonight. We're home free there."

"Yeah," replied Mann, "I guess so. Si, you tell Tim I want some free time before we go, even if he has to keep the locals out with a ball bat. I want to call home."

Alec McGregor had taken advantage of Mann's campaign trip to ask Clem Boise for a special meeting of the Forecast Commission. His own work on it was top secret and not known even to Senator Mann—not yet. He hadn't liked the transfer from his work on the border to his present assignment. He hated what he thought of as baby-sitting politicians but, as usual, the old man was right. Some interesting things were turning up in Washington, and his assignment made it possible and plausible to be there.

He was particularly concerned that his work on the joint intelligence commission be kept under wraps because of the outsiders in his detail. The borrowing of security men during a campaign is not publicized. As far as the public is concerned all the men guarding a candidate are Secret Service. Sometimes even the candidate isn't told that they are not. If he were from the party out of power, the candidate might think he was being shortchanged. And sometimes they are, Alec admitted to himself. The men from Sentry Central were not men he would have picked to guard a future vice-president. But what could he do? They had been Mann's bodyguards before he was vice-president—hired, he understood, by the senator's brother, who was worried by the increasing number of terrorist attacks.

Alec McGregor thought of himself as a Treasury man. He was proud to serve in the oldest department of the United States government and quick to let people know that the first responsibility of the Secret Service was the integrity of the United States revenue and currency and the security of its borders. Guarding the president and officials had come much later as a Treasury responsibility and, to Alec's mind, was not nearly as important as tracking money. He had come out of college with honors in economics, and the flow of money was his abiding interest.

The Treasury investigators are its detectives, so Alec had always told himself. His father had been a police detective, and as a boy he had been enormously proud of that fact. He had wanted to follow in his father's footsteps, and in a way he had.

The Forecast Commission had been formed after the attempt on the life of President Reagan early in his presidency. Although the FBI knew of John Hinckley's presence in Washington, the men responsible for the safety of the president had never been informed. In fact, lack of cooperation between the agencies had become so widespread that the FBI refused to tell the Secret Service the caliber of the bullet the doctors had to search for in operating on the president. The hospital authorities were outraged, and they made their outrage known to the congressional committees on intelligence and to the press.

In response, congressional oversight committees on intelligence became more critical and vigilant. Proposals to unify the intelligence services followed one after the other. But the intelligence services, never very cooperative, and wary of each other, responded with more lip service than actual change. Although their directors participated in an administration commission chaired by Vice-President Bush to study a coordinated response to terrorism and its prevention and agreed to its conclusions, no overall authority was in place or effective when President Batchelder took over and faced new outbreaks of hijackings and bombings.

In the end, the Forecast Commission was set up as an interagency instrument for the exchange of any information that might be useful in predicting trouble in the future. And it became the duty once again of the vice-president to chair the committee and enforce cooperation.

Vice-President Boise tackled the job with surprising zest. He had long been on the side of those who felt that better internal and external intelligence was the answer to terrorism, rather than the interdiction of nations and military reprisals. Through the Commission he felt that he could prove his point. He laid down the law to the gathered directors of the various agencies at the first meeting.

"Most presidential study commissions in the past have had little effect because the appointed members have left the real work to a hired staff and have had little real involvement themselves. The outstanding exception was the commission studying the Challenger disaster under former Attorney-General Rogers, who made the commission independent of the agency studied and who saw to it that every member was committed in public hearings and took part in task forces specializing in different aspects of the investigation.

"Ladies and gentlemen, I have the president's mandate to use that approach here. You are not here as advocates of your agencies. You are here as persons with knowledge of those agencies to find a way to make them better serve the United States of America in the present crisis and in the future. Every one of you—or a member of your agency who has complete access to you and can be considered your 'alter ego'—is to be here at each and every meeting and is to be a member of an inter-agency task force. Only by cooperation here can we prepare for true cooperation among the services."

"I'm appointing you as our representative, Alec," the undersecretary had said, "because of that canny intuition of yours—it must be your Scots blood—and because you have the doggedness to keep after those guys for details. No detail is insignificant. You're the guy who knows that."

In a way Alec looked forward to getting back to it. He enjoyed piecing together bits of information. It was like working on one of those huge picture puzzles—the kind you leave out on the table for everybody to take a crack at as they go by. The picture comes clearer bit by bit. He looked forward to seeing the vice-president again, too. Boise was a politician one could respect and he was a very sharp man despite his age.

They met in the vice-president's official office in the Capitol building. It once was the only office a vice-president had—a series of high-ceilinged chandeliered rooms off the ornate and vaulted Senate reception room. Ostensibly the committee gathered there because their coming together was less apt to be noticed in the hustle and bustle of the Capitol—tour groups in and out and gawking, constituents and delegations arriving in the hope of calling senators off the floor. Alec thought that the real reason, though, was that old Clem Boise liked the Capitol and was at home there. This commission was his responsibility, and on the Hill, which had so long been his world, he felt completely in charge.

They were almost all there when Alec came in, gathered around a conference table looking for all the world like a board of directors—Regan from the FBI, Asgaard from CIA, Mullan representing the director of DEA, the Drug Enforcement Agency, Richardson from Protective Services, a buttoned-down type he didn't know who turned out to be from State, the chief of the Capitol police, Owens from Immigration, and DiCarpio from Customs. That was the lot today. They were the members of the task force on the relationship between drugs and terrorism. They nodded or said "hi" as he went round them to say hello to the VP and make his excuses.

"Alec McGregor, sir," he said, "Secret Service."

"Glad to have you back, McGregor," Boise said, and Alec thought he meant it. At least, his next words made it clear that he remembered him. "Thought I saw somebody familiar behind the Manns at that White House dinner the other night."

Alec sat down feeling good about that and sorry as hell at the same time that the old man was being replaced. Nobody had to tell McGregor how much that hurt. He knew how he would feel in Boise's place.

"You were saying?" The vice-president nodded at Regan, who had been talking when Alec came in.

"The director feels that the terrorists are being fed by the drug and gun trade. He wanted me to emphasize that, and the fact that unless we make an all-out commitment now—a massive commitment in money and men—we might as well forget the whole thing. Intelligence isn't enough." He looked at a paper on the table in front of him.

"It is almost twelve years since Director Webster said that the illegal drug trade generates 'tremendous corruption' in our society. He pointed out that the amounts of money available are extraordinary. The various terrorist organizations feed on this money. Yet drug production is protected on the highest levels—marijuana, for example. It's a relatively harmless substance and the use is down but the money in it alone could support any number of Red Brigades. Marijuana is growing all up and down the Mississippi Valley. We at the Bureau have had every reason to think that the mob is organizing its growth and transport. If we could cut off just that one product we'd dry up a significant flow of money. But we're continually told that it's a small-potatoes operation and to stay away from it."

Regan's face was flushed with earnestness and he was unaware of his effect on the others. Asgaard was glowering. DiCarpio from Customs kept opening his mouth to interrupt. The vice-president had started a slow drumming on the table with his long bony fingers. But Mullan from DEA took up where Regan left off. "And what about the big pharmaceutical firms? They've got to be aware that the uppers and downers they produce could fill the needs of the medical profession twice over. And heroin—it's all over the streets."

DiCarpio couldn't stand it any longer. He broke in, riding Mullan's voice down. "What about those Canadian mobsters who have been bringing Quaaludes into this country for years? I tell you our problem is imported. The terrorists are foreigners or illegal aliens and the stuff comes in along the coasts and over the borders. Terrorism isn't an American product—not yet. We've got to concentrate on cutting the flow into this country first. We've nearly five thousand men trained to do that and we can hardly make a dent—"

"And even after all this time," broke in Owens angrily, "we're not getting decent cooperation from the Mexicans. The corruption and ineptitude of their officials which your Customs Commissioner von Raab talked about more than a half dozen years ago still exist. The air strips built by Colombian smugglers are still there—only a 100 miles from the border—and the warehouses; the paid-off Mexes are the freight forwarders and the protective services for drug-smugglers and they can be for terrorists, too. It's time we deal with the Mexicans!"

"You're damned right," Mullan interrupted. "Every time we find one of those coke factories in the Florida Glades or the Louisiana swamps—or the Maine woods, for that matter—it's José and Jorge and Julio or Pierre and Jean-Louis that're running the cooking. We need planes, planes and more planes to intercept the boats and the flights. My God, it's like a flight of bumblebees coming out of the Caribbean at sundown every night."

The vice-president's voice cut through the discussion. The relaxed Western tone was gone and the group came to attention. "Gentlemen, gentlemen, we're going beyond the mandate of this committee. Policy is up to the administration. Funding and legislation belong to the Congress. Our job is to exchange and coordinate information so that they can make the proper decisions. So far I gather that you agree there is a strong and direct connection between the drug traffic and the increase in terrorist incidents in this country. That's a point worth emphasizing. The next question is, what do we know about how this connection is made? I understand that agent McGregor here has been working on something like that at the Canadian border. Tell us about it, McGregor."

Alec was not sure he was ready to talk about it—or that he was supposed to. And though he didn't like Regan much, he thought the bureau man was right about the pervasiveness of the corruption brought about by the trade. He had no doubt that it reached to those in the highest places. The amounts of money were staggering. And these days it took staggering amounts to start a business or mount a political campaign— or to start up in farming for that matter. There were all sorts of ways to launder that money. Until very recently it was relatively easy to launder it through respectable banks. It could even be reaching someone on the committee.

"Well, sir," he began slowly, "what we've been doing is looking for the connection, and what we have isn't hard yet. What we see is sort of a spider web. There's a spider there in the center somewhere but the cross strands don't lead to him. That's where we are now—locating the strands that will lead us to that spider. That's the best way I can put it, sir."

"Very vivid, McGregor. Now, can you give us some examples of what you're talking about?"

"I'll try. What we see is a centralizing development. Somebody, somewhere, is bringing things together and getting a lock on everything. I mean *everything*. Take Regan's marijuana-grower, for instance. Say he's like the guy who leased access to that Missouri farmer's cornfields a while back. He gave the farmer $20,000 to use a little over an acre of land and he had a crop growing between the corn rows that was worth $400,000. Multiply that all over those central river valleys and you know somebody—or a bunch of somebodies—is putting up hundreds of times $20,000 and getting back the bigger share of $400,000 many times over. He's got a big transport operation. We think we've traced some of it to a barge operation on the rivers—the tonnage of commodities moved by those barges is awesome. And he's got a big coordinated selling operation—probably through the American mafia, and the Canadian mob DiCarpio mentioned; the illegal traffic in legal drugs like Quaaludes is another part of the operation.

"Or take Mullan's Jorges and Josés in the Glades. They're the small fry. We know that. But what we're beginning to see by tracing the money flow is that behind the guy funding that operation in Missouri and behind the guy funding that little factory in the Glades may be the same spider."

He could see DiCarpio nodding. Vice-President Boise was listening intently. And Alec said a little more than he intended to.

"Mr. Vice-President," he said, "I think that spider wants to invite us into his parlor. I think he doesn't like the United States of America. And I think he is in Canada."

"Why?"

"I can't tell you why. It's a hunch. But there are a lot of indicators. The underground money flow, for one thing. It's going north. And it seems to be coming back in investments. Then, if you look closely at the INS—the immigration figures—more and more illegals are coming in over that northern border. They're not Canadians. They're Latins from the Caribbean, Belfast Irish, God help us, and Pakistanis, Pacific Islanders, Asians, what-have-you—a lot of them the kind of people who have grievances and join terrorist groups."

"Anything else?"

"Yes," Alec said. "I think our spider is important and has lots of help down here—from people who probably don't know who it is they're helping. But that's a hunch, too. And here's another—there's something big in the works. I get a feel of a buildup."

They chewed it over. When they left, trailing out again one by one, the old vice-president held Alec back for a moment.

"I think you're on the right track, McGregor," he said. "Stick with it."


There was another meeting that day, in the library of the Metropolitan Club. The man who sat waiting looked like an ambassador; he was not, although he was at home in the spots where diplomats gather all around the world. He was so tall that, as he sat in the deep leather chair, his thin and tailored knees were raised to the level of his chin and made a convenient support for the book through which he was leafing. His brown hair, which had never grayed, was combed close to his narrow head; his long bony face was somewhat lopsided. People never remembered the color of his eyes.

He put down the book and rose to his feet when he spotted the white-haired man from New York lingering uncertainly in the doorway. Harrison Crawford, always called "Pete" by friends and initiates in the world of international finance, advanced on him, his broad ruddy face and blue eyes alive with apparently genuine pleasure.

"It's been a long time, El," he said.

"Since the IMF meeting in Tokyo in 1985 to be exact," said Ellis Murat.

"Good Lord, yes," said Crawford, "just after the bottom fell out of the dollar. What a time that was!"

"Yes," said Murat dryly, "but you have the look of a man who came through all right."

Pete Crawford was unoffended. He waved a hand. "Oh, yes, I was ready—it's my business to be, isn't it? I had good holdings in Swiss francs, the Deutschmark, some metals and, of course, land in the Canadian Rockies. That's hot now, you know. Lots of people holing up. Most of our big depositors came out pretty well, too, I'm happy to say. We took care of them." He paused. "And you? I expect you've been pretty busy since then with all that's been going on."

"You might say that." Unconsciously Murat raised his hand to his right cheek. Crawford, following the gesture, looked questioningly at the thin white scar.

Murat, embarrassed, turned his face away but explained, "The embassy bombing in Pakistan. That was in '85, too."

"I know," said Crawford. He changed the subject. "I grabbed the shuttle as soon as I got your call. I gather you've got a top-priority proposal in mind."

"You're open to one then, I take it?"

Crawford laughed. "You damn well know we are. I'm sure you had our liquidity checked out, didn't you?"

Murat's smile was thin. "As I might say in my turn, it's my business to know. General McLeod is to meet us in the dining room. Shall we go in? I wanted to confirm your interest in this thing before we got together with him."

Pete Crawford laughed aloud. "Always cloak-and-dagger, aren't you? Lead on, Macduff, lead on, I'm ready."

Murat spotted the general at a table in the far corner at the same time McLeod spotted them. As they made their way toward him, Murat thought that he had chosen the time well and that the general had done equally well in choosing the table. It was late and the lunch crowd was thinning out; the corner table was adjoined by others ready for clearing. There would be no one in earshot.

He shook hands with the general, whose military bearing was unmistakable even in his gray sack suit. Pete Crawford was effusive in his greeting.

"Bob! It's an honor. Haven't seen you for a long time. We'll have to get you up to New York for one of those briefing luncheons. You always get rave reviews from our board members, you know. They appreciate your frankness."

The general's voice was gruff but he was pleased. "I like to shake them up. It's damned important that they understand the crisis we're in. Come anytime."

"Oh, they're beginning to understand all right," rejoined Crawford. "That's why I'm here."

"Let's order," said Murat. "Then the general can give us his report." He indicated the general's ruddy tan and the white mark across his upper brow just below the short-cut gray hair. "You can see he's just back."

They waived cocktails and made short work of ordering.

"Now, let's get to it," said Crawford. His geniality had been laid aside; he was a businessman at work. The general leaned forward and spoke in an undertone.

"I looked at everything. The training centers in Honduras and Guatemala and the bases in south-central Mexico. They're using the ones we closed down a while back. They were never really closed down, of course, just held in readiness with a skeleton maintenance force. There are two—no, three—points I want to make. First, this is no ragtag mobilization, no bunch of half-trained guerrillas. They're international in makeup. There's your usual mix of some Cubans, some PLOs, Eastern Europeans and so on. But the main body is largely Canadian (mostly French), Caribbean, a lot of our own ex-service people, and they've been trained to the hilt by officers who learned what they know in our old school in Panama or in our own army. They're fit. They're disciplined. They're ready.

"Two"—he tapped his forefinger on the table slowly—"they're well armed. They've been getting regular shipments. Some from the CCs"— Pete Crawford looked puzzled and General McLeod explained—"the Christian Contras. And some from God knows where. My sources are closemouthed about some things. But I've got a pretty good guess. They have everything they need—tanks, armored cars, howitzers, mortars, rocket launchers, air-to-ground missiles, patrol boats, landing craft—" He paused for breath, then continued. "They've got planes. About sixty combat aircraft. Some old Zeros. A lot of our A-37 Dragonfly bombers. About twenty AC-47 gunships with rapid-fire capacity. They've got new planes coming, and the Contras are seeing that trained pilots come with them. Frankly, I was astonished at their state of readiness.

"Three. They're at the peak of preparedness. Too much delay and they won't be as effective. An operation to overthrow—even one as good as that—can't hold if it's put on the back burner. What they have to have now is money and lots of it so they are assured that the men are paid and the supplies keep coming as long as they're needed."

The waiter arrived with their food and the three fell into silence. When he had gone, Murat spoke.

"Your assessment is that you have no doubt they can do it?" McLeod nodded. "And how long would it take? Are we talking coup or are we talking protracted bloody revolution right next door?"

"From my knowledge of Mexican readiness," said General McLeod, "they'll have control of Mexico City in a week. It'll be like the Germans rolling into Denmark."

It was Crawford's turn, and his question was addressed to Murat. "What about our intervention? Won't the president have to move on that? Won't public opinion force her hand?"

Murat shook his head. "In my judgment it isn't likely. She's convinced that the flood of immigration, both legal and illegal, is tied to terrorism. She'll have to deplore and denounce publicly but she'll drag her feet about any intervention. Interference in the internal affairs of a neighbor. The example of Afghanistan. Our bad history in Central America—all to no purpose—et cetera. I think the public will back the delay. People are worked up about all these aliens still pouring into the country."

"But, good God, man," Crawford broke out, so intense that he forgot to keep his voice low, "the way I see it, any uprising down there will send even bigger hordes over the border. And immigration will have nothing to do with it. They'll come in as refugees." Murat lifted a warning hand, and he lowered his voice. "We just can't go on being the international dump heap. Why, I read an article the other day which made the serious projection that by 2025 this country will be more than half black and Hispanic. That's not the country our forefathers built. More and more we see that John D. Rockefeller was right when he spent his last years concentrating on braking the population boom—right to promote abortion as a worldwide solution. A lot of people thought he was a bit obsessed but he was right. We can all see that now. I can tell you we're not going to fund anything that will have any more fleeing people coming in here like lemmings!"

Murat's voice was calm and judicial. "That's exactly the point, Pete. What we want is a government in Mexico that will cooperate with us in stemming the flow. That—and let us take over the oil production. That's a mess now, as you know, and we need to assure the supply."

At the mention of oil, Crawford's face became thoughtful. But he needs to know more than that to come through, Murat thought. "There are certain tactical solutions to the refugee problem, aren't there, Bob?" he asked.

The general nodded. "The Contras and our planners have considered that. Depending on your point of view, the Soviets made alarming or remarkable progress in experimenting with chemical warfare in Afghanistan. Since nothing like that can stay secret in the scientific community for long, we have profited from their experimentation. To take only one example, they have refined a liquid form of mustard gas, which is applied directly rather than let loose in the air. It can be used target fashion with aerosol means for either individuals or groups. It is fairly quick-acting. There are other products that are slower-acting and less traceable, which can be introduced into the food or water supplies of concentrated populations who pose a threat to the general welfare—overcrowded refugee camps, for instance. Population experts have been considering such use for some time. It is part of the plan that a certain judicious use of such agents would be effective in pacifying the populace and eliminating nonproductive elements as well as reducing the threat you speak of."

Crawford looked stunned. "I see," he said. "I see."

Murat smiled. "More effective than a population crusade, wouldn't you say? And much quicker. Shall we have dessert and coffee?"


Celia flew to the phone. It had to be Johnny, she thought, calling to share his elation at his reception out there—just as he always used to.

"Celia?" In the established habit of a long marriage, they felt no need to identify themselves to each other. They knew each other's voices better than they knew their own.

"Oh, Johnny, Maura called." Celia was talking almost as soon as he had said her name. "The reception in Chicago sounded wonderful.

Right where it counts this year, too! How is Lake City? Are the Machanskys with you? And Adam? How was Annunciation?"

"Hey—one question at a time." Johnny sounded amused in spite of
himself. "No, the Machanskys aren't with me but they'll be at the dinner
tonight. Adam, too—and I'll remember to say hello for you." His voice
hardened a little. "And your precious Annunciation almost gummed up
the works, I can tell you."

"Johnny! How? Didn't they have a good turnout? When I talked to
Helen she said the student committee had been planning it for weeks . . ."

"Oh, the turnout was good, all right, but they almost turned it into a
rally for that outfit of yours. I tell you, Celia, this is getting serious.
You've got to pull out, and pull out now."

How much should she say? Celia wondered. Perhaps she should just
agree. But Jim was coming over later to argue with her about Peace Day.
It would be best if she could say that she had talked to Johnny.

"Johnny, I am," she said carefully. "I told you I would. I just have
this last talk on Peace Day—just a brief introduction to make. And then
I'm through until after the campaign."

The force of his exasperation was so great she could almost physically
feel it.

"You're not going to speak there or anywhere! No, get that straight.
Good God, Celia, I don't need this aggravation!"

"Johnny, listen, please . . ."

But he had hung up.

Celia's hands shook. She was surprised at the rage she felt. Did no
one care that Peace Work was *hers*? That she had spent days and
months and, yes, years studying the nuclear threat and putting together
this women's force to curb it? All of them—Jim, the president, that
odious old Cromfield Haines—all telling her to stop. To put everything
aside as if her work were a toy. And now Johnny—*ordering* her. Well,
she had tried to be reasonable. But she was not going to be pushed
aside and ordered about. She was *not*.

# . 9 .

THEY SAT that night, Celia and the four men, in the wainscoted dining room at the polished table and ate in virtual silence. Celia had been depressed by her husband's call but tried to rally herself to her duties as hostess. She looked around the table. The men seemed constrained. Jim made surly by his earlier disagreement with her, Celia guessed. Sam subdued by his surroundings. Dr. Grant, Jim's friend and officially their family doctor, was never very good at small talk, but Maurice Chouinard was not usually as quiet as this. Celia rather liked the Canadian doctor, whom she had seen from time to time over the last few years. As if sensing her thoughts he roused from his abstraction.

"This is a very pleasant setting, Madame," he said, "and I am sure that you are the one responsible."

Celia's glance followed his around the room; she was pleased once again with the effect of the glowing dark gold paint of the walls and the fresh white silk of the curtains against the dark oak woodwork. "Do you really like it, Dr. Chouinard?" she asked. "People bleach the wood-work in these old houses, but we liked the more traditional look of the oak as it was. We just took off the shiny varnish and had it sanded down." Maurice nodded approvingly.

"Tell me how things are now in Canada," Celia said. She had never lost the fascination of her childhood with what she, as a native of the Ohio urban center around Lake City, always called the other side of the lake. "Things do seem to us down here to be very unsettled there lately. And our two countries don't seem to be getting on as well as they should."

"There is, of course, as you know, a long and unfortunate history behind our present situation," said the doctor, giving her remarks the grave consideration he seemed to give every statement. "You under-

**96**

stand that I myself am very much in sympathy with the aims of my French-speaking compatriots."

"But surely not with the terrorists who are demanding a separate Quebec again," Celia protested. "Terrorism never seems justifiable to me."

Maurice did not waiver. "There are terrorists and terrorists, Madame," he said. "Sometimes theirs is the only way against overwhelming power. And often the terrorists of one generation are the respected world leaders of the next. What of the early leaders of the Irish Republic? And what of Menachem Begin? Many of the figures legendary in your own early history would be thought of as terrorists if they lived today."

Celia was doubtful but took his point. "Well, I suppose you mean people like Ethan Allen and his Green Mountain Boys," she said, "and Marion, the Swamp Fox. I guess they do fit your description in a way." She laughed.

The dinner went on pleasantly enough, although Sam seemed very restless. He was obviously anxious to get down to the business discussion. After dessert, Celia rose. "I know you are anxious to get to the shop talk," she said. "I'll have Juanita bring in the coffee and I'll just get back to signing those notes the office has been doing for me. Campaigns take an awful lot of thank-you's, you know," she said to Chouinard. "It's been very nice to see you again."

The door to the butler's pantry had hardly swung shut when Grant burst out: "Wait until you hear what Chouinard has to tell us. He has fantastic news about the prospects for our international syndicate." All three looked expectantly at Maurice.

He felt a real distaste for these American doctors. He at least had a purpose behind what he did, while they, with their investment syndicates, seemed only to think of money. Greed seemed to be their only motivation. For the present, however, he still needed them. So he answered their unvoiced question.

"I have every reason to believe that the market for our arms investment has expanded greatly. The people interested in what we have to trade now have the money to buy."

"That's great, just great!" exclaimed Jim Fifield. "Add that to the possibility of our getting the contracts for most of the Moonlab stuff for our domestic corporations and we're talking billions, and I mean *billions*."

"Johnny will see to the Moonlab stuff," said Sam.

Dr. Grant laughed out loud and rubbed his hands.

Did they think it ended with the money? Maurice asked himself. He had an overwhelming desire to remind them of the realities.

"And we have also the satisfaction that we help the oppressed of this world," he said icily. "I propose a toast. To the New Revolution!" He raised his wineglass. "To a New Bastille Day when the fortress of oppression falls!"

The others echoed him uncertainly. Dr. Grant was openly confused. "Bastille Day?" he said. "That's the fourteenth of July, isn't it?"

"A metaphor, *mon ami*," answered Maurice. "A mere manner of speaking."

"A metaphor, I'll bet," said Sam recklessly. He poured himself another glass of wine. "Well, here's to that Bastille Day of theirs. We don't care when it is as long as the Swiss banks hold."

On the other side of the door Celia Mann stood frozen, holding the coffee tray. She had reached the kitchen to find it set up on the counter and the coffee hot on the warming burner of the stove. One of Juanita's infrequent, semiliterate notes was propped against the tray.

"*Señora,*" it read, "*es necesario yo voy a apartamiento con dinero*"— Señora, it is necessary for me to go to the apartment with money. Celia shrugged. These emergencies of Juanita's seemed to be coming more often of late. She had an amazing number of relatives who depended on her for help. Celia had taken up the tray and turned to the dining room, pausing in the butler's pantry to search for the coffee spoons Juanita had forgotten. She had listened to Maurice, at first absently, then in horror at what he seemed to be saying. And the others! What they said was worse.

Celia went into the dining room. (Later she would be unable to recall the volition that had propelled her there.) The tray and its contents clattered in her hands. Chouinard jumped to his feet and the others, less automatically courteous, half-rose from their chairs. All three looked at her with a mixture of surprise and chagrin, which she pretended not to notice. "Juanita seems to have disappeared, but she did leave this ready." She put the tray down. "Please sit down, all of you—this really is my last appearance. Goodnight again."

I will think about it later, she told herself. I just cannot face it tonight. I will think about it tomorrow and I will talk to Johnny. She went into Susan's room, where a small night-light glowed from the baseboard. Susan was sleeping, as she usually did, flat on her stomach, embracing her pillow. Celia straightened the covers as best she could. Her hands still trembled. She kissed Susan lightly and went to her own room.

Downstairs the men heard her door close. They looked at each other.

"She couldn't have heard enough to matter," said Fifield uncomfortably.

"I don't like it," said Grant. "I don't like it at all."

"All we need to do is get her suspicious," said Sam. "She's already asking questions about"—he paused, then finished—"other things."

Maurice stood up. "I must get back to my hotel. I take the first plane in the morning. This complication I leave to you to resolve. It is your responsibility."

After an early conference with Sam Drottman the next morning, Dr. James Fifield asked Cromfield Haines to accompany him to the airport to meet the senator on his return from Chicago. He would need Haines's presidential clout to convince Johnny of the steps that must be taken. They were closeted with Johnny in the presidential Air Force One, which had been lent him for the campaign trip, for over an hour before he finally emerged to meet the pool reporters whom Sam had been keeping occupied with a genial and jesting banter. "What's taking so long, Sam?" asked the *Washington Post* reporter. "Classified stuff on the latest from the heartland, Cliff—what'd you think?"

"Your wife's name is on the flyers, Senator," said Haines, "and in the letter that went out to the peace group lists. Can you imagine the attention it is going to draw if she is actually there—and two weeks before the election? The headlines? 'Vice-Presidential Candidate's Wife in Demonstration Against Administration Policy' . . . 'Mann and Wife at Odds Over Policy.' That sort of thing."

"You were just lucky yesterday with that award thing at the college, Johnny," Fifield interposed. John Mann, who had been doodling on one of the notepads with which the conference table was furnished, looked up sharply. Privately he was chagrined. So Fifield knew about that. He should have known that Fifield's Lake City contacts would keep him informed. Fifield went on. "Once the press picks it up, it'll be follow-the-leader all over again—one of them rewriting the other. Remember what the Eagleton flap did to the McGovern campaign—and that was early on. And don't forget how the Ferraro thing set Mondale's campaign back. He never did regain the momentum he needed."

"The president certainly can't afford anything like that at this stage. You can surely see that," added Haines.

Mann knew they were right. Even now, it was hard to see how the potential damage could be controlled. He tried to keep the vexation out of his voice as he directed his attention to the presidential adviser, ignoring his brother-in-law.

"What do you suggest?"

"I gather you have persuaded Mrs. Mann to withdraw?"

Mann hesitated and picked his words carefully.

"We talked last night. But the details have to be worked out."

The hesitation confirmed Haines's suspicion that Celia had been intransigent. He began again slowly.

"Now, mind you, this is just a thought. Suppose she is willing to withdraw, as you say. That very fact might in itself create a different kind of problem. Is she withdrawing under pressure? Has she changed her convictions about nuclear armament? We've discovered that she turns out to be on record in some pretty positive ways. There'll be interviews. Statements from the peace people. Lots of publicity. They'd love it, as you can well imagine. That kind of thing could be as bad as her appearance, don't you agree?"

John Mann stared at him, baffled. He shook his head as if to clear it.

"Well then, what's the answer?"

Haines nodded at Fifield.

"Celia could be taken sick, Johnny," said the latter.

John Mann didn't understand. "But she'd never play sick, Jim," he said irritably. "Celia's too up-front. You know that as well as I do."

"I know, Johnny, I know. That's why she'd have to be really sick. And there are medications that can make her sick without hurting her. And keep her sick just long enough. We think it's worth the try."

"It may be the only way open to us," added Cromfield Haines. He was studying the senator closely.

Mann met his look for a moment, then let his gaze slide away.

"I see," he said. His voice was flat.


Senator Mann went straight to his car, smiling, waving and holding up his briefcase in an explanatory gesture as the Secret Service held off the reporters. In a low voice he said a final word to the men accompanying him.

"All right. I'll think about it, but I can't decide right now. I've got an intelligence briefing coming up." He stepped away from them and got into the car without looking back. They saw him speak to the driver and then open the folder he had been carrying.

Sam looked at the others and grinned mirthlessly.

"He's decided to agree. He just doesn't want to say it to you directly. It would spoil his good-guy image of himself. I'll get the word from him later on—you can bet on it—and I'll pass it on. You can decide just how you're going to do it, Jim. We'll leave that to you experts."

He went back to pacifying the now-outraged members of the press.

The day had turned wet and dark. One of the season's tropical storms raged off the Carolinas and the tail end of its winds and rains swept the Potomac valley. In the late morning Celia stared out of the study window, watching huge drops form and fall from the branches of the maple outside the window. She felt drained and depressed.

Johnny had not called since his return—a sure sign that he was still angry about their conversation. And she was worried. Morning clarity had not lessened the threatening import of the discussion she had overheard. But it had made her doubt her own jump to conclusions. There had to be a sensible explanation. But what could it be?

Sam had laughed—the sound came back to her—but it was a cynical laugh. And what had he said? "We don't care when it is as long as the Swiss banks hold." Maurice Chouinard's voice had been mocking but his words were serious. And all of them had been obviously disturbed at her reappearance. Could they really be involved in dealings that would bring about revolution? Supporting subversion? It sounded like it. But where? It must be an action supported by our government, Celia told herself, or Sam and Jim would not be party to it. A Communist country? A top-secret government operation? Or one of those destabilizing maneuvers like the aborted Bay of Pigs invasion of Cuba or the overthrow of Allende in Chile in which one part of the intelligence community had no idea what the other part was doing?

Once she would have taken the problem to Johnny without hesitation. She would have been sure that he'd have no part in one of the CIA's peace-threatening destabilizations of a foreign country. But now she was not sure.

Whatever the operation, it was something about which the men she had heard were neither idealistic nor patriotic. They had been interested in the money that could be made. And it was clear that Johnny was helpful to them. Still Johnny might not know everything that was being done, or that these men were profiting from it. She did not trust Sam, and as for Jim—Celia sighed. She tried not to think about it, but she knew her brother's weakness. He would look to his own advantage whatever the cost to Johnny. If only she could talk this over with someone—someone safe!

She had made a tentative try earlier when Maura McGinnis had come from the office with her schedule and letters to sign. "Maura," she had said when her friend began gathering up the work and preparing to leave, "don't hurry. Let's have a cup of coffee and talk. I'm so cut off from what's going on in the office these days. I need to catch up, and I want to hear how it is working out for you."

"We-ell," Maura hesitated, "I guess I have time. But Jule wants this back pretty soon so she can synchronize your schedule with the senator's. Things are moving pretty fast these days." There was a trace of importance in her voice. Celia smiled inwardly. So it had infected Maura, too, the feeling of reflected glory that came from being on the staff of an important man—even Maura, who had known Johnny as a friend ever since his university days.

She poured the coffee and motioned Maura to a chair at the breakfast table.

"So it's going well then for you," she asked, "being on the staff?"

"Oh, yes," Maura said enthusiastically, "very well. It was a little awkward at first. I think they thought I might throw my weight around because of my former relationship with you and the senator." Surely Maura had never called Johnny "the senator" before? "But I was very careful about that from the beginning. We don't see much of the senator in the outer office anyway and when we do I never make any bid for attention, you know."

"But Maura," interjected Celia, "why do you say '*former* relationship'? We're just as much friends as we were before."

Maura's voice was gentle but it was firm. "No, Celia. It's not the same. It can't be. I'm not the wife of one of your husband's golfing friends and contributors now. I'm an employee. A friend—yes, always—but in a different way." She raised her hand to stop Celia's objection and added quickly, "Don't think it isn't a good thing. Because of the work and being on the Hill I've got new friends and new interests. And working with the campaign staff is fascinating. I've been helping Bill Cuddahy analyze the opinion polls from the Midwest. He says I have a flair for interpretation. It may open up a whole new field for me."

Celia sipped her coffee and listened. She heard the words behind Maura's spoken ones. I'm not your office friend anymore, Celia. I can't be your eyes and ears. I have an agenda of my own. Well, what had she expected? She did not really know. But she felt rebuffed and hurt.

After Maura left the day dragged on. Celia dreaded the coming evening and the reopening of the argument with Johnny, which she was sure it would bring. She was almost glad when Jule called to say that the senator would be staying on the Hill for dinner. She had decided during the afternoon that, even if it made him more angry, she would have to tell him about the conversation she had overheard and ask what it meant. Now she could put that off until tomorrow. I'm getting to be a regular Scarlett O'Hara, she thought ruefully. She ate with Susan, helped her with her homework, and went to bed after the ten o'clock news.


She woke with a start when she heard Johnny in the bathroom. He was moving things around in the medicine cabinet. He's trying to do it quietly, bless him, she thought. He's being considerate again, so he must be over his anger. She waited sleepily, wondering whether he would come in. When she heard him leave the bathroom by the opposite door and close it softly, she wondered whether she should get up and follow him. Now might be the best time, especially if he was less upset about her and Peace Work. But the effect of the long day and the ebbing of tension made her drowsy and reluctant to move. In only a few minutes she was asleep again.

When she awoke it was barely light and Johnny was coming into the room. "Hi," she said sleepily. He started guiltily. "Hi," he answered. "I didn't mean to wake you. Early breakfast meeting today. I was going to leave a note." He crossed the room and kissed her lightly. "I'll see you tonight."

Everything is all right, she thought. It's as if our disagreement had never been. Relief made her bold.

"I hope you'll see us, for heaven's sake," she said only half-joking. "Susie is forgetting what you look like."

She regretted saying it immediately, because his small laugh was forced, "Okay, okay, I said I'd see you. Tell Juanita to cook something special—"

Her first migraine started before she could finish dressing.

The pain was sudden and intense. She went to the bathroom and took two aspirin. Then she lay down again thinking that it would pass. Juanita came with the coffee tray and she waved it away. She asked Juanita to help Susan get ready for the car pool and to see her off. "Say Mommy's sick . . . *enferma*."

At ten-thirty she called her brother's office.

"Tell Dr. Fifield it's his sister and it's urgent." Pain sharpened her voice.

By the time Jim came on the line she was made almost breathless by her fight to control the waves of pain, dizziness and nausea that swept over her.

"I've never felt anything like it, Jim," she gasped. "It's terrible. I don't think I can stand it." Her voice cracked.

"Steady on, Celia. It sounds like migraine—the kind Grandmother Cleary used to have. Have you called Grant?"

"No," she said tearfully. "I can't see numbers! Jim, you've got to come."

"I'll call him and I'll get there right away. Now listen, Sis, lie down again and don't move. The trick is not to move your head if you can help it."

She hung up and sank back. Migraine? Grandmother Cleary?


"It runs in families," said Dr. Grant the next day. They stood in her room where she lay, pale and exhausted, on the bed. Jim was just behind Dr. Grant and Johnny hovered in the background.

"Sometimes they show up very early, at the time of first menstruation for instance. Sometimes, as in your case, much later. Usually the later appearances are brought on by stress. Fortunately, there's a very good new medication for control of the pain. And it's important to control the stress to prevent recurrences. We'll have to try different tranquilizers to see which works best."

"I don't like the idea of tranquilizers," said Celia weakly.

"It's a tradeoff, Sis," said her brother, "if it's stress that's caused the migraine. We'll do some tests, of course . . . when you feel better. Let's let her sleep now," he said to the others.


When they were downstairs and out of earshot, John Mann gave voice to his misgivings.

"Lord, she was really sick. I didn't think the effect would be that severe."

"It's hard to control the dose doing it this way," said Grant.

"It didn't really hurt her," said Fifield, "and it's certainly had the desired effect. It's distracted her from Peace Day. As long as she's worried about recurrence she'll probably suggest that they get a substitute. We may have to switch jars again and precipitate another episode. But I doubt it."

"I hope you're right," said Mann fervently.

That was how it started. In the weeks that followed Celia felt lethargic. She thought of herself as going through the motions. It was not that she lost interest in Peace Day, but the dread of another headache took precedence. No very strong protest was raised when, finally, she withdrew for reasons of health.

On Peace Day itself she watched the proceedings on television. The cameras were concentrated on the enormous crowd. Polly, who took her place, was a tiny figure on the distant stage. "See, it wouldn't have mattered if I did it, Johnny," she said to him later. "They would have hardly seen me."

"Don't you believe it," he answered. "If the vice-presidential candidate's wife was up there the cameras would have been in close. And that would have been only half of it."

"If that's so, I *should* have been there," said Celia with something of her old conviction.

In the years to come Celia was never able to call up a clear, consecutive memory of the last week of the campaign. It came back to her like a kaleidoscopic montage of airport arrivals and departures in places as far apart as Portland, Maine, and Prescott, Arizona; of banquets, receptions and endless receiving lines; of head tables and stages where she sat, alternately smiling or serious, listening, listening to introductions by local politicians, and speeches by Lily Batchelder, or John, or both; of "photo opportunity" visits to day-care centers, nursing homes and housing projects.

There had been, after John Mann's first campaign swing, the hasty assembling of a staff for her. The staff was headed by Maura, who was given temporary leave from the Senate office to serve as her personal aide and liaison. There were two young secretaries drawn from the campaign volunteers to answer the phones and mail, and a young man named Wade Haney, who came over from President Batchelder's press office to handle all her press releases and interviews. They commandeered the den in the Chevy Chase house and Celia often, as she passed the door, heard with some wonderment the busy ringing of the phones and the brisk answers, "Mrs. Mann's office, one moment please," or, "Mrs. Mann's office, can you hold?" With the staff in the house and the Secret Service and its Sentry Central assistants housed over the garage, Celia had the bewildering sense that she and Susan were alone, surrounded by strangers.

At a strategy session with Senator McElwain of Illinois, who had been drafted as the president's campaign chairman, it was decided that Celia would accompany her husband on all trips of more than one day in duration and that she would always be with him when he appeared on the same platform or at the same event as President Batchelder. Celia, who sat in on the session, demurred halfheartedly. "But Johnny and I have always had separate campaign schedules except for the big rallies and the finale," she said. "Don't you see, Roy, how that doubles the impact?"

She saw Roy's quick look at Johnny and her husband's slight shake of the head. She felt a brief spurt of anger, but she could not quarrel with Roy's response.

"Well, yes, Celia," he said, "that's usually true, but this time you've got your handsome young husband campaigning with a pretty widow lady. That has to be handled mighty carefully. We can't have people beginning to ask, 'Where's Mrs. Mann?' "

The election was never in doubt. The two rather pedestrian Republican candidates from the conservative wing of the party did not attract the press, which had grown weary of the conservatives' alarms and excursions. The relative novelty of the Batchelder-Mann team, and the fact that Lily Batchelder's first term had ended with high approval ratings in the polls, kept the focus on the Democrats. The election seemed almost a matter of form and, although there was no concession until after the polls had closed in the Western states, it was clear to Johnny and Celia, watching returns in their suite at the hotel in Lake City, that John Mann had been elected vice-president of the United States.

Mann and Batchelder had chosen to await the returns in their native states as a concession to the constituents in each. Celia felt a pang of sympathy for Johnny as he watched Lily, surrounded by smiling, cheering Mississippians, appear on the screen to make her acceptance speech. She realized, as she followed him out of the suite to go down to the ballroom where he would make his own, that for him everything was a bit flat. He had a victory, yes, but it was a victory for the second place, and not only that, he had not really had the joy of the contest. There was a sense of repetition about Lily Batchelder's reelection. She and the people had been there before. It had been an evening of desultory election news, and the campaign veteran in Celia knew that Johnny could almost physically feel, as she did, sets being turned off all across America before he had his chance at that nationwide audience.

That sense of the secondhand persisted throughout the period that followed. After a short and almost obligatory vacation in the Caribbean with Susan and Peter, John and Celia returned to Washington, where John Mann was to participate in the carefully orchestrated restructuring of the new Batchelder-Mann administration. Resignations were accepted and new appointments made, all with an eye to dominating the news as much as possible.

Celia was occupied with the move to the vice-presidential residence on its hill on the Naval Observatory grounds high over Massachusetts Avenue. She and John had lunch there with retiring vice-president Boise, who gave them a tour of the house. A comfortable shabbiness, curiously suitable to the old widower's personality, seemed to have settled on it during his tenure. Celia, who had been a guest there during the Rockefeller, Mondale and Bush occupancies, marveled once again how soon a house takes on the stamp of those who live in it. She was seized with a sense of pity when Clem Boise showed them his study. It was packed with mementoes; the pictures of associates and heroes cherished through a long political life had obviously been selected and placed with care. It was clear that the rugged old man had settled in here and was being uprooted before he had planned. But Clem Boise showed no disappointment and made every effort to make them feel that it was their house and he a temporary lodger, anxious to move on.

After a while Celia began to enjoy the daily trips to the house and the planning for their post-inaugural entertaining.

President Lily Batchelder, using the precedent set by the last Reagan inaugural, had drastically scaled down the festivities at the time of her own first inauguration. The unusual cold of 1985 had forced the cancellation of the parade and the traditional outdoor inaugural address. Lily Batchelder surmised, as did other people, that the elderly Reagan, robust though he was, had welcomed this cancellation of exposure to the elements.

"It turned out to be a moving and beautiful inauguration as the nation witnessed it on television," said Lily to the planners and press after the election in 1988, "and I would like my inauguration to be that way. After all, we will only be accepting the technological realities of our era in a way that Thomas Jefferson, the great founder of our party, would have done." Privately she had said to Clem Boise, "I think it's a better reason to give than to acknowledge that we are concerned about security." The protective services of the government heaved a sigh of relief and the era of the small inaugural began. Lily Batchelder's first inaugural had had, however, the excitement engendered by the election of the first woman president. There was no real excitement about her second one, and John Mann's first. Celia knew that Johnny felt this way, although he affected to ignore the preparations and to bury himself in briefings for the upcoming tripartite meeting of scientists making the final arrangements for Moonlab. She tried to distract him with plans for festivities in the vice-president's house.

"I thought it would be nice, Johnny, if we had some old friends and Chevy Chase neighbors for our first open house. Sort of a private, informal christening of our occupancy. Of course, we'll have to have a congressional reception to mark your presiding over the Senate. But perhaps we could have another dinner just for the class of '76—the year you were elected, and I could have a lunch for the '76 Congress Club . . ."

Johnny kept his eyes fixed on the bowl game he was watching. "Do whatever you like, Celia. Work it out with Jule," he said.

On the first day of his occupancy of the vice-presidential office John Mann studied the schedule on his desk and shouted into the intercom for his private secretary, "Jule, in here! What *is* this?"

Jule arrived at the door unruffled. "What's the trouble, Mr. Vice-President?" she asked with a touch of irony.

"These things scheduled for the house, that's the matter," exploded John Mann. "Look here, you've got that peace group of Celia's just at the time we open the Moonlab conference. Can't you see what the press is going to make of that?"

Jule knew well enough how to deflect his irritation. "You left that schedule for Mrs. Mann to arrange, Senator," she said, falling back on the old and more familiar title, "and that's what she wanted. I didn't think it was up to me to raise any objection. She said you had told her to work it out with me."

"Well, work out a cancellation or a postponement then, and quick— before anyone gets hold of this!" He was reluctant to let his anger subside. Celia again, he thought. Would she never be reasonable?

"I'll do my best, Senator," said Jule noncommittally. She looked at her watch. "That CIA man is waiting for you in the Capitol office."

Murat, waiting in the anteroom to meet the vice-president, was feeling a little keyed up. He noted his own feeling clinically. It was to be expected, he supposed. From long experience he was an expert at maintaining the delicate balance between truth and half-truth, discreet bullying and persuasion, with which the top men of his agency had learned to manipulate government executives and members of Congress when the requirements of the agency made it necessary. This was big. Bigger than anything they had ever done. And Mann was the key. The president had to be kept in the dark until there was no turning back. And Murat knew she was a lost cause. Too cautious. Too convinced that negotiation was the key to all problems. But they needed executive authority for some of the steps that had to be taken. Not for Mexico, thank God. The machinery set up in the previous administration, when Central America preoccupied the president and his advisers, was still there and working once again with the cooperation of special branches of Lily Batchelder's own Defense Department. But they needed cover for Canada. And Canada was known to be Mann's baby—put into his arms by the lady herself. Murat smiled his thin smile.

Ellis Murat had at last fallen heir to that mysterious section of the CIA in which covert actions were planned and directed. Within his realm his authority was absolute and his reach worldwide. The politically appointed directors of the CIA, except for the feisty and bullheaded William Colby, had, out of prudence, left the section pretty much to its own devices. There was tacit agreement that it would be best not to know too much about what went on there and in what foreign countries its agents were involved. Among America's allies and client nations there were those whose intelligence operatives would deal only with Murat and his men.

The effect of the crackdown on the CIA following Watergate had long since worn away. Now the section was riding high again, almost without restraint, and Murat shared the fine-edged, scornful arrogance of men of his type—men who had been the aristocrats of the agency from the beginning—who felt that they, rather than the elected officials of the country, held its welfare in their hands and knew what was best for America and for the world. In his view, elected officials were necessary evils. They were the facade of democracy. The important thing was to assess them accurately, use them if possible or go around them if they were not usable. In his opinion John Mann was eminently usable.

He heard the quick click of heels on the tiled floor outside and rose to his feet. Mann burst through the door followed by his Secret Service man. His greeting was brusque and without warmth.

He's turned off the charm, thought Murat, following him into the inner office. Upset about something. Something's on his mind. Well, I may have to work a little harder. But I wager I'll soon have his complete attention.

John Mann waved Murat to a chair and sat down behind his desk. His voice was irritable.

"Well, let's get on with it. What have we got today? The names of twenty terrorist groups all laying claim to the same bombing? Why can't you people tie these things together? We're not getting anywhere with the problem as far as I can see."

"That's why we have worked out a different approach, Mr. Vice-President," said Murat smoothly, ignoring the intentionally offensive words. Mann had given him a perfect opening. He paused and looked around the room. "You're sure we are secure?"

"Swept every morning and twice a day after that," said John Mann. "Fire away." His irritability was subsiding.

Ten minutes later the vice-president was sitting bolt upright in his chair, his attention riveted on Murat.

"Good God, man," he said slowly, "what you're talking about amounts to overthrowing the Canadian government."

Murat shook his head. "Just assisting the overturn in the Province of Quebec, sir." The more deferential the better, now. "Chouinard's men are in place and ready. We have to have a government there which will take the stringent measures that are needed. Once Quebec is under control, Ottawa will fall into line."

John Mann shook his head. "Chouinard," he said in disbelief. "It's hard to believe that he has that kind of power. I knew he was an operator, of course—"

Indeed you did, thought Murat with irony.

"We are sure that his organization is impressive and effective," he said aloud. "All he needs is the restraint on our side which will allow him the freedom to move. Our agencies have to be called off their co-operative investigations with the Canadians. Our forces up there have to be thinned out. Our planes have to be called home. We have to give him breathing room." He paused again. This was the tricky part. "You can see why the president had to leave it up to you. She can't even seem to know about it. But she has perfect trust in your ability to carry it off." Will he swallow that? he wondered. It's a little thick even for an ego like Mann's. And he's been protecting his behind for years.

The vice-president drew a deep breath. "I wish I could go over it with her all the same," he said, but his voice held no hint of disbelief.

Murat relaxed. Hooked. The man was hooked. Now reel him in.

"The country will be in your debt, Mr. Vice-President, although it will never know it. You will join the long line of those who have done what had to be done to save our democracy for a people who will never know or understand what has been done for them. I won't deceive you. There are risks. If there are slips there will be an uproar and Congress in full cry calling for investigations like hounds baying after the fox."

The vice-president's face was solemn. "I guess you fellows know all about that," he said. "I see the risk. But I count on you to see that there are no slips."

Murat nodded, solemn in his turn. "We can only do our best." Then he turned to business. "The way we see it, Mr. Vice-President, is that you arrange the pullbacks, agency by agency, service by service, enjoining utmost secrecy every time. Each one will think it's just another small move expressing our government's discontent with the Canadian government's performance and a way of backing up the president's pressure on the PM . . ."

When Murat had gone the vice-president sat alone in his office, his thoughts whirling. He was seized with a genuine admiration for President Lily Batchelder, which was unlike the grudging respect he had granted her until then. Good God, the lady had guts he had never suspected. She was playing hardball with the whole goddamn hemisphere. And Maurice! Playing it close to his chest like that all this time! John Mann was not so sure that he liked that. If only he could brace the guy—ask just what he thought he was doing, keeping his American allies in the dark. But better not. Maybe Leo knew. Maybe Adam—even Sam.

Although he didn't like to admit it, it was better that he himself had not
known. Still it made him uneasy to think of the shadowy, cool French-
Canadian dealing with the government of the United States of America.
These were bad times, he told himself, more soberly reflective than was
his wont. He shook his head. An almost irrelevant thought crossed his
mind. He had real reason now to see that Celia kept quiet. He fished in
his inside coat pocket for the microrecorder he was never without these
days. Did Murat really think he wouldn't have protected his ass? He
grinned to himself. A good thing Celia would never hear this tape.

But Celia did hear the tape. The night of his talk with Murat, Jule
called to say that the vice-president would be late. Celia gave up waiting
for him about eleven. She was almost asleep when she heard him come
in. Here in the vice-president's house they shared the large master bedroom, but the room across the hall had been transformed into Johnny's
dressing and exercise room. It also held a comfortable single bed where,
in his words, he could sack out without disturbing her. Although he had
slept there more and more often, it had not exactly served that purpose.
The steps and floors in the old house creaked tellingly under their thick
carpets. She always woke when he came in.

She heard him stop on the landing. Why? she wondered drowsily—
then remembered and smiled to herself. The old wall safe. Did Johnny
use that? She remembered how they had laughed at their discovery of
that archaic feature in the old mansion. The small cylinder safe plas-
tered into the wall and designed to be hidden behind a painting seemed
such a pathetic effort at securing valuables in the face of modern
technology.

"Let's hang Spiro Agnew there," she had suggested mischievously. A
misguided benefactor had donated portraits of all the former vice-
presidents, and their predecessors in the house had placed them in the
stairwell. Johnny had laughed again and agreed to her suggestion. Later
Celia had put her pearls there, thinking the safe safer than the dressing-
table drawer.

She heard the cautious scrape as he moved the Agnew portrait aside,
then the faint squeak as the little round door yielded to the combination
and the slight thud as it closed again. Johnny must be using it for things
he doesn't want to have in the office. What kinds of things?

It was several days before she thought of the wall safe again. Curiosity and a growing suspicion impelled her to open it one afternoon when she was fairly sure she was alone. She found it empty except for her pearls and a stack of tiny microtapes. Hurriedly she took the one with the latest date and put the others back. She had barely closed the safe and let the sardonically smiling portrait of Agnew fall back into place when she heard one of the navy corpsmen who staffed the house clattering down the third-floor stairs. A minute later she slipped the tape into the knitting bag she kept in a corner of the sofa in the small downstairs sitting room. But it was more than a month before she thought of how she could play it. And when she had heard it she did not know what to do.

First she tried to bring it up with Johnny. Indirectly. Johnny had come home early and was in his own bed tonight. Now was her time. Celia hadn't listened to the whole tape, but her every instinct told her that something was very wrong. President Lily Batchelder would never have agreed to that plan. It smacked too much of games—men and their deadly games. But she would have to be careful about what she said. Johnny would explode into anger if he thought she had looked for the tape and found it. He would call it spying. She breathed a prayer, then got up and crawled into his bed.

He rolled over in sleepy welcome, putting his arm around her, and one hand on her thigh. Not too fast, she thought silently. I need a few minutes. She snuggled against him.

"Johnny," she said, "I worry about it. Have you ever told the president that something might happen in July—that there was talk of an uprising of some kind?"

"Celia, I told you before that that was all nonsense—just Maurice being flamboyant—showing off." So she hadn't forgotten. She *had* brought that up after she overheard Maurice and Sam and the others, but he had been pretty sure the induced migraines had driven it out of her mind.

How much did she dare? Celia asked herself. She took his face in her hands. "But Johnny, there might be other things—couldn't you talk to Bill Haskins? Isn't he chairman of the intelligence committee?" If she could plant doubts—make him think of checking—make him think of other ways—

"Don't worry about things like that, Celia," he said with finality. Silently he told himself that he would have to deflect her attention once again. Then, as if softening, he said, "At least, not now. Mmm, your hands smell good." He would have to switch creams.

He was up the next morning before her. And the next morning she had another migraine.

# PART
# 2

# . 10 .

"I DON'T THINK it's necessary, Johnny," said Celia. She sat at the table in the window of their bedroom, where they breakfasted regularly. Her voice was a little desperate. Johnny sat across from her and her brother stood beside him holding a coffee cup and staring fixedly across the lawn at the Naval Observatory.

"I don't see why I can't just go in and out for tests instead of checking into the hospital. Susie still doesn't feel at home in this house and I don't think I should leave her. I don't *want* to go to the hospital, Johnny." She looked pleadingly at her husband, but he was avoiding her eyes. He did that when he was uncomfortable about what he was doing, she thought, and when—but she did not let herself finish the thought—when he is lying. She had always tried hard to believe that Johnny didn't lie to her. Sometimes he forgot—and sometimes he avoided the unpleasant and the difficult. That was all. That was what she steadfastly told herself.

"Your aunt will come to be with Susie," said her husband. "I talked to her. And you must see that you can't stay here as long as you're having these blackouts. It's too dangerous."

Celia sighed. She looked past her brother, out the window at the driveway going down the hill. Had she really walked—or perhaps run— down that hill yesterday? They said she had. But it was so hard to believe. And so frightening.

"I could have a nurse or a companion," she offered, looking from one to the other. They exchanged glances. Before they could reject the suggestion she thought of another. "Wouldn't it be better if I went home to the hospital in Lake City? Dr. Corbeil has taken care of me most of my life. Wouldn't he be the best one to look into what's the matter with me—especially if the migraines, which started all this, are hereditary,

**117**

as you say?" She looked at her brother. "All the family records are there."

"We *know* what's the matter with you, Celia," said Dr. Fifield with exaggerated patience. "It's a drug interaction and not at all uncommon. You forget how many pills you've taken and you take more—and more—until it's too many. Lots of people begin to show addictive symptoms that way. And that's what you're showing. The pattern is clear. Dr. Grant concurs."

"Jim, I am *not* addicted," said Celia indignantly. "I've taken only what you told me to take!"

"You can't be sure when you're out of it half the time," he said brutally.

Celia gasped. With growing panic she turned to her husband again, casting about for an argument that would win him over. "Johnny, the publicity! Think of the publicity! No matter what we tell them, they'll say I went into the hospital with a drug problem."

"It won't be any worse than if you got run over kiting down the avenue, would it?" said her husband.

That publicity is exactly what we need, he thought. But there's no sense getting her more upset than she is already. He got up and put his arm around her shoulders.

"Look, Celia, it's the best thing. And it's only for a few days—a week, ten days at the most." He knew it would have to be longer to keep her out of the way during the crucial time ahead, but it was best to ease her along by stages. "I'll come home this afternoon and we'll go and get you settled. Jim has alerted the hospital. The country will just have to get along without me for a while." He kissed her lightly on the cheek. "Come on now, get ready. Juanita will help you."

Celia got up. She knew she was defeated.

"It really is the conservative medical approach, Celia," said her brother with relief. "If you like, I'll call old Corbeil and ask him to come down to have a look at you."

She did not answer him directly. "If you'll excuse me," she said, "I'll get dressed now. There's a lot to do if I'm to be out of commission for a while."


It was almost five by the time the vice-president and Dr. James Fifield left the hospital. Curious nurses were grouped around the desk and patients peered from doorways as they emerged from the VIP wing and walked down the hall toward the waiting elevator blocked off by the Secret Service. They were about to step in when John Mann heard a familiar voice calling his name.

"Mr. Mann! Mr. Vice-President!"

He turned and saw a tall young man in a white coat hurrying toward them. The stethoscope hanging around his neck bounced as he moved. A doctor? The vice-president frowned, trying to place him.

"Bill Cratte, Senator—I mean Mr. Vice-President," said the young man as he caught up to him. He was smiling broadly, sure of his welcome. "From Hartport."

"Bill! What are you doing here?" John Mann shook his proffered hand automatically.

"I'm on rotation from medical school in Boston. Only been here a week. I didn't quite know how to get in touch with you folks—didn't know if I should now that you're vice-president and all. But I did want to see Mrs. Mann. It's a piece of luck that she's checked in here." He flushed, suddenly aware of the inappropriateness of the remark. "I mean it's not luck for her, of course," he stumbled, "but luck for me that I can visit with her. It's not serious, is it? I mean, it's just for observation, isn't it?" He floundered. He needed help.

"Oh, yes, yes," the vice-president said hastily and reassuringly. Inwardly he was dismayed. Bill Cratte, of all people. The boy had been in and out of the house for years. He knew Celia too well. Sometimes he had seemed as much her friend as Pete's. And the kid was sharp—with medical training he might suspect something.

"I'm not sure she can have visitors," he said. "What do you say, Jim?" he turned to Fifield. "This young man is from our summer place, Hartport. This is Dr. Fifield, Bill, from the National Institute and head of the president's commission. He's Mrs. Mann's brother."

Bill Cratte looked impressed, but he did not wait for Dr. Fifield's answer. "Oh, I don't mean as a regular visitor," he said cheerfully. "I take the histories and do the preliminary exams on this floor." He waved the clipboard in his hand. "They just gave me Mrs. Mann's chart. That's how I knew she was here—and then I saw you."

Jim Fifield had opened his mouth to answer Mann's question, but he closed it again. He had been about to say that his sister's room was off-limits except to specially assigned hospital personnel. But it was too late for that where Cratte was concerned. They would have to trust to luck. Cratte was only a student, after all. If he formed any contrary opinions, he could easily be overridden.

If Bill Cratte detected any uneasiness in the atmosphere, he did not show it. He drew back.

"I mustn't keep you," he said. "I know you're very busy. Say hello to Pete when you talk to him, won't you? It's nice to meet you, Dr. Fifield," he added. He waited respectfully as they entered the elevator and waved as the doors closed.

Celia Mann's reluctance to go to the hospital had been instinctive. She feared a further loss of independence and privacy, and from the minute she walked in the door of St. Simeon's she realized it was going to be worse than she thought.

They were met by the administrator, Sister Anna, whom she knew from her years of service on the hospital board. Sister's normally deferential attitude had undergone a subtle change. She was kindly but dismissive. She directed her welcoming remarks to Johnny and to Jim as she led them to the reception desk, and Celia detected a strong note of sympathy toward them underlying her professional remarks. The usual check-in procedure had been waived for Mrs. Mann. Her room was in readiness, the floor supervisor was expecting her, she had only to have the chest X ray—a matter of minutes. When that was over, Sister Anna took them to the elevator and said vaguely that she would be up to see Mrs. Mann later.

Once John and her brother had accompanied her to the room and taken their leave, Celia found that control over the details of her life was quietly but firmly being taken away from her.

"I'm not sick, you know," she said to the floor supervisor, Miss Hutzler, who announced that she would help her undress and "get comfy." "I'll wait until after dinner to undress, if you don't mind. I've brought some books and some notes to answer and I'll just sit here by the window."

"Now, now, Mrs. Mann," said the nurse, "we like our patients to be ready for the preliminaries. They'll be in for blood tests and to take your blood pressure and your medical history. It's better for you to be in bed for all that. The doctor has to use his stethoscope and test for chest sound, you know." Her tone was patronizing and she was busy opening and unpacking Celia's bag as she spoke. "What a pretty robe! And here's your gown. Now I'll just pop out and get a thermometer while you get into these." She was out the door before Celia could protest again.

They think I will wander off, thought Celia. She had a momentary urge to stand her ground—to refuse to undress, to rebel. What would happen? she wondered. Would they send for Sister Anna or a doctor? Would they call Johnny? Would the nurse try to undress her forcibly? She had a hysterical impulse to laugh aloud as she imagined the scene— she in her proper spring suit struggling with the fat sandy-haired nurse. Resignedly she took her robe and gown and went into the bathroom.

When she emerged, the nurse was waiting with the covers on the bed turned down. She pulled out the bed stool and helped Celia up with a firm grip on her arm.

"I'll get your books and your notepaper," she said as Celia demurred. "Are these the ones, in this portfolio?" She made a rather long business of taking them out and putting them on Celia's bed table. "Now, here's your purse. Just take out your makeup and a dollar or two and I'll have the rest locked up in the hospital safe." She watched as Celia took out compact, lipstick and pen. "Now let's see, where are your medications— here in your tote bag? They'll have to go in our drug cabinet."

Suddenly Celia understood. She's searching my things! She thinks I have pills hidden away. What in the world had her brother or Dr. Grant told the administrator and the nurses?

"Miss Hutzler," she said indignantly, "I have only the prescriptions the doctor—my brother—ordered, and they're in my little medicine bag. You needn't rummage through my personal things. Just give me that bag and I'll find them for you."

The nurse surrendered the bag, but Celia felt she had already seen everything in it.

"Of course, Mrs. Mann," she said, "whatever you say. But people do carry aspirin, you know, and cold tablets. They usually don't realize that those are medications, too, and could interact badly with what we give them here."

She is soothing me down, Celia told herself, but what she says is true, I suppose. A moment later her indignation returned when Nurse Hutzler put a thermometer in her mouth and went into the bathroom. She could hear her opening the medicine cabinet. Checking to see if I've secreted anything, thought Celia angrily. Her cheeks were hot and she stared stubbornly out the window when Miss Hutzler returned to retrieve the thermometer. She ignored the nurse's cheerful farewell and instantly regretted doing so. Acting childish would only confirm their suspicions. She looked at her flushed face in the mirror across the room and fought back tears of frustration.

* * *

Bill Cratte found her sitting in the half-dark of the fading afternoon. It took her a minute to realize who he was, and he felt that her pleasure in seeing him was forced. He himself was aware of their distance from the sunny world of Hartport; he had been made distinctly uneasy by the preliminary report given him at the nurses' stations. Although he tried to be matter-of-fact and professional as he settled himself to take Mrs. Mann's history, he knew his voice was too heavy. Celia's voice, initially warm, dulled to a monotone. They went through the routine mechanically as Bill dealt with his dismay and confusion. Mrs. Mann on drugs! It was hard to believe.

Age. She was forty-four years old. Bill Cratte, despite his own youth, knew that was young in terms of today's maturity. Peter's mother had always seemed young to him—almost a contemporary. She was lithe and active and laughed easily at simple things—sometimes just because she felt good and happy at the Cape. His own mother was ten years older. She was a little heavy and she was weathered as women often are who live year round by the sea. He loved her but they were not close. He could not talk to her easily. He had always, until now, been able to talk easily with Mrs. Mann. He tried to look at her objectively, observing signs as he had been trained to do. Her color was good. Her eyes— perhaps a bit dull?

Childhood health. Always excellent. All the right immunizations. The right nutrition, he surmised. Good dental care. Parents' health good until shortly before their deaths, so she thought. Was she concealing anything? A hereditary pattern that would predispose her to drugs? He didn't think so. Both parents dead but not in unusual ways. And her muscle tone was good; her skin tone, too. No signs of overindulgence in food or alcohol. There he felt himself on sure ground. His last rotation had been at a Veterans Hospital.

When they came to the reasons for her hospitalization, he fumbled for words. He could not be blunt in questioning her about this. Anything might be the wrong thing to ask.

Celia felt his hesitation. She roused herself—he was Peter's friend, after all. This could not be easy for him. At least he didn't act like the nurses.

"I started having migraine headaches, Bill," she said, "quite suddenly, last fall—not too long after we came back from Hartport."

Bill seized on the information eagerly. Migraine was a covering name for various head pains from different causes. They could also be excruciating. People suffering from them would grasp at almost any relief.

"They're usually hereditary," he said. "Do you remember any history?"

"Jim—my brother, Dr. Fifield—said my grandmother had them. It's funny, though. I don't remember that at all." Celia's voice was puzzled. "Anyway, mine were awful."

"And what helped?"

"My brother prescribed Demerol to begin with—then lithium and Haldol for the stress he thought caused them."

Bill Cratte looked astonished. "Are you sure? Lithium and Haldol?"

"Yes," said Celia, "I'm sure. I could show you the containers but the nurse took them."

Bill Cratte looked unconvinced. He did not write the names down. She must be wrong, he thought. I'll ask at the desk.


Bill Cratte went from Celia Mann's room to the nurses' station, where Miss Hutzler sat working on a pile of charts. She looked up and smiled without warmth.

"Oh, good, there you are. I need your notations on Mann's chart and we'll have them all," she paused and added, "every one of them in, doctor."

Bill flushed. It bothered him that the still-unearned title was used in hospitals for medical students on rotation. The practice was intended to be reassuring to patients but he felt that the nurses, especially the older ones like Miss Hutzler, used it with a hint of mockery. He tried to show no signs of diffidence when he said, "It'll be a minute more, Miss Hutzler. I want to check the patient's medications. Could I have the key?"

Miss Hutzler produced it with no sign of impatience. The magic of the white coat and the stethoscope is working again, Bill thought to himself with some amazement, and turned to the cupboard where the medications were kept under lock and key at all times. He checked Celia Mann's twice. She was right. They were all there and had been renewed in the last month. And they weren't on the chart. Something was wrong here. Really wrong. He would ask about it at rounds in the morning.

# . 11 .

WHEN Bill Cratte left the room Celia was at a loss. She had no feelings at all. She did not know how she should feel, she realized. It was so strange that she should be here—that Bill Cratte should also be here. She had a disturbing sense of distance from reality. Could that person she could see in the mirror really be herself—Celia Fifield Mann?

"Time for dinner!" The aide's artificially cheery voice interrupted her depressed reverie. "Let me fix your table and crank you up so you can eat comfortably." She was doing just that even as she uttered the words. Why does she even bother to say "Let me," Celia thought fretfully, but mindful of her resolution, she thanked the aide and asked her to turn on the television.

"Here's your remote control," said the aide instructively, "right here on the bed console. And this button is for dimming the lights so you can see the screen better. Call me if you need anything else." She went out again.

A clatter of trays in the hall announced the arrival of the food service cart. Another aide came in with a tray and was gone again with only a quick "Good evening," a curious appraising look at Celia, and a mechanical smile. Hospital clockwork. It was so depersonalized. Even the most privileged of us have to struggle to maintain our individuality, Celia mused as she inspected her tray. Instinctively she was trying to distance herself from the experience. To reflect on it and to generalize it was to hold it off so that it could not really hurt her. She would watch TV while she ate, she decided, and concentrate.

The TV set suspended from the wall just above eye level had flickered

124

into life. The smoothly modeled head with its close-cropped hair, the bland brown face—it was Donna Chase with the local evening news.

"—and so tensions with Canada continue to mount despite the supposedly friendly meeting between President Batchelder and the prime minister only six months ago. Today a White House source said that the president has authorized a stiff representation to the prime minister asking for forcible action to control the French-Canadian terrorists and what she terms their 'intrusions' across our borders—"

That would upset Johnny, Celia thought automatically. He was so proud of his work on Canadian relations. But Donna Chase was going on.

"—Vice-President Mann, to whom the president has given special responsibility for ironing out our difficulties with our neighbor to the north, is understandably otherwise preoccupied today. Joe McClelland has that story. Joe—"

Joe McClelland was supposed to be the funny man of the evening news team. He owed his job to his time-tested ability to amuse local Washington with his puns and his supposedly spontaneous quips. But tonight his broad, massaged face was solemn, to indicate that there was nothing funny about the news he had to impart.

"This city was stunned today by the revelation that the wife of the vice-president, Mrs. John Mann, has been hospitalized for treatment for drug addiction. Bill Shields, WTEC's reporter on Capitol Hill, talked with the vice-president today."

Celia sat shocked, as her husband appeared seated, leaning back in a desk chair. Behind him were cases of handsome leather, gold-lettered lawbooks. His office in the White House, she thought, not his hideaway in the Capitol. Johnny's boyishly handsome face looked worried. Both hands gripped a pencil, fingering it as he talked. His voice was subdued, grave.

"Well, Bill," John was saying, "it's not a thing I can talk about very easily. It's too close to me. My wife has been under a lot of strain. She was on medication—tranquilizers and sleeping pills—but no one, not even our doctor, thought she was addicted." His gaze seemed to meet that of each viewer. "Well, I have to be totally frank—not until about ten days ago. It has gone beyond home treatment. There'll be a full medical report tomorrow."

While he talked, an action shot appeared on the screen. Celia had seen it more than once—she and John together at the convention, acknowledging the cheers of the delegates, each with one arm around the other and one arm upraised, waving.

"Do you think your wife found the national campaign too much of a strain, Mr. Vice-President?" asked Bill Shields, his voice professionally sympathetic.

The senator's face was sober, thoughtful.

"Maybe. Maybe that was it."

Bill Shields again. "We have more on this story. Stay tuned. Now this—" A commercial.

Celia sat in her bed, stunned, unbelieving. Johnny—how could he do it? How could he say things like that? He knew it wasn't true. It's as if I am hardly a person, she thought. They discuss me as if I am not alive, not real. How easy it was for him to make people think this thing of her . . . everyone would believe it. The children . . . they would surely hear it . . . she thought of Susan facing that horrid little Elly. Why? Why did he want to do it?

That familiar voice . . . was she dreaming again? . . . No, it *was* Hannah Steinman. A panel. She recognized Sheila McCrady, network reporter. Sheila McCrady, so very young . . . fully aware of the useful curving of her body outlined in a blue silk blouse as she leaned over the desk, and of her lips moving as she questioned, coaxed and cajoled the people she was interviewing. "Now, about Celia Mann," she was saying . . . they were talking about her again. The realization focused Celia's wandering attention . . . Hannah Steinman looking nervous . . . her hair looking teased, stiff and set . . . the scarf around her neck, an effort to soften the effects of age, looked bunchy . . . Hannah, her friend, so earnest, talking about Celia as if she were some case she'd studied at the university . . . and Father Antonio, the psychologist on the St. Simeon's board, there, too . . . wearing the Roman collar and the black rabat, which he hardly ever wore . . . his hair combed so carefully across his balding head . . . sounding so authoritative, so knowledgeable . . . and Sheila, summing her up, filing her away . . . just a case study. "Is Celia Mann still another to bow and break under the burdens of political wifehood? Did the strains and stresses that have affected so many other prominent Washington women finally reach her just as her husband has assumed one of the highest offices in the land? These experts who knew her think it might be very possible. This is Sheila McCrady in Washington for Capital Coverage." Celia despaired. Everyone will believe it, she thought—and no one cares.

\*    \*    \*

By the next morning, Celia's hospitalization was the talk of the capital. Washingtonians were inured to the troubles of political wives. There had been, after all, Martha Mitchell, Joan Kennedy, Betty Ford, governors' wives, mayors' wives—all spread out in the headlines. This was no different but it was news. It stood out in the bold headlines of the morning *Post*: MANN'S WIFE IN HOSPITAL / ADDICTED, DOCTOR SAYS.

And so the town buzzed. At the White House, President Batchelder received the early edition with her breakfast tray. She read the story carefully, then reached out to the telephone console and pressed a button. In a house in Georgetown a buzzer sounded and Cromfield Haines picked up the white phone beside his bed. He heard the very faint whine which indicated that a scrambler protected the call. He smiled.

"I've just learned that Celia Mann is in the hospital," said the president.

"Yes," said Haines. "Her brother called me. And she's somewhat discredited, I would judge, and her movement, too."

"I'm sorry about it," said the president. "I hope John handles it well."

"Oh, he will," said Haines. "He'll know how to play it for sympathy."


The Haskinses sat at the breakfast table in the high bay window overlooking Cumberland Avenue. The network news was over and Bill Haskins used his remote control to flip to cable news, which was making the most of the Mann story. A picture of Celia Mann lit the screen. He turned up the sound.

Polly Haskins stood stock still at the sound of Celia's voice. "Why, that's our organization meetin' in Louisville," she said. "They must have got that from that one little local station that covered us."

Celia Mann stood before a small group of women in what appeared to be a school hall. The women set on folding chairs. A scattered few held Styrofoam coffee cups. Most of them were young—the age of PTA mothers—but here and there a gray head was also visible. In front of them, beside a folding table stacked with brochures, Celia stood, vivid in a red shirtdress.

"I'm so glad for this opportunity to tell you about Peace Work," she said. "We've played with the name, you see—called it for piece work, the kind of work women have always done, like 'piecing' a quilt. We women, we put things together. We pick up the pieces. Look at the women of the South after the war between the states—"

Bill Haskins laughed. "She sure knew where she was," he said.

"Oh, sure, Celia's smart," said Polly.

"They were a nation of widows. They farmed the farms, they took in roomers, they rebuilt their families. Women have always buried their dead, grieved for the young lives snuffed out, and started the business of living all over again. And most of them have lived to see it happen again. Well, never again. Because we aren't going to pick up the pieces after the next war." Celia's voice was deadly earnest and her eyes, fixed on the camera, had a faraway look as if she looked into the future. "There won't be any pieces. There will be hundreds of millions dead and dying and only a few ratlike survivors crawling about a cold and silent planet."

"She sure can fling words around," observed Haskins.

"We're piecing it all together now, *right now*, piecing together women like you—women who opt for life, women who will see that their children have a future. Kentucky women, Ohio women, women from Maine to California, women in Asia, Africa, the Islands, European women— yes, Soviet women, too! We're piecing together a world that will not accept war. War never again!"

Celia's last words were drowned out in a burst of applause as the women came to their feet clapping and calling out. The scene faded from the screen and the commentator's pseudosolemn face appeared.

"And now Celia Mann, head of Peace Work, is confined to a hospital room fighting drug addiction instead of nuclear war. Will that mean the end of Peace Work? Only time will tell."

"I can see now that you ladies were really making waves," said Bill Haskins to his wife thoughtfully. "No wonder old Duckett was on the attack."

"And don't think the president liked it either," said Polly, "or Johnny Mann. Essentially Celia pulled out during the campaign. I think Johnny was giving her a hard time. He's not like you."

"Honey, it's not that I'm so tolerant of you," said her husband. "I wasn't in Johnny's position. He couldn't buck the president and she sees the peace movement as weakening her position." But Polly wasn't listening.

"Maybe I shouldn't have tried to talk her out of pulling back," she said.

"Maybe. But I can see how you might think you needed her."

Polly Haskins sighed. She was essentially an honest woman, and she was not sure that was why she had tried to persuade Celia against her will.

The telephone shrilled. The senator answered and handed it to his wife without comment. He turned back to his *New York Times* but he could hear the high-pitched voice as clearly as if he still held the receiver.

"Oh, Polly, Polly, what are we going to do? This is so awful about Celia!"

It was Millie Prescott's voice. The wife of the senator from Kansas was upset.

"We'll just have to go on, I guess. What else can we do?"

"But, Polly, I mean about the publicity. There will be the reporters and all the questions. That attack of Senator Duckett in the Senate was bad enough. Now they'll be saying we're all on dope or something. You know they will."

Polly sighed. She sought her husband's eyes but he did not look up. "Look, honey," she said soothingly, "taking too many tranquilizers isn't exactly being on dope. We just have to make it real plain that it is very sad about Celia. And, of course, that it has nothing at all to do with how we feel about nuclear arms." She paused. "It looks like it was a good thing she wasn't with us on Peace Day—and not much at all these last months," she added.

"Oh." Millie was quiet for a moment. Then she was off on another worry. "But who *will* take Celia's place? It can't be anyone but you, Polly. No one else could do it the way you can. You did so well on Peace Day!"

Polly did not argue. "We'll see, Millie. We'll have a meetin' and decide. Now you just take it easy, you hear? It's too bad Celia got herself in this mess but we just have to make the best of it."

She gave her husband the phone to replace in the cradle and he looked at her quizzically.

"This thing is affecting more than the administration, I gather," he said in his slowest drawl.

"It most certainly is," rejoined his wife. "What do you think? I'll bet the prez is regrettin' her choice of vice-president right now."

"I don't think," he said—and there was an implied warning in his voice—"it's our business, is it? And I thought you and Celia were real good friends. You didn't sound right friendly just now."

" 'Course Celia is my best friend the way all us wives are friends. But you're the friend I care most about." She began to gather up the dishes.

Bill Haskins sat deep in thought. The woman he had just seen speaking on television was certainly in control of all her faculties.

In the Haines bedroom on the top floor of the big double house in Georgetown, Deborah Haines had gone to bed early. She sipped a glass of milk and idly switched the television from channel to channel. The news was the same—mostly what she had seen that morning.

Life for Deborah Haines was a series of repetitions of what she had done for years and years. Weekday lunches at the Sulgrave or in a neighboring Georgetown house with women friends, dinner parties with an ever-changing cast of ambassadors or office-holders, weekend lunches in the country with the powerful and the press. Face followed face— they were all the same.

The cable newsclip with Celia Mann caught her attention. Really, the girl should not have been speaking out like that. It certainly couldn't have helped her husband. And yet— Convention had bound Deborah Haines for a long time, but something stirred in her as she listened to what Celia was saying.

Her eyes turned to the silver-framed photos on the dresser. Crom in his World War II major's uniform. Always well connected, he was an adjutant in Washington when she had come down from Boston to visit her aunt. Crom, Jr., in his navy flier's uniform. He had rejected his father's offers of influence and served on an aircraft carrier during the Vietnam war. Officially he was still listed as missing in action, but her daughter-in-law had remarried and gone to live in Hawaii—of all places. She and Crom seldom saw their grandsons. Deborah Haines stared at the picture of the two boys, older now—good heavens, Billy must be nineteen and Tom was seventeen, at the very least—and listened to Celia Mann.

In the city by the lake, they had just watched the noon news. It carried the clip of John Mann's interview. Now an elegantly tailored Adam Mann lounged behind his desk in a tower office and nodded patiently at the conference telephone transmitter. An authoritative, faintly accented voice was coming from the speaker, holding his attention and that of Sam Drottman, who was leaning against the wall behind him. They had watched the interview and so had their caller.

"So far, so good. Johnny handled it all right, but there can't be any slip-ups now. The deal is on and it's the biggest deal ever. I want you to tell Johnny that, Adam."

"Yeah, yeah, Leo," said the listener reassuringly. "Johnny knows that. Johnny's okay. You can bet on that."

"Maybe, maybe not," said the disembodied voice. "I don't like this with Celia. It's got to be a sure thing. She knows something she shouldn't, she's got to be kept quiet. What's with Johnny—he can't keep his wife quiet? A woman stands by her man."

"Sure, sure, Leo," said the listener easily, "but things are a little different these days. You don't need to worry, though. Johnny and Sam have everything under control."

"They don't—my boys take over."

Adam sighed. "Don't worry, Leo," he repeated. "Johnny's going to be mighty careful. He won't let anything blow it—not *anything*, Leo. I promise you that."

"He'd better be careful. He'd better," repeated the voice. "I count on you for that, Adam." The transmitter went dead. The listener swiveled in his chair and looked at Sam.

"For a man who operates on three continents, Leo is still old-fashioned. He's got old-country ideas," he said wearily.

"What are you going to do, Adam?" Sam asked. The tone of his voice, a mixture of overfamiliarity with just a hint of deference, was the mark of the indispensable staff man. "It was bad luck that Celia overheard us. Celia's smart. She can put two and two together."

"You heard the man, Sam," said Adam. "Celia has to stay sick. A sick wife is a safe one."

"A dead one is safer," said Sam and laughed.

Adam Mann's face was impassive. "It's not smart to talk like that," he said, and dialed a private number. "You'd better get back to Washington, Sam," he added over his shoulder. "You've got to stick close to Grant now. He's apt to lose his nerve."

The number Adam Mann had dialed set a telephone ringing in Maurice Chouinard's office in a city on the other side of the lake. It was a private line and, as the doctor lifted the phone, he nodded crisply to his nurse, who stood by his desk with some reports in hand. She inclined her head and withdrew, shutting the door softly but firmly behind her. Only then did he speak.

"Hello, Adam?" he said in English, sure of the source of the call.

"Hello, Maurice," came Adam's answer over the wire. "I suppose you've heard about our friend's little setback—his family trouble?"

"Yes, Adam, I have. I was in Washington yesterday. It was on the television here, and I saw the vice-president just now. He handles it well. But it makes little difference, I think, to us. Our business goes forward, no?"

"Of course, Maurice, of course." The American's voice was hearty. "Just wanted to touch base with you, Maurice."

"Naturally, Adam, naturally. I understand." The doctor put down the phone and sat still, staring out at the great gray lake.


Alone in his own office Adam Mann slumped in his chair. He was tired, he felt old, and he was worried. Things were not going well. He did not like dealing with Maurice Chouinard. The man made him uneasy. Adam's instinct told him that Chouinard had an agenda other than his own, which had always been simple enough: acquiring money and the power that went with it. And fulfilling their mother's dreams for Johnny.

"Look after him, Adam," his mother had said. She had lain wasted and gaunt in the hospital bed, indomitable as she had always been even in her defeat by the cancer she had battled so long. Her hand was bony and dry in his but her clutch was tight and strong. "With you behind him he can go anywhere. Make us proud. Promise me you'll help him, Adam."

"Sure, Ma, I promise," he had answered. "Johnny can be anything—governor, president. We know that. But," he had added miserably, "hang on, Ma, we need you."

She had looked at him once more with the measuring gaze he knew so well. "No, Adam, you don't need me anymore. You've done well and you've done what you had to. You're strong like me. We got us out of the flats, Adam, you and me together. I did want more. I would've liked to live to see us held in honor because of Johnny . . ." Her voice trailed off and she loosened her hold on his hand. "I'm tired, Adam"—her voice was almost a whisper—"and you'll see to it." She turned her face toward the window and did not speak again.

It was true that they had done it together, he and his mother. His father, Adam Mankowicz, for whom he was named, had worked in the plants when he could, but Adam remembered him as chronically unemployed, sullen and taciturn in the little time he spent at home. He was seldom there, preferring to hang about in the hiring halls or drink with his mates in the Slovenian club down the street from the dingy three-decker in which they lived.

It was their Canadian-born mother who had provided the iron and drive that made the family different. She had registered Adam as Adam Mann when she took him to kindergarten and Mann gradually became the name by which they were known in the neighborhood.

She went out sewing when she had to, and that was often, especially in the early years when they were small. The old families of Lake City still followed the custom of having a seamstress in every spring and fall to mend the linens, turn some faded draperies, split and turn and re-seam worn sheets for the servants' rooms, let down hems and alter waist-bands for children who had shot up or grown larger in the preceding season. Wanda Mann was exceedingly deft with the needle and had a surprisingly good eye.

In time she became more a dressmaker than a regular seamstress, and a few of the wealthier families monopolized her services. She toiled over their daughters' wedding dresses and the correct, rich dark silks and velvets worn by the older women. "Wanda is a genius with the right materials," they told each other, and congratulated themselves on hav-ing secured her devoted attention to their needs. In later years the approval she thus earned was transferred to her sons—first Adam, then Johnny—who were perceived as equally dutiful and hard-working.

She was a rawboned, plain woman who spoke seldom and showed little affection. Her love expressed itself in her determination to get them "out of there"—out of the flats, into the world she entered only on sufferance and through side doors. She had pushed Adam through high school and into the grim, soot-smeared buildings of City College.

Adam had struggled through law school at night and, as his mother had said, did what he had to do to buy into the Addison practice and rebuild it. As soon as he made some money he had invested in real estate—first parking lots, then apartment and office buildings, and finally shopping malls. Leo Santini, whose organization was gradually gaining control of the local building trades—partly through muscle and partly because Santini's political connections gave him an edge on city and county contracts—gave him tips on where and what to buy. In return, Adam saw to it that the firm did useful work for Santini.

Johnny, the child of his parents' midlife and fifteen years younger, was the final focus of his mother's hopes. Perhaps Adam should not have insisted that Johnny came back to the family law firm even though Johnny had good offers in the East. But it was what their mother had wanted. Lake City was where he had the possibility of a political base, and where Johnny could get the backing he needed.

All the same, Adam was sure that Johnny had no idea how much they owed to Leo Santini. It was better that way. Johnny was on his own track, using his own connections. But Leo Santini was always in the background.

Adam Mann and Leo Santini had grown up together in the flats. They played stickball in the streets and they went to the same parochial school. Later, when they went separate ways, they went right on knowing each other. They went to the same weddings and wakes and funerals. But each had his own turf. Adam was legal and Leo wasn't. They had kept it that way. But Adam wasn't above doing legitimate business with Leo. And Leo did favors for Adam. That's the way it worked in a town like Lake City. People from the neighborhoods didn't separate into good guys and bad guys. Their lives touched in too many places.

With Johnny it was different. He didn't really belong in the old neighborhood. He knew Leo, of course, as every politician in Lake City did. He knew Leo helped behind the scenes. But it was kept perfectly legal. If there was money, it went to the right committees. If there was muscle, it wasn't traceable.

And everything had been under control until Johnny—or more likely Sam—got connected up with Maurice Chouinard.

Adam Mann sighed heavily.


On his side of the lake Maurice Chouinard was giving the hospitalization of Celia Mann the careful, detailed examination he gave every development that might affect his plans. Like Adam Mann he had had an arduous climb from his origins; like Adam he had taken his family with him.

The crowded flat in a Montreal slum was always at the back of his mind. His mother, attended by an ignorant midwife, had died giving birth to his younger sister Jacqueline; another brother and sister had succumbed to childhood diseases before they reached their teens— killed, he was convinced, by the lack of health services and medical care for the French-speaking poor. These family tragedies informed his childhood decision to take up medicine, but it might have been only a dream if his father had not spent years as a manservant to members of the English-speaking establishment, and if Jacqueline had not left school at fourteen to work in a garment factory. Well, he had made it worth their while. He had set Jacqueline up in business. And his father, Marcel Chouinard, was now a gatherer of intelligence and a proud leader of The People—a man of authority. They worked together. Nothing would stop them. Celia Mann might have been a problem, but she was being taken care of. She might even be useful.

# . 12 .

DESPITE the efforts of those who had hospitalized her, Celia Mann, despairing in her hospital bed, was wrong in thinking that everyone believed the published stories. There were a few, if only a few, who were not convinced by the doctors and the experts.

"I don't believe it! I simply refuse to believe it!" Janie Fraser had said that first morning, waving the *Washington Post* at her husband as he came through the door of the breakfast room.

"What don't you believe, dear?" asked the Canadian minister absently as he sat down. He was used to his wife's bouts of indignation, brought on by anything from the price of breakfast tea to the plight of the Eskimos near the pipeline.

"That my nice Celia Mann is a dope addict," said Janie. "It's just too absurd. I *know* Celia Mann. I can't imagine—how could anyone"—she gave up—"just *read* that," she said, pointing at the front-page story.

Angus Fraser sighed and read. He had long since given up trying to make Janie conform to the conventional diplomatic pattern. She refused to accept the view that frequent moves made it unwise to invest too much time in emotion and friendships. She made friends easily, loved them all, and was disconsolate at each change of post. Still, he had to acknowledge that most of those who returned her affection were very nice people. Mrs. Mann had certainly seemed that, and he himself had felt a little smug about the easy access he and Janie had to the vicepresident, in whom his superiors at the Foreign Office had more than a casual interest. This *was* disturbing news, certainly, he acknowledged. Perhaps he should get the intelligence men at the embassy on it. Ottawa would want some idea of the political effect—Mann's chances for succession and so on. Aloud he said, "Well, it's certainly odd, I grant you."

"Angus, it's more than *odd*," rejoined Janie. "You know I went to

Middleburg with her just after the convention. We spent the whole day. There never was an inkling—of course, we had wine at lunch but—oh, Angus, I just know it isn't true!"

"Don't see what we can do about it, old girl. I don't suppose they'll let you see her," said her husband peaceably. "You can send flowers, of course—"

"Oh, *Angus*!" said Janie in exasperation. She sank into silence. There must be some way to get more information. Perhaps Yanni would know something. It was Celia Mann who had recommended him to her, and he was proud that Celia was his client, she knew. She had cancelled her own appointment with him that very morning in order to play a pre-breakfast game of tennis with Angus, who had just gotten back from Ottawa the night before. Poor Angus, she thought—this separatist and terrorist thing keeps him going back and forth like a shuttlecock. One should be glad the Americans are finally taking it seriously. But all the same, he has no proper schedule of work and play. He needs to get out and whack the ball around, and it's up to me to see he does.

Well, the cancellation gave her an excuse to give Yanni another call. She would have to think how to bring up the matter of Celia Mann.

When Angus left the breakfast room, having given her a perfunctory peck on the cheek on his way out, she settled down to careful thought. She couldn't remember quite when, but sometime during that lunch with Celia their conversation had put their relationship on a different plane. It was as if Celia were saying something without quite saying it, as if she were telling Janie something without fully telling it. She felt that Celia wanted something from her, hoped for something from her and could not ask for it. What had made her feel that way? Could Celia have wanted to talk about her "problem," as they say—if she had a problem, that is? Not likely. No, it was more as if Celia were worried about someone else.

They had been having a good gossip about Elena Andovian and her latest marriage. It was always fun talking about Elena. One almost felt it a duty because Elena loved being talked about so much.

"How does one do it, I wonder," Celia had mused. "Start all over, I mean, in a relationship? It seems to me you would have to become an entirely different person. So much of what one is depends on the person to whom one is *married*. You become half of something that is one thing. I expect that's why widows have such a hard time. You must feel cut in two, as if part of you will never be there again. You reach for it, but it's gone." Her voice was almost sad.

But Janie had been too busy thinking about Elena. Elena was such a fascinating subject. She realized now that she had run on, oblivious of the undertone in her friend's voice. "Oh, I don't think it's like that for Elena," she had said airily. "Well, I shouldn't say that, maybe it *was* the first time. But I think for Elena people, even husbands, are supporting players. She's center stage, and if life takes someone away from her, well, it's a nuisance but she herself isn't really diminished in any way because she's never given that much of herself to any other person."

"Yes"—Celia had nodded thoughtfully—"yes, I can see it is possible to be like that. To be completely yourself, not identified inside yourself with what another person does, as if you yourself were doing it. I can see that it would be better to be like Elena."

And then she had changed the subject. Or had she changed it? She had asked abruptly, "Do people change, Janie, really change? Or does our perception of them change? I mean, have you ever looked at someone you thought you knew inside and out, as well as yourself, and seen somebody completely different?"

At last, then, Janie had sensed an underlying urgency and preoccupation. "I'm not sure," she had said. "I suppose we don't always know people as well as we think. Sometimes I'm quite sure that nobody knows me, not even Angus—or I suppose I should say, especially Angus, but then men never really know women, do they?"

Celia was silent. Her blue eyes were so fixed on Janie's that her friend felt uncomfortable and looked away. Yes, that was strange, thought Janie, remembering. Perhaps she was really going to tell me something then, and I spoiled it. Then they had both started to talk again—this time about something else.

Janie Fraser stood up. I don't suppose I'll ever know now, she thought. But I suspect there is some strain between her and Johnny. That's what it sounded like. Well, I'll call Yanni tonight.

While Janie Fraser pondered her friend's fate, things had not been going well in Yanni's shop. The woman from Kalorama burst through the door labeled simply "Mr. Jan" in discreet cursive gold script. She was late. She was really late and disturbed about it. One never knew what sort of mood Yanni would be in on a Saturday morning. She crossed the marble-floored foyer heading for the spiral staircase without pausing to check in at the reception desk.

"Mrs. Stone—Mr. Jan is expecting me," she said over her shoulder.

Lars, the receptionist, looked after her despairingly. Sometimes letting clients go up like that was all right; sometimes it wasn't. Today, he
was sure, it wouldn't be. He didn't know if he could stand another day
of not doing one single thing that suited Yanni and then probably sitting through dinner in one of Yanni's sullen silences. It was getting to
be a bit too much. It had all seemed glamorous that night several months
ago when he had first met Yanni at the bar and heard about his clients.
Yanni had talked so knowledgeably about Cabinet wives, Senate wives,
the wives of presidential candidates, the beautiful people on television.
He *did* know them—that was true. And they did come into the shop
laughing, confiding in Yanni, and getting special favors. But what good
was it doing Lars? He sat down and stared moodily at the desk.

Once upstairs, Mrs. Stone found her trepidation justified. In the center of the elegant blue-and-gold salon, where shampoo girls scurried and
smock-clad clients sat patiently awaiting his ministrations, Yanni stood,
large, brown, muscular, his handsome face angry, talking to an abashed
salesman.

"I can't talk to you now," he said. "That must be perfectly clear to
you. Look at all these people. I can't *imagine* why Lars sent you up.
Saturday is always a madhouse. And on top of that, I have late clients
holding up the whole schedule." This last comment, Mrs. Stone knew,
was for her benefit. She shrugged and slunk into the cubicle reserved
for changing. There was another woman there, trying to struggle into
her dress without undoing Yanni's handiwork.

"Will you help me with my zipper?" she asked.

Mrs. Stone obliged and queried in a low tone, "What's with the mae-
stro? He seems to be in a terrible mood." The other woman reached
for her tote bag and pulled out a copy of the *Washington Post*. She
unfolded it and pointed to the headline and picture. "My God!" said
Mrs. Stone, "his fair-haired girl. No wonder."

The day had started badly for Jan Michal, once John Michalowski of
Pittsburgh. Behind the chichi professional facade he had carefully con-
structed over the past ten years, he was at bottom a warmhearted Polish
American, still close to his own roots and genuinely fond of the women
who depended on him. Often they seemed to him like so many more
mothers and aunts and sisters. He understood their need for a little
cosseting, attention and sympathy. Many of them were truly his friends
and had been coming to him ever since his first years in Washington,
when he had found that his peculiar combination of talent and personality was perfectly suited to that changeable city. Over the years they

had come to understand and extend an unspoken tolerance for his own emotional needs.

Of all his clients, his favorite was Celia Mann. She was always quiet and pleasant, slipping in and out unobtrusively, often unrecognized by the other clients. She joked occasionally about his sporadic efforts to make her adopt a new and trendier hairstyle. She never talked about her personal life except in the most general way, exchanging with him comments about the health and well-being of their respective families, news of comings and goings, and chitchat about presents and celebrations of birthdays and holidays; yet he knew she counted on him as a friend. He was profoundly disturbed by the picture on the front page of the *Washington Post*. He simply did not believe the story beneath it. And he was bewildered by it.

When Mrs. Stone emerged from the dressing cubicle, Yanni was combing out a small white-haired woman who was something of an oddity among his fashionable clients. Sister Margaret Rose was a nun of the order that staffed the parochial school Yanni Michal had attended. She had taught him in the eighth grade and, when she was missioned to Washington for graduate study and then to medical social work at her order's hospital, she had called him at his mother's request.

"I don't think John goes to church anymore, Sister," his mother had said worriedly. "Maybe hearing from you would remind him, like." Sister Margaret Rose had doubted that, but she made the call and found Yanni evasive but friendly.

A little later, when she, like the other nuns of her order, shed her habit and adopted modern dress, she had quite sensibly decided that she needed help with her hair and had turned as a matter of course to her former student. She came to the shop at monthly intervals, resisted any suggestion that she call the proprietor anything except "John," and insisted on paying, over his protest.

"No, John, I can't accept it as a gift from you. We don't do that anymore. We have learned that we must function as mature women and we all have salaries now. We share them, of course, and only use what we need for our personal requirements. But we have learned to manage our money and to pay our way." She insisted on tipping, too, a precise fifteen percent.

Now Yanni, working rapidly and watching her face in the mirror, was unburdening himself to her.

"I can't understand it. I really can't," he was saying. "I saw her just two days ago. She's no drug addict. I'd know if she were. Why would they want to say that?"

"Well, it *is* strange," said Sister Margaret Rose. "We know Mrs. Mann quite well, too. She has served on our hospital board, you know. It's not at all like what I have heard of her. She was once quite a close friend of Sister Patricia. They were classmates in college. You know Sister Patricia, John—she was the one we had such trouble finding and getting out of prison in Latin America. Through Mrs. Mann we had a great deal of help from the senator's office on that."

Yanni nodded. He was impatient for her reaction to the newspaper in her hand.

She studied the caption under the picture and then the headline, and she read some of the lines below it aloud, as if to plumb their meaning. "Mrs. Mann's physician, Dr. Elwood Grant, issued a brief statement saying that Mrs. Mann was suffering from an overdose of sedatives to which she has become addicted during treatment for a nervous disorder. Dr. Grant added that Mrs. Mann would probably need extended hospitalization." She paused as if to digest what she had read. Then, "That sounds just horrible," said Sister Margaret Rose.

"I don't know why they have to make things sound like that," said Yanni. "She told me she was taking something her brother prescribed— for headaches, she said—some sort of tranquilizer. But she didn't act addicted like they say. She just seemed quieter—as if the life had sort of gone out of her, you know. But this—this just doesn't add up. I would have noticed. I've seen plenty of druggies in my time."

"Well, maybe, John"—Sister Margaret Rose was tentative—"there's so much of this kind of thing nowadays . . . but I will ask at St. Simeon's. I have my office there, you know. Maybe they will even let me see Mrs. Mann . . ." She rose from the chair.

"Let me know what you find out, Sister," said Yanni. "You have my private number, don't you?"

Sister Margaret Rose nodded, inspiring a silent fury in Mrs. Stone, who was listening avidly, and had been trying to get that number for years. It was available only to the privileged few who could call Yanni personally to make or change appointments, or to ask him to come to their homes to comb out their hair for special events.

# . 13 .

THE MEDICAL TEAM moved down the hall. Dr. Sauro, chief resident, joined them as they turned into the VIP wing. Patients in this wing were still at breakfast. The clatter of trays being removed from the carts covered the low-voiced conferences of interns and students. Dr. Alwell, the intern who was head of the team, paused a good distance from the door of Celia Mann's room. He was a little flustered by Sauro's presence but proceeded as if the vice-president's wife were just another patient. His voice was as matter-of-fact as he could make it.

"Mrs. Mann is a forty-four-year-old white female, a patient of Dr. Grant and Dr. James Fifield. They present her for evaluation of mental status changes. Mrs. Mann was a rather vague historian of her own condition and most of the facts I have here are from Dr. Grant. Apparently she was well until about six months ago when she complained about severe frontal headaches occurring in the mornings. There were no vision changes nor did she associate nausea or vomiting with these headaches. She has no history of hypertension. The headaches were thought to be migraine, with a possible component of chronic tension, and her doctor prescribed Elavil 150 mg. and Valium 10 mg. prn. At first she improved, according to Dr. Grant, but in the past several weeks she has been experiencing temporary blackouts and confusion. Her exam, except for showing confusion and lethargy, was normal."

He looked up. Sauro, behind the students, was staring at the ceiling and biting at a hangnail. He looked irritated—always did lately, thought Alwell. In his opinion the chief didn't have his mind on his work. Nevertheless, he speeded the pace of his presentation.

"What is the differential?" he asked rhetorically. "The most worrisome cause for headaches and changes in mental status is glioblastoma—

142

a primary tumor. Mrs. Mann is the right age for that and the gradual onset of these headaches and her confusion are typical signs. Another possibility might be the metastasis to the brain of another kind of tumor—one in the lung or the breast. Tumors in either site are metastatic. But she has never smoked. Her chest X ray is normal and her breast exam appears normal." He drew a breath.

"Still other possibilities might be endocrine dysfunction such as hypothyroidism or possibly normal pressure hydrocephalus . . . but, of course she's on heavy medication. It's a little hard to tell what she's really like. I mean, this is a lot of dope. Grant says she's already had a CT and LP, although I couldn't find her records. Maybe it's agitated depression and she's a candidate for St. E's." He paused and looked at Bill Cratte. "Cratte, you did the history. Any additions?"

Bill Cratte cleared his throat. He spoke carefully. "One addition. Mrs. Mann seems to have a family history of migraine according to Dr. Fifield. Isn't there a hereditary factor in right-sided morning headaches of that type? And wouldn't that be a contraindication of morbidity of any kind?"

Alwell flipped through his papers. He saw Sauro's impatient gesture signaling him to cut off the presentation. But he was stubbornly methodical. "Grant didn't mention any hereditary factor. Anything else?"

"Yes." Bill Cratte sounded nervous. He was aware of Sauro's impatience. "I noted that Mrs. Mann has been taking thyroid 1 gr. daily for some years and that she has a prescription for Placidyl given her a year ago by Dr. Grant. Don't those two interact badly with Elavil? Couldn't the interaction and the buildup of Elavil account for the severe symptoms?"

"All right, all right"—Sauro broke in harshly—"all that's been looked into. Mrs. Mann is a special patient and the rest of you can forget about her. I'll be going in for the morning check myself. The rest of you can go about your business." He broke off, aware that his abruptness had startled them. "You can come with me, Alwell," he said in a milder tone. "It's your floor after all."

"No, better not," said Alwell. He was put out but determined that the students shouldn't know it. "We don't want to freak the lady out, do we?" he added lightly. As they moved off down the hall he patted Bill Cratte's shoulder. "That was a good contribution, Cratte. You were right. Those things didn't show on the record. Sometimes these big guns are a little high-handed about not sharing all the information."

Bill nodded gratefully. At least Alwell wasn't offended. He was still confused and worried, but his instinct told him not to press the point even though he hadn't had a chance to bring up the prescriptions in the cabinet but not on the chart—the lithium and Haldol.

Later Bill Cratte lay, fully clothed, on the bed in the "on call" room. He could not sleep. His mind kept wrestling with the problem. They had drugged her. He was sure of that. All that dope . . . But she never would have taken the stuff if it weren't for the headaches. And the head-aches were real. What had she said?

"They were just pounding agony, Bill, and I would be all confused just before and afterwards . . . little things got all mixed up. My hand cream jar would seem to me to be half-empty . . . and then it would be almost full . . ."

Hand cream! He sat bolt upright. His last rotation. In the Veterans Hospital. The orderly had come running.

"The old guy is going," he said. "I think it's his heart again."

When Bill had got there the nurse was working frantically over the old repeater they had brought in from the streets that afternoon.

"His blood pressure's out of sight," she said, and handed Bill the reading. He did what he had been ordered to do in a case of this kind when he did not know the patient's history.

"Lay on an inch of nitroglycerine paste," he directed.

The nurse squeezed it onto the tape from the tube. She worked gingerly.

"I hate this stuff," she said. "If you get the least bit on your hands, you get a hellish headache—"

That was how they did it! Nitroglycerine paste in Mrs. Mann's hand cream.

I could demonstrate it if I have to, he thought. But who could he tell? After this morning, he had to assume Sauro was mixed up in it. And Fifield and Grant of course. Also the vice-president. It was heavy.

Sister Margaret Rose sometimes felt guilty about it, especially when the younger sisters were holding forth on the women's movement in the community room, but she *did* miss teaching boys. Compared to the self-conscious, moody and critical junior high girls in her classes, the boy students had seemed uncomplicated, a bit zany and given to easy enthusiasms. She had been an only girl in a family of four and, as a young teacher, she had felt most at home in her homeroom after school. There were always a few boys there cleaning the blackboards or seeking help with assignments. They sensed in her an ally and delighted in breaking through the nun's decorum with which she, in those days, felt bound to disguise her natural heartiness and good humor. It pleased them that she was easily reduced to fits of laughter by their simple jokes and that she could listen raptly to their play-by-play account of the school football and basketball games, then off-limits to the nuns.

The interns and medical students at St. Simeon's soon learned that they would find a welcome and a willing listener in her little social service office in the basement. Behind the partition that screened her desk from the waiting area there was, for their sake, a table always supplied with hot water, instant coffee and a supply of what she called "sticky buns." "Sugar gives quick energy," she would assure them. She knew that they were always hungry and tired. A few had even been known to catch a quick forty winks on the padded bench she had scrounged from somewhere and embellished with mismatched cushions. She tried to be evenhandedly welcoming to the young women putting in their time at St. Simeon's, but she could not help feeling more at home with the men. They seemed to her more open—more apt to talk out their problems. And, like her junior high students, they were often very funny.

She was not surprised, then, when Bill Cratte came into the office one night just as she was about to lock up and flung himself into the chair opposite her desk.

"I've got to talk to someone or go nuts," he said.

"Talk away then," said Sister Margaret Rose, putting her arms on the desk in the attitude of someone with all the time in the world. Bill Cratte had not been around long but she had already developed a special liking for him. A nice boy who worked hard and liked to talk about his family. He was probably having trouble with the chief resident. Most students and interns did. Dr. Sauro's temper was uncertain, but Sister Anna thought him brilliant and he seemed to be a protégé of Dr. Grant. Sister Margaret Rose, however, was of the private opinion that something should be done about Dr. Sauro. He did not belong in a Catholic hospital.

But Bill Cratte's trouble was not Dr. Sauro, it seemed. He was worried about Mrs. Mann.

"Maybe I'm not clinical and dispassionate enough because I know her. Nobody else seems worried about the discrepancies. Not even Alwell, and he seems so careful . . ." He went on, explaining his connection with the Manns—"I keep thinking about how Pete must feel"—and detailing his worries about Mrs. Mann's prescriptions.

Despite her hospital association, Sister Margaret Rose had little medical knowledge and only a rudimentary grasp of the jargon, but she understood from Bill's outpouring—his talk of milligrams and dosage as needed, his mentioning of names like Placidyl, Elavil, Valium, nitroglycerine, and his explanation of interactions ignored—that there was something indeed wrong. Yanni's suspicions might well be justified. But what could she do? Sister Anna had made it clear often enough that she did not appreciate suggestions from what she called "nonprofessionals," let alone criticism. A medical student could be seriously set back—even have his career wrecked—if he became known as a troublemaker on rotation. She chose her words carefully.

"Sometimes older doctors aren't too careful about medications for women of a certain age, Bill," she said. "There is quite a lot of feminist writing on that subject. I could lend you some. And I'm afraid it's more or less hospital custom not to be too inquiring about the methods of the better-known staff doctors." She paused. "I could make some inquiries, though, without mentioning your name." It was what she had promised Yanni.

Bill sat up wearily. "Would you? That would be a relief. But," he added stubbornly, "it seems almost like they've been overdosing her on purpose."

"Oh, it doesn't seem likely that they would do *that*, Bill," said Sister Margaret Rose comfortingly. But privately she thought that it did sound very much like that.


Sauro was waiting for Sam when he came back from Ohio. He was obviously agitated.

He started talking even before Sam closed the door. Grant was going soft—he could sense it. He was nervous as a cat about this Mrs. Mann thing. And it had brought too much attention to the hospital. If Grant got too edgy and began backing out, they stood to lose everything just when they were getting into the big time . . .

Sam held up his hand. "Let's get a cup of coffee and then talk about it," he said warningly.

Sauro subsided but continued muttering and mouthing obscenities as they went.

Outside Sam growled at him. His voice was forceful although it was just audible.

"You goon—that whole place is bugged. You know what would happen to you if some guys I could mention thought you were getting loose-lipped?"

Sauro paled a little and kept his voice down, but he was persistent. "Look, it's serious. There's this medical student who's some sort of friend of Mann's kid. He's talking to her and asking questions. He's beginning to put two and two together. And we don't know how much the woman knows."

"Plenty probably," said Sam unhelpfully. Then he grinned and slapped Sauro on the shoulder. "Cheer up. So we stop her talking."

"How?" asked Sauro. "You don't mean—"

"Naw, not yet anyway," said Sam. "Say she's off-limits to anyone but Grant and Fifield. Get private-duty nurses. Say she's had a relapse or something." He paused and thought. "Can't you stick her with something that will knock her out—make her unable to talk?"

"Sure," said Sauro. Then he added, "But I want some backup. I'm not just going to stick my neck out and walk in there on my own for everybody and anybody to finger."

"I'll fix it," Sam answered.


Celia was alone in the hospital room when it happened. The night-duty nurse had come and gone, leaving her medications. They trust me now to take them myself, Celia had thought happily. She became aware that it was very quiet in the corridor. She could hear none of the far-away sounds of a working hospital. Were the doors at the end of the wing closed? And then the two strange men came into her room.

"You must have had a suspicion—some sort of warning," Alec McGregor was to say to her later. But she had not. She truly had not. Nothing could have prepared her for the shock she felt. This could not be happening. Not to her! Struggling with the two hard-handed strangers—unable to call out—struggling futilely against their callous, indifferent manhandling—one holding her down, yanking at her clothes, the other pushing the needle into her tensed muscle and laughing. Laughing! Shame and rage at her helplessness flooded over her in a hot wave as the door slammed behind them. It suffused her from the top of her head to the soles of her feet, until she felt she might drown in it.

It was only with great effort that she forced herself to sit up, and she did it slowly, like someone very old and fragile. Her mind was still clear. It told her that she had only a short time in which to help herself. But her body was weighted down, made leaden with the burden of betrayal and her conviction of guilt. She felt as if she had connived in her own undoing.

The bedside telephone. If it was still connected, it meant they expected the drug—whatever it was—to act swiftly. She had only this one chance to reach someone who might help. Someone who would believe her. But the effort was so great. Afterwards Celia would never remember how she got to the phone and made the call before one of the strange men was back, cursing her, slapping her aside. The last thing she remembered was a familiar voice from the corridor saying, "I told you it was risky—you don't know her. Did she get through?" And the rejoinder, "Naw, only the operator—the line was dead." And then the drug had taken over. Her last thought was that the first voice was her brother's.

Celia rose to consciousness very, very slowly. It seemed to her that she was in a tunnel, whirling and turning. Voices reverberated as if from the walls of the tunnel and words echoed and reechoed and died away. "Awa-a-a-ke . . ." Then, "Take care . . . care . . . care . . ." A bright light, red as blood, seemed to pierce the thin skin of her eyelids. She struggled to turn her head from it and pain pounded at her temples. The light went out. "She's coming around." It was a familiar voice, very close. Jim? The smell of starched linen and antiseptic. She was still in the hospital, she thought with relief. Johnny would be nearby. Like the other times. After the babies. She wanted the reassurance of his big hand covering hers.

She tried to say his name. She thought she said it. It sounded loud in her own ears, "Johnny! . . . Johnny?" But no one answered her.

"After I've checked her reflexes, nurse, you give her another injection—and not so strong this time. We mustn't take any chances." It was Dr. Grant's voice now. She tried to open her eyes, but she could see only a slit of light and figures moving. Her eyelids were very heavy.

The doctor's hands, competent, impersonal, were on her wrist, then lifting and flexing her arms—first one, then the other. Why couldn't she move them herself? Then he was tapping her knees, the left one, the right one. She felt her legs jump. The stethoscope, cold between her breasts, then under them. Hands were turning her over—uncaring, ungentle hands. Like those men—how long ago? Those men who had come into her room.

Surely Johnny would come now. Dr. Grant must have called him. Then she felt a hand stretching her skin and the sting and thrust of the needle going in. But before she slid down again into the whirling dark, she remembered. Johnny had wanted her here. At first she could not remember why. Then, Johnny didn't care—didn't care anymore. She was alone . . . alone. Alone. The word was an echo, a hollow sound in her ears as she slid once more into unconsciousness.

That must have been in the night, she thought later, trying to remember. It was morning when she woke again. There was a faint gray light edging the window blinds. All alone, she felt miserably ill, but the climb to consciousness was not as difficult as it had been before. There were voices, at first seemingly indistinct and very far away, but then quite clear, close, recognizable. Dr. Grant. And Jim. This time she could open her eyes without difficulty. They were standing in the doorway talking to each other. Jim, her brother, big, ruddy, healthy. Dr. Grant, smooth-faced, gesturing. They were talking about her.

"I assure you, it's quite safe. They've been using it in Argentina and Central America for some time now. It keeps the subject very controlled, very docile." Dr. Grant spoke rapidly. "But we've had to reduce the dose a good bit. After all, we have to see that she is fed. We have to follow the hospital routine so as not to arouse suspicion. The nurses are my own. And with the guards, it's as safe as one can be here, but I think, as I have always thought, that it would have been better to take her to a hospital across the river. Involuntary commitment is easy in Virginia. There is always an element of risk here."

And Jim's voice, matter-of-fact, easy, but a little impatient, "I know, I know, but there are other considerations. We've got the press to deal with. And it's known that she's on the board here. As soon as the reporters and the president are satisfied, we can move her."

He turned and looked at her then. She knew he saw that her eyes were open. She tried to say his name, to call to him. Her lips were stiff and cracked and swollen, but she could hear herself whispering it, "Jim . . . Jim!" He came toward her, smiling. He did not look angry but his eyes evaded hers. He patted her hand and then he turned away. He nodded to Dr. Grant and went out the door. She could hear his footsteps, heavy on the terrazzo floor. Then Dr. Grant went out and closed the door. Involuntary commitment! This is a dream, she thought, a bad dream.

The hospital room was darkening. Blue-white light flickered on the walls. Celia Mann lay very still. The woman Dr. Grant called "Nurse" sprawled facing her in the one big chair, but her head was turned toward the television on the wall and her eyes were fixed on the flickering screen. With half-shut eyes, Celia watched her fearfully. If she does not realize that I am awake, she thought, I may be able to figure things out. The hours behind her were a blur of sleeping and waking. She thought Johnny had been there, but she was not sure. Johnny looking concerned, kissing her forehead, talking to Sister Anna. Yes, Sister Anna. She was sure she remembered the tall sister behind him. "Steady on, Celia, you'll lick this. We'll lick it together." Had Johnny said that? What a funny thing to say. But she was not sure. She had to think. To remember.

Since the lunch tray had come at twelve o'clock and the woman had elevated the top part of the bed and roughly fed her some half-cold soup, which she could barely swallow, there had been no injection. She thought the nurse had been frightened.

"Got to eat, got to eat," the woman had muttered, mopping at the liquid that spilled from the corner of Celia's mouth. She had let the bed down again cautiously and Celia, eyes closed, had felt her standing there, watching, for long minutes. Then she moved away. No injection! Celia's mind felt clearer now and she thought that the power of movement was coming back to her. Cautiously, she tried to move her right hand. It flexed a little. She must make some sense of what had happened to her. If she could only . . . if she could think . . . rather . . . if she could only understand . . .

With a start she realized that the light behind her bed had been turned on. The bulky, ill-smelling nurse was beside her once again, holding a needle up to the light, squinting at it. Celia Mann could move now, but she could not struggle. As she began to sink into darkness once again, she thought of young Peter—he would see the marks . . . he would believe . . . As the mists deepened she forgot . . . she left the present . . . she thought she had had a baby . . . she smiled faintly . . . so vivid was her dream of the small head butting blindly at her, the small mouth seeking her breast . . . When the night nurse came on she lay quiet, her breathing almost inaudible.

\*    \*    \*

The hospital press release, issued jointly by Dr. Elwood Grant and Dr. James Fifield, was brief and terse.

We regret to report that Mrs. John Mann, wife of the vice president, has apparently taken a turn for the worse. The interaction of drugs in her system has brought on a state of extreme passivity and weakness. It is our consensus that there may be multiple causes for this condition and that it will be some time before we can ascertain the appropriate remedy. Mrs. Mann is, however, taking nourishment by mouth and is resting comfortably.

"That says something and nothing," said Sheila McCrady. MANN'S WIFE SUFFERS RELAPSE, said the headline in the *Washington Post.*

# . 14 .

AT NIGHT the cavernous halls of Old Main at Annunciation are dimly lit and quiet just as they have been throughout the hundred years since it was built. There is only a pool of light at the glassed-in cubicle where a nun handles the calls coming in on the few lines left open after the offices have closed for the day.

On the Sunday night of Celia Mann's call the cubicle was occupied by a young probationer, affectionately called Sister Polly—short for her religious name, Pauline. Sister Polly was a young Samoan woman who had been a student of the Sisters of Annunciation at their school in Apia. She was desperately homesick.

When she finally reported the call to Sister Helen, Sister Polly's instinct told her that it had been a mistake to ignore the frantic caller with the confused and terrified voice. It was not quite true, what she told the college president, that she had not understood. It was true that she had not understood the import of the call; she still did not. But the words were clear. "Please, please, call Sister Helen quickly! She must help. Tell her it's the Fife. Tell her not to believe—what they say. They have . . ." There was a curious dry sob. "They have injected something . . . oh, please . . ." There had been a sound like a blow and a moan. There might have been more, but Sister Polly broke the connection as she had been instructed to do on crank calls and obscene calls. But she had heard that. The next morning, she remembered every word. She repeated them carefully to the older nun and told her what she had heard. A sharply indrawn breath was the only sign of Sister Helen's impatience.

"Was there no way to tell where the call came from, Sister?" she asked.

Sister Polly shook her head.

"What time was it?"

"Eleven—or half after, Sister, no later."

"And you're sure she said 'the Fife'?"

The question was pure form. Sister Polly could not have drawn the nickname from her own associations and memories. In the days when Celia Fifield was called that, Polly was a baby in a village in the Pacific. The president of Annunciation College was talking, she acknowledged to herself, to cover her own anxiety. What could have happened to Celia? Why was she calling for help? What could Sister Helen do? Call Washington? Call Celia's aunt? Her thoughts flew, but out of long habit she concealed her concern.

"Well, thank you, Sister," she said. "It's always best to report these things promptly, but I think there's been no harm done. I'm afraid some of our girls have had experience with drugs in spite of all we can do. We will just have to await developments."

Sister Polly, obviously relieved, slipped away.

Sister Helen sat down to think. She had always been a woman of method and precision. Her life for years had been measured in bells and hours, all preordained, scheduled, laid out for her by tradition and obedience. Throughout the years of change in her church, she had been an executive bound by the calendar, conference schedules and a planned order of classes and meetings. Although she had accepted change with seeming ease, the very even tenor of her life in academia had left her need for structure untouched. She exercised authority well, easily and sympathetically because for her the real order of the world had not changed.

No one but Sister Helen herself could know how alien to her nature was the sudden need she felt to respond, somehow, to this wild plea in the night from her friend. Although they had been best friends in college, she and Celia had not seen much of each other in the early years of Celia's marriage, the years in which she herself had been completing her doctorate and advancing in the order. But for the last ten years or so they had been growing closer again.

At first Celia had started dropping by for a late-afternoon chat whenever she and her husband were in their home state. Sister Helen admitted to herself that she had been pleased. Celia Mann brought onto the campus the aura of a larger world and always caused a mild flurry among the members of the administrative staff. Did Sister Helen think

Mrs. Mann could help with this grant or that? And perhaps she could find a place in Washington for this alumna or that? At first Sister Helen had been diffident about broaching such requests, but Celia brushed aside her apologies. "It's one of the pluses, Helen," she said. "There are many times when I wish Johnny was out of politics and we could lead a normal life, but then I think how great it is to be able to help people. Honestly, I don't mind asking him to see what he can do about these things."

Then, over the last few years, Celia had taken to spending time on the campus, staying for a few days at a time. She flew in from Washington at least once a year, ostensibly to make a private retreat but really, Sister Helen thought, to spend time talking with her and visiting with some of her old friends among the faculty. Little by little, in the course of their late-afteroon walks, she had begun to talk with Helen about the things that troubled her. In the last year her confidences had been up-setting. Sister Helen had not liked to hear them. She did not like to think that John Mann, a hero to the young of Ohio, a role model to its ethnics and Catholics—one of their own as glamorous and charismatic as a Kennedy—could be flawed; as flawed as any other alumna's hus-band. But she had listened.

So she knew what others did not—that Celia Mann had been worried about her husband. That she was not as sure as she had once been that his motives were idealistic. Or that his aim was social justice. True, Celia defended Johnny. She made excuses. Helen could hear her now.

"You see, it's so hard, Helen. The interests in conflict are so powerful. And, of course, it's so, what Johnny says—compromise is the stuff of practical political progress. But there are times when it seems to me that the compromises go too far. And it's as if Johnny doesn't really listen anymore. He's riding so high, I feel as if we're traveling too fast."

That was after the convention but before John Mann was elected vice-president. Sister Helen's first reaction when she heard of Celia's hos-pitalization was that the ride had indeed been too far and too fast for her. It was common enough for people whose lives were stressful and demanding to resort to tranquilizers and artificial stimulants, and then to overdo it. Still, it was hard to think of Celia as weak and addicted. Celia had always been a person to whom others turned for help. And now this phone call—Sister Helen sighed. She reached for the telephone. Perhaps Sister Mary Linda, who had taught them both, could tell her what to do.

\*   \*   \*

They sat looking at each other—two women very different in appearance, bound by their membership in the same community. Sister Helen Lincoln was handsome. Everything about her—her neatly coiffed, gray-streaked brown hair, her crisp flannel suit, even her practical but fashionable gray suede shoes—bespoke a woman of competence, authority and efficiency. Only the hands tightly clasped on the desktop to control their slight trembling showed that she was disturbed.

Across the desk from her, Sister Linda's face was half-hidden by the white bonnet tied beneath her chin. She sat relaxed but erect, no part of her back touching the chair cushions. It was an ascetic practice taught her by a novice mistress long ago.

Sister Linda's early anthropological studies had given her an understanding and appreciation of native cultures unique to her missionary generation. "We have as much to learn as we have to teach," was the axiom she repeated over and over in the intervals when she came home to teach missiology at the mother house of the Annunciation Sisters.

In the field she had steadfastly refused to be part of any government-assisted project no matter how worthy. Later, she was among the few who refused to be "debriefed" by the CIA.

"In our missionary work we have to choose between God and Caesar," she would say. "We cannot serve both. That does not mean that we love our country any less. But in the field we are citizens of the world." Most of the younger Annunciation missionaries followed her lead. The wisdom of Sister Linda's way became apparent when news of some of the CIA's unwise "destabilizing" projects began to surface. When other missionaries were deported by new governments that considered them secret agents, the women of the Annunciation community were often allowed to stay. "And the work goes on," noted Sister Linda with satisfaction.

It was Sister Linda's prescience that Sister Helen Lincoln was relying on now.

"What do you think, Sister?" she asked, having recounted Sister Polly's story of Celia Mann's frantic telephone call.

"She used the old nickname to identify herself, you say?"

Sister Helen nodded.

"She was being both cautious and resourceful then. That doesn't sound as if she was confused."

"Do you think it possible"—Sister Helen hesitated—"do you think it *likely* that someone drugged her against her will? She said, 'They have injected something.' "

Sister Linda was calm. "Of course it's possible. Such things are being done every day. Whether it's likely, I don't know. I suppose it would also be possible to suspect that Celia was hysterical or under the influence of alcohol and that the doctor had to . . . take certain steps. And we have to ask ourselves why she would call here. Why not call her aunt? What do you think?"

Sister Helen spoke carefully. "Well, she *was* planning to come here soon for a short visit—and then I think, although I am not sure, that I am the only one who knows she has had doubts about John. Celia is very loyal. She doesn't want people to think that she would question Johnny or, for that matter, that there is anything to question. It isn't the way it was when they were younger and such a wonderful political team. They have become rather separate in their interests, I think."

"Interests like the peace movement?"

Sister Helen nodded again.

"I wondered whether the vice-president's commitment was as deep as Celia's," observed the older nun. Celia Mann would not have been the first woman to foster her husband's stated ideals, only to find herself alone when he abandoned them.

Sister Helen went on. "I don't think Celia ever admitted any doubts to her family. I don't think her Aunt Susan was ever very happy about their connection with the Mann family."

"I know, I know." Sister Linda's voice was dry. "I can hear Susan saying it: 'Blood will tell, blood will tell.' "

"I think of Celia as always a little too intense—and yet, someone very trusting," Sister Linda mused. "On the surface there would seem no reason to doubt the official story. She *has* been under severe strain. She *has* been unhappy according to what she has told you. She would no doubt be very dutiful about taking whatever a doctor prescribed and we know they have been very careless—at least many have—in over-prescribing sedatives and tranquilizers for women they consider over-wrought or hysterical or depressed.

"But, on the other hand, she did appeal for help—to you. And she did ask you not to believe what was going to be said. A plea for help, and the trust that we will answer it, imposes an obligation, Sister. Do you want to help her—to risk helping her if she is really in need of help? And do you believe her?"

The direct personal import of the questions startled Sister Helen. Her hand flew to her mouth as if to check an answer that might come too quickly.

Sister Linda watched her younger colleague with sympathy and interest. She knew that prudence and caution had become second nature to the college president. And, as an anthropologist, she could not help wondering whether the bonding of Helen Lincoln and Celia Mann would hold.

She had often thought that it was a form of bonding peculiar to women of the Western world. Few women in other cultures enjoyed the period in early adulthood provided by the women's colleges, when, almost entirely free of the pressures they experienced in the world of men, they could learn and explore, develop talents and achieve. In those years and in that atmosphere, enduring and altruistic friendships were often born.

Sister Helen spoke. Her voice was tired.

"I guess it comes down to this, Sister. Celia turned to me for help."

Sister Linda nodded. "Yes, I think we must go to Washington right away and find out what we can." She rose with surprising spryness. "St. Simeon's? That hospital is run by the Regulines, isn't it? I know their provincial quite well. We were in Burma together."


It was after sunset when the wide-bodied jet lifted clumsily off the runway on its way across the last of the plains and the ranges of the Appalachians. As the plane gathered speed and soared above the clouds still whitely radiant in the light of the sun, Sister Helen, nearest the window, could see that it was night below. Through an occasional break in the clouds, clustered towns, white and, for the most part, metal-roofed, were bright in the sun's last light. On the farms, steel cornsheds, round silos and white houses caught at the light. The higher parts of contoured fields and the straight section-line roads reflected it. An undulating river was glistening blackly. Sister Helen caught her breath, struck with the strange unreality of the world turning beneath her. It seemed to underline the strangeness and unreality of her own position.

Who could know whether what she was doing was not as totally ridiculous as it seemed on the face of it? Here she was, the president of a college, a woman in her middle years, setting out hastily without plan or knowledge to face a situation she had no way of measuring. She looked sideways at Sister Linda, who had shed her habit for the journey, as was her custom whenever she left the convent. Her anthropologist colleagues would have recognized Dr. Eva Marwood in the strangely sexless older woman with the smooth-cropped gray hair wearing a neat navy blue suit and white blouse. They would have recognized, too, her attitude of total concentration on the book in her hand. But what she held was not a scholarly monograph but an old copy of the *Little Hours of Our Lady* (Sister Helen could see that it was the old Latin text), and her lips moved steadily as she recited the ancient prayers to herself. So must she have sat, thought Sister Helen, in huts of Indian villages at the end of the day, guarded and shielded from the strange world about her by the familiar, the prescribed and the traditional.

Sister Linda seemed to see nothing strange at all in their journey. It was she who had insisted on it and immediately made the arrangements, calling ahead for their accommodations, arranging introductions to the authorities at the hospital through the Reguline provincial superior. She had also remembered a Reguline alumna of Annunciation who might be useful and asked the alumnae office to locate her.

Had she never questioned the verities by which she lived, her companion wondered, even when she was surrounded by people so convinced of other verities? So many younger sisters had found the idea of the life-long fidelity to vows insupportable once they ventured forth from the old rules in the old cloisters into the free marketplace of ideas.

It occurred to Sister Helen that Sister Linda might be so fixed on the eternal, so sure that it existed and that it was her destiny, that she passed through all things of this world, both good and bad, thinking them equally strange. Certainly all of her religious life she had been at home in strangeness and unflustered by it.

It was as if Sister Linda sensed her uncertainties. She lifted her head and looked at Sister Helen.

"Don't worry, Sister," she said. "We are doing the right thing. I have prayed over it and I am certain of it. I think Celia Mann needs us." Her voice was firm and clear. The steward passing down the aisle, taking drink orders, caught the name she mentioned and turned to look at the little nun. Interesting, he thought, and made a mental note.


The nuns had gone from the airport to the old Annunciation Academy on North Capitol Street, because it was not too far from St. Simeon's Hospital and Sister Anna Kempel could easily meet them there.

Sister Anna, on arrival, was inclined to be skeptical and a little testily on her dignity. She was also completely predictable. Sister Helen and Sister Linda heard her out with resignation. One could imagine exactly what she might say from the way she looked, thought Sister Helen, observing Sister Anna's portly figure and her garb, which was an uneasy compromise between old and new. A white-edged half veil covered her hair, leaving only a fringe of gray permanent visible around her ruddy face. A short-skirted black habit fell straight from the shoulders, over her ample bosom and well below her knees. Her sturdy shoes were planted well apart and as she talked she grasped the arms of the wooden armchair she had chosen.

"I think you are overreacting, Sisters," she was saying. "I can understand that a lay person with little medical knowledge might take alarm, but I can assure you that everything is in order. Dr. Fifield, Mrs. Mann's brother, certainly wants the best care for her. Dr. Elwood Grant, our chief of staff, is eminently respectable and an authority on drugs. Our staff resident, Dr. Sauro, has also been involved in drug research. He has already published two papers on drug interaction. Just now he is working on developing a synthetic which will be as effective as heroin in easing pain and depression for those terminally ill of cancer. He is taking special interest in Mrs. Mann's treatment. Mrs. Mann is having the very best treatment Washington affords—outside of NIH, of course."

She faltered momentarily, remembering that she herself had wondered why Vice-President Mann had not availed himself of the splendid resources of the National Institute, but she rallied quickly. "Why, Dr. Grant is nationally known in the drug field and is frequently called on as a consultant at the Institute. In fact, he serves on the President's Committee on Drug Abuse." Her testiness was mounting again.

"I'm sure you are right, Sister," said Sister Helen Lincoln, "but I'm sure you realize that we feel a special responsibility to Celia Mann. She is not only an Annunciation alumna but, in my case, a lifelong friend, and she has no family in Washington or in Lake City now. We are, I suppose, her family in these places."

"And," interposed Sister Linda smoothly, "Celia *did* call Sister Helen for help. It would, we feel, be unchristian for us to ignore that." She turned toward Sister Helen, "What were the exact words, Sister? 'Tell her not to believe what they say. They have injected something . . .' Isn't that right?" Sister Helen nodded and Sister Linda turned again to Sister Anna. "It was Sister Pauline, our little Samoan sister student, who took the message. You know, Sister Anna," she added as if appealing to an authority, "how very accurate the aural memories of the islanders are. Sister Pauline was very certain that that was the message."

Sister Helen took up the theme. "Then, too, we had other reasons for belief. It isn't very much to go on," she added to Sister Anna, "but we had been told both by Celia and her aunt that Celia had certain differences with her husband these past years."

Against her will Sister Anna's certainty was being shaken, and Sister Linda's final appeal increased her uneasiness. "We are so glad you can assure us that everything is all right and that we have no cause for concern. You don't know how relieved we are. You do assure us of that, don't you, Sister?"

Sister Anna cleared her throat. "Well, of course, I have not seen Mrs. Mann myself since her turn for the worse." She paused. Dr. Grant had been rather unreasonably peremptory when he told her that no one, *no one*, except the special nurses were to see Mrs. Mann. And there were those men outside the door. Security, of course—and yet . . . And then there had been that visit from Sister Margaret Rose. Something about that hairdresser. And prescriptions. She had thought it nonsense at the time, but still . . . She made a decision.

"I won't take the responsibility for assuring you that you have no cause for concern, Sisters, until I have seen Mrs. Mann, and I intend to do that as soon as I go back to the hospital. I won't deny that there have been questions raised. There is always the press, of course. And our Sister Margaret Rose seemed to have had reason"—she paused—"well, very slight reason, to doubt Dr. Grant's public statement. I would not want to have any harm to Mrs. Mann on my conscience either, Sisters. After all, we Regulines have felt close to her, too. She has been very helpful to us on our board. And a great help to Sister Patricia Black. You know her—she got quite a lot of notice when she was held prisoner." There was an indication in her voice that Sister Anna had her doubts about *any* connection with Sister Patricia. Sister Linda took mental note. Patricia Black was an Annunciation graduate, the alumna she and Sister Helen had counted on for help. It would complicate things if she was in difficulty with her own community, the Regulines.

But Sister Helen took quick advantage of the crack in her armor indicated by Sister Anna's hesitations.

"If you *should* find something awry, something irregular, Sister Anna, hadn't we better plan what our next move would be? If Celia is drugged and cannot communicate with us, what shall we do? Who else has access to her room—besides yourself, I mean?"

Sister Anna was quite comfortable with practical details. They were the very meat of her existence. "At the moment the floor supervisor does not have access, I believe, but according to Board of Health regulations she has legal access to the room at any time. Then, of course, the linen room workers and the cleaners must also have access."

"Are any of them trustworthy people in whom we could confide?" asked Sister Linda.

"We have some of Mother Camilla's nuns working in the hospital, just 'til they learn English. They are Bengali, I believe, and wear the blue sari. They do linen work among other things."

"I speak a little Bengali," said Sister Linda.

Without Sister Anna's realizing exactly what had happened, or how she had gotten into it, the three sisters set about making a plan to move Celia Mann if that should prove necessary.

When Dr. Elwood Grant entered the hospital that evening for rounds and a proposed special examination of his most distinguished patient, he was met by Sister Anna Kempel's secretary. "Sister Anna would like to see you before you start rounds, Doctor," she said. The doctor pointedly looked at his watch. It was a large, gold-banded digital watch, she noted, and thought that it must have been very expensive.

"Can't it wait until after rounds? I'm in a bit of a hurry this evening."

"I don't think so, Doctor," she answered. "Sister Anna was most specific."

Sister Anna rose from her desk to meet him, picking up a pad and pencil as she moved away from it. "Good evening, Doctor. I haven't made the regulation rounds with you for some time now, and since I want to look in on Mrs. Mann with you, this seemed an ideal time."

"I'm not sure that's wise tonight," said Dr. Grant. "Mrs. Mann is very confused and seeing you might confuse her further. In a day or two she will be in better shape."

Was there a faint note of bluster in his voice or was she imagining it? Sister Anna wondered. She kept moving massively toward the door and Dr. Grant could do nothing but stand aside and let her go before him. "Oh, a patient coming out of a drugged state is bound to be confused, Doctor," she said airily, "and I'll feel better about making the necessary statements to the press and to VIP callers after I've seen her. You know how all that goes."

There was no sense making waves, Dr. Grant told himself. There was no way he could keep the woman out of Mrs. Mann's room if she insisted on going in. It was her hospital after all, and he could not afford to risk his own standing at St. Simeon's. He had been too long building it up and it was an ideal cover for his own extracurricular activities. He had things worked out very nicely with this young Dr. Sauro. Well, he thought glumly as they emerged from the elevator on the sixth floor, the thing to hope for was that Sister Anna would not recognize the source or symptoms of his patient's state. Behind her back he made shrugging gestures to the two men on either side of the door, signifying to them that there was nothing to be done.

Inside the large room, Sister Anna was every inch the correct hospital nurse-administrator accompanying an eminent doctor on his rounds, but she was taking note of every detail. She had noted with inward disgust the lazy truculence of manner shown by the private-duty nurse, that her uniform was none too clean, and that she rose very slowly from the chair where she had been watching the patient's television set. While Dr. Grant made a show of reading the chart, Sister Anna stood at his elbow, a little to the rear as was correct, but she was aware of the rumpled bed and the faint odor in the room, evidence to her that the patient's private needs were not being properly cared for.

Celia Mann lay flat and inert without a pillow. Her dark hair was tangled and tumbled about her head. Her breathing was slow and labored and her eyes were half-closed, but Sister Anna could clearly see the gleam of the eyes beneath the lids, eyes very much alive and filled with fear. During the doctor's routine respiration and pulse count, Sister Anna moved aside, as if more interested in the hospital room than the patient. She ran her hand over the bed rail and an exploring finger along the edge of the dresser beside the bed.

"Tut," she said easily into the air of the quiet room. "I wouldn't like to have the vice-president see this, or Mrs. Mann's aunt, either. I must speak to the maid service. This room is filthy." She turned to the nurse, who was looking a little disconcerted by the nun's quiet assumption of authority.

"I see that they haven't provided you with clean linen or a clean gown for your patient, Nurse," she said. "I'll just help you clean her up. It won't take us a moment and it will make her a lot more comfortable. Does she have gowns of her own?" The nurse nodded and moved reluctantly toward the dresser. To Dr. Grant, Sister Anna said, "Don't let me hold you up, Dr. Grant. I'll be with you in a moment. I'll catch up with you on Ward 2." Skillfully she began to make the bed in the way she had learned as a probationer long ago, folding back half the covers at a time so as to protect the modesty of the patient. The nurse, perforce, began to follow suit. Without comment Sister Anna accepted the blue charmeuse gown the nurse thrust at her and a clean draw sheet. Throughout the operation, she was taking quick inventory of the condition of the patient.

"I really think we must give her a quick bath, Nurse," she said. "You'll find the basin and everything you need in the bathroom." In her brief absence, Sister Anna made a quick examination of Celia Mann. She looked at the fading bruises on her upper arms, at an angry bruise on one buttock, at the marks of the injection needles. She made a quick inventory of the medical equipment on the bedside table. She took one of the ampules she found there and slipped it into the capacious pocket of her habit just as the nurse reemerged with bath sheet, basin and water.

Sister Anna took over the ministrations. Skillfully and soothingly she cleaned and dressed the inert woman. She smoothed the tangled hair with her hands—looked around for a pillow, found one and put it beneath Celia's head. Then she patted her on the shoulder reassuringly. Did she imagine it, or was there a gleam of relief in the half-open eyes? To the nurse she said, "I forgot to get your name, Nurse—Miss Purcell, is it? You're on 'til eleven, I gather. I'll look in a little later." And she made her exit.

She caught up with Dr. Grant as promised on Ward 2.

"You'll be with us at staff meeting tomorrow, Doctor, I suppose, to report on Mrs. Mann's condition," she said to the nettled doctor, who was checking surprised patients perfunctorily.

"And afterwards I will need your help in filling out the narcotics report. You know the commission insists that we make them now for each case like this. They want to know blood counts and all that. I suppose it is better that you provide them yourself rather than one of the residents."

She was matter-of-factness and naturalness personified, but Dr. Grant was made profoundly uneasy. Yet he knew there was nothing he could do. He could not even recommend a quick move now with the specter of the narcotics report raised. He would have to go through that, farce though it would be. His mind was racing over the details.

Once Sister Anna had seen him to the door, customarily deferential
as was seemly for an administrator dealing with such an important doctor, she went into her office and shut the door firmly. She dialed the
number of Annunciation Convent.

"Let me talk to Sister Helen Lincoln, please," she said to the portress
answering the phone.


St. Simeon's is an old hospital. Many of its facilities have been fitted
into a labyrinth of rooms under the buildings, which are connected by
tunnels rather euphemistically called "subways." The floors have been
newly tiled and the walls brightly painted, but a bewildered patient or
visitor is glad for the arrows implanted in the floor and the correspond-
ingly color-coded stripes leading to X ray or to therapy or to the laboratory and the blood bank. Black arrows and a black trail lead past all
these to the oldest building of all and stop abruptly at double black steel
doors labeled "PATHOLOGY–No admittance without permit."

Dr. Grant's steps sounded hollowly in the deserted corridor and his
shadow moved tall before him in the dim light thrown by low-energy
fluorescent tubes. He moved quickly through the double doors and
through the record room where one of the nuns, who wore a blue sari,
was tidying up in preparation for her all-night stay. Patients usually
died at night, if they were to die, and at St. Simeon's there was always a
nun in the area where the bodies were received—sometimes for autopsy,
sometimes for temporary storage in the hospital's small morgue. (Sister
Anna had issued the edict after her first few months at the hospital,
during which she had had wind of the casual handling and ribaldry
with which some interns dealt with death. "The human body will be
treated with respect here—it has been the temple of the Holy Spirit,"
she said.) Mother Camilla's nuns were ideal for the duty. They could
study. There was little to do and little need of English.

The nun bowed and made the Hindu gesture of greeting. Dr. Grant,
brushing past her, growled a curt reply. In the mood he was in, he found
it a further irritant to have to deal with one of these foreigners. Any
inquiries, he knew, would be met with half-comprehension and efforts at
reply in broken phrases. He opened the door to the autopsy room, knowing full well that the man he sought would be there. It was a delivery
night. He passed through the autopsy room, ignoring the sheeted corpse
on the table and fishing in his pocket for the key of the door labeled
"Tissue Room" at its far end. He opened the door quickly and shut it as

quickly behind him. Young Dr. Sauro, his black hair glossy under the bright light over the laboratory table, did not turn around. No one not entitled to a key came this far. The threat of infection was even more potent than the lock.

"El?" he queried, intent on his work.

The older man grunted assent.

"It's a sweet batch, just like the real stuff," said the younger man. "This new retort is something." He turned and smiled at Dr. Grant. "Ryan and Smalley's man is picking him up out there—and this—at eleven. How about helping me get it into the bags?"

Dr. Grant did not return the smile, but he moved toward the table and mounted the stool at Sauro's side. He had never been averse to acting as a cover for Joe Sauro's operation or to taking his generous cut of the profits, but he did not like to be part of the actual process. Still, he wanted Sauro's cooperation. He took up one of the small scoops.

"You"—he began, then corrected himself—"we've got to shut down for a while until we get the Mann woman out of the hospital. The superintendent's got her wind up. She's got the narcotics people coming in here tomorrow." He flinched at the younger man's violent gesture and added hastily, "Nothing to do with this, just checking the patient's treatment, but that involves doctoring blood samples, and if there's the slightest slip, there'll be a lab check."

He had expected an explosion but he was unprepared for the fury unleashed in his colleague by his announcement. Sauro was literally shaking with rage, his face working, spittle forming at the corners of his full-lipped mouth. He brought his face so close to Grant's, cursing, that Grant could see the network of veins surrounding the surprising bright blue of his eyes. Noting them clinically, Grant wondered, not the first time, if Sauro had been more affected than he knew by the drugs of his own manufacture. His volatility was becoming dangerous, Grant thought. Not that Sauro had not always been a source of risk. His experience as a military adviser in Central America had left him with an indifference to law and its enforcement and the callousness that allowed him to use dead bodies as a means of delivery; and that had been useful, up to a point. But he was increasingly hard to control. Too greedy, thought Grant. He stood up so that he could look down at Sauro.

"Joe, be reasonable," he said. "It's only for a week or two. I know it would have been better not to bring the woman here just now, but that was the way Fifield wanted it, and that was the way it had to be. He's useful to the whole network."

Sauro was still expostulating loudly. They were so close, so close to the really big time. The lighter-than-air craft they had been able to order were on the way from France via Quebec—Grant knew that. Everything in place and millions to be made. They couldn't shut off supply now. Goddammit, they just could not shut off. Better that Grant increase the dosage and get rid of the woman once and for all. Now. Tonight. If Grant would not, he, Sauro, would.

Sauro's frenzy made Grant wonder if the younger man had made assurances in the deal for the planes that would bring reprisals swiftly if the deal was not kept. The thought induced a touch of cold fear. Sauro could be dangerous. He decided not to argue the matter. Sauro was capable of carrying out his threat. He would be more manageable in the morning.

"Okay, Joe," he said ambiguously. "You're right, of course, but first things first. Let's take care of this shipment. The buyers are waiting." He had diverted Sauro's attention and assured Celia Mann one more night, thus unknowingly answering the prayers of her friends.

In the outer room the Bengali sister relaxed as the loud voices subsided. These American doctors frightened her. Such things had not happened in the hospital in Japan where she had had her first training. It was a weakness on her part, she knew, but she did not think she could continue to work in this place. She would speak to her superior tomorrow. The decision fortified her to face the rest of the night, and it was with outward calm that she opened the doors a few minutes later to let the undertaker's men pass through.

The small community of Regulines who managed St. Simeon's were housed on the top floor of the main building. A small chapel, a community room, a kitchenette and ten single bedrooms sufficed for their needs. Sister Margaret Rose, coming from the telephone, went into the chapel. As she expected, she found Sister Anna there. As she slipped into the pew beside the kneeling administrator, she touched her on the shoulder and whispered.

"John will come tomorrow. I think he understands already."

The face Sister Anna turned to her was worried.

"Sister, don't you think we should consult the police? This is all so irregular."

Sister Margaret Rose shook her head. "The sisters from Annunciation have thought of that," she said. "They know more about the Mann family than we do, and they must have reasons for distrusting the authorities. Besides, what could we say?"

That was just it, thought Sister Anna. There was so little to go on. But she had still another worry.

"I don't like the look of the patient either, Sister. Her pulse is irregular. I don't know how conscious she is, but if she has lost trust in her husband, she may have little will to live. You know how that is. If anything should happen—if she should die . . ."

Sister Margaret Rose nodded. "We can only pray tonight, Sister," she said. "Maybe things will be clearer tomorrow."

They both turned toward the altar where a single votive candle glowed in the half-light.


Below them, in the lobby, the volunteer manager of the hospital gift shop, locking up for the night, was mildly surprised to see Dr. Grant emerge from the pay phone booth. She greeted him respectfully—she was somewhat in awe of the doctors at St. Simeon's and proud to be involved in the hospital even in a peripheral way—but he passed her unseeing. He was telling himself that he had done the only thing he could do. Sauro was out of control. Their backers could not tolerate a source who had become a user. He was a danger. Yes, Grant thought, it was necessary to let them know.


Yanni was often up and about early, long before the shop opened and long before Lars, who was still given, like many young people, to "sleeping in" at every opportunity. Today, Yanni did not find that annoying. He was glad there would be no need to explain his journey across town to the convent on North Capitol Street.

As he went up the high steps to the old, narrow building, he felt again the mixture of trepidation and curiosity with which he had begun his weekly appointments at the convent in Pittsburgh for music lessons. When the door was opened by a young, rather severe-looking woman, he recognized the familiar smells of wax and varnish and cooking. And as Sister Margaret Rose moved down the corridor to greet him, only the swish of habit and the jangle of rosary beads was missing. She ushered him into the room at the right, a sort of conference room that had been updated somewhat, with orange plastic-and-chrome chairs arranged around a Scandinavian teakwood table. He recognized Sister Anna. He had given her her permanent and noted her arrangement of it with some dismay. He was introduced to Sister Helen Lincoln and Sister Linda and to a small dark woman with tight-cropped, curly iron-gray hair, who was smoking a cigarette so far down that it was almost burning her misshapen fingers.

"Sister Patricia Black," said Sister Margaret Rose. The other waved her hand abruptly.

"Pat," she said abruptly, "call me Pat."

"Now that we are all here," said Sister Helen Lincoln, "shall we review the situation?" Sister Anna reported briefly on her observations of the night before, and her conclusions.

"I am afraid there is no doubt that she is being forcibly held and that she is being drugged to keep her quiet. I don't know yet what the drug is. I did manage to reduce the dosage last night, but whatever it is, it is so powerful that it is bound to have serious side effects unless we can take her off it soon." Uncharacteristically, Sister Anna's voice trembled and her eyes filled with tears. The very foundation of her world had been shaken. A doctor she respected and trusted was apparently involved in something so nefarious that she could not take it in. Her hospital, of which she was so proud, and her staff, had been infected with deceit and betrayal—how, she did not know. She continued.

"I looked at the preliminary lab reports this morning. I'm afraid that they've been doctored. They indicate traces of heroin in the bloodstream and a mild sedation. I know from observation that they cannot be right."

"Could we not get a lab report of our own, somehow?" asked Sister Linda.

"Well, at least I have the ampule I took last night," answered Sister Anna, producing it from beneath her scapular, "but I don't know where to get it analyzed. At this point, I don't know whom we can trust."

Yanni cleared his throat and they all turned to look at him.

"What about the street clinic in Georgetown?" he asked. "They're very good about keeping things confidential. And I could have one of my friends take it in. I think we'd get a pretty quick report there."

The suggestion set things in motion and made the unbelievable possible to contend with. It restored Sister Anna's power of practical decision. They agreed that time was an important factor and that the most important thing was to get Celia Mann out of the hospital and into a place where she could be cared for. Sister Anna noted rather gloomily that, once free of the drug, Celia might well be too depressed to help herself or to help them to help her. It might take days, it might take weeks, she added.

"I would feel much better if we had some support from Mrs. Mann's family. I don't know how we can take this on ourselves. I really don't," she said.

"Mrs. Raley, Celia's Aunt Susan, has agreed to join us," said Sister Linda. "I have talked with her and she will see us this afternoon—here, if you like. She doesn't know what we know, but she is very much concerned."

Sister Anna brightened, but went on.

"Then we have to have a place to take Celia right here in Washington where she'll be safe—it can't be a convent or one of our schools. Once we get her out of the hospital—if, please God, we do—they are bound to suspect that we are somehow involved. And I have to think of the hospital, and the other sisters."

What had started in somber and uncertain inquiry and conjecture was beginning to take on purpose. The atmosphere in the room had lightened. They looked at each other with a sense of growing comradeship. They felt the excitement of conspiracy, all the more heady because it was strange to them. Only Patricia Black held back. She broke in harshly.

"Stop it, all of you, and listen to me! I can't *believe* this. You all act as if this were a game . . . as if you were living in a story. How can you be so naive? If this is what you think it is . . . if the wife of the vice-president is being held against her will in the very center of the city of Washington . . . doesn't that tell you something? It means that some of the most powerful people in the world are part of it. I'd just like to remind you that these people have experts to remove people, to intimidate them, and to . . . torture them." Her voice shook. She stopped a moment.

"They train people to do that—right here in our own country—right here in Washington. They have all the resources of the CIA . . . and the FBI . . . and the police . . . and Immigration . . . and subagencies we haven't even heard of. People they trained have been behind the maiming and assassination of people in these very streets. And they tell you it's for your security. To safeguard your *liberty*!" Her voice was shrill and bitter. She almost spat the words.

"I can't see you—any of you—really going against them. It isn't in you or people like you. If you do it, if you even try to do it, you will be crossing over. You'll be on the other side of the line. You'll be where I am. And you're too safe and comfortable to want that."

Sister Linda was studying her as she talked. The others sat silent, embarrassed by her intensity. They stole glances at each other. In light of her words their planning did look childish and inadequate. Suddenly they saw their efforts as puny and absurd in the face of powers and designs they could only dimly discern.

Oddly enough, Sister Patricia's words only seemed to confirm Sister Anna in her resolve. "Oh, come now, Sister," she said crossly, "we're only trying to find out what's wrong. It needn't be any big plot having to do with the government, for goodness' sake. I'm sorry to say that it's not unheard-of for husbands to try to have their wives committed—or wives their husbands, for that matter. It's being done all the time, but these days it isn't as easy as it once was. This particular case seems different just because Vice-President Mann is such an important person. But to say the administration is mixed up in it—that's just plain nonsense. This isn't South America."

"I know it continues to be news to you that what happens in Central and South America starts right here," Pat rejoined heatedly. "It starts with those international corporations you're always getting piddling little grants from—sops thrown to people like us to keep us quiet! But I tell you, if you get into this thing with Celia Mann, you will find you are into something bigger than you know. Getting her out of the hospital is only one step. If you want to save her, you're going to have to change her appearance and get her out of this country. She may never be able to come back. There has to be something she knows that made them risk this. The president may be in it, or she may not, but she won't risk her administration or her policy. Believe me. Too many powerful people have a stake in it."

Sister Linda looked from one to the other thoughtfully. It is the classic confrontation, she thought—it's going on in every religious community in the Western world. We thought Christianity had penetrated the institutions of our civilization. A generation ago our missionaries never questioned it. And now they go out—simple, middle-class people from Cleveland and Buffalo and little towns in Iowa—and the culture shock they experience is too great. Because they really see the poor as people with rights to a better life. Why didn't they see them that way before? I wonder. But the rhetoric is the same. Good and evil. All the good on one side, all the evil on the other. It is tearing us apart.

Yanni listened to the two nuns in growing puzzlement. The sense of return to the familiar he had had when he first came into the convent that morning was fast disappearing. The sisters in his school had had individuality. He remembered the nicknames their pupils used behind their backs, unkind names fixing with the uncanny accuracy of childhood on any idiosyncratic weakness of character or appearance—"Nosy-Nosy," "Pink Petunia," "Flat Foot" and worse. But they were truly sisters unified in their purpose, undivided, and the embodiment of the church and its teachings. He looked at Sister Margaret Rose and could see her in front of the classroom, a commanding presence in neat black and white, her hands folded as she led them in morning prayer, her arm outstretched, her face respectful as she led them in the salute to the flag. God, church, country. That was the way it had been. That was what the sisters taught. Now that they had taken off their habits they seemed to have turned into different people.

I came to help Mrs. Mann, he protested silently. I didn't bargain for any trouble with the government or anybody else.

There was an awkward silence. It was broken by Sister Helen. Her voice was reasonable and placating.

"It's hard for us to understand, Pat. I think I know how you feel . . . no, I shouldn't even say that. How can I know . . . how can any of us know? . . . We didn't share your dreadful experience in South America. But we can only take one step at a time. We all agree that we want to help Celia. In a way, we have been chosen to help her because she turned to us, and because we can, or think we can. And because there is no one else. Right now the most reasonable assumption is that legal authorities won't or can't help us because they have been successfully deceived by the doctor or by John Mann or both. We don't have to go any further than that."

She paused and looked around the room, pulling them together once again by her very calmness. Then she looked at Sister Patricia Black and added earnestly, "This may lead us to where you are, as you say. But we do need you to help us, Pat."

Patricia Black took a deep drag on her cigarette.

"Oh, why not," she said impatiently. "God knows you need me. You're babes in the woods where this kind of thing is concerned. You have to have a network. And if it does come to getting her out of the country, I can help, I think. But where she will go, where she will stay, what she will do—all these things have to be decided."

Yanni thought of Janie Fraser's call on the day of Mrs. Mann's hospitalization. Canada? But he said nothing for the moment because they had moved on to the very immediate problem of getting Celia Mann out of the hospital.

After half an hour of orderly discussion led unobtrusively by Sister Helen, they had agreed on a course of action. Sister Patricia stood up.

"All right then. I will make contact and ask my friends for help. They may go with us, they may not. If they do, it will make everything easier because they have the resources. I should know when we meet again this afternoon. From what Anna says about Celia's condition we have to move fast."

It was only an hour from the time Yanni had entered the convent door until he took his leave, but it seemed longer than that because it also seemed that something important had happened to him, although he was charged with nothing more than getting the ampule analyzed and locating a van they could borrow with no questions asked. He was keyed up but content. He had been reassured by Sister Helen's quiet competence. He was involved in something grave and serious, with people who trusted and accepted him. And under his arm he carried something Sister Margaret Rose had pressed upon him—a copy of *Dignity*, a magazine for gay Catholics.

Patricia Black had become a familiar figure in the employees' cafeteria at St. Simeon's, where she could be heard speaking in fluent Spanish with the Latin Americans among the laundry workers, maids and maintenance men on the staff. She was known as the sister who could be counted on to help them through the myriad difficulties they encountered as they struggled to make new homes in a society complicated beyond their comprehension.

So she attracted no attention as she dropped money into the coffee machine and took her cup into the telephone cubicle near the cafeteria entrance. She dialed a number, heard the ring and an answering machine's tinny message. She waited for the tone.

"Patricia," she said crisply. "I must talk to Frank. Emergency. 357-0216." She hung up quickly, before the call could be traced mechanically. Then she stood sipping her coffee. She had to allow him time to get to one of the pay phones he used to return calls like hers.

When the phone rang she lifted the receiver quickly, looking over her shoulder to be sure no one was standing near the booth.

"Frank here." She could hear the noises of the street behind his voice.

"We need help to get someone out of the hospital."

"An illegal?" His voice was matter-of-fact.

"No, an Anglo." She was businesslike. "She's helpless. We'll need transport. And disguise. And a safe house."

He was silent, thinking. Finally, "That's unusual. I'll have to clear. Is this person high-level?"

She hesitated. Frank's intuition was uncanny. "Well, highly connected, at least."

"Hmnn." He was unflustered. "Sounds as if it's a job for Ralph. And usual conditions when we break cover. If you don't hear from me at this number at three, he will be at the meet for briefing before four. Now, what place?"

She told him and the line went dead. She stood a minute. With whom did Frank clear? she wondered. At last she shook her head as if to empty it of questions and went out to take her place in the cafeteria line for lunch.

Less than five minutes later the telephone rang in the servants' quarters at the Canadian Embassy. Shortly thereafter a stocky, gray-haired man could have been seen emerging from the service entrance, walking briskly up Rock Creek Drive, and taking the turn toward Massachusetts Avenue. He crossed the bridge toward the mosque, whose reconstruction was under way. He looked neither right nor left. It was a trip he made with some frequency, to the exasperation of the ambassadress, who thought her butler was called away too often on "urgent family matters," as Mme. Gophin, the housekeeper, was no doubt explaining once again.

Marcel, the butler, entered the telephone booth on the corner by the construction site. His connection was made quickly. Speaking in a rapid French patois, he conveyed his message. The answer was quick.

"But that is interesting. Very interesting. If it is as you think, it could prove very useful. Proceed, of course. But with great caution."

Marcel hung up. He dialed another number and spoke only one word, "Cleared."

He turned back to the embassy. Not long after, the housekeeper announced to the ambassadress, "Marcel is back and the luncheon guests do not yet arrive. See, Madame, no harm done."

When they met again in the afternoon, Sister Patricia had with her a tall, brown-skinned young man who moved, Yanni noted, with the grace of a dancer. She introduced him only as Ralph, and said, "As I told you this morning, Ralph is my contact with the people who help with our undocumented workers. He is affiliated with a theatrical group here and his specialty is disguise. But his friends—and he will be our only contact with them—know a great deal about getting people out of the city and, when necessary, out of the country."

She stood before them, like the high school teacher she once had been. Her voice was low, her speech measured and pedantic, but her words were unsettling to her listeners.

"I owe my life to the people whom Ralph represents, and Ralph is literally risking deportation and, perhaps, death by coming here today. He is only doing it in return for what some of us in the Regulines and in your community, too"—she nodded at Sister Helen and Sister Linda— "have been doing for them. He asks that you all take the oath, and the consequences of breaking it can mean—and again, I am being quite literal—death. Now I know that for most of you taking this oath will seem unnecessary and even blasphemous. But Ralph cannot help us unless you do. And I have taken this oath. I know what it means to have been betrayed."

She held up her hand and for the first time Yanni realized that there were only scars and black, scaly protrusions where the nails should have been. He felt queasy as he looked from one to the other of his companions, who sat very still.

Sister Helen and Sister Linda were next to each other on the sofa. Sister Linda was concentrating her attention on Ralph, observing him with the detached interest of a scientist. On the chair next to the sofa sat Celia's aunt, Susan Raley. She was exactly what he would have expected from their conversations about her. She wore an elegantly cut, apple-green pantsuit, the traditional attire of the affluent, retired resident of the Southwest. Her slightly curly, salt-and-pepper hair was cut short and she had the almost leathery, tanned skin of the older woman who has spent a great deal of her life out of doors. She was small, alert, direct, and now she sat very straight, with her hooded blue eyes fixed on Sister Patricia. Sister Anna sat in a straight chair at the other end of the sofa. Her face was astonished and horrified. Sister Margaret Rose, beside Yanni, looked steadily at the floor.

Sister Anna broke the silence. "Sister Patricia," she said, "this is going beyond anything I can condone. It is highly irregular. It borders on the criminal—if it is not criminal. We may think we have reason for moving Mrs. Mann and getting a second opinion on her condition, but there are perfectly legal ways to do that. Mrs. Raley has only to swear out a complaint and we can ask for police help in the matter. I really must protest our even discussing these lurid matters—the taking of oaths, indeed." She stopped, unable to find words for what she thought of such matters.

Ralph, who had been lounging in a chair beside Sister Patricia's, stood up. "I'm getting out of here right now, man," he addressed himself to Sister Patricia. "You told me these people were ready to go."

Sister Linda noted that his voice was trained but she thought she detected the traces of a singsong rhythm. Trinidad, she thought to herself.

Ralph was continuing, looking at Patricia. "I've blown my cover coming here," he said. "It's your responsibility, Pat."

Patricia nodded and spoke as if the others were not there. "I know, Ralph. They told me they were ready to go. It's the risk you take."

Mrs. Raley broke in. "Sister Anna, this is nonsense. If I thought going to the police would do any good, I would have done that instead of coming here. You yourself have said that my niece is in danger and that what the doctor says is not true, and that is your professional opinion. It may be only the doctor who is mistreating Celia for reasons we cannot imagine, but if there is any possibility that my nephew-in-law is involved, we are dealing with forces that frighten me to contemplate. Some very strange things have happened in our country in the last decades. You are acting as if those things did not happen and could not happen again. I intend to help my niece in any way I can and I will take any oath that is necessary to do it. Are you willing to risk her life to uphold rules that no longer seem to have any validity?"

Sister Anna wilted. Susan Raley's voice held the authority of the kind of people Sister Anna respected, the kind of people who served on her hospital boards, chaired their benefits, and occupied the best private rooms. If one of them had come to the conclusion that all this was necessary, Sister Anna was not disposed to dispute her. But she was not happy.

"Well," Pat said to them, "are you ready to take the oath to satisfy Ralph?"

Sister Helen Lincoln was as unwilling as Sister Anna, but she could sense that Sister Mary Linda thought it all a matter of course and even interesting. She nodded with the rest.

Ralph stepped forward. "Raise your right hands," he said, "and repeat after me, phrase by phrase. It is very short. I swear by the God I believe in—"

"I swear by the God I believe in—" they chorused.

"I swear by the lives entrusted to me—"

"I swear by the lives entrusted to me—"

"I swear by my own life, which I devote now to the service of The People everywhere under the sun—"

"That I will never betray, by word, deed or gesture, any person in the same service."

A sigh—as if of one person—sounded in the room when they had finished. The atmosphere seemed to lighten again, and in a few minutes they were immersed in the practical details of their task.

Ralph explained, with occasional interpolations from Sister Patricia, that the essential technique of disappearing from under the noses of the most stringent security forces was to learn, as they put it, to 'swim in the sea.' It meant altering one's appearance completely in every way, including facial habits and body movements. "One must make oneself so totally invisible that one is not noticed," said Pat.

And Ralph added, "It's easier than you think. Patricia Hearst did it for months. Abbie Hoffman did it for years. All around you insignificant people are doing it every day."

"But," said Sister Margaret Rose, almost timidly, "Sister Anna thinks that Celia Mann won't be in condition to help herself."

"That's why we try to alter her appearance first," said Ralph patiently, "and take her someplace where she can be nursed along and helped until she can run for the border, if she has to. And," he added matter-of-factly, "she will have to. I guarantee you that. This is too big, I think, for anything else."

"Now," said Pat, resuming the instruction, "the first thing is to get her out of there. There are some people in the hospital already who will help us." She looked at Sister Anna's surprised face and smiled for the first time. "But Ralph has explained to me that there must also be diversionary tactics. It must seem that it was possible for her to be taken in several different ways. He will attend to that. Now, each of us has an assignment—"

Sister Helen Lincoln lay awake, not quite comfortable in her unfamiliar bed. The planes thundering over the convent at regular intervals kept her from falling asleep, but she doubted that she would have slept in any case. She had been deeply disturbed by the day's events. Before advancing to administration, Sister Helen had taught government with enthusiasm. What a marvel, she used to tell her classes, that in a nation of hundreds of millions of individuals with fierce desires, wants and hopes, there could be this synchronization of human effort. She had believed then that most politicians—those who brought it about—were of good will. Well, nobody seemed to think that these days. Watergate, Abscam—people took it for granted that the people they elected were capable of almost anything.

She turned restlessly in her bed. If Sister Anna was right, surely John Mann was corrupt . . .

But could anyone be guilty of what they suspected him of? Could he allow his wife to be put away—sent to a living death—for some nefarious reason of his own? Her mind told her that, yes, he could. Just such an attempt seemed to have been made on Martha Mitchell back in the days of Watergate. There seemed to be real evidence of that, although Martha Mitchell had been hard to believe. So much of her talk seemed silly, attention-getting prattle. But she had gone to her death sure that her cancer had been caused by injections forced on her in that motel in California. And what if the doctor there had not recognized her? Who were the people guarding her? Nobody seemed to know.

No, what she and the others suspected might be almost incredible, but it was not impossible. Helen Lincoln could accept that fact intellectually, but her emotions fought the acceptance. All her instincts, all her training, all her professionalism had conditioned her against that which was not orderly and charted. Even if what they suspected were true, could they justify what they were planning to do? She gave up trying to sleep. Perhaps if she got up and read for a while—

She snapped on the light beside her bed. She would, she thought, get up and do a few stretching exercises, then read until she got sleepy.

She stood up, a tall woman, neat and trim in her white cotton pajamas, and watched herself in the mirror as she stretched high and clasped her hands over her head. She bent forward, back, to the right and to the left, counting absently as she did so. She thought, a little crossly, that Sister Linda was probably sound asleep.

It was a rabbit warren of a building on the 13th Street heights. Its windows looked down on the sweep of Washington and on the procession of monuments from the White House to the lighted white dome of the

Capitol on its hill. Once it had been very grand. Coaches of the important and the wealthy had pulled into the porticoed U of the driveway and befurred ladies and top-hatted gentlemen had walked the marble-tiled halls on their way to dinners and concert parties.

Now the apartments were cut up, the tiled halls dingy with the dirt of decades. Despite the best efforts of a struggling tenants' association the halls smelled of poverty, of garbage and urine and cheap wine. People wandered in and out all night long without question or challenge.

At ten that evening a couple in one of the larger, cleaner apartments on an upper floor were expecting company. Their children had been forcibly torn from the television an hour earlier and put to bed. The parents sat at the large wooden table in the center of the room and waited stolidly. Everything was ready. There were tacos. There was beer and there was a soft drink for the padre. They sat quietly, neither thinking nor speaking. They were used to waiting.

Across town Marcel left his apartment above the garage at the embassy and took his car from its parking space. At the New Zealand chancery a resigned second secretary was filling in for Fiame, the islander, as officer of the day. Downtown at the Washington Hotel near the National Press Club, Belfast-born Hugh Swampscott, stringer for the *Irish Times* and various Australian papers, dropped his key at the desk and went out to look for a gypsy cab. He was wary of the Yellows and the Diamonds and their carefully kept logs. Near Howard University, Ralph and two of his housemates caught a late bus. Nearby, Frank was walking the few blocks from his combination storefront mission and home. He was well known in these street and he was not afraid.

He arrived first and the faces of the two waiting brightened at his arrival. "Good evening, Olaya; good evening, Francisco; all is in readiness, I see," he said in Spanish and took his place at the foot of the table. One by one the others arrived, nodding to or greeting their hosts with varying degrees of cordiality. Last of all was Marcel, who took his place at the head of the table. He looked around at those assembled.

"We are one," he said in English.

"We are many." The chorused reply was perfunctory, a matter of routine. He nodded. The council of The People, Washington branch, was in session.

At the conclusion of the meeting, Frank did the summing up.

"All right. This is it. Ralph and Richard serve as van drivers to stay outside as a distraction. Francisco and his cousin will serve as stretcher bearers. I will select and train the maid. Hugh will serve as chauffeur. Olaya will alert Leora and help at her place. And all procedures are changed enough to take control from the hands of the amateurs. Correct?"

Marcel nodded. So did the others. One by one they went out into the night.

# . 15 .

SOMETIME between six and seven o'clock the next evening Celia Mann disappeared from her room at St. Simeon's Hospital. It was some time before her absence was discovered. The early evening hour is a relatively quiet time in a hospital—the lull between the bustle surrounding the delivery of the absurdly early dinner trays and the arrival of the patients' evening visitors.

Precisely at a quarter to six Sister Anna rose ponderously to her feet, locked her desk, and prepared to leave her office. Having decided on a course of action, she was not one to vary from it. As she made her way to the elevator, she was troubled only by the changes that had been made in the plan since yesterday's meeting. They had been conveyed to her by Pat in hurried whispers during the sisters' morning mass. As the elevator rose she mulled them over once again.

She could see that the sooner all connection was broken to the original group who had met at the convent, the better. But she was troubled by the people from outside—the extra "helpers" as Patricia had called them. Would they fit into the hospital scene as easily as Patricia thought? Well, it was too late to worry about that now.

Miss Purcell had just finished her haphazard effort to feed her helpless and unresponsive patient when Sister Anna came into the room.

"Good evening, Nurse," she said pleasantly. "I don't know if you know that this is a feast day at St. Simeon's. The floor nurses are having a little celebration in the kitchenette down the hall. I thought you might like to join them while I take your place here. They have all sorts of goodies," she added archly, "and wine."

She counted on that last word. Her trained eye had spotted the indications the night before. By this time of evening, she knew, Miss Purcell would be badly in need of a drink. She only hoped the need was strong

**180**

enough to overcome the nurse's fear of disobeying her orders. Conflict was immediately apparent in the woman's raddled face.

"I'm not supposed to leave the patient," she said crossly. She had the sort of stubborn but limited intelligence that causes people to blame others for their own dilemmas.

Sister Anna smiled gently. "Even with the hospital administrator? I can't believe that," she added easily. She gave Miss Purcell's shoulder a little pat. "Now go on before they've eaten and drunk everything. Go on and enjoy yourself a little. I'll be right here. I'll tidy up your patient for the night."

"Well," said Miss Purcell slowly. Sister Anna knew that the inner struggle was over. She followed Miss Purcell to the door, listened to her explanation to the guard, and nodded at him to confirm it. Miss Purcell went down the hall, walking faster.

"It's the room beside the nurses' station," Sister Anna called after her. She nodded to the guard again and moved back into the room, pulling, as she did so, the so-called privacy screen between the bed and the door. The guard, incurious, could hear her moving about the bed, addressing the patient soothingly as though she were a small child.

"There, doesn't that feel better? We'll just get you into a fresh gown, won't we? This arm, that's it, that's it, now this one," her insistent murmuring went on.

The guard was bored. And, like Miss Purcell, he had begun to think about a drink. It was the only time of day when he was alone. He and his mate took half-hour turns going out for the evening meal. It gave them barely enough time to get a beer and a hamburger in the little joint across the street from the hospital. But it was all the time the boss allowed. It rarely occurred to him to question the boss, but it didn't take two men to sit here guarding one silly woman. He did like a decent meal. He shifted his weight on the hard chair and decided to stand for a while. He consulted his watch. Five minutes, maybe ten, and Benny would be back. He looked down the long corridor. It was empty except for a cleaning man slowly pushing a waste cart before him, sweeping as he went. The service elevator door opened and two maids appeared. They took the long, narrow tray cart standing beside the nurses' station and began to move it down the hall, pushing it part way into the rooms as they collected the trays. He sat down again and tilted his chair against the wall. The women with the tray cart reached Mrs. Mann's room. One left the cart and went into the room across the hall. He watched her go, sourly. Her hips, he noted, were bony and her rear flat under the thin nylon uniform—nothing like the figure of the one he had observed appreciatively the night before. Her partner had pushed the cart halfway into the doorway beside him.

"Is that you, Maura?" came Sister Anna's clear voice. "Come in here a minute. I want to talk to you about the tray service."

Maura looked at him and rolled her eyes and shrugged. "What now?" she said sotto voce, made as if to go around the cart through the doorway, then, apparently deciding that entry was too narrow, pushed the cart ahead of her all the way into the room, bumping the doorstop as she did so, so that the door swung halfway shut. She came back at once to open it and secured the door once more.

"Sorry about that," she said to him pleasantly. He heard them talking in low tones, Sister Anna's peremptory and scolding, the maid's defensive and placating. He did not listen. He was watching the two men who were bringing a laden stretcher out of the elevator. They were making heavy work of it, he thought scornfully, sure that the short dark men in white trousers and uniform shirts were foreigners. They stopped at the desk. One left a chart on the counter; no attendant was visible— probably all at the party. He was aware again that he was hungry. The men approached, passed him, and went on.

The other maid reappeared with more trays piled one on the other.

"Where has she got to?" she asked complainingly. "These things are heavy." He jerked his head toward the room.

"The Big Sister called her in there," he said.

"Well, I like that! We're not supposed to push that thing into the patients' rooms. And what am I supposed to do with these?"

He looked at her. She was not so bad head-on, he reflected—in fact the red hair, bold blue eyes and round breasts stretching her uniform were promising. He grinned at her—"Oh, go on in, won't do no harm."

She went in, and Sister Anna and Maura came out and moved away from the door, continuing their talk. He heard trays clattering in the room. In a moment the red-haired maid came out. She pushed the unwieldy cart through the door, banging the jamb as she did so, and began complaining as soon as she saw Maura. "Don't go off and leave me with this thing—it's too big to take into the rooms." She ignored Sister Anna.

"Look," said Maura, "it was just this once. Sister Anna called me in and you know we're not supposed to leave the trays unattended. There are special diets . . ." They moved off toward the elevator.

He sat down again and watched without interest. As the doors opened, they had to pull back to let one of the tiny Bengali sisters off with a linen cart. It seemed too big and loaded for her to handle, but she managed it efficiently, wheeling it quietly and quickly into the rooms and out again. She kept her head bent modestly and the blue sari half-obscured her features.

Inside the room Celia Mann had understood what Anna was saying in the rapid, whispered undertone with which the administrator interspersed the mundane, rather fatuous monologue she kept up for the benefit of the guard. She understood that efforts were being made to help her; that she was not to be frightened at what they would have to do. But she was weak and sick. She had an irrational desire to be left alone. In just a little while the people who had drugged her would do away with her. And she could quit struggling . . . she was tired . . . and the pull toward oblivion was strong.

She was barely conscious of the maid called Maura coming in with the cart, or of her loud conversation with Sister Anna . . . or that they had left the cart beside the bed as they moved toward the door . . . but she was startled into consciousness again by the loud bangs with which the strange maid slammed her trays down on the cart. She found herself resisting weakly as she was expertly lifted and placed in the center section, legs folded under, head on knees. "That's it . . . keep your head down . . . don't panic . . . the door is open a crack on both sides for air . . . five minutes and you'll be out of here . . . here we go"—the voice was efficient, impersonal. The cart was rolling. It banged against the door, jamming her head against the end of the compartment with a painful bump . . . rolling again . . . and rocking . . . she could not breathe . . . she could not breathe . . .

When the two in maids' uniforms opened the compartment in the basement, she rolled out unconscious. They looked at each other but did not pause. Each had her task. The stranger lifted Celia into the express elevator and was gone, down the corridor toward the exit. Maura watched the indicator until it reached the top floor. Then she wheeled the cart toward the kitchen where she wiped it clean. There would be no fingerprints but her own.

The Bengali sister had barely gone into Mrs. Mann's room when the hospital loudspeaker crackled.

"Code blue, code blue, room 147!" The metallic voice was flat and mechanical. But as it repeated, the sound of hurrying feet came down the hall. Doctors and nurses were running for the elevator. The guard watched with interest as Sister Anna, who had remained standing by the door, turned and hurried toward the nurses' station where nurses were already converging from the kitchenette. He saw Miss Purcell among them. He stood up again, the better to observe the action.

With her usual detachment Sister Linda thought, as she worked quickly, that the sari made a practical habit. She could see why first Mother Teresa and then Mother Camilla had adopted it. It concealed but it allowed for complete freedom of movement.

There. She stood back. Yes, that looked convincing. Now, back to coach the little Bengali whose sari she wore. Surprising how willing she had been to cooperate. Well, the poor things were not used to asking questions.

She took the linen cart, pushed it before her, stopped at the door to be sure the sari veiled her face sufficiently, and went out.

The guard was mildly diverted. All up and down the hall, ambulatory patients were poking their heads out of doorways, curious about the excitement. But the Bengali sister trundled the linen cart out of Mrs. Mann's room and into the room across the hall with no sign of interest. She seemed unaware of the commotion. Nor was the cleaning man interested. He kept wielding his broom and pushing the trash cart before him. He stopped at the door of Mrs. Mann's room and said abruptly, "She says I got to sweep this one every night." He jerked his thumb toward Sister Anna, clearly and massively visible in the center of the hall by the nurses' station. The guard nodded. He was more concerned with the reappearance of Benny, who had just come off the passenger elevator, toothpick in mouth, hitching his trousers, diverted by the action in the hall. Sister Anna and Miss Purcell joined him as he came. Sister Anna was obviously explaining things.

"—a lot more of them are saved this way. I don't think we've lost a heart attack victim since it started. But this one is old Father Gunderson. He's had so many little seizures. It may be a different story."

The hungry guard did not wait for their arrival, but passed them with a curt nod and "See ya."

Benny looked in the door of Mrs. Mann's room, decided there was no need to check further, and sank into the chair just vacated. Sister Anna, still talking volubly, detained Miss Purcell at the door.

"You'll find her all tucked in. I really enjoy taking care of patients once in a while, you know. Administration involves too much paper-work."

Inexplicably, Miss Purcell yawned in her face, then mumbled a hasty apology.

"Well now, Miss Purcell," said Sister Anna with what sounded like satisfaction, "you're really tired, aren't you? And you have to stay on 'til eleven, too. You just sit down and I'll have one of the nurses bring you a cup of coffee. Let me just turn off the light near Mrs. Mann's bed and you can sit right there, where it's comfortable." She suited the action to the word and went in, pulling aside the privacy screen so that both Miss Purcell and the guard could see for a moment the quiet figure in the bed with its dark head on the pillow. Miss Purcell acknowledged that she was tired and she did think that she would sit down, but she didn't want coffee. She wouldn't sleep a wink if she had that. Sister Anna moved away.

In a very short time, Benny heard sounds from the room behind him, sounds that could be nothing else but the rhythmical, even sound of Miss Purcell's snoring. Benny wondered idly if he should wake her. She was supposed to be keeping a close watch on the dame. Then he decided that there was no harm done, for the time being at least. He was feeling a little sleepy himself.

It was ten minutes later when a nurse appeared with coffee. Sister Anna had evidently decided to ignore Miss Purcell's objection. The nurse, young and, it seemed, a little frightened, proffered the coffee to Benny.

"Will you take it in, please?" she asked. "I know I'm not supposed to go in there." Benny bestirred himself a little grudgingly. Miss Purcell was sprawled in the armchair so sound asleep that her cap was askew and her head thrown back, mouth open. Benny gave her a disgusted shove, pushing her upright, but it did not waken her. The stupid old bag, he thought. The Doc or Mann might show up at any moment. He shook her again with no result. It was only then that he began to be alarmed. Her sleep was unnatural. It looked as if she'd been given something. He went to the door and summoned a passing nurse. She also tried to waken the sleeping Purcell, shaking her less vigorously, but firmly. She stooped to sniff at the inert woman's breath.

"Well," she said to the guard, "I'd better get the supervisor. She's either drugged or drunk. She's been drinking, that's for sure."

The night supervisor came, calm and unhurried. She regarded the still-snoring Miss Purcell with distaste. Then, "How is Mrs. Mann?" she asked in a first-things-first voice. They turned as one to look at the quiet figure on the bed. Too quiet. The supervisor approached and reached out her hand, then let it fall again.

"That's not Mrs. Mann," she said flatly. "That's not her hair." Benny pushed her aside roughly and pulled at the covers.

"What the fucking hell?" he said violently. Under the covers were two pillows overlapping each other so as to simulate the curves of a human body. He held up the head—a stuffed wig. Cold fear sharpened his wits. He moved to the door and pulled it open.

"You two ain't seen nothing," he said to the frightened women. "This thing has got to be kept quiet." He jerked his head at the junior nurse. "You go get that Sister Anna."

# . 16 .

THE VICE-PRESIDENT did not hear of his wife's disappearance until well after nine o'clock, a fact which was of use to the friends of Celia Mann in that it gave them much-needed time. Because of the delay the hunt did not begin in earnest until well after ten.

The delay, as Benny, the guard, was to protest later, was not his fault. Benny had called Sam first of all. He knew that technically his boss was Alec McGregor, as head of the Secret Service detail, but like every guard at Sentry Central he knew that his real boss was Adam Mann and that Sam was his voice.

A frantic Sam had finally reached the vice-president at the Canadian Embassy dinner for the visiting Canadian delegation. John Mann had dressed early in his office lavatory and then, passing through the outer office, had nodded at Jule Andvik, his appointments secretary. It was a signal arranged long ago, a signal that he needed to unwind and wanted her to come in for a drink. Jule, like Mann, was from the Lake City flats. The brief affair that had flared between them when she first came to Washington to work in his office had burned out long ago, but an undemanding friendship remained. Jule accepted John Mann as he was. With her he felt no need to live up to his image or to any expectations. So they had lingered, laughing and talking, in the comfortable inner office. He had been late leaving for the embassy, and the men waiting for him in the car outside, also from Sentry Central, made no effort to hurry him.

"Why do they have me so mixed up with these Commonwealth countries?" he had asked Jule half-seriously. "Canada tonight, New Zealand Thursday—it can get damned dull."

"You're the expert on those international organizations—that's what your press releases say, isn't it?" she said pertly and waved him off.

**187**

Sam picked up an incredulous McGregor on his way to the embassy. They were still trying to decide on the best way to begin the search when they turned into the driveway.

Inside, the diners were just finishing the first course. John Mann, aware that his tardiness had held up the others, was doing his best to make amends by listening with flattering attention to Ambassador Hightower, who held forth on his favorite subject—the difference between Americans and Canadians.

"I always try to tell our American friends like the vice-president here," he said to the guests at the table in general, "that it's hard for them to understand our present situation because they do not understand our psychological history. Americans from the beginning thought of themselves as creating a new country and believed that the American, as Crèvecoeur put it, was a new man. That's not it, not it at all with us, you see, is it, Pickens?" He turned his pink smooth face to the head of the delegation but did not wait for an answer. "No, not at all. The Canadian has always felt that he represents England, or Europe, if you will, on a new continent. Very different point of view. We always relate to our origins."

John Mann, thinking of Maurice Chouinard, was genuinely interested. He was about to pursue the subject when the butler came hurrying in and spoke to the ambassador in a low tone. The ambassador listened, then indicated Mann with a nod of his head. The butler came to his side and whispered, "An urgent message, sir. Please come with me." Mann rose, murmuring excuses to those beside him. Once he had heard what Sam had to say, he made no effort to return but left his excuses to the butler. Marcel watched them out the door and waited until they joined McGregor by the car. Only then did he return to the dining room with the vice-president's pro forma message for his dismayed host.

Now John Mann was at a complete loss. With McGregor in the front seat, turned halfway round so that they could talk, there was no way to communicate with Sam. Celia gone from the hospital—kidnapped, McGregor said—it was impossible! His first thought was of Adam. For years he and his older brother had communicated by indirection. Adam took care of his problems and smoothed his path, sometimes in ways— it was tacitly agreed between them—that it was best he know nothing about. This agreement was even more important now that he was vice-president. Had Adam picked up a signal he had not meant to send, and had Celia removed from the hospital? The guards were Adam's. Adam had insisted on that and, at the risk of arousing the suspicion of the

Secret Service men, John Mann had agreed. It must be Adam. He raised his eyebrows questioningly at Sam. But Sam indicated by a very faint shake of his head and turning his palms upward that he had no answer. Sam, then, he thought, knew no more than he.

"It's a real puzzler, Mr. Vice-President," McGregor was saying. "There was no ransom note, no call—but, of course, we may get one at any moment. If we can keep it from the press for a reasonable amount of time we can eliminate the usual cranks. Then we can be fairly sure that whatever comes in is from the real kidnappers. That will cut down the leads we have to follow. You didn't get anything—any kind of threat recently that we don't know about, did you, sir?" He looked searchingly at John Mann. The worried spouses of victims were apt to conceal such things under threat from extortionists.

The vice-president shook his head. "No, no, I know that's usually the first thought, but there's been nothing like that—not that I know of. You don't know of anything, do you, Sam?" he asked, appealing to his aide. Sam shook his head, this time visibly and decisively.

If it wasn't Adam, could it be some of the firm's shadowy backers, grown impatient with the risk Celia posed as long as she was still in Washington? No, that would be absurd. They could hardly have her reemerge in a sanitarium elsewhere after disappearing so mysteriously. Or was it absurd? There were people, he knew, who thought it would be best to have Celia out of the way entirely. He had often thought that Sam was one of them. It was not that Sam didn't like Celia. She had always been very friendly toward him, with no hint of the condescension some official wives showed toward their husbands' staff people, and Sam, on his part, admired what he called her "class." But John Mann knew very well that Sam Drottman had only one criterion for everything he did: whether it furthered his boss's career and ambitions and his own.

Whichever way you looked at it, John Mann decided, this was a bad development and a frightening one. It could be that whoever held Celia knew he was the key to John Mann's destruction.

"For God's sake, McGregor," he said violently to the agent, "we've got to find her!" And he meant it.

It was only eight o'clock and the sky in the west was still faintly light outside the window of the headmaster's office at the Clarke School in Ohio. The headmaster sat at his desk talking to the athletic director about what had happened during spring football practice.

"Well, it's an unfortunate way to do it, but it solves a problem for us," he was saying. "Having the Mann boy available was beginning to draw the press like flies. We couldn't have held them off forever. Sensational publicity. Our directors and parents aren't going to like it. Confined to the infirmary, he's off-limits for the time being."

The other man nodded. "Neither is hurt that bad but I thought it would be best to put them there. Nobody gets by Nurse Byam if she can help it. Young Forsythe had to have stitches taken over his eye and he may have a broken nose. He'll have two black eyes by morning." He chuckled. "I didn't think Peter Mann had it in him. He was all over Forsythe like a demon. He's bruised but he probably got some of that in scrimmage. And he's got the beginning of one shiner himself and a scraped ear."

"What caused it?" asked the headmaster.

"According to Coach Feeney, Forsythe said something about Mann's mother. Sort of rotten of him. But he wanted the position Mann got on the team rather badly. And he was getting the worst of things in practice. Mann's faster and heavier."

"They're not used to disappointment—boys like Forsythe," said the headmaster absently. "And nobody's taught them there are some things that just aren't done. Slurring other people's mothers, for instance." He paused, then, "I've been wondering how Peter Mann was taking this. He's not a charmer like his father but I like the boy. He seems solid."

"Feeney says he's been very quiet, ever since he heard."

"Probably just exploded." The headmaster nodded, satisfied with his own unremarkable insight.


In the infirmary Peter Mann lay fully dressed on his cot and stared miserably into the dark. Mom, he thought. It wasn't true. He knew it wasn't true. There was nothing wrong with her. He could still hear her clear voice on the telephone when they talked the last time. That was only last week. But then why had his father said it was true? And the way they had talked about her on the news shows . . . asking those questions so glibly . . . and how his father had looked answering. Involuntarily he squeezed his eyes shut as if, even in the dark, he could still see him.

Something, *something* was very wrong. Peter Mann was proud of his father but he had given up trying to get his real attention. Oh, he knew his father loved him in his way. Dad goes through the motions, he thought, asks about grades, knows my friends' names, is glad I do well in sports. He was grateful that his father played golf with him occasionally and always took him out at the opening of the duck season. It was more than some fathers did. But it was his mother who was really there. Who knew who Peter was. To whom he was not just a son but a person.

Under his misery lay a dark thought he could not yet bear to examine. Over the years young Peter Mann had heard his father fend off importunate constituents with evasions and half-truths when he thought it necessary. Peter could always tell when his father was not being square with them and he had always been made uncomfortable by the note of false sincerity in his father's voice. That tone had been in his father's voice yesterday when he called Peter about his mother. "You'd better stay where you are now, son," he had said, "and come to see Mother when she's a little better. Your Aunt Susan is on her way here—and I don't think Mother would want you to see her now." That last was smooth, as if Dad had practiced saying it, Peter thought. He turned restlessly. If he *could* just see her—

The door to his room creaked and a sliver of light crept in from the hall.

"Pete, you awake?" It was Jim Forsythe.

Peter didn't answer. He was shaken again with the same anger and sense of betrayal that had swept over him on the football field. Jim Forsythe was his Chevy Chase neighbor and his oldest friend. Jim's mother, a divorcee, had sent him to Clarke because it was Peter's school. For Jim to say what he had—

"Christ, Pete, I'm sorry." Jim was in the room now, beside the bed. "I don't blame you for being mad. I like your mother, you know that. I know she's no druggie. I don't know what came over me."

Peter Mann lay still in unrelenting silence.

"Pete, I *know* you're awake." Forsythe's voice, not quite changed, squeaked. "Listen, Pete, you've got to understand. I think I'm jealous sometimes. You've got so much—your father and everything—and, well, first team and everything."

"Well, okay then." Peter Mann said it reluctantly.

"Pete, listen." Jim Forsythe's words came out in a rush of relief. "I've been thinking. Let's go to Washington and see your mom. I know you want to.

"My car's in the parking lot and it's easy to get out of here without Byam knowing. I've done it before. We just drop out the bathroom window onto the roof of the equipment shed, wait 'til the security guard is over at the other building, and we're home free. It's still only eight o'clock or eight-thirty and we can be there in five hours."

"What about the Secret Service?"

"One guy is sitting out in the hall, and the other just parks in the gatehouse watching the television covering the exits. I've watched him. He just sits there—half the time not looking. We won't go out the regular gate. There's a piece of fence they lay down sometimes to bring in the trucks and the rollers near the athletic field. We can get out there. I've done it before, and I don't think it's wired."

Peter Mann was on his feet.

"Wait 'til I get my windbreaker," he said, then, struck by a sudden thought, "You got any money?"

"Fifty dollars," said Jim Forsythe happily.

They had been at it for hours.

It was after midnight. Alec McGregor sat behind Sister Anna's neat, uncluttered desk and looked from one to another of those gathered in her office. The vice-president. The vice-president's aide, Sam Drottman. Sister Anna, massive in the chair opposite him. Dr. Elwood Grant. The chief of police. He was making a mental count.

In the anteroom were the two weary nurses from Mrs. Mann's floor, the private-duty nurse, Miss Purcell, and the chief hospital security guard. Upstairs, the two private guards still sat beside the closed door to Mrs. Mann's room. Counting himself, that made twelve who knew about Celia Mann's disappearance. And, oh yes, the nuns they had questioned. And the interpreter. Three, four more. Too many. And, of course, there were the others—those who had taken Celia Mann.

"How long do you think we can hold it?" he asked the police chief. He had his own idea about that, but he wanted to gauge just how far the able black politician was willing to go with them.

"Twenty-four hours at the outside, I would guess, if we're lucky." The chief looked at him levelly.

That was about right, Alec thought, and it was probably as much as they had any right to expect. The police could explain twenty-four hours of silence to the press in terms of concern for Celia Mann's safety. But no more. Aloud he said, "I think you're right. There are too many who know about this now. We can count on Dr. Grant, of course, and Sister Anna." He noted that Sister Anna flushed at the sound of her name, not for the first time that night. She was at that age, he supposed, and upset at what had happened in her hospital. It certainly didn't look good for St. Simeon's. Or for her. It had happened right under her nose.

"I think we'll leave it to her and to you, Chief Potter, to convince those two nurses of the need for discretion. We don't want to make any federal presence too obtrusive at this stage. Is there any way we could keep them here for the night, any plausible way?" he asked Sister Anna.

"Well, it's so late now," she said. "I think we could suggest that they stay in the nursing students' residence tonight. It's just a wing of the hospital, you know. Mrs. Davies—she's the supervisor—lives alone in her own apartment, and Miss Hollings has already called home to say she was held up by an emergency here. She lives with two other nurses and I don't think they worry much about each other." She was thinking of the others who knew about Celia Mann's disappearance; she had known this part would be difficult, but she was not an imaginative woman and she had not really realized how difficult. There was a heaviness in the pit of her stomach that would not go away.

"What about your security chief?" asked McGregor. Sister Anna was quiet, trying to think.

"I don't really know what to say, Mr. McGregor," she said. "Mr. McCoy came to us from the security service, of course. But his sister is one of our nuns. I think he's very loyal, but he does talk a lot. He's Irish, you know," she added vaguely.

Alec McGregor smiled for the first time. "Well, we'll just have to hope that you and Chief Potter can put the fear of God into him. I'll have to call the president again now," he added.

During this exchange, Vice-President Mann had been sitting with his elbows on his knees, his face in his hands. He straightened up.

"The president knows?" he asked.

"The president *had* to know, Mr. Mann," said Alec McGregor flatly.

John Mann nodded. It was true then, he thought. The service watched and reported as much as they protected.

"I'll just use the phone in the car and be right back; we need to sum things up," said McGregor as he went out the door. He passed through the outer office quickly, looking neither to right nor left but fully aware of the eyes fixed on him as he went. He stood on the hospital steps and immediately the black car parked just to the right pulled up smoothly. He went around and got in beside his deputy.

"How are things going?" he asked.

The deputy shrugged. "They've pulled the list of all the crazies and they've started the questioning. So far there doesn't seem to be anybody who fits this method of operation. If we get into the terrorist groups— well, that's another can of worms. The snitches and the plants are report- ing in now, those that aren't undercover and can't be reached until they report in as usual." Alec nodded and took up the car phone and gave a curt command to the operator.

"Get me Magnolia."

Although the police chief was still there, studying the notes he had made, the constraint in the office seemed to lessen in McGregor's ab- sence. The vice-president and Drottman fell into low-voiced conversa- tion. Sister Anna, with a half-hearted "May I?" to the chief, lifted her phone and called the page. "Have you heard from Dr. Sauro yet?" she asked. She shook her head slowly at Dr. Grant, indicating the reply she had received, then said, "Well, there's no use repeating. Cancel it for now. I suppose Dr. Farrow is covering." Chief Potter waited for her to finish before he put down his papers and cleared his throat.

"All right," he said quietly, but the tone of his voice brought them to attention. "I've made a schedule here and while we're waiting for Spe- cial Agent McGregor, we might as well go over it. If you have anything else to add to it, or if you notice anything out of line, now is the time for us to get it straight." He consulted his notes.

"Here it is," he began, alternately reading and watching them.

> *5:25 p.m.* Guard Benny Furoso leaves guard Tom Greider alone on duty and goes across the street to Angel's Grill. Both guards and Nurse Purcell testify Mrs. Mann in room, and physically unable to leave bed at that time.

> *5:30 p.m.* Evening trays are distributed to rooms by maids Maura Moynihan and Preta García. Purcell says she fed Mann, who could not feed self.

He saw John Mann flinch at this further reminder of his wife's help- lessness.

> *5:50 p.m.* Administrator arrives and relieves Purcell. Gets Mann ready for night.

Sister Anna was looking at her hands.

> *5:55 or 6:00 p.m.* Maids come back and start collecting trays. Cleaning man also appears on floor.

*6:00 or 6:05 p.m.* Maid enters room with tray cart at Sister Anna's request.

Potter paused. Sister Anna nodded hastily, as if he had questioned her.

At same time two men dressed as orderlies appear on floor pushing stretcher cart with covered patient. No explanation for men or patient at this time.

Potter paused again but no one moved.

*6:06 approximately.* Other maid enters room at guard's suggestion. Administrator and first maid emerge. Other maid evidently deposits trays and follows with cart. Not more than two minutes overall according to administrator and guard.

Potter paused once more. Sister Anna made no sign.

Mrs. Mann now apparently alone in room.

Potter went on without emphasis.

*6:07 approximately.* Nun enters room with linen cart.

Potter looked up and saw that McGregor was back, standing just inside the door. He signed to the chief to continue. Potter nodded and turned back to his paper.

*6:08 p.m.* Code Blue sounds. Sister Anna goes down the hall. Nun with linen cart leaves room. Cleaning man enters room.

*6:10 p.m.* Administrator, nurse and guard Furoso on way to room pass guard Greider in hall. Mann apparently alone and unguarded at that time.

*6:11 p.m.* Purcell and administrator enter room. Administrator, concerned with Purcell, who allegedly shows effects of drinking, notes nothing unusual.

He looked at Sister Anna, who flushed but nodded. She was surprised that she was so calm. Except for coloring, which she could not control, she was not finding the disguised interrogation difficult. She had a methodical mind and she was well prepared. She did not even think it strange that she was bent on deceiving the police and the representatives of the federal government. Some things were wrong only in degree in Sister Anna's scheme of life.

*6:15 p.m.* Guard enters rooms to bring Purcell coffee. Finds her asleep. Thinks she is drugged. Sends for supervisor. Supervisor and guard find Mann missing.

*   *   *

Chief Potter put down his paper. "I shortened it up there at the last," he said mildly, "because it looks like that time ain't so crucial."

To McGregor's surprise Vice-President Mann was the first to react.

"There are obvious ringers in that list," he said, and began ticking them off his fingers. "The orderlies . . . and the patient on the stretcher— if there *was* a patient, that is—the one strange maid, but she was hardly there long enough to do anything—"

Sister Anna interrupted him a little breathlessly. "The maid wasn't exactly strange, Mr. Vice-President, she just wasn't one of our regulars, I understand. She's on our list of fill-ins from the Hispanic Center."

He nodded. "Well, that leaves the cleaning man—"

"—and we think there's no way a human being could be stuffed into his cart," said Chief Potter.

The vice-president paused a moment, then said, "But we don't really know that he had a regular cart, do we? It just looked like one."

That's true, thought McGregor, he has a point there.

The chief was unsatisfied. "It just doesn't hang together. You're sure, ma'am," he said to Sister Anna, "that Mrs. Mann could not have gotten out by herself?"

Sister Anna looked shocked. "Oh, I don't think that could be possible in the condition she was in. No, I don't think so. I don't think she could have deceived us about that, do you, Dr. Grant?"

The doctor, who had been staring at the wall lost in thoughts of his own, was startled back into professionalism. "Oh no," he said. "On the basis of my examinations and observation I would think that highly unlikely." He straightened up, struck by a sudden thought. "Unless, of course, there was some collusion with one of the nurses—Purcell, or Brennan, who went off duty at four . . ." He sounded almost hopeful.

Great, thought McGregor. More possibilities. This was not going to be easy. It must have been carefully planned. All those decoys. They had to come from outside. But there had to be inside help. With the rapid turnover in lower-level personnel at the hospital, it was going to be difficult to identify any ringers on any particular day.

They had been at it since Benny had notified Alec McGregor and also, Alec McGregor was sure, Sam Drottman, at seven o'clock. Whatever he himself thought privately of Sentry Central's strong-arm boys, they had come through in this instance. The nurses, thoroughly frightened into cooperation by the guards, had emerged one by one from

Celia Mann's room. The two hospital nurses had been told to resume
their work and to act as natural as possible until they were replaced and
called for. The supervisor had explained to the nurse working on charts
at the nurses' station that Miss Purcell seemed to be drunk. The other
nurse said that Miss Purcell had seemed to like the wine very much at
the little celebration in the kitchenette.

"But she must be one of those people who can't take liquor very well,"
she added. "She certainly didn't have that much. But then, you never
know," she added indifferently.

"Anyway, they're sending somebody to replace her," said the supervisor, as she had been told.

It was Sister Anna who had suggested that they explain the interrogation by saying that Mrs. Mann's room seemed to have been robbed, and
she had sent her own secretary home with no explanation. Her inven-
tiveness and alacrity had rather surprised McGregor when he arrived.
His first impression of her on the day Celia Mann was brought to the
hospital was of someone more ponderous and slow in her thinking. The
story she suggested was quite good, he had to admit. It even gave an
excuse for Chief Potter's arrival at the hospital. Theft from people on
the Manns' level was enough for a little special attention. Not really, but
so people might think, the cynicism about people in office running as
deep as it did these days. It also gave him an excuse for questioning
people who had been in or near Celia Mann's room. The chief had had
the investigation well under way when McGregor, Mann and Drottman
arrived.

The one clear thing was that the cleaning man was nowhere to be
found. He should have been doing corridors until midnight, according
to Sister Marie Josephine, who was in charge of maintenance personnel.
She could not even describe, him, however.

"You see, Mr. McGregor," she had said, "I don't interview them or
hire them. We depend on the cleaning service to do that. And this man
was new today." Sister Anna had spread her hands apologetically.

"I know it sounds strange, Mr. McGregor, but with labor troubles and
all, hospitals have taken to contracting out services. There was a time
when I knew everybody who worked in this hospital and all about them.
But not anymore." She shook her head sadly. He had a feeling that she
had said this many times before, that the topic was well worn. The topic
was, in fact, comforting to Sister Anna. Here, at least, she was on familiar ground. They had finally tracked down the day cleaning man, whom
the missing man had replaced.

"Yes," he said, "the guy was new, sort of a big dude, thin." That's all he could say, he argued belligerently.

Alec McGregor could almost hear the unspoken dialogue between the man and the chief:

"You gonna hassle me in front of these honkies, just because some brother got back some of our own?" It was implicit in the man's surly, closed face and his stubborn insistence despite the chief's repeated questions. The new cleaner had been big; he'd been black; he'd worn the usual uniform; and that was all he could remember. How black? He couldn't rightly say. Any marks? He couldn't say. He had closed ranks with the vanished man and expected the chief to do the same. And why not, thought Alec McGregor. As far as he knew, it was a standard rip-off. If the brother had gotten away with it, more power to him. The chief was going to be handicapped, Alec saw, as long as the wraps were on. Washington had become a black city and was run by a black administration, but for most of its citizenry, the memory of "white niggers" who betrayed their own and the belief that there was one kind of justice for blacks and another for whites still conditioned the attitude toward official questioning.

There were political dangers for the chief and his boss, the mayor, in this and the chief must struggle with these dangers every day, McGregor thought.

Chief Potter was saved from his dilemma by an excited report from Sister Marie Josephine. The man who had disappeared must have been an imposter. The regular night cleaning man had just been found, unconscious but unhurt, locked in the cleaning cupboard on the first floor.

"If he'd been there much longer, I think he would have suffocated," she said. "We have one of the junior residents there and he's coming around now, I think." The Secret Service man and the chief looked at each other and nodded.

"That seems to settle it," said McGregor.

"I don't like it," said Sam Drottman suddenly. "It's too neat."

McGregor did not like Drottman. He was much too hand-in-glove with the Sentry Central people for one thing, and he had seen enough in the past few weeks to know that Drottman was the man—the kind necessary for any politician to have, he supposed—who handled the unpleasant things John Mann would rather not know about, who brought pressure to bear and who eased people out of their jobs, made the promises and broke them if they had to be broken. Alec McGregor was not really tolerant of such men. He didn't understand what motivated them, but he was inclined to agree with Drottman this time. It was too open and shut as far as suspects went.

Something was not right. He did not see how one man alone could have wrestled an inert, almost paralyzed woman into the narrow confines of that cleaning cart or how he could have concealed her as he went down the hall. The food cart was a more likely possibility. It was wider and the doors rolled back smoothly and quietly on ball-bearing hinges. It was made of heavy steel and could easily have sustained Mrs. Mann's weight. He reviewed, in his mind, the facts gained from earlier questioning.

"I can't see any reason why the man with the waste cart would be going into the patient's room," Sister Anna had insisted. "That simply isn't done; it isn't the way we do it. But the food cart—I called Maura Moynihan in myself. I wanted to know how things were going with her. It was the first chance I'd had to see her in several days, and I didn't think I should leave Mrs. Mann. Of course, I don't know why she pushed the cart in, but they do take it into the four-bed rooms. It's easier to serve that way." Sister Anna was huffy and a little fussed, he had thought. She had evidently not liked having to explain to Protestants like himself and the chief that Maura Moynihan was an ex-Reguline sister who had been reduced to maid's work to keep body and soul together.

"Well, ma'am, if you didn't want to leave Mrs. Mann, why did you leave her a few minutes later?" the chief had asked. The same question had occurred to McGregor, but he had known what Sister Anna's answer would be.

"A Code Blue takes precedence over everything. That's our rule, officer," Sister Anna said firmly, "and lives depend on our sticking to it. As chief administrator, I went to be sure the rules were fully carried out—and the guard was there." She was defensive again.

It hung together. The people in question corroborated each other. It was a dead-end lead anyway. The cart had been found, cleaned, polished and standing in its numbered place in the big hospital kitchen during their quick check of the premises, and it had been there, as far as anyone knew, ever since the two maids had taken it from the floor.

The linen cart was bigger than the cleaning cart too. There were big hamper spaces at each end. If a room was vacated in the afternoon, or if someone died, the little Bengali sister stripped the bed on her evening rounds, so she had explained through the interpreter Sister Anna had summoned.

"I know most of the people think that the people in India and Pakistan—Bangladesh was part of Pakistan, you know—speak English," she had said to them. "I thought so, too, before these sisters came here. But it seems that only the upper class of civil servants learned English even in the British times, and most of the ordinary people never learned it at all. These sisters were born since then. We will need Sister Linda's help to get the story clear and to keep her from being frightened," Sister Anna had continued.

They had all been a little disconcerted by Sister Linda, so small, withered and strange-looking in her black habit, but so matter-of-fact in eliciting just the information they needed.

"She goes into the patients' rooms because it is her vocation to do so. She was chosen to give love and help and comfort to the sick and dying. Here, she can only do it by smiling at them, perhaps patting them a little, until she can learn English. But she feels she should do that at least." The Bengali sister added something and Sister Linda hesitated before translating. Then she said quickly, "She says she does not think the English-speaking nurses are always very kind to the old and the troublesome. I'm sure that's just a cultural perception, Sister," Sister Linda added apologetically to Sister Anna. The Bengali sister had gone on. "She takes the cart into the room with her because even here, in this rich country, she has heard that people steal things. Tonight was the first time she was able to get into Mrs. Mann's room. She was glad she could do that as the poor lady seemed very sick indeed." The Bengali sister's passport had checked out, of course, and she left after exchanging *namaste* with Sister Linda.

McGregor found all these nuns and their different modes of dress confusing. The vice-president and his aide seemed to take them in stride. They were Catholic, of course. The little one in the black habit seemed to know the vice-president. It was not clear to him what she was doing here. She evidently lived in Lake City.

Suddenly the whole thing seemed fantastic. The wife of one of the best-known men in the country could not disappear from a quasi-public institution like this one without a trace. Yet, here they sat accepting that fact. He looked from one to another, searching the strained faces, unnaturally white under the fluorescent lighting, looking for clues to what they were feeling and thinking.

The doctor could only be called a wreck, McGregor thought. Perhaps in these days of malpractice suits his reaction was understandable. But the glistening sweat which covered his face and which he tried to control with ineffectual dabs of a wadded handkerchief, and the uncontrollable twitching of his hands, seemed signs of an excessive reaction. With a leap of intuition, McGregor wondered whether the good doctor might not be involved in something else here at the hospital that he wanted to keep quiet. It would be best to keep an eye on him.

McGregor was close to the truth. Dr. Grant's nervousness was in part owing to his fear of discovery. Sooner or later a search of the whole hospital would be made and no one knew what trained eyes might see despite their careful cover-up. But he was more afraid of what his resident, Joe Sauro, might have done. Sauro was nowhere to be found. The page he himself had instituted two hours before had echoed with monotonous regularity from the corridor outside the office in which they sat until Sister Anna cut it off: "Dr. Sauro . . . Dr. Sauro . . . please respond to page phone . . . Dr. Sauro . . . Dr. Sauro." Celia Mann was missing and Joe Sauro, too. There had to be a connection. Surely these men would note it before too long. The people he had called had not got to Sauro in time after all. How long would this go on? Lord, he needed a drink.

Sam Drottman and the vice-president had contributed little to the interrogation. They had sat silently for the most part, looking at the people questioned, and listening. Occasionally Sam had expressed, by a growled query or an abrupt movement, his impatience with the pace of the investigation. Obviously he wanted to be somewhere else. There are people he wants to talk to, thought Alec grimly, people he doesn't want us to talk to first. The vice-president had said nothing at all until his response to the chief's summary, but he often nodded reassuringly at the people being questioned, especially the nuns, Alec noted. It was, he supposed, an instinctive political response. Now both men sat quietly, seemingly lost in thoughts of their own. Sister Anna shifted from side to side. She looked increasingly worried and nervous. McGregor could not know it, but Sister Anna's thoughts were not with the people there in her office. She was beginning to feel that she could not bear it if she didn't soon find out what was going on above them in the hospital.


Sam Drottman was not only impatient; he was frightened. He was sure that the disappearance of Celia Mann was not the work of Leo's organization. Benny and the other guard were too frightened to have had any part in it. He was sure that if it were not for the controlling presence of the Secret Service detail director they would have been elsewhere by now, battered and cringing, pleading their innocence without much hope to Leo's enforcers. Their time would come, he thought. And maybe his as well. Sam Drottman had long served as the organization's eye on John Mann. More than that, he had served as the facilitator who translated Mann's position into advantage for the organization. How had that come about? He could hardly remember.

In the beginning he had just been John's man Friday. He had not been able to finish law school—he couldn't get a scholarship and odd jobs didn't give him enough money—and had been hired as an investigator by the Manns' firm. Adam had approved his work and taken a shine to him. He was the chief advance man in John Mann's first campaign and, when Mann was elected governor, had gone with him to the state capital. Eventually, he had become his chief administrative aide. Like most aides of people in power, he had been open to the blandishments of lobbyists. He had enjoyed the free dinners and lunches, the gifts at Christmastime, the use of clubs and planes and pleasure boats and, eventually, the envelopes of money. At first those envelopes were just laid on the desk; then they were passed under the table and, finally, handed over casually. Because of those envelopes, he thought dully, he had become no longer John's man, but Leo's. Adam and the others were fools to think they could keep John's shirttails clean. He realized that he was sweating lightly. He had to figure out who could have snatched the woman. And how to get her back. His fear merged into fury, a fury directed at Dr. Grant and Sister Anna, the two he held responsible for not keeping Celia Mann safely locked away. He had never wanted her brought here in the first place. These places run by nuns gave him the creeps.

Despite his calm exterior, John Mann was sunk in gloom. It was his nature to face any difficulty or setback in his political life by accepting it as a given, a hurdle to be overcome. He would then immediately set his mind on taking the next step; figuring out how to use what had happened or find a way around it. But what had happened now was so dire and unexpected that he was at a loss. Although he had not been able to talk to Sam, by now he was equally sure that this was not the work of Adam and Leo. And, if not, he himself faced possible ruin and a fall from the heights to which he had climbed. In this mood it was his instinctive reaction to blame his wife for the situation. If Celia had been different this would never have happened. It never would have been necessary for her to be here in the first place.

But Celia in the hands of terrorists . . . he hadn't counted on that. He had never meant anything really bad to happen to her. He had just wanted to stop her. Unbidden memories of a younger Celia raced through his mind . . .

It was a huge gray stone, turreted Victorian on the lake road. An incongruous arched porte cochere sheltered the high double front door with etched windows through which the brown glazed tiles of the entrance hall could be seen as if through a frosty forest inhabited by ghostly antlered stags.

They had met there for the first time, he and Celia. He was crunching up the graveled drive just on time for an appointment with her mother to discuss some business about the Fifield property. Celia Fifield, bursting out of the door in a hurry, almost ran into him. "Oh," she said, polite if breathless—he sensed that she had run down the stairs and across the big entrance hall—"you must be Mr. Mann. Mother is expecting you."

She was unexpectedly vivid against the dimness behind her and the gray stone. She wore a red coat and the black of her hair, the dark blue of her eyes and the fresh color in her white skin, mark of her Celtic forebears, were almost startling. He had seen photographs of her in the society section of the *Lake City News* and had not thought her regular features especially pretty. Now he was genuinely taken aback at her appearance and momentarily speechless.

"You are Mr. Mann, aren't you?" she asked, smiling. "Not the Fuller Brush man?"

"Yes, no," he said laughing. "I mean, yes, I'm Johnny Mann and, no, I'm not the brush man—wrong equipment." He lifted his briefcase. "But I've been one—and a lot of other things, too—when I was working my way through college."

"Oh, I know," she said and blushed. "I mean I know quite a bit about you. We all think it's splendid that you're doing such good things for the city now—like helping Mother's committee to clean up the lakefront. The lake means so much to everybody. The lake really *is* Lake City, I think. I'm always homesick away from it."

He followed her gaze out over the water, slaty blue now in the morning sun.

Johnny did not say that people growing up on the flats did not see much of the lake. He was warmed by her admiration and pleased by her assumption that they had common interests. She reminded him of the college girls he had dated cautiously while he was at Yale. She had their assurance but not, he thought, the same sophistication.

"Well," she said quickly, extending her hand, "it was nice to meet you."

He watched her go down the drive as he waited beside the door she had left ajar for someone to answer the bell. He was thoughtful. She was certainly good to look at and there was something in the way she walked, a sturdiness about her shoulders, that pleased him. She would make someone a very good wife.

He called her the next evening.

He had really fallen in love, he had to admit that. He could hardly believe his good fortune. To be engaged to a Fifield—and a girl like Celia into the bargain! His mother, awkward and ill at ease with Celia and her family, nevertheless was astute in her judgment. "She's a good girl, Johnny—and smart. She'll be the help you need."

The early days of their marriage were dim in his memory. He would have been hard put to describe their wedding or honeymoon or even the first five years in any detail, but from somewhere deep in his consciousness a picture flashed into his mind.

Celia breathless with suppressed laughter when they checked into that inn across the lake on their wedding night.

"I can't help it, Johnny," she said. "You were so stiff and proper."

His own sheepishness. He was nervous—he had to admit it.

Later they lay and looked at the moon reflected on the water just beyond their window. They were very content with each other.

He tightened the hold of his arm around her shoulders.

"You're something, Celia," he said.

"Did I make you happy, Johnny?" she asked.

He had been surprised and delighted at Celia's frank, innocent ardor and the sure intuition with which she followed his lead.

But that was a long time ago . . .


McGregor rose to go. Just then there was a sound of scuffling and an outcry in the outer office. The door burst open and one of the Sentry Central guards thrust a bedraggled young man into the room.

"This kid tried to force his way into Mrs. Mann's room," said the guard to McGregor, ignoring the police chief.

"Let go of me, you goon," said the boy furiously. "I tell you I'm Peter Mann and I want to know what all of you have done with my mother!"

Sam Drottman swore under his breath. "All we need—" he said.

The vice-president rose uncertainly. "Son," he said and paused. McGregor guessed that he was uncertain what to say. The boy did not look at his father. "Where is she?" he demanded of the chief. "My mother is not any dope addict. I know her better than anybody and I know that."

It was easy to see why Peter Mann had come into the building unrecognized. He was wearing wrinkled chinos and worn running shoes. A dirty T-shirt was visible under his faded blue windbreaker. One eye was half-closed and black with bruises and one ear was swollen. A light stubble covered his cheeks and chin. Not what you would think of as the son of a vice-president, McGregor thought wryly with some amusement. At the same time, he felt annoyance at the guard. Slack again. The boy evidently had seen enough to know that his mother was not in her room.

Sister Anna took charge. "You can go," she said severely to the guard. She took Peter's hand. "You remember me, Peter," she said, "Sister Anna. I was here when you were in with appendicitis last year. I think you have every right to know that we are afraid your mother has been kidnapped."

It was only then that the boy turned to his father.


It was three o'clock in the morning. A pale moon was setting across the Potomac, sinking toward the newly sprouted forest of concrete and glass that is called Rosslyn. Between Capitol Hill and the White House the city was eerily quiet. The mall stretched empty in the faint moonlight. The great national galleries and museums were tomblike on its border. Only a few guards moved here and there in the slablike government buildings on the great avenues and manned the entrance doors. The projecting upper floor of the ugliest of these, the FBI building, seemed to beetle out in a perpetual frown over the streets below. The two men in the solitary car coming down Pennsylvania Avenue saw windows spring into light as they approached.

The car made a wide U-turn in the empty street and rolled to a stop. Alec, getting out, said to the driver, "I have no idea how long this will take," and closed the door quietly. The car slid away and came to a stop again at the curb a block down the street.

"McGregor, Secret Service," he said to the guard at the door. An agent who had been waiting beside the guard's desk stepped forward.

"Ingersoll," he said, introducing himself without extending his hand. "They're waiting for you in the director's suite."

Alec nodded and followed Ingersoll into the elevator.

In the office on the top floor, four men were seated at a table covered with green felt. McGregor noted the tape recorder and the one empty chair placed on the side of the table opposite the others. The members of the Forecast Commission had been hastily assembled—and others, he noted with some surprise: Haskins, chairman of the Senate Intelligence Committee, and Wilcox, the minority chairman, too. He nodded to Regan, top interrogator for the bureau, who was seated at the table. Next to him was his own chief, Simmons from Treasury, then Tom Fergus, director of the DEA, and finally, a gray man with an almost anonymous face, Paul Robard, new head of the FBI. No one moved at his approach. Ingersoll indicated the lone chair but McGregor remained standing.

"Is this an interrogation?" he asked, addressing himself to Simmons, ignoring the others.

"No, not really, Alec," said Simmons uneasily. A banker and a bureaucrat at heart, he was not at home in his capacity as head of the Secret Service. He had never really understood why it should still be the responsibility of the Treasury Department.

"You can call it that if you want," interrupted Regan roughly. "When the wife of the vice-president of the United States disappears, and it's got all the earmarks of an inside job, you can bet we're going to question the guy responsible."

"Correction," said McGregor evenly. "We're responsible only for the vice-president. Protection for the family is a courtesy extended by the president. In any case, questioning or interrogation, I must insist on the usual safeguards."

"Now, look here, you—" began Regan, but Robard cut in.

"Special Agent McGregor is entirely right." His voice was low, cold, clear. There was a trace of accent which McGregor could not identify. Robard indicated the chair to his left. "Come, sit here. The tape is for Secretary Boise. We didn't like to roust him out at this time of night. Is that all right with you?" he asked Alec. Alec nodded.

It was a matter of form. McGregor was sure the whole room was wired. They had to play their little game, he thought. He sat down and kept his eyes on Robard.

"We need to know about the process of investigation so far," said the director, "and anything you can tell us about the situation prior to what happened tonight. The president thinks we will make better progress if we all cooperate and bypass the usual formalities in the matter of a kidnapping."

"We don't know yet that it's a kidnapping," said McGregor stubbornly. "Or that she's been taken out of the District."

"What else could it be?" Regan, who had been momentarily rebuffed, was back in character. "She couldn't leave under her own power if the medical reports are accurate. She disappeared from under the noses of your own guards." McGregor saw Simmons reddening. "It has all the earmarks of a professional snatch with accomplices positioned inside—like I said before."

McGregor ignored the implication. There had been enough fencing. At this stage the more help the better. The important thing was to get Mrs. Mann back and to get her back unharmed.

"I'm not sure," he said wearily, putting into words the thoughts that had been nagging at the back of his mind since he was first told that Celia Mann was missing eight long hours ago. He was bone-weary. "It's not clean the way a professional operation usually is. Too many coincidences, too many people with the opportunity. People walk in and out of that hospital day and night. Relatives of patients, friends, employees, paper boys, doctors, nurses, undertakers, all kinds of nuns—priests, too."

"Nuns are up to their eyeballs in political capers these days," said Regan sourly, his heavy black brows pulled together in one straight line. You should know, McGregor thought. You've got that old Boston College look if ever I saw it. But he wasn't willing to concede the point.

"And I can't figure the motive," McGregor added. "With regular hoods after money or terrorists with a political objective of some kind, we'd have heard by now. Unless there's been something from the vice-president while I was on the way here? He hasn't heard anything, has he?" He directed his question to Simmons, who shook his head.

"We think the motive is more directly connected with the lady herself," said the director. "She may know things she shouldn't. She was mixed up with the peace people not so long ago. And some of her brother's connections are questionable. And if she's addicted and just coming off the stuff she's going to tell everything she knows not so many hours from now. Tell him"—he nodded at DEA Director Fergus—"it might help him remember things, or see something he's noticed in a different perspective, something he saw without knowing it."

"We've been working on the biggest bust in history," said Fergus. "It's bigger than the Florida-based cleanup of the Southeast a few years ago. Some of the most untouchable guys in the organization are going down if it works out. And some of those top Canadians who are supposed to be our allies. It's a real mess. We pull the string and a whole house of cards will come tumbling down. At least, it could have. This dame could blow it all. We've had some of our best people working on the inside for five years. And we won't even have time to reel them in." His voice was bitter.

McGregor was silent. It hadn't occurred to him that Celia Mann herself might have been a threat to dangerous forces.

"We need to get some sort of profile on Mrs. Mann," Regan was saying. "What she was like, who she was in touch with, who would know her comings and goings . . . you know the drill. Just start from the beginning."

It made sense, McGregor knew. Somewhere in what he and the others had observed in Celia Mann there was a clue to her disappearance. Since the 1970s, the Bureau had almost perfected the means by which they could tell precisely what kind of person had committed a crime and where to look for him or, as was probably the case now, *them.*

"Well," he began slowly, "I don't know much about women. We're assigned to the husbands, as I said. But it did seem to me that sometimes she was like two different people . . ."


When he finally arrived at the bare one-bedroom apartment on New Hampshire Avenue where, as his sister said, he hung his hat between hours on duty when he was in Washington, Alec took a beer from the refrigerator and went out on his balcony. He was tired but not ready to sleep. A few streaks in the sky to the east foretold the coming of daylight. He sank into a chair to think.

The loose ends . . .

What was Celia Mann really like? He didn't really know the answer. He remembered his first sight of her. A nice woman—he thought that then—a nice woman in a roomy comfortable house whose colorful chintzes and fresh flowers reflected her style. A sensible woman, too. And clear-headed, then.

"I have the lists you'll want to see here in my desk," she had said when he first came to see her. "Sit in that red chair, Mr. McGregor—

it's the only man-sized chair in the room—and I'll get them out. I'll ask Juanita to bring us some coffee. And I think she has some fresh blueberry muffins."

They were not supposed to fraternize with the people they were guarding. It was considered unprofessional. But he hadn't stopped for lunch and he thought he could explain the policy later. He needed the coffee and, anyway, in that atmosphere refusal would seem discourteous.

Her lists were neatly typed and in logical order. They included all the names security would need. A list of the people who came to the house on some sort of regular basis. The milkman. The paperboy. The postman. The florist. The delivery man from the neighborhood market. Her hairdresser. The seamstress who did alterations. A list of babysitters, with the telephone numbers at which they could be reached. Beside some of the names there were number notations—"8½, 17, 22." She saw his puzzled look and laughed.

"Sizes and ages, Mr. McGregor. For Christmas presents. We've been in this neighborhood a long time and some of these people are old friends. Just giving them Christmas tips doesn't seem enough."

There were the names of the people from the senator's office and their home addresses. A list of family friends and neighbors. And a list made up only of women's names. "My committees," she explained.

"It's going to be nice having you here, Mr. McGregor," she said when they were finished. "Those two men Adam sent us aren't as professional as you are in the service."

"I've wanted to ask you about them," he said. "Why were they sent? Had you had any threats?"

She frowned a little, as if trying to remember. "Not anything unusual, Mr. McGregor. Unless Johnny didn't tell me—not wanting to worry me, you know. Adam uses that agency to protect his real estate holdings. He's a heavy investor in property in our home state, but I suppose you know that. He's my husband's older brother—very proud of him and"— she hesitated a little—"very protective."

He had gone back to the coach house feeling a little better about the assignment. The lady, at least, he had thought then, would be easy to work with.

He finished his beer and went back inside to check the log sheets he had brought home with him. As was the usual practice, the Secret Service had monitored all calls to and from the Manns. A matter of security. He looked at the telephone logs covering the calls to and from Mrs. Mann's room in the hospital. Not many. He leafed through. Yes, here it was—the day of Celia Mann's alleged relapse. Incoming calls? Yes, one. From the vice-president. After that, only one outgoing. He studied the entry:

> 11:30 p.m. Dial-direct call to Lake City. Mrs. Mann's voice. Too brief to monitor.

Another loose end, that phone call. According to the doctors Mrs. Mann was barely able to walk and evidently not able to speak that night. Could she have dialed a long-distance call and had it completed? He had better check the call.

Joe Manfuso, when queried, was helpful if ungrammatical. "It didn't make no sense, Alec. I figured the poor girl was out of it. That's why I didn't put down the details. She got some place called Roseau Hall in Lake City. She said something about a fife . . ."

"A *what*?" Alec interrupted.

"A fife. It's a musical instrument you blow on," Joe added helpfully, "and then she says something about injections. And the other party hung up on her. I tell you, Alec, she was out of it. I felt sorry for her."

"Okay, Joe. But remember, after this everything, *everything* goes down."

Alec hadn't thought it merited a stronger rebuke. A fife. And injections. Joe was right. She must have been out of it. He, too, felt sorry for Celia Mann, very sorry. But what was wrong? The doctors had never reported a diagnosis. They were probably in disagreement. Still, all that had to be checked into.

He looked at the other log sheet for that day, the one recording the movements of all who entered and left the wing where Mrs. Mann was staying.

> *8:30 p.m.* Dr. Fifield, Mrs. Mann's brother, arrives to see Mrs. Mann. Accompanied by Dr. Elwood Grant and Sentry Central bodyguard, all with proper identification.
>
> *11:00 p.m.* Two Sentry Central men arrive on orders from Dr. Fifield.

Why all these guards? Did they need more security because she was worse? Or had they suspected foul play? If so, why had he as head of the detail not been informed? He put the logs aside. There were certainly theories to explore. But first he needed some sleep.

* * *

Secretary Boise had the commission's report the next morning. He was profoundly disturbed. He had not begun to act when he should have. He had long sensed that this new generation of politicians spelled trouble for his party. Lily Batchelder had, it seemed, no awareness that their shoddiness, their sharp dealings and less-than-clean backgrounds could rub off on her administration, could spell disaster not only for her but for all she stood for. The secretary could only suppose that the president had been conditioned early by the hard and personal politics of the boardroom and the boss-ridden politics of the old decaying industrial centers of the South. Both were politics, Clem Boise knew, whose history did not bear close examination.

He had long since ceased raising the question with her. As his interests and hers became one, he had simply set about dealing with the problems as they arose. He set up his own system of checks. When a man looked like too much of a risk to have around, or even if he simply seemed apt to cause embarrassment, Clem Boise exerted pressures of his own. Sometimes a financial threat inspired in the right quarter would do the job. The trouble now was that he had not begun early enough to make inquiries about John Mann.

The truth was, he admitted to himself, he had taken the president's announcement that she was seeking a new vice-presidential candidate badly. He had known it was coming, he had seen the sense of it—and yet he had let himself be hurt. All the more, he acknowledged to himself, because he had opposed the president on sending more military aid into the Latin countries and he had lost—for the first time. When he looked around that day at the faces around the table at the National Security Council meeting, he saw that some of them avoided his eyes and others looked—even now he could scarcely bear the thought—others looked pitying. In their eyes he was a man without power—a man already gone from their circle. And for the first time he knew that he was an old man.

He had holed up in his office and his residence like a wounded and toothless tiger, and he had let things drift. He had watched idly as his potential successors vied for precedence and had taken little interest. When Governor Quinn of Ohio, whom he had favored if he favored anyone, inexplicably withdrew his name from consideration, his old political instincts were aroused. He had smelled something wrong. But he had done nothing.

No politician in Washington is without his "bitter-enders," those associates who have risen as he rose, or whose fortunes depend on his— and many of them go down fighting, hoping to reverse destiny until the very last. Cabinet member through courtesy though he might be, Clem Boise had a sizable cadre of these on whom he could call for help. In addition to that there were those, in and out of government, who had guessed that he might serve elsewhere in a position of some importance in Lily Batchelder's second term and had hedged their bets accordingly. Relying on all these, Clem Boise pulled himself together and began to look into things. So far he had turned up nothing that would really incriminate John Mann, but there were shadows . . .

He looked at the clock. Ten. Not too late. He put in a call to the Washington bureau of an Ohio newspaper chain and listened while the resourceful White House operator was shunted from one number to another until his quarry was tracked down. He heard the shout as she asked for his party: "Grady! Hey, Grady—phone over here!" A neighborhood bar evidently. He had a nostalgic desire to be there with Grady and his friends, whiling away the hours in the fustiness of the place he imagined, talking and joking and drinking beer while the jukebox thumped in the background.

"Jack?" he said when Grady came to the phone. "Clem here. I need to pick your brains a bit. Can you meet me at my house? Half an hour from now?"

# . 17 .

WHILE THE SEARCH was launched Celia's rescuers had been busy.

Yanni Michal was nervous; his hands sweated and slid on the steering wheel as he guided the florist's van into the no-parking zone in front of the hospital. But he was on schedule. His watch told him that it was exactly seven. He left the motor running.

"Boldness is important," Ralph had said. Mindful of that, Yanni took the two chrysanthemum plants—one white, one bronze—from the back of the van and strolled casually toward the entrance. His tight black stocking cap was rolled down to his eyebrows, effectively covering his hair. His brown eyebrows had been reddened and he now wore a false, full red mustache, which trailed into fine, thin muttonchop whiskers on either side of his mouth.

"What do you remember from a face?" Ralph had queried. "The eyes, the mouth—sometimes the nose, if it's distinctive. So those are what you change, that and your clothes." Yanni was wearing a blue uniform coverall and earth shoes. He was well inside the front door when a man dressed almost identically emerged from the garage entrance of the hospital, got into the van, and drove it away.

Yanni went to the reception desk and turned over the flowers to the receptionist. She was arranging files in preparation for the nightly visiting hour and hardly noticed him. He asked if there was a water fountain handy, and she pointed back down the corridor over her shoulder. He walked slowly toward the fountain, passed it, and went through a swinging door just beyond. He found the entrance to the fire stairs and started climbing. He encountered no one, but he was breathless by the time he

**213**

reached the seventh floor and emerged into the corridor leading to the quarters of the Regulines. Sister Margaret Rose was waiting there.

"Oh, I'm glad you came," she said into thin air, although there seemed to be no one around to hear her. "We've been having trouble with this one bathroom for ages."

Yanni nodded. "Better not to speak unless it's necessary," Ralph had said. "People remember voices."

Sister Margaret Rose whisked down the corridor, opened a door, and motioned him through it. It was Sister Anna's room, bigger than he had imagined it. On the bed, covered with a white knitted afghan, lay Celia Mann.

He caught his breath at the sight of her. Until now, nothing about the venture had seemed totally real. This neglected-looking, forlorn woman could not be Celia Mann! His mind sought for words to express his feelings . . . she could be . . . she could be anybody! And his emotions told him what his mind could not: his previous feeling for her was bound up with his perception of her as a woman secure in her position, a woman who went from his hands into a world of power and importance and, in an indefinable way, took him with her.

But the woman lying on the bed was nondescript in her helplessness. Her arms were thin, her eyes sunken. Her face was gray and damp with the perspiration of weakness. A faint smell of sickness permeated the room and hovered about her. His stomach lurched.

She opened her eyes and smiled at him feebly. Her eyes were the same deep blue as ever, and at the recognition he saw in them, Yanni felt a surge of tenderness. This was, after all, his friend, and he was touched by her need. Instinctively he reached out and smoothed her tangled hair—he had never before seen it unkempt and it troubled him to see it matted and uncombed.

Oblivious and intent, Sister Margaret Rose was talking in a rapid undertone, "—stuffed in the warming compartment of the food cart, poor thing. We weren't sure she knew what was going on even though Anna whispered the plans to her while she was taking care of her. It was a near thing. Maura and the other girl had only a minute to get her on the express elevator before the kitchen supervisor began to make the nightly count of the carts."

She was looking anxiously at Celia Mann as she talked. "She was unconscious when Pat and I lifted her out of the elevator. Her heart was so faint that Pat had to give her an injection of adrenaline. She looks better now, I think, don't you? It's so hard for me to know . . . I'm not a nurse. And we must get her out of the hospital in the morning. Do you think she looks all right, John?"

Yanni nodded, more to reassure Celia Mann, whose eyes were on them both, than in answer to the question. It irritated him that Margaret Rose went on as if Celia were unable to hear them. But according to the timetable, he had only a few minutes to spare. He pulled a red wig from the pocket of his coverall. It was coppery, soft and feather-light. "There isn't time to color your hair. That will have to come afterwards. You see, I'll get to do it after all," he said to Celia, who smiled again. "I decided on red because her skin is so very fair," he added to Sister Margaret Rose, tying and pinning back Celia's hair as he spoke. He was expert at it. And careful. It never did to take a chance on a lock straying below a wig under any circumstances, let alone these special ones. He adjusted the wig. Then he reached into his pocket and pulled out a small jar of bleach. "We'll just lighten the brows with this," he said. "They're so very black that they'd be a dead giveaway." He worked quickly and carefully. "Now, Sister," he said, stepping back, "let it set for fifteen minutes and be very careful that she doesn't toss her head and get it into her eyes. But I don't think she will. She understands."

"Thanks, Yanni." It was a faint whisper, but it came clearly from Celia Mann's barely moving lips.

"Thank heavens," said Sister Margaret Rose. "That's the very first time she's spoken since we got her here!"

A weary but rather triumphant Sister Anna was conferring with Sister Patricia and Sister Margaret Rose in the latter's room. She could not help feeling that her evening's work had been a job well done. But there were still problems to overcome.

"Yanni's lab report indicates that she was injected with heavy doses of Prolixin. That makes for confusion—especially with the residue of the other drugs in her system—and extreme weakness, as you know," Pat reported.

Sister Margaret Rose nodded emphatically in agreement. "She's very weak. She wanted to go to the bathroom and she fell right over when I tried to help her stand up. It was a good thing Pat was standing by," she added.

"Prolixin—" Sister Anna considered the problem. "That means a week—maybe two—before she can get about by herself."

"She can't go to the safe house like this," said Pat. "We'll have to take her where she can having nursing care. What about the priory?"

"I didn't want to involve any more sisters," said Sister Anna weakly, "It's so risky for all our works."

"But we can't keep her here," said Sister Margaret Rose.

"Sooner or later they're going to search the hospital," said Pat, "and Sister Kathleen Keating at the priory has always been willing to help in a pinch." What kind of pinch, it was just as well Sister Anna did not know, she thought to herself. Ever since Thomas Merton had roused them, cloistered nuns had been advocates of the poor and oppressed, and fearless in their opposition to war. The powerless of Washington knew they had friends in the nuns who lived, apparently isolated from the world, in the walled convent on a hilltop in the far northeast section of the city.

"We *could* transfer her to one of the reserved rooms," said Sister Anna slowly, "and take her out dressed in one of their habits tomorrow."

"It's tricky, but we'll have to risk it," said Sister Patricia, getting up. "You get her down there in a wheelchair and I'll make the arrangements with Sister Kathleen. I'll have to call off the other people, too."


Miss Babb, night supervisor of surgery, was very busy. There was a new colostomy in number 16, a gallbladder in 4, and in 20, a four-bed room, a Mexican construction worker had emerged from anesthesia to discover that he had lost a hand. She was too busy to have more than a mild interest in the comings and goings during the night in number 23, one of the small rooms at the end of the corridor reserved for nuns. She noted Sister Patricia and Sister Anna herself. A nun in one of the old habits, too. A strange one. Probably the superior or companion of the one who had been brought in for observation. It was only much later that she remembered she hadn't seen a doctor.


Inside 23 Celia lay quiet. Pat had administered the shot of cholinesterase that Sister Anna had said was indicated by the blood analysis. "It inhibits the action of the Prolixin on the nerves and muscles," she had said. "I gave her one before we took her from the room and it seems to be acting quickly. That's one good thing about it. But it should only be used by a trained anesthetist. We could get a bad reaction any minute, because we don't know how much they used, or how often, or whether we're using the right amount of the other . . . oh, Sister, it's such a risk."

"It is, but we have to take it," Pat answered. "I'll be careful."

Sister Linda slipped in quietly and smiled at Celia Mann.

Celia's eyes opened wide for the first time.

"What are *you* doing here?" she asked faintly. It was her first full question.

"Sister Helen and I got your message, Celia," said Sister Linda matter-of-factly. She continued talking, explaining what had happened step by step. Pat kept her hand on Celia's pulse and observed her respiration while Sister Linda talked. When she judged that the pulse was nearing normal, she nodded briefly at Sister Linda, who rose.

"I'll have to go so as not to arouse more suspicion than necessary."

Celia Mann clutched at her hand. "Don't go, don't leave me here. Take me with you," she said fearfully. "I'm afraid here."

"We know," said the old woman calmly, "and Patricia is going to get you out. But you will have to help. First, though, we have to know who it is you're afraid of."

"That doctor. And those guards of Adam's. They were the ones . . . the ones . . ." She faltered and shook her head.

"The ones who injected you?"

She nodded.

"Does your husband know about this? Is he part of it?"

Celia nodded again. "I think so." Her voice was a faint whisper. Patricia and Sister Linda looked at each other. So what they had surmised was true. Sister Linda bent and kissed Celia on the forehead. Then she slipped out of the room, her assignment finished.


Sister Anna herself came to take the emergency patient on second-floor surgical down for discharge. The daytime supervisor was in no way surprised. Babb had filled her in when she came on duty and she had glanced at the chart, which had been hastily and sketchily completed in a strange hand. Patient, Sister Rose of Lima, OSB—no last name, just like the old days. Severe and sudden pain indicating an inflamed appendix. Evidently a false alarm. Temperature down. White count okay. Sister Patricia Black acting as private-duty nurse.

Mrs. Norris was an old-fashioned Catholic. She wished nuns were still the way they had been when she was young. Not that she ever wanted to be one. God forbid! But she had had a romantic interest in them then. She remembered her grade school teachers. There was an aura of mystery about them as they brushed by with their folds of skirt trailing the floor and long silk veils floating. One could imagine all sorts of interesting stories as to who they really were and why they had escaped to—or perhaps even run away to—the convent. But today! Those short skirts and scraps of veil, more like rags than anything, made them look like a bunch of old maids. Which they were, in fact. But cloistered nuns were different. They kept to the old ways. Her Catholic newspaper said that vocations to the cloistered orders were increasing even as vocations to the active orders had almost come to a standstill. Mrs. Norris thought it no wonder.

She watched with curiosity as Sister Anna emerged from 23, wheeling the patient carefully and keeping up a steady murmur of reassuring conversation as she did so.

"If the pain recurs, Sister, I've told Sister Kathleen to bring you right back to us. None of that nonsense now of suffering silently and not complaining. Pain is nature's way of telling us that we must pay attention to our bodies—"

Mrs. Norris eyed the nun in the wheelchair approvingly. She was covered head to foot in a simple black habit and black veil. Her face, banded by the white coif, looked young. But she did look sick. Her face was very pale and her eyes behind the standard steel-rimmed, slightly tinted glasses were half-closed. She had probably let things go too long, just the way Sister Anna said. A saintly young nun suffering silently. Mrs. Norris felt quite inspired.

Inside the elevator Sister Anna's voice changed. "So far, so good," she said. She pressed the button for the basement. "We're taking you out through social services," she said. "They're used to seeing the priory van there. And that is where our charity and welfare patients check out."

The van labeled "St. Benet's Priory" carrying the departing patient and the companion who had come to fetch her drew away from the entrance marked with a small sign, "Social Services," just as a huge television truck drew up before the plate-glass front entrance of St. Simeon's.

McGregor did not need the police chief's agitated call to alert him to the fact that the news had broken. He already knew it.

"The shit has hit the fan," the chief had said, almost shouting. "All hell has broken loose at the hospital. You better get over here. We've got a mob scene to deal with."

"I know. I'm on my way. Hold the fort," said McGregor, and put down the receiver. He looked down the drive and gloomily surveyed the milling crowd of reporters and cameramen being held at bay at the gates of the vice-president's residence by two of his men. They had started arriving over an hour ago. The report from the men inside the hospital was that one of the "Gray Ladies" on duty the night before was the mother of one of the younger reporters at television station WTEC. Her suspicions had been aroused by the unusual coming and goings from Sister Anna's office. She had seen Vice-President Mann and guessed that all was not well with his wife. On the pretense of delivering flowers to a patient, she had gone to the VIP floor, looking for any kind of telltale sign she could discover. There seemed nothing amiss at the nurses' station. The door to Mrs. Mann's room was tightly closed and the two guards were in position. But as she boarded the elevator to return to the first floor, a large disgruntled-looking maid with a load of linen got on with her.

"There seems to be a lot of commotion downstairs. The police are there and everything." She had offered the conversational gambit tentatively, uncertain whether she would get any reply from the woman with the stolid, blank face. She had found unwittingly a sympathetic ear.

"They here all the time," said the maid. "Seems like they're always blaming folks in this here hospital, saying somebody took this, somebody took that. They saying now that somebody stole somethin' out of that Mrs. Mann's room. How they do that, I'd like to know, with them two men sittin' outside the door and nobody allowed in?"

It was enough to confirm the Gray Lady's suspicions. As soon as she got home, she called her son. There was something strange going on in connection with Mrs. Mann. Something was happening or had happened and the hospital's story did not seem to hang together. The son called his producer and the producer was impressed enough to suggest that the young reporter stake out the hospital. The latter had spent a long and shivery night, watching those who came and went, first at the front door, then at the back. Then, just after dawn, he struck pay dirt. The injured cleaning man, who had spent an uncomfortable night on a cot in a cubicle off the emergency room, emerged. His head was freshly bandaged and he had been advised to go home and spend the day in bed. Since he had been unconscious the night before, when Chief Potter

and Alec McGregor had first heard of him, no one had thought to remind him of the importance of secrecy. He responded to the reporter's
questions about Mrs. Mann with a simple statement which, to the reporter, was electrifying. "She gone, they say."

"Gone! Gone where?" the reporter exclaimed.

"Don't know. I jus' heard 'em talkin' about it. You better ask them
inside. I got a splittin' headache, man," the other replied indifferently.

It was enough. The reporter called the station for reinforcements and
the night hospital workers were interrogated relentlessly, one by one, as
they straggled out. A hint emerged here, a fact there. When they had
pooled their information, there seemed enough to warrant a team of
reporters being sent to Police Headquarters. Chief Potter had remained
incommunicado, feeling the pressure increasingly through the long
morning. He had finally resorted to going to the hospital with the object
of forcing Sister Anna and Dr. Grant to make a statement. He brushed
by the reporters, muttering unhappily in answer to their questions, "I
have no statement at this time."

Again it was enough. Whatever the facts, WTEC had enough for a
cautiously ventured scoop. Sheila McCrady led off on the noon news.

"WTEC has learned today that there is a strong rumor, yet to be confirmed, that Mrs. John Mann, wife of the vice-president, has been spirited away from her hospital room, destination unknown. There are
some disturbing implications of foul play. Mrs. Mann was hospitalized
only recently. Her doctor, Dr. Elwood Grant, alleged that Mrs. Mann
was suffering from addiction to drugs brought on by overuse of prescriptions for a nervous condition. WTEC is monitoring this story and
will bring you details as soon as possible."

McGregor switched off the set wearily. Twelve hours sooner than he
had hoped—twelve hours that they had needed badly. Lord, a hospital
was nothing but a sieve when it came to security. Increasingly, he was
aware of the ease with which people came and went, the multiplication
of the activities of those who served within the hospital and those who
serviced it. Without a break of some sort, it was going to take a long
time to track all the threads to their sources.

Well, maybe it was just as well. At least they could search the hospital
thoroughly now—something they could not do before. And interrogate
all the help—go over everything with a fine-tooth comb. The trail was
cold—but perhaps not too cold.

He went to tell Vice-President Mann, now virtually a prisoner in the
residence, that he had better accompany him to the hospital. Somebody

was going to have to make a statement and it seemed to McGregor that it should be the hospital authorities. Then the vice-president could take questions if he had to. But it would be better if they could protect him a little while longer.

There was pandemonium in the parking lot in front of the hospital entrance. Camera crews were jockeying for position; press photographers were squeezing and pushing their way between them; reporters with notebooks were crowded against the sawhorses that had been hastily erected as a barrier. The police and two Secret Service men were doing their best to hold them back, but as the car bringing Vice-President Mann and Alec McGregor drew up, the crowd of men and women bearing minicams on their shoulders or carrying recorders and microphones broke through the barriers and surrounded the car, shouting questions, beating on the window to attract the vice-president's attention. The cacophony of voices was deafening, but a few of the questions, some of them brutal, came through the general noise. "Is your wife dying?" . . . "Has she been taken to a mental hospital?" . . . "Do you think your wife has been kidnapped?"

McGregor held his charge within the car until a path could be cleared. Then he hustled him out past the waiting reporters, who kept up the barrage of questions as they passed. Sam Drottman brought up the rear, shouting angrily at the press, "Get back! Get back! Let the man through!"

They had barely reached the door when Dr. Elwood Grant, escorted by Chief Potter, came out. The chief looked levelly at McGregor.

"The doctor's going to make a statement," he said. "We can't wait any longer. They're going wild." He jerked his head at the screaming press people, who had now been pushed back behind the barriers again. "Get the vice-president inside," he said. "It's better that way."

Dr. Grant's face was pale and the paper he held in his hand shook and rustled like something with a life of its own. He had never thought it would come to this. In his own mind, he was sure that Sauro had taken things into his own hands after all. Getting Mrs. Mann out of the hospital would have had to be done from the inside. He was certain of that. The one shred of comfort he found in the situation was that the uproar might distract attention from his and Sauro's own operation. He was fairly sure that he and his aides had covered their tracks effectively, but they had had to improvise so hurriedly that he needed time to go back over each step.

Chief Potter had borrowed a bullhorn from one of his officers. He was bellowing through it, but his words were surprisingly courteous.

"Ladies and gentlemen, ladies and gentlemen, quiet, please! Quiet, please! As soon as you are in order Dr. Grant will have a statement. I said, Dr. Grant will have a statement. Ladies and gentlemen. Ladies and gentlemen, quiet, please! Quiet, please!"

They gradually quieted down and Chief Potter supervised the hospital public relations man as he set up a small platform and brought forward a battery-powered microphone. Dr. Grant mounted the little platform and, in the sudden hush, began to read his statement.

"Ladies and gentlemen of the media. It is my sad duty as representative of the staff of St. Simeon's Hospital to tell you that Mrs. John Mann, wife of the vice-president, who was hospitalized here two days ago, has been kidnapped from the hospital by persons unknown. As far as we can determine, she was taken sometime between six and seven o'clock last evening. It was the quiet, after-supper time in the hospital and because her private-duty nurse was drugged, again by persons unknown, her disappearance was not discovered for several hours. We have withheld this statement until now at the request of the police and the Secret Service, who had hoped to safeguard Mrs. Mann's life by making it possible for the kidnappers to contact us or the vice-president. There had been no contact and the FBI is now at work on the case. That is all I can say at the present time." He stepped down hastily and made for the hospital entrance. Chief Potter followed and uniformed policemen fell in on either side as he did so. The clamor broke out again, the high, metallic, familiar voice of Sheila McCrady soaring over the others.

"But what about the rumors, Doctor? What makes you think she was kidnapped?"

Inside the foyer, Sam Drottman heard that. There was no help for it. John Mann was going to have to hold a press conference as soon as they could put one together. The sympathetic mood of the press of only a few short hours ago had disappeared. They were raging now, fighting each other for information, fighting for "the right to know," which, he thought sourly, really meant fighting for their jobs.

# PART
# 3

# . 18 .

SOMEWHERE a rooster was crowing. The rough pillowslip against her cheek smelled of fresh lavender. And from somewhere nearby came another teasing scent—lemon soap? She ached with an overwhelming fatigue but felt wrapped in comfort and peace.

Celia opened her eyes to a small white room where early sunlight streaked the floor. On a chair near the foot of the bed sat a nun in a long veil and a black robe who was writing away busily on a yellow legal pad. Celia studied her. A nun in the old-style habit but not one Celia recognized. There was no white coif around the face under the veil. The only touch of white was that of a folded kerchief around the neck. The robe was belted with a tie of its same material rather than a cincture, and no rosary dangled from it. Celia's glance, traveling downward, rested on the nun's rather shabby Nikes.

A legal pad and Nikes! The queer illogic of a dream. Celia accepted it as people do in the time just before waking when they know they are dreaming but are not yet ready to enter the day.

"Good morning," said the nun.

"Good morning," said Celia.

"I thought I'd just scratch out a bit of this while I waited for you to wake up," said the nun, lifting the legal pad slightly.

"Oh," said Celia politely, "what is it?"

"A paper on Thomas Merton for the Conference of the Cloistered next month," said the nun, adding suddenly, "I think I've just thought of a title—*The Inner Room in the Demented Inn.*"

"I see," said Celia sleepily.

The nun's laugh rang out. She put aside the pad and got up to stand beside Celia.

"No, you don't see, Mrs. Mann—and why should you? You probably

**225**

think you're hallucinating. Do you know where you are?"

Celia shook her head.

"This is the Priory of St. Benet. You're in the infirmary and I'm Sister Kathleen Keating, president of the community here. You've been asleep ever since Sister Gertrude brought you here yesterday. I've been waiting here for you to wake up because I wanted you to know how welcome you are." She looked at Celia a little anxiously. "Are you fully awake now?"

Celia nodded. "I was before," she said, "but I wasn't sure. It was your shoes," she added, feeling a little cross. Surely it was unusual to wear running shoes with a habit. Anyone might find it strange.

"My shoes?" said Sister Kathleen, looking down. Then she laughed again. She had an easy, infectious laugh, and Celia found herself smiling in response. "My running shoes, you mean? I thought I'd take my run after Prime so I put them on. I try to run every day. When you live the confined life of the cloister you really have to work at being healthy. I see I'd better explain things before Gertrude comes in with your breakfast."

By the time Sister Gertrude, a tall lean young nun, arrived carrying a breakfast tray, Celia was quite prepared for the sight of jeans and boots under the habit, which was shorter on the younger nun than it was on Sister Kathleen. She knew that Sister Gertrude would doff her habit and go out to work in the garden in T-shirt and jeans as soon as she had sung the hour with the other sisters.

The Benectines of St. Benet's had arrived at a happy compromise between *aggiornamento*—the word Pope John XXIII had used for the updating of the church—and the desire to conform to the fifteen centuries of tradition that distinguished their order. "When we do our individual work, whatever it is, we dress for it," explained Sister Kathleen; "when we are a community functioning as one we put on our choir robes." They had designed both the circular robe, which zipped up the front and fell in deep folds over whatever else they were wearing, and the veil, which banded the forehead and fell around the face when held in place with an elastic cord. "Then a nice crisp kerchief around the neck, a belt at the waist—and in two minutes flat, we look like our foremothers."

"You do," agreed Celia wonderingly.

Sister Kathleen turned serious. "When you get out of bed—and we don't want you to do that for a while yet—it would be a good idea for you to wear one, too. For the time being, you're Sister Rose of Lima, here for health reasons from our sister foundation in Pennsylvania. That's the name in the hospital files and the name Sister Gertrude was given. *Only I* know that you are not. You won't be questioned. We practice silence here—and you are supposed to be here for a complete rest."

"Sister Rose of Lima—" Celia nodded.

And then Sister Kathleen had called Sister Gertrude.

"Sister Gertrude is part infirmarian, part gardener," said Sister Kathleen. "She's a wonder with herbs and health foods, and she purées raw vegetables with all sorts of the right vitamins in them. She'll have your system back to normal in no time. She has a wonderful concoction she calls a stress formula that's full of brewer's yeast and orange juice and heaven-knows-what. She makes me drink it after I run. I'm her guinea pig." She smiled affectionately at Gertrude, waved to Celia, and was gone.

Gertrude made Celia comfortable, put the tray on her lap, and said she'd be back right after office. She went out, leaving the door ajar.

In a few minutes Celia heard the pure thin rise and fall of the chant in the distance. The psalms of Prime. The nuns of St. Benet's were singing the morning Divine Office.

> The-fears-of-my-heart-are-*mul*tiplied/
>   Deliver-me-from-my-ne*cess*ities . . .
> See-mine-enemies-how-*many*-they-*are*/
>   They-hate-me-with-an-*un*just-*hat*red . . .
> Preserve-my-life-and-de*liver-me*/
>   Let-not-my-trust-in-thee-be-*put*-to-*shame* . . .

Fifteen centuries, thought Celia, and ate her breakfast.

All through that week she slept and ate, slept and ate. Toward the end of the week she dressed and, feeling a little foolish, covered herself with the habit to walk morning and evening around the grounds with Sister Kathleen. She marveled at the little world the nuns had made on that hilltop surrounded on all sides by the standard subdivisions in northeast Washington.

The priory was a white frame, V-shaped building. At the angle of the V was the chapel; in one wing were the nuns' rooms or cells, in the other the visitors' parlors and rooms for retreatants. Behind the priory bordered paths led to a weaving shed, a small pottery, the "printery" and a garage where tiny Sister Jean—"a whiz of a mechanic"—tended the convent cars and took in neighborhood lawn mowers and leaf-blowers for repair. There was a chicken yard, a large vegetable garden, and an orchard of dwarf apple and pear trees with beehives in a neat row.

They stood near the hen house. Below them they could see the stream of cars bearing people homeward through the rush-hour traffic, but on the priory hill it was very quiet. They could hear the faint homely sounds—the cluckings and stirrings—of the fowl settling down for the night.

"What is it like to be a contemplative, Kathleen," asked Celia, "now, I mean, in this century? I know the old explanation."

Sister Kathleen smiled. "I think about that every day. I redefine our task every day. But right now I think it amounts to this: we are the world's memory, never meant to forget the source of all being, from whom or which we came and to whom we shall return. We call it God. Each day we hold the world and all its creatures up before the Lord in praise and petition."

She stared down at the cars moving and stopping, weaving in and out, but Celia knew she did not see them.

"In this century? In this *terrible* century you mean, I think—but it is not much more terrible than any other, Celia, except that it may be the last. Well, in this century we have come to see that we have to know the world in its pain—in all its pain—and all its wonder, too. We have to know, to *contemplate* that which we bring before Him. So we have to know humankind, too—the humankind we are to believe created in His image. We have to find the traces in the deformed image and the one half-formed, in the shattered, broken image and, yes, the reverse image which is evil—and hold them up, too."

"I see," said Celia, a little stunned, "I think I see."

"Do you?" said the nun. "When I say it, it sounds to me like a lot of meaningless words. And yet I stake my life on it—on its reality."

"We used to have goats for milk and meat," said Sister Kathleen, resuming their walk, "but when the neighborhood grew up around us they were zoned out of existence. I still think it unfair. They were nice, clean, quiet goats."

It is a quiet, lovely world, thought Celia.

But the guardhouse at the gate and the guard patrolling the perimeter with the savage-looking Dobermans were reminders that St. Benet's was an oasis in a world made desertlike by the rising tides of barbarism.

\* \* \*

"I wish I could stay," said Celia on her last night. They were sitting in the library after vespers watching the sun set.

"You think so now because you aren't quite ready yet for the struggle out there," said Kathleen, "but if you did stay you would find a different kind of struggle here—an interior struggle just as perilous, just as wearing. Only those who are called to the life here—really called—can cope. It is not a place of escape. That was what killed cloistered life in the old days. The cloister was used as a retreat from life for the weak and the wounded and the afraid. St. Teresa was right, you know. The contemplative life is for the brave and the strong and, of those, only those few chosen by God. The others we heal as best we can and send them forth again."

Celia was reminded of something. "What were you writing, that first day," she asked curiously, "about a 'demented inn'?"

"Oh, that." Sister Kathleen was thoughtful. "That's what Merton called the world. It is full of horrors; it always has been. I can't quote him exactly but it goes like this—'Into this demented inn, in which there was absolutely no room for him at all, Christ came uninvited. . . . Christ is present in this world. He is mysteriously present in those for whom there seems to be nothing but the world at its worst.' You see, He did not live one time only—or suffer one time only. He lives and suffers now. We are both Christ praying and the place he prays. We are the inner room in the demented inn. He brings his agony here. Our peace is at its core."

She saw Celia's stricken face and reached across the table to take her hand.

"Oh, don't look like that, Celia. It is a real peace—and sometimes a joy. If you are ever called to it, you will be specially welcome. It's been good to have you here."

She got up and turned on a light, dispelling the early twilight. "I'm going to share your supper tonight. Sister Gertrude is preparing something special. Let's hope it isn't vegetable fritters!"


Sister Patricia came for her in the morning.

"A car is waiting," she said, "You must leave now, while the sisters are at Prime. I will stay behind, ostensibly for a day's retreat. That way there will be the same number here if anyone is watching, and the same number in the car.

She gave Celia an appraising look. "Better put a scarf on to hide that red hair."

Feeling a curious numbing reluctance Celia obeyed and took up her things. I'm not ready for this, she thought. I don't think I can go out and face whatever is coming.

"But, Pat, where am I going?" she asked, her voice shaking a little, "And who is taking me?"

Pat took her by the elbow and led her out the door and down the corridor. "You're going to a safe place, Celia. Trust me. The man taking you is called Frank. Better not to ask his last name. He's a clergyman, I think, but I don't know for sure. He has worked with us in the Sanctuary movement ever since the days when the immigration service began deporting refugees from El Salvador. He is good. He is trustworthy, and he is working with us to help you."

At the door of the monastery she gave Celia's shoulder an admonitory pat. "Here you go," she said, "get into the car quickly."

As Celia slid into the front seat of the waiting car her social training of years asserted itself. "How do you do," she said to the pleasant-looking man behind the wheel, "I'm Celia Mann."

"No," he answered, and handed her a small wallet, "now you are Marguerite Bowman. Better look over your credentials. Everything's there but a passport and you'll soon have that." He slid the car into gear and turned down the drive.

Automatically Celia inspected the wallet. A driver's license with a blurry picture of someone vaguely like herself. An American Express card. Charge cards for local Washington stores—Garfinckel's, Hecht's, Woodward and Lothrop. Even—she had a wild urge to laugh—a library card. All with the address of an apartment building on 16th Street. Was that where they were going? She looked at Frank. He was driving at deliberate speed, staring straight ahead.

"I guess I should say thank you," she said. Then thinking that ungracious, she added hastily, "I do thank you. It's awfully good of you to spend your time helping me—and people like me."

"Not really," said Frank, "it's what I have been called to do. I found that out way back when I joined CALCAV."

"CALCAV?" Celia echoed uncertainly.

"Clergy and Laymen Concerned Against Vietnam," said Frank.

Vietnam, thought Celia. That's so long ago. She sat staring out the window in silence.

He took her not to the apartment building of her new address but to a hidden apartment in Leora García-Smith's home. It was a huge old place, just off upper 16th Street in the area above the Spanish Embassy. The little car stopped openly in the short circular driveway and Frank escorted Celia to the entrance with no appearance of hurry. They went through a series of imposing high-ceilinged rooms. There were floor-to-ceiling windows and Celia could see, beyond the formal dining room, a terrace and a sheltered garden glowing with tulips, potted geraniums and bearded iris. Frank led her down some narrow steps to the basement, into the old marble-floored laundry and past a wine cellar. There was a storage wall for canned goods. Frank stepped on a lever, and one section of the wall swung open to reveal the apartment behind it.

Celia sank into one of the vinyl-covered chairs in the small living room, feeling lost and not very welcome. All of a sudden she was very tired. Leora García-Smith came in carrying a tray. She was a tall, bony, blond woman, not at all Latin in appearance. She acknowledged Frank's introduction rather coldly and immediately made it clear that she was not what Celia might think.

"*No soy Angla*," she said proudly, and translated immediately and rather disdainfully, "I am not Anglo—I am Mexican-born but it is useful that I look like my mother's people."

"Leora calls herself *Mrs.* García-Smith because it is also useful," Frank explained. "It lets people think she is Mexican only by marriage. García was her father's name, Smith her mother's." Celia was to learn that Leora García-Smith took bitter amusement from the fact that the same people who were frightened by the tide of Latins flooding over their border had no qualms at all about using their services.

"How charming, Leora," she would quote the friends she had made at the Sulgrave Club and the Washington Club. "Really, you have done wonders. Wherever did you get the people to do this work? It's so hard to find good workmen nowadays." And Leora would explain how she had just happened to find this little carpenter, or that little plumber, and yes, she thought he just might do things for her friends.

"You have to pay him in cash, of course," she would say, "because of the taxes, you know."

She also found maids for those friends who were happy with maids who did not want any Social Security payments made or records kept. "They think it's such a nice economy really," she said to Celia, biting off the words.

Ostensibly, as far as social Washington was concerned, Leora García-Smith was one of the colony of wealthy Latin Americans who, for various reasons, had made the capital their home. They were ex-diplomats who preferred Washington to their home countries and, like "Bill" Martínez-Schwenger, knew how to use its resources to increase their wealth; they were exiles from Cuba or other countries where the rich and upper middle classes were threatened; they were of mixed Latin and American ancestry. Their wealth and presumed status gave them easy entrée into Washington's fluid and undiscriminating social circles.

Unlike most of the others, however, Leora García-Smith quietly associated herself with the poor Latin Americans who were less welcome. She was known to them as a protector of illegal aliens, as someone who was of aid to the Sanctuary movement resisting the deportation of those who had fled the Central American upheaval. She had her own agenda. She lived for the day when she could avenge her father, who, she felt, had been deprived of his right to lead Mexico by the strongmen in the PRI, Mexico's dominant party. Insofar as The People's goals coincided with hers, she was one of them.

Frank visited Celia each day that she was there. At first she was puzzled by his gentle probing. Then she began to understand that he thought her finding out about Johnny and what Johnny was willing to let others do to her had been a terrible shock.

What Celia really felt, however, was not shock but rather something more like relief. After uncertainty, she knew. She did not suspect and wonder as she had for so long. In a strange way she felt that she finally understood Johnny; that his feeling for her had turned to dislike she had found hard to bear, but she saw now that there was a reason for that dislike. She had been a danger because of her unwillingness to recognize that he was not the selfless idealist of her youth's dreams, that he was a man seeking power and doing what he thought he had to do to achieve it. And Johnny had resented the knowledge that she expected more than he was able to give and the feeling that she was calling him to account.

As her mind cleared in the quiet of Leora's hidden apartment, she realized that Johnny's love had lessened because she had separated herself from him by questioning him, by ceasing to believe that what he did was right just because it was he who did it. What she had failed to understand was that Johnny loved, in the only way he could love, those he saw as parts of himself.

Each morning Frank sat opposite her, tall and solid in his brown suit, his hands on his knees. Celia noted the hands absently as she talked, trying to explain herself to him and to reassure him about the way she felt. The hands went with Frank, she thought—white, indoor hands with a fine sprinkling of pale hair and short spatulate fingers. Frank was watching her earnestly, his hazel eyes behind the gold-rimmed glasses fixed on hers, solicitous. And uncomprehending.

"Don't you see, Frank," she said earnestly, "I *understand* Johnny even though I know he's wrong. Johnny thinks in terms of personal loyalties. It's almost like a clan mentality, you see. It's the world he comes from. You help people and they help you. You choose sides and you stick to your family and your friends and your party—no matter what. In politics it is like that, I think. It mostly works like that and that's why Johnny was so good at it. People like Johnny don't think in abstractions."

But, looking at him, she knew he didn't see. Frank's face, like his hands, belonged to the indoors. It was broad, smooth and pale under the thinning brown hair with only a slight darkening at the angle of the jaw and the tip of the round, smooth chin to indicate a beard. If he had a beard, she thought inconsequentially, it would have to be a small Van-dyke. It was a face that had shown patience and interest through thousands of committee meetings, hundred of counseling sessions. It was the face of a man who lived with abstractions. The poor. The hungry. The dispossessed. Minorities. The Third World. No, Frank would never understand the feudal loyalties of Johnny's world.

"What really bothers me," Celia said, "and what hurts me, is that I am so helpless. Frank, for the last twenty years I have lived among the most powerful people in the world, and yet when I was in danger myself, I couldn't do anything for myself. And strangers"—she put out her hand to stop his quick protest—"strangers had to help me."

Frank reached out and took her hand.

"Everyone has been the recipient of more than he or she deserves," he said. "That is why it is so important for us to answer a call for help when it comes, from wherever it comes. It is our job to stand in readiness."

It was more difficult to explain things to Pat. Pat had been very brusque with her at first. She doesn't like me, thought Celia helplessly as they sat side by side on the sofa in the little apartment, drinking coffee, on the morning after her arrival. She looked at Pat's appraising brown eyes and closed face, at the twisted hands holding the coffee mug, and felt something like dread. She is so fierce, she thought. She demands so much. I never measured up, even in school. She thinks of me as neither hot nor cold, like the lukewarm people Christ spat out.

But little by little, Pat's attitude changed. Like a person who has taken in a wandering, lost puppy and become responsible for it, she began to develop and to show a kind of offhand affection for Celia. Nevertheless she was very direct when Celia repeated to her what she had said about her helplessness to Frank.

"People who help are people who have been helped. They have debts. You were helped because there were some people who believed you were worth the trouble. Now you have to prove that is true by helping yourself. Self-pity is a luxury you can't afford. Others have endangered themselves to help you. Now help yourself."

At Leora's Celia began to assume her new identity—that of Marguerite Bowman, the name on the forged Social Security card and driver's license Frank had brought her. Marguerite Bowman, she was told, was a single office worker from Iowa, one of the thousands in Washington moving from temporary job to temporary job.

She began to summon her strength under Pat's bracing direction and to learn how to help herself. In those first few days, she dressed in the clothes Leora brought her and went on simple errands to the shops on Columbia Road. It was a small triumph of sorts to make a list, go to the Safeway, and return with the right articles and the right change, to have run the gamut of the eyes watching her on the street and from behind the curtains of the windows that she passed. She began to take on the skin of the woman with the red hair, loose cotton skirts and low-cut blouses—the woman whose pale reflection she saw in store windows, the woman who was now herself—Marguerite Bowman.

There was one bad moment when she was in the post office getting a money order. Leora was always sending money orders to friends or relatives in El Paso, in Brownsville, Laredo, Nogales, Miami.

She felt someone looking at her. The sense of eyes fixed on her was as strong as if someone had actually touched her back. When she turned from the window she saw no one behind her. But there was a woman standing at the high desk studying the Zip Code book. She had her back to Celia and she never turned her face. But the yellow linen dress she was wearing had been Celia's favorite shirtdress of two summers back. It was Juanita. Had she recognized Celia's back? She showed no sign—

she did not look up as Celia passed to the door and continued on her way. No, she told herself—Juanita could not have recognized her from the back of her head. Still it was an odd coincidence. She should have realized that Juanita might be anywhere in this part of Washington where the Spanish-speaking made their world.

"Don't worry," said Pat when she told her. "Even if she did know you, she won't tell anyone. Latins are used to taking things without question where Anglos are concerned. And they stay away from the law. They're used to protecting people."

Pat was less comforting about Celia's efforts to come to terms with her husband's part in her hospitalization. It made her frankly irate.

"Celia, that is outrageous nonsense. That man used you for years. When you began to act like a person, he was willing to throw you away like a discarded tool. Don't you realize, Celia, what he was willing to do to you? If he had his way, you would be locked up for the rest of your life! You'd be a nonperson! Forgotten! What kind of man would do that to his wife? Keep asking yourself that question—keep the answer in the front of your mind. Then you will begin to be somebody, Celia Fifield!"

Her words stung Celia and stirred her to a healthy anger. She had felt it start at the scornful tone of Pat's voice. It grew in her after Pat had gone, as she reflected on what the nun had said.

Her past seemed to have been shattered into a thousand shards by Pat's scornful words. She could not see it whole. She could not see Johnny whole.

The images whirled in her mind. Johnny's hand, resting on her knee as they drove from town to town during campaigns. Johnny's hand, large, broad, tanned and strong, with heavy fingers. His blue alligator shirts, the ones he loved for golfing, piled on the dryer. His voice booming back from the microphone as she sat beside him on the podium. Johnny turned and waiting for her at the bottom of the ski run, approving then, and proud. Then Johnny's eyes, watching her with dislike. Johnny walking out of the hospital room without looking back. Sometimes these days she grew so angry, thinking of that, that she shook. Still she knew Pat was not wholly right.

When Pat returned she confronted her. "You say Johnny used me, Pat. But I used him, too. There were a lot of things I could do through Johnny and because of who Johnny was. I helped him and he listened to me. In a way I was his eyes and ears on important matters. He couldn't be informed on everything. Don't you see, that's how marriage works. People can't do everything alone. And Pat," she added, "no matter what you say, I was a person when I worked for and with Johnny. I didn't just start being a person when I began work in the peace movement."

Pat was not inclined to yield.

"Oh, your peace work—" Pat waved her hand, dismissing that too. "It was more wife stuff. The only difference was your sticking to it when he didn't like it."

Celia felt outraged. "My peace work was important enough to land me here, even if it was 'wife stuff,' as you call it. And it was wife stuff that got you out of South America, Pat, whether you like to think so or not!"

Pat's face darkened. "I see it's no use talking to you," she said. She got up and left the room. Let her go, thought Celia, I don't care.

But Pat was back the next morning. Neither of them referred to the day before.

During the night Celia had come to a decision.

"Pat," she said, "I've been thinking a good deal about it. I can't be grateful enough for what you all have done and I know you are right— that I must get out of the country for the time being, at least. But, don't you see, I'm going to have to take charge of my own life sometime. I have to know more than I do now about what's ahead and who it is that is helping me."

Pat looked at her for a moment. Then she nodded. "Yes, I think I see what you mean. And I think you've reached the point where you can begin to be active. The aftermath of a drugged state is prolonged passivity, you know, and we had no way of knowing when that would begin to pass. But you must realize, too, that the less you know the better. I'll tell you what I can."

She stood up. "Let's go outside," she said, "and walk in the garden." Walking to and fro between the beds of tulips and iris she told Celia about The People.

When she came back from South America, Pat said, she could not bear the way things were in her own community or in the country. As a nun who had been imprisoned by the rightists, she found herself something of a celebrity. At first she believed that her story would waken people to the terrible injustices in South America and to the plight of the poor. But, she told Celia bitterly, she found that people were curious, interested in knowing about the torture, but not really moved. They didn't want to hear more or feel any requirement to do more. Oh yes, there were some nuns in her order and others, but a handful only. She wanted to go back, but her superiors would not allow it. She was persona non grata in too many places and she would endanger the missions, they said. Finally, because it was something, at least, she began to help at the Center for the Spanish-Speaking. It was there that she began to try to help undocumented workers and political refugees escaping from the military dictatorships. Ever since the Reagan administration had re-asserted friendly relationships with their governments, they had had to be smuggled into the country.

At the Center Pat met Frank. She really didn't know much about Frank except that he was the connection to The People. And she thought he had organized the new underground railway that now used the routes of those who had helped runaway slaves to save aliens in danger of deportation.

The People was the name for a powerful and effective international network. She knew they had been accused of terrorism, but she did not care. They were on the side of the little people, the wretched, those whom she was dedicated to helping. They—The People—gave help only in the most desperate cases, however. Frank usually decided when to call on them. He cleared it with someone higher up, she thought, but who that was she did not know and she did not care.

"Truthfully, I went to him about you with not much hope. I was surprised that he got the clearance to help you and that he has devoted so much time to it himself. Not that your case wasn't desperate enough—" She looked at Celia and shrugged and her voice faded away. "Maybe they just liked the idea of testing themselves against the power of the government. I don't know." She was quiet, still wondering about it, Celia supposed. Celia felt once again the familiar need to apologize for the undeserved fate that seemed to make her more fortunate than others.

And on a Sunday, only two weeks after she had been spirited out of St. Simeon's Hospital, Celia Mann saw Alec McGregor. At first she didn't recognize him. She was walking up 18th Street, idling a little in the soft air of the clear, warm spring afternoon.

She noticed the man in the blue plaid hunting shirt sitting in the battered gray car at one of the pumps in the service station and looked at him idly as she passed. An Irish fisherman's hat with a limp brim and a fish fly stuck in its band partially shaded his face. Until then, she had seen him only in the sober three-piece suits affected by the Secret

Service and at the wheel of the dark shiny Secret Service cars, but something about him seemed familiar. She looked a little more closely, recognized the gray eyes watching her and the lean, fresh-colored Scot's face. She looked away quickly.

Had he seen the leap of recognition in her eyes? She hoped not. But the impulse had been strong for a moment. The impulse to appeal to him for help. He was a decent man, she knew that. He might believe her story and get to someone who could help. But who? There was no one.

She tried not to hurry obviously but she quickened her pace and kept her face averted for fear that Alec might turn her way when he came out of the station. She did not think he had recognized her but she knew that her own flash of recognition had been obvious. His trained mind would turn the matter over and he might come to the conclusion that she was worth checking out. She fought down fear as she realized that this very possibility would make it impossible for her to stay any longer in Washington.

She sensed rather than saw his car pass her, but she was sure of it when she noticed the gray car U-turn. She bolted down a side street and into a pet store, where Sunday shoppers were streaming in and out.

# . 19 .

ALEC MCGREGOR could have seized her then but he didn't. He wasn't quite sure. No, damn it, he *was* sure. He had seen her every day for more than six solid months. He knew her gestures, her walk, the way she held her head. He could not mistake those level blue eyes even disguised as they were by the out-of-character sunglasses with their tilted frames, or the fine sturdy set of her shoulders. It was a funny thing, that last, to find attractive in a woman, but it was one of the first things about her he had noticed.

When he passed her it was clear to him that she was hurrying. The way she kept her head turned was a dead giveaway. She hoped she had not been recognized. But Alec had a feeling that she knew he knew—that she was as sure as he was. Once past the Columbia Road intersection, he made an illegal U-turn and came back. She had disappeared. That didn't worry him. An APB would have turned her up in no time. The police knew the neighborhood like the backs of their hands.

But too many things weren't hanging together. If she had been kidnapped, why was she here in the middle of Washington disguised and alone? Why was she not in touch with her husband or her son or her aunt? Young Peter Mann's voice came back to him: "What have *all of you* done with my mother?" If she was on drugs she might be paranoid—see everyone close to her as an enemy. There was always that possibility. But the boy's voice had rung with conviction. "My mother is not a dope addict." And the woman he had just seen was a woman in control of herself.

He drove home slowly, thinking it over. By the time he reached the apartment he had decided what to do. He picked up the scrambler phone and punched out a private number. Secretary Boise answered almost as soon as it rang.

239

"McGregor," he said. "Are you alone, sir?"

"Yes," answered Boise, "and the phone was swept today."

"I think I've seen a certain lady," Alec said.

There was a pause while Boise digested the information. Then he said, "You let her alone, I gather."

"Yes. I have reasons."

"You'd better come over here right away."

The secretary had not sounded surprised, but if he also knew that Celia Mann was walking free in the city—not being held by ruthless abductors—he had learned it only in the last few days. Alec had been working more or less directly with him in the last two weeks. His superiors had sympathized with his insistence that, since Alec was the one nominally responsible for Celia Mann when she had disappeared, he must be allowed to devote full time to the search. And the secretary had taken full charge. They worked well together. Boise knew, when Alec took the weekend off to go fishing at his sister's place on the Patuxent, that he needed the time to be alone and think.

"It looks bad, Alec, I agree," he had said. "This thing with the doctor is our first clue. And it certainly looks as if violent people are involved—probably psychopaths."

The resident, Dr. Sauro, who had disappeared at the same time as Celia Mann, had been found dead. His body had been found floating in the Potomac, hands tied behind him and a bullet through his head. Not the work of psychopaths, Alec thought. It had all the appearance of an execution. But he saw no point in disagreeing with Boise. He knew Boise thought at the time as he himself did then, that Celia Mann was also dead.

She had called early that morning and taken Clem Boise by surprise.

"Deborah Haines, Clem. It's a nice warm day here in Georgetown. Would you join me for coffee in the garden?"

He hesitated. An invitation from the Haineses. Out of the blue. What was behind it?

"It's been a long time, Deb, and I'd like to. But I'm up to my ears in papers—and not really in the mood for a party."

"It's not a party—it's just me. Crom is gone to the country and I have something I should tell you. It may be important."

Deborah Haines had always struck Clem Boise as a no-nonsense woman. Her flat statements now were characteristic. No flurry of apologies. No beating around the bush. What she thought important was likely to be really important.

"All right. I'll order the car. Should be there in fifteen minutes."

When she had seated him comfortably in the garden, where tulips, lilies and early roses bloomed, and had seen to his coffee, she was true to form in wasting no time.

"You're in charge of the search for Mrs. Mann." It was a statement rather than a question.

He nodded wearily. "And it's going nowhere. Whoever took her seems to have taken her off the face of the earth. I just hope to God she isn't dead—or—" He stopped.

"Or being tortured somewhere by some sociopath," she finished for him. "That's what worries you, isn't it, Clem? God knows we've heard enough about such things. But I wouldn't worry about that if I were you. Maybe she doesn't want to be found. It may be better if she isn't found."

"You're saying that you know something, Deborah?"

She met his inquiry with a level gaze.

"I don't know anything, but I strongly suspect something. I'll tell you what I know and you can see if you come to the same conclusion."

She told him about the conversation in the White House private quarters after the state dinner for the Canadian prime minister. The implication that both her husband and the president found Celia Mann a problem. The suggestion that they would have to find "another way." About her husband's subsequent telephone conversation with Dr. James Fifield and his talk with the president on the morning of Celia Mann's hospitalization.

"Good God," exclaimed Boise, "no wonder she's hiding out, if she is. She can't trust her own brother or her husband—or, for that matter, the president of the United States. For all Celia Mann knows the president was behind what happened whether she was or not." He swore softly. "You're sure of this, Deborah? They said these things right in front of you?" He looked at her. Her face was without expression but her hands were tightly clasped before her on the tabletop.

"Why not? I'm just part of the furniture, Clem, and I've never made waves before. Making waves—isn't that the expression?"

"Why now?"

"Because she's right about nuclear war. The generals—Crom—they're like boys playing with their great big perilous toys." Her voice slowed. "And because they shouldn't have treated her that way. As if she didn't count. As if we're as disposable as—as"—she searched for a comparison—"as disposable as a paper handkerchief."

Time was when she had been a slender, fine-boned, blond New England girl whose pale skin flushed rose at any hint of admiration. And time was that a young congressman from the West, who had been too busy to get married, had entertained the idea of asking her to marry him. But her aunt, and Deborah herself, had seemed to prefer Cromfield Haines, who so clearly had the right credentials, and Clem Boise had taken temporary leave of Congress and had gone off to war in time to serve in the Normandy invasion. He had met and married his Angela, a Red Cross girl from Wyoming. He had been happy enough, as things turned out, and he had taken it for granted that Deborah was, too. Her bleakness now aroused a sense of deep pity in him. He reached across the table and covered her hands with one of his own.

"I'm sorry, Deb," he said. The words hung in the air.

She nodded. "You've got to find her and protect her, Clem."

"We will if we can, Deborah," he replied, "but it's been two weeks. It helps to know that she may be cooperating with whoever got her out of the hospital. But why did you wait so long to tell me what you knew? Time is important in a case like this. She might be anywhere by now—South America or, well, Lord knows where."

"I know," said Deborah Haines. "I know. But forty-six years of being a wife . . . the habits are hard to break, Clem. You don't want to believe what you know." Her voice softened a little. "Clem, Crom wasn't always so . . . so cold-blooded, you know. In the beginning he believed he was serving with no thought of gain. I know he did. But then it was the power, and knowing he had the influence. And now—now"—a note of distaste came into her voice—"money seems to have become so important. I tried to tell myself that it was natural to be concerned about building your estate as you got older. But this—this is different. I can't be part of this," she sighed. "Well, I've done what I had to do." She withdrew her hands and stood up. She looked very old in the late-morning sunlight. "I think I'll go upstairs and lie down now. You know your way out, Clem. And thank you for coming."

Secretary Boise met Alec at the entrance to the office on the third floor of his townhouse. He was unsmiling. "Sit down," he said. "You've got a drink coming. Join me in bourbon and branch?" Alec nodded. Only when he had the drink in hand did the secretary begin to talk. He told McGregor what Deborah Haines had confided to him that morning.

McGregor drew a deep breath. "That explains a lot, sir."

Boise indicated a pile of documents on his desk. "I've been going over these reports ever since I talked to her—looking for threads, looking for tie-ups. I'm not sure there's *anyone* we can trust. I've had some old friends checking into things because I wasn't sure of Mann or the agency. The FBI seems straight under this new man but we can't be sure. There may be some rotten apples left. My men are oldtime muckrakers. They've got long memories and they know where to look." He sighed and put his big hand heavily on the pile of reports. "I tell you, Alec, the trail of greed and corruption runs through these reports in tracks of slime from one person to another.

"First, there are the greedy farmers leasing their fields for marijuana growing. And there are the men in Congress who protect them—paid off in campaign contributions, I suppose—and helped by the president's science adviser—Mann's brother-in-law—who gets his some way, you may be sure. And there is the so-called 'organization' which can market it and move it. Then there are the big commodity movers who don't question the bales of other substances that move up and down the big rivers on barges under legitimate cargoes of coal and wheat. And there are the law firms who represent the businesses that are nothing more than laundries for the 'organization'—law firms with a senator's, even a vice-president's, name on the door—and then there are the big-time lawyers who do their Washington business for them—lawyers important enough to have the ear of the president. And that's only the trail spreading from the marijuana grown in the Mississippi Valley. Small-time stuff in comparison to California and to the other traffic. Supposedly respectable financial institutions from the Bank of Boston on the east coast to the Bank of America on the west were laundering money—or at least some of their people were—for the mob and the drug dealers until we caught up with them. That's history, but cocaine and heroin are still pouring in from Latin America and the Middle East—"

Alec nodded. "I know. The stuff we were trying to track on the border. Synthetic cocaine and counterfeit money—and other things. It's hard to pin it down—but you can feel a connection."

"But the bad thing—the really rotten thing—is that every segment of American society is penetrated by this corruption. And the lady was in the middle—in more ways than one. She and her peaceful friends annoyed the president. There are always people willing to spare the president annoyance." He looked at Alec directly. "And she was a danger to her brother's friends. No reason to think Mann was in direct collusion. He could have just let it happen." He paused. "You're sure you saw her? Where?"

"I'm even more certain of it now, sir. She's disguised, in a way— enough to pass with most people. But I saw her every day for months and I'm trained to look for the things that don't change much—or that are hard to change. It was her eyes I noticed. She was off guard, too. I know she recognized me."

"But if you recognized her, others could, too. I'm glad you didn't take her, though. You didn't know then what you know now. If you brought her in we'd have no choice but to turn her over. There'd be the investiga- tion—who helped her—all that." He sank into thought. "No, there's only one way, McGregor. You've got to find her yourself and take her away before the others do. I'm behind you for what it's worth—but for all general purposes you're on your own. How close do you think the others might be?"

"With the organization, who knows? But I'm pretty sure the police are still floundering. I don't know about the FBI for sure, but they've been pretty straight with us. So has Drug Enforcement. As for Lang- ley—well, again who knows?"

The old man nodded slowly. "But you have the advantage of knowing that she's capable of operating on her own and what she looks like now—or did today. I agree, God knows what that outfit at Langley is doing. They report no progress, but I think they're on to something. Good Lord, every time we get that outfit cleaned up, something even more devious turns up. Or those madmen they employ take matters into their own hands. The FBI is working more responsibly in this. That Robard may turn out to be the ticket after all." He returned to the subject of Alec's investigation. "Yeah, I think you've got to get going. Don't worry about the details here. I'll have you assigned to special duty."

# . 20 .

ALEC MCGREGOR could not have known it when he discussed the possibilities with Secretary Boise, but he was only half right about the Washington police. They were coming closer to the truth about Celia Mann's disappearance than he thought. Every police chief in America's big cities has been forced to make an uneasy truce with crime. He has to set priorities. Doing that means he often lets the small lawbreakers run—within limits—while he concentrates on the big ones. Every once in a while, just to keep things under control, he will ordain a sweep in one area, a crackdown in another. But when a big crime occurs, one that threatens the social fabric and his whole department as well, he knows how to enlist the help of the people on the other side of the line. Chief Potter had no doubt that the disappearance of Celia Mann was a crime of just those proportions. The president of the United States had told him that she wanted her found and found *now*. So Chief Potter gave orders. He sent out the word. None of the petty thievery, none of the fencing, none of the pimping and prostitution, none of the street-corner gambling with which Washington ordinarily lived, would be tolerated any longer. Every person who so much as looked sideways would be pulled in, until Celia Mann was found or the persons who took her apprehended.

His officers fanned out and got in touch with their sources. He himself had a meeting that Monday morning with "Big Daddy" Dawson, whom he had known since childhood. "Big Daddy" operated out of a back room in the near northeast. Nobody was sure what he controlled, but it was generally assumed that he had a connection to whatever unlawful business regularly went on in the metropolitan area.

"It's a crunch, Big Daddy," said the chief. "There can't be no fooling around. We gotta have all the help you can give us."

Big Daddy snorted. "Don't like to see you so set on helpin' them feds, Roosevelt," he said.

Chief Potter winced. Officially, he was known as R. Benjamin Potter. He was a little ashamed of that first name, given to him by his parents as a grateful tribute to a white president. Big Daddy was reminding him he had "known him when" and that he had been brought up by his mama to be respectful to his elders. But he answered patiently, "It's not for them. It'll be better for all of us if we beat them to it."

"Beatin' *them* ain't that hard. Look how we fixed 'em when they tried to trap old Mayor Tillman." Big Daddy laughed richly and people on the sidewalk turned to look at the big old man who seemed strangely happy to be sitting, as he was, in the back of the police car. Big Daddy relished the memory of the confusion of the FBI men who, encouraged by their success with ABSCAM, had used the same methods to entrap local officials. They had fitted an operative with bugging equipment and sent him out to bribe the black mayor of Washington. The mayor had had the FBI man searched and jailed and had denounced the bureau in his most self-righteous and orotund tones, and all Washington had laughed. Big Daddy was still laughing. Big Daddy subsided into chuckles, and then said, "Well, Roosevelt, if I was you, I'd check around on who is helping these Mexes they're always trying to track down, and some of these church people could stand a little lookin' into."

"You got to do better than that, Big Daddy," rejoined the chief.

The big man opened the door and heaved himself painfully out of the car. He was fond of saying to anyone who would listen that his legs weren't what they ought to be. Once out, he half-closed the door and spoke through the narrowed aperture. "Well, you look around. Meantime, I'll see what I can do. Take a day or two." He stood up straight, finished closing the door, and gave the car a friendly slap on the side, as if it were an old horse. The chief watched him lumber off, looking neither to right nor left. People on the crowded sidewalk veered to one side or the other to let him pass. They didn't mess with Big Daddy in his own neighborhood.

Chief Potter nodded to himself. He thought he knew now where to look for Celia Mann.


On the same day out in Langley, Virginia, in the building that had been plainly marked "Central Intelligence Agency" ever since the revulsion against secrecy in the '60s, the director was listening to the report of two men. They were members of a task force that had been established after the hostage crisis in Iran that made it clear that the United States was a helpless giant in the face of international terrorism. The task force had been given added responsibility after Reagan's election and the insistence of his secretary of state and director of intelligence that worldwide terrorism was supported and instigated by the Soviet Union. The agency was to be geared to anticipate acts of terrorism, spot trained terrorists, establish a method for dealing with them, and establish a linkage with the Communists. In the ensuing years, the men assigned to this task had never fully established the linkage, but they had learned a great deal about individual terrorist bands throughout the world.

The director listened to what they had to say. When they finished, he was silent, considering.

"So you think there's no doubt," he asked finally, "this thing has the mark of an operation carried out by this group you call The People?" They both nodded. The more senior of the two answered.

"I don't think there's *any* doubt. There's the number of people who had the opportunity, for one thing. And there's reason for suspicion pointing in several directions. The People always try to cover an operation like that. In this case, it should have been difficult—when they were getting a helpless woman out of a well-guarded hospital room. But it really wasn't. Look at the possibilities, the ones they wanted us to consider, anyway. Somebody sits in a van with the motor running near the back entrance of the hospital during the time frame of the disappearance and drives away again. Nobody gets the license number of the van. There's a new cleaning man who evidently knocked out the regular one, stuffed him in a closet, substituted himself, and later disappeared. He was in Mrs. Mann's room, but he couldn't have taken her because the cleaning cart would never have concealed or contained a woman's body, or even a child's. There was no other way he could've gotten her out of the room. The maids with the food cart were not the regular maids, but they *are* employees of the hospital and frequent substitutes on that floor. Then there's the foreign nun. She would've had to have help. You see, sir, more than one possibility, and one of them, at least, a clear diversionary tactic. That's the mark of The People."

"What's their purpose?" That was the second man's field.

"A power play of some sort. They operate in so many countries and their ties to each other are so loose that it's hard to say just which bunch of guerrillas they're working with this time. But their aim is always to turn the screws on some top politician or businessman. Here, it has to be Vice-President Mann. He still insists that they have made no attempt to get in touch with him. But it's very likely he's playing along with them to keep his wife safe."

"Do we have a line to any of them?" said the director.

The two men looked at each other. This was delicate ground. The fact that the agency had cooperated with subversive foreign groups when it seemed in the interest of the United States to "disestablish" regimes thought unfriendly was a fact of history. That it had quietly resumed doing so, after the purges in the early '70s, was not openly admitted.

"Yes, we do." The senior man was again the speaker. "Some of them are helpful when they think it is in their own interests. They seem to have one general aim, but a lot of differences over actions taken by individual units. Our contacts are working on it."

The director lined up the pencils on his desk in an even row. "I suggest they work harder and faster. We don't have to be too careful about the woman's safety. The important thing is to clear it up. And to keep to ourselves that we are working on this angle." He stood up. The two men went out silently.


The bureau had not been looking there. They had no reason to think that there was a connection. But their first break came in the form of a tip from the gay community.

Lars had gone to Mr. Henry's alone on the Sunday night of the day Alec had seen Celia. It had been days since Yanni was good company. He kept reading things and wanting to talk to Lars about religion! Privately, Lars thought Yanni was cracking up. He confided this gloomily to Anders, the airline steward whom he ran into now and then. Anders was also alone. They took their glasses of ale to a table and sat there talking. Anders listened sympathetically.

"He keeps talking to this nun about joining one of those gay Catholic organizations," said Lars disgustedly, "and then he's all upset about this Mrs. Mann being kidnapped. You'd think there was nothing else in the world news."

"Yeah, I heard some nuns talking about her on the plane a while back," Anders volunteered. He said it more to say something than for any other reason. He saw no real connection to what Lars was saying.

It interested Lars, however. "You did?" he said. "What did they say?" It would be some little scrap to take home to Yanni, something that might arouse his interest.

Anders tried to remember. "I don't know exactly," he said. "Something about her being in the hospital and they were doing the right thing. Maybe they were going to see her. Let's get another ale."

That was all. But the man with earrings and elaborate chains who had been sitting alone at the next table thought it was interesting. He thought he knew somebody who might like to hear that scrap of information, too. He got up and left the bar.

Out of consideration for Adam Mann, Leo Santini had not dispatched his operatives to find Celia. His own operation had been contained and protected, the mouthy young medic disposed of neatly, and his contacts had assured him that Celia was in the hands of The People, where she posed no danger for the moment. The People's interests sometimes coincided with his and he had been content to let things ride. If they had use for her, so be it.

But now they had lost her. It was time to stop the fooling around. He had taken things into his own hands.

Benny, the guard from Sentry Central, stood before a desk in a bleak warehouse office in Lake City. A flexible desk lamp was directed so that the light shone full on his face. The face of the man sitting behind the desk was lost in shadow and the men standing on either side of him were only large menacing shapes. Benny, trying to avoid the light and see his interrogator, was sweating profusely.

"We got no time for more mistakes," said the man behind the desk. "It destroys respect."

"I know, I know, Mr. Santini," said Benny desperately, "but maybe I can help you find the dame."

"You do, maybe we let you off, maybe not. The way we figure it, whoever got her this time must be people she knew, connections maybe Sam or Johnny didn't know too much about. We got to find somebody our enforcers can lean on—somebody who can maybe lead us to the brains of the operation. You were at the house long enough. Now, who like that came to see her?"

The terrified Benny tried to think quickly. The women who came—

he had never sorted them out. He hadn't figured they mattered. Anyway they had been over all this before. Then a thought struck him.

"Well," he said, "there was that fruit hairdresser."

The same day agent Martin Murray waited nervously in the anteroom of the director's office. He was unsure of the step he was taking. It was a very big step. First of all his asking for a D-O would get around and cause suspicion among his fellow agents. They would be sure he was ratting on someone. Director Robard had been determined to clean up procedures and illegal operations when he took over the bureau. The word had gone out. No more ABSCAMs. No more computerization of raw data. No more meetings of advisory boards, secret and closed to the Congress.

Robard had let it be known that anyone in the bureau could have a private appointment with the director if he knew something important but of potential danger to himself or herself. These appointments were known as D-Os (Director-Onlys). They were made on a special telephone and the summons to the director's office made under another pretext. They had been fruitful enough from the director's point of view but not as secret as he thought.

The potential danger to Murray lay in explaining what he had been doing in a gay bar. Theoretically there was no longer any discrimination against gays in government agencies, even in the so-called sensitive ones like the bureau. In recent years the National Security Agency under the pressure of the Supreme Court had had to reinstate a gay who had been dismissed. So had the CIA. There was even speculation when gays got together about the probability that Paul Robard himself was a homosexual.

Murray doubted that. He thought it the kind of thing gays liked to say about prominent people, past and present, in order to reassure themselves. Privately he thought the director that rarest of men, a celibate by preference and totally dedicated to his work. For his own part Murray, like many others, thought it the better part of wisdom to assume a straight and buttoned-down appearance in the workplace. It was only prudent to fit in if one hoped for advancement.

Caution was still warring with courage as he stood there waiting for the director to call him in. But, whatever else he was, Murray was an FBI man. The patriotism and "the bureau-gets-its-man" spirit that had drawn him to the agency were still strong. This matter of Mrs. Mann's disappearance was too important for him to ignore what he had overheard. She had been gone two weeks now—the wife of the vice-president! The agencies of the United States must be the laughingstock of the world.

He wondered once again why Lars's friend Yanni was so upset about Mrs. Mann and why he was mixed up with nuns. Was there a connection? He thought grimly of what Franklin Kameny, dean of Washington's gay activists, was fond of saying: "Whatever the group is, ten percent of them are us." That would go in this case, too, he supposed.

In the director's office at the bureau, Paul Robard was reviewing the latest development with Regan, his top interrogator.

"It ties in then with what our informant told us," the director said in his quiet, colorless voice. "It seems pretty clear that Michal, or Michalowski, was mixed up in it in some way. Our agent identified the man he overheard as this Lars Stedman."

"Yeah," said Regan eagerly, "and he tied them up to the nuns. I said from the beginning that those nuns were up to their necks in it."

The director fixed him with a level gaze. He preferred to take things step by step. Regan subsided reluctantly. He had trouble adjusting to this new man's style. Arrogant old goat, he thought to himself, not for the first time.

"And the organization is somehow mixed up in it too, if the execution of that hospital resident, Sauro, is any indication. The coincidence in the times of Mrs. Mann's disappearance and his killing seems too fortuitous to have been accidental."

"We've got pretty good evidence that that guard group, Sentry Central, has ties to the organization," said Regan.

The director nodded. This was the way he liked to do it. To tick off one thing at a time. "So we have to ask ourselves why a man like Vice-President Mann employed a group like Sentry Central."

Regan was patient now.

"Well, we have that old evidence that the Mann firm was fronting for the organization when they took over legitimate businesses for money-laundering purposes."

"Nothing we could bring them to court for, as I remember it," the director said.

Regan shook his head. "No, but it's probably only the tip of the iceberg. Chances are the organization has a hold on the Manns. They would have seen to that. They don't do business with anyone who can afford to be too independent."

The director nodded. "And they take a long view. According to our information, the connection goes back almost thirty years. A good investment for them. They ended up with a vice-president of the United States as part of the bargain."

Regan stared. "You mean you think Mann is their errand boy?"

Robard shook his head. "Nothing that direct or obvious. But it stands to reason that over the years he smoothed the way for the businesses his family firm represents. It's the normal thing in political life, isn't it? Favors for friends. A tax fix here. A contract there. No laws broken. Just a timely word to the right person in the right place. He might not even have known they were organization errands. He'd be valuable to them, though, and if anything was threatening the connection—" He paused and frowned at Regan. "Doesn't it strike you that whoever took Celia Mann might have been helping her to get away for a good reason? That might be where those nuns come into the picture."

Regan simply stared at the director. He was working it out.

"Might be," he said finally. "What's our move, then?" he asked.

"We'll keep the hospital nuns under surveillance. They might lead us somewhere. Are we watching any of them?"

"Not that I know of," said Regan, "but there's a sister of that order, Sister Patricia Black, who was accused of being in Latin American leftist movements a while back. She was imprisoned and supposedly tortured. Getting her out was hairy, and I think, if I remember it right, the Mann office was involved in that. She's stationed in this country now, but not at the hospital, as far as I know. And, of course, there's strong indication that nuns generally are mixed up in helping illegal aliens."

"If they have her," said the director, "it might be best to let them run with her until we know more about what's going on. Just keep track of it and uncover any connections you can find." Regan felt himself dismissed. He was half-satisfied, but he was beginning to feel the direction his superior was taking.

When he had gone, the director put in a call to Clement Boise. "Robard here, sir," he said when he had been put through. "I didn't want to bring it up in the general meeting, but I thought you'd like to know that we have nothing solid, but we think we know who has—or at least did have—Mrs. Mann. It's possible that it might be in our interest"—he paused and changed his phrasing—"*your* interest," he continued delicately, "to leave it at that for the time being until the big picture clarifies. I hope you understand my thinking." He outlined his theory in a few brief sentences.

There was a short silence at the other end of the line, then a satisfied chuckle. "You know best, Director. I think we can work together on that." Clem Boise hung up. So the director of the FBI had chosen sides, he thought. For the time being at least, he's on my team. The secretary was deeply satisfied.

# . 21 .

JUANITA, still seething with indignation and with her fears aroused, decided to talk to the *monja*, the nun, at the hospital. Not the young one who helped the *pájaros*, the people in flight, but the one with little Spanish who had helped her when she had her operation. That one knew Señora Mann—she had said so.

"*Vieja*," Old One, Manuel had called her! Just after she had bought him the fine jeans with the label, and all because she had said she did not have the money for a new leather jacket as well. It was almost summer. Why did he want a brown one when he already had the fine black one she had given him at Navidad? He had been happy enough with that one then, strutting and preening before the mirror. A cock, that Manuel—a rooster of a man.

"Keep your money, Vieja," he had said. "Soon it will be all you have. I will be in Mexico where the girls are pretty and I will be a soldier with a fine uniform and plenty of money of my own."

In his anger he had said many things. "You will have no job. Your fine Señor Vice-Presidente will in all likelihood be dead—and your fine Señora will be far away where she cannot help you."

At her startled look he had sneered, "Aha, you thought I did not know. But we of the *insurgentes* know many things. We know that La Rubia, the Blonde One, keeps the Señora. She will be *insurencia* for La Rubia and the leaders. Soon, very soon, they will take her away. You, Old One, will not see her again."

When he had slammed out the door, Juanita, shaking and tearful, had opened a Coke and sat down at her fine new chrome-and-red-plastic dinette table to think. In her way Juanita, as the preferred housekeeper of the American *vice-presidente* and an American citizen herself—no mere holder of a green card—was a woman of prominence in the Adams-Morgan district.

254

"She seems to be thoroughly honest and industrious. She owns her condominium free and clear," noted the agent writing up her security clearance. He gave the details of her bank accounts, her hospitalization, her income tax and Social Security. He also made note of the fact that she paid her bills in cash, carried no installment debts, and occasionally took in roomers for extra money.

The agent did not note that these roomers, at least two or three of them, were Juanita's lovers. He was Irish and it did not occur to him that a middle-aged woman like Juanita—sober, hard-working, a regular churchgoer—would have that kind of relationship with such young men. To the Spanish-speaking neighbors and friends he had interviewed it was not worthy of mention. *Claro*—if a woman still vigorous and a young man in his full strength were under one roof, what could one expect? As for Juanita, the roomers filled her maternal and womanly needs. She enjoyed the noise they brought into the house. She liked cooking for them. She liked listening to their boastful man-talk of soccer and fights. Within limits she liked to spend money on them.

José Méndez, the first one, however, had taught her to be careful. She had been younger then, in love with him and bent on keeping him. She had believed him too easily and he had made off with her savings. Now she was more practical and cautious.

That Manuel—he was, like most men, all braggadocio and talk. She had listened but paid little attention to his talk about great things happening soon in Mexico. But she knew that some of the young Mexicans had recently been returning to the country they had made such efforts to leave. And not only Mexicans but others—from El Salvador and Colombia and other countries. Even, it was said, some of the *morenos*, the blacks, had gone. It could be true that a big revolution—something bigger than usual—was about to happen.

But what had that to do with the Señora? That the Señora had taken refuge with La Rubia for reasons of her own Juanita had not questioned. La Rubia was the acknowledged *protectora* of the Spanish community and a personage among the Anglos as well. Still, it was known that she was not to be trifled with. If she demanded repayment for her favors in tasks she assigned—sometimes dangerous ones—it was best to comply if one valued one's own safety or the safety of one's family and friends. If La Rubia was using the Señora for *insurencia*, as Manuel had said, that could be very bad.

Yes, Juanita decided. She must talk to someone safe. The Señora had been good to her. And it would serve Manuel right. *Vieja* indeed!

*    *    *

On Tuesday, when Sister Margaret Rose donned the perky short veil she seldom wore except when she had to deal with the Hispanics—it was useful then, she found—and boarded the bus going up 16th Street, she felt ridiculous. Juanita's warning seemed so—so lurid. But then the whole business was lurid, she reminded herself. As she rode she reviewed the sketchy information Sister Patricia had shared with her and Sister Anna. She must use the names easily and naturally.

She told the stolid brown man who answered the door that she had a message from Sister Patricia for Señora García-Smith. She told Leora, when she appeared, that the message was really for "Miss Bowman—Marguerite." It was about her family, she added.

"It is not regular, Sister," Leora had replied, looking, thought Sister Margaret Rose, somewhat mulish. She held her breath. After a frowning pause Leora said, "Well, very well, but I wish you sisters would observe the rules. You endanger all of us."

"I understand. I really do, Mrs. García-Smith, I really do," said Sister Margaret Rose gratefully.

After a long wait Celia appeared.

"You have news for me—about Peter and Susan? There's nothing wrong, is there?" The anxiety in her eyes made Sister Margaret Rose regret her glib explanation. "Oh no," she said hastily, "but it's a rather long story. Could we go somewhere and sit down?" Her poorly concealed perturbation was now very apparent.

"We could take a little walk," suggested Celia. "It's so nice out." She noted that Pedro, Mrs. Smith's "man," looked disapproving as he let them out, but he did not try to stop them. There must be a reason why Pat took me into the garden when she talked about The People, thought Celia. Even that wasn't really safe with the equipment they had now-adays, she knew, but I am not that important, she thought, and anyway, this is the best I can do. The traffic, continuous on busy 16th Street, was noise cover of a kind.

Sister Margaret Rose was relieved that Celia took Juanita's warning at face value. "She wouldn't have gone to you if she wasn't pretty upset and pretty sure," she said. "She knows what's going on in this neighborhood. She knew I was here, didn't she—or, at least, that Leora had something to do with me?"

"It was the talk of *garantía*, or *insurencia*, as she called it—they do speak such a mixture of Spanish and English, don't they?—that's what worried me most—as if you were a hostage . . ."

"I suppose I am. It explains the trouble they all took. It wasn't for love or the desire to do good, you know . . . Nothing surprises me anymore," Celia added bitterly. She saw the look on Sister Margaret Rose's face and added quickly, "Oh, I don't think Sister Patricia knows. She said herself that she didn't know why The People had bothered to help me." She took Sister Margaret Rose by the hand. "Don't think I don't know what you and Yanni and Sister Anna and all the others did for me. I can never be grateful enough. I was so without hope. And look what you've done just now—endangered yourself for my sake."

Embarrassed and touched, the nun withdrew her hand. She had been trying all afternoon to forget the oath dictated by the strange young man and Pat's words, "The penalty for betrayal is death." It had not seemed real then. It seemed real now. But I am not betraying them, she protested to herself, I am just trying to help Celia.

"What will you do? Juanita said something will happen soon."

Celia remembered Johnny's tape. There had to be a connection.

"I think she's right. I'll pack tonight and get up early and slip out. I was thinking just today that I ought to get out of the country somehow. I'll try to do it as soon as I can—perhaps to Italy. I have a cousin there. If I could get to Aunt Susan she would help me. And maybe I could see Susie," she added wistfully.

Sister Margaret Rose marveled at the change these few short weeks had made in Celia Mann. She was entirely different from the depressed and passive woman the nun had helped into Sister Anna's room. She was capable of making decisions, of planning.

"The best way would be a rental car. They watch the planes and buses. Frank gave me some credit cards, but I would need cash—to use in case of emergency."

"I thought of money," Sister Margaret Rose assured her. "I brought a hundred dollars out of the ready cash in the office."

Celia did not argue or demur. She just said, "Thank you," and, "We'd better get back."

At the door she kissed Sister Margaret Rose, gave her a quick hug, and went in without looking back.

As she packed quickly, putting her few new clothes into the small bag in which Patricia had brought them, Celia realized that the reason she had so easily accepted the warning from Juanita through Sister Margaret Rose was that she had never been at ease with Leora. She had seen little of her in the weeks she had spent in the apartment. Leora saw to Celia's needs and cooperated as was necessary, but she kept to herself when she was not gone from the house, busy about her many social and organizational activities.

Celia found it impossible to like Leora and she was sure that Leora did not like—maybe even hated—her. There was an undertone of bitterness and contempt in Leora's comments and instructions, even though the words in which they were couched were formally correct. Is it because I am one of the despised Anglos, or because I am Johnny's wife? Celia asked herself. She knew from sad experience that simply being the wife of a prominent man sometimes inspired unreasonable dislike. Well, never mind, she thought. Tomorrow morning I will be gone from this place. The apartment was no longer a haven. It was a prison.

At six o'clock the next morning she stood dressed and ready to go, bag in one hand, purse in the other, looking around the apartment to see if all was in order. She wanted to be a good guest even in flight. Then she heard the faint dragging rustle of the concealed door opening.

"And just what do you think you are doing?" Leora's voice was harsh and biting. She stood in the doorway in her dressing gown, her hair still in the rollers she wore at night. Celia froze.

"I thought there was something—*cómo se dice*—phony about that little nun, your friend." Leora advanced into the room and the door swung shut behind her on its silent hinges.

She came toward Celia. She is going to attack me, Celia thought wildly, and hold me by force. How had she known? Movement in this place must be monitored. The intercom! I should have thought of that—the suitcase snapping shut, drawers closing. She said the first thing that came into her head.

"She came to tell me that the Secret Service man did recognize me . . . I told you about him . . . she heard it at the hospital . . . she thinks he knows where I am . . ."

Leora stood close, eyeing her.

"Don't you see, Leora," she said desperately, "I must go. I am a danger to everybody."

Leora stood back. "And where will you go, eh? Wander about the streets? Come now. Let us have some coffee and talk this over. Put down your things and sit down with me like a sensible girl."

There was a forced reasonableness in her voice. She doesn't believe me for a second, Celia realized.

Leora went on talking. "Yes, a little coffee, a croissant, and things will seem much clearer. It is always so." She was edging toward the bedroom.

"Our little guest leaves things very orderly, very neat, I see," the older woman said as if in admiration. She went into the bedroom and opened the closet door. "No, she leaves no traces, a good thing . . ." The intercom was on the bed table. She was turning toward it when Celia dropped bag and purse and rushed. If she could push Leora into the closet . . .

She caught Leora around the neck. She must not cry out . . . I cannot let her cry out! Leora struggled fiercely, throwing her weight back, twisting, clawing at Celia. She caught at Celia's blouse; Celia heard it rip. I am younger, she thought, stronger . . . all that tennis . . . Little by little she maneuvered Leora through the closet door. Then she relaxed her hold on Leora's neck, pulled her around, and put all her strength into a fierce blow to the solar plexus. She watched, half-amazed, as the other woman doubled over, retching. How did I know how to do that? Watching Jim box? Television? Her mind seemed separate, an observer, as she closed and locked the closet door.

She was trembling and shaken. What next? She must disconnect the intercom—in a moment Leora would be screaming and pounding—here and in the kitchen. She pulled at the wires of the bedside instrument with all her remaining strength. They gave way at last. She could hear sounds from the closet. She rushed to the kitchen, closing the bedroom door as she went—another barrier to sound.

The intercom in the kitchen was wall-mounted. How to get it loose? She had seen tools in one of the drawers. Fumbling, she found a screwdriver. No hammer. No matter. She took off her shoe—how many times had she done this?—and used the heel to drive the screwdriver between the intercom and the wall. She pulled the handle of the tool toward her, exerting all the leverage she could. She heard a crack as it gave way. Plastic, she thought. She fished out the wires and cut them with the kitchen scissors.

She looked at the wall clock. Seven-thirty. Time was running out. Pedro was due at eight but he often came early. He would look for Leora. She must not risk running into him. She must give herself time to get as far away as possible. In the adjacent room Leora had set up a steady piercing howl. It was horribly loud in the little apartment. She heard steps on the other side of the false partition. Celia panicked. Her bag and purse were in the bedroom . . . no time to go back . . . she was cut off from the basement entrance . . . the emergency exit hidden by the garden hedge . . .   She clawed at the multiple locks on the back door, gasped with relief as she got it open. She heard the concealed door in the wall swing on its hinges as she fled.

While his mother fought for her survival only a few miles away, Peter Mann, now home on vacation, moved restlessly around his room. He ached for his mother's warm presence in the big, quiet house. He tried not to think of where she might be and was successful most of the time, except in the darkest hours of the night. He missed Susie, too, and her bright, ceaseless chatter. He wished that his Aunt Susan had not taken his little sister to her home out west as soon as school was out, although he knew it was better for Susie to be away from all the publicity and the hullabaloo surrounding their mother's disappearance.

He stared out the window at the topiary elephant, which had been a gift to former vice-president Bush, and the topiary donkey his parents had had planted at its side. Stupid. He thought they were stupid things. Politics made people do stupid things. He had decided that long ago, when he was a very small boy, and nothing had changed his mind since.

He turned away and began rummaging in his desk drawers. What a mess! Yet he was glad that his mother respected his privacy and would not let Juanita straighten them out as she was always wanting to do. Juanita's devotion was sometimes smothering.

His electric pencil sharpener. The battery was run down. He should get another. Rubber bands, paper clips. An old transistor radio. He got that on his tenth birthday, he remembered. Still in its box, the micro-recorder his mother had given him for Christmas. She had remembered his fascination with his father's.

He thought of her pleasure at his enthusiasm over it. "You're a gadget-lover like your father," she had said, laughing. Things were pretty good for a while at Christmas, he thought. He hoped his mother wasn't hurt that he hadn't taken it with him to school. He hadn't wanted to tell her that it would probably get stolen there. She would have been shocked to know how much stealing went on at a good school like Clarke.

He noticed that there was a cassette half-played in the recorder. He knew he hadn't left one. His mother must have been trying it. Automatically he ran the tape back and pressed the "play" button. He heard his father's voice—then another man's. His mother spying on his father!

He felt sick. He got up and closed the door. Then he listened to the words.

"You understand, Mr. Vice-President, that the government involvement in this thing is very closely held." The man's voice was warning, even a little threatening. "Only the director and I are privy to it out there in Virginia. Your staff can't know—not even your wife." He laughed as if Peter's father had made some gesture. "*Our* wives take secrecy for granted, but I have known political wives to be different," he said placatingly, then went on, "Now this is the situation to the south of us . . ."

But his mother *did* know if she had this tape, Peter Mann thought dully. Had that put her in danger? They said men in the CIA would do almost anything—some of them.

What had Bill Cratte said when he was trying to buck him up the other night? "Look, Pete, maybe somebody was doping her." He had said it as if it were just an idea, but maybe Bill had reason to suspect something. Anyway, Bill was the only person in the whole world he could think of to talk to—and he seemed to have gotten over that French business. He was more like he used to be. He's been darned good to me, Peter thought; if it weren't for him, I'd go nuts. Now this thing. A faint hope stirred. Maybe it would help find his mother.

His fingers shook a little as he dialed the hospital number.

They sat in his bedroom that night with the door shut and talked in low tones. Peter had played the tape for Bill with the volume turned very low, and then, at Bill's insistence, played it again.

"It's the CIA all right," Bill whispered. "We've got to talk to somebody about this. We can't talk to your father."

Peter caught the uncertainty in his voice. Did Bill think he didn't get it?

"No, of course not"—he tried to say it matter-of-factly but his voice shook—"don't you think I know he's mixed up in it?"

Bill gripped his shoulder but said nothing for a minute. Then he spoke cautiously. "Paul Robard is a cousin of mine. I found that out a summer ago in Manchester. He would listen to us."

"The director of the FBI is a French Canadian?" Peter's tone was surprised. He spoke out loud.

"Yes he is," began Bill defensively. "What's wrong with"—he broke off—"oh, I see," he said smilingly, "you're thinking about when I was hooked on that oppression stuff. He's not like that. He had me to dinner when I first got here and straightened me out on a lot of things. We've done all right. I see that now. And there's nothing better than being a good American."

"Okay then," said Peter. "But how are we going to do it? Those goons follow me everywhere and I think all the phone lines here are bugged."

"You can be taking the visiting fireman on the FBI tour. I don't think they'd follow you in there. Anyway, Paul can arrange to see us alone. Special deal for the vice-president's son and his guest. You know the drill. I'll call him from a pay phone—just like in the spy movies."

"It's not a joke, Bill. Be sure you aren't followed."

"Sure, I was just trying to . . ."

"Yeah, I know—but I'm not a kid anymore."


Celia walked rapidly, trying not to look hurried or agitated. Her heart was beating wildly. She could feel a pulse throbbing in her neck and she knew that her color was high and her hair disheveled. She must not attract attention, but how could she not? She was without a jacket or purse and her blouse had ripped under one arm in the struggle with Leora. She was afraid to inspect the tear there on the open street. Perhaps if she kept her arm pressed to her side it would not be notice-able. Walk straight ahead with purpose, she told herself a little wildly, remembering Frank's instructions and Pat's. Walk like a person with a definite destination, they had said. Avoid eye contact.

Almost blindly she turned off 16th Street at Columbia Road and, as soon as she could, turned right again. If she remembered correctly she could find her way through the side streets almost to the place where the bridge on Calvert crossed the park and then she would be almost out of the Adams-Morgan district, where The People had so many eyes and ears. They were everywhere, she knew, but she felt in these first moments of panic that she could deal with things better in her own part of town. What *was* my part of town, she corrected herself bitterly. To encounter an old friend and to be recognized would be as dangerous as to meet one of The People.

Her breath was beginning to come more evenly and she slowed her pace. There weren't many people on the street. She passed a few elderly women pulling shopping carts on their way to the Safeway market. An occasional young man or woman hurried past. Office workers off to a late start, she guessed. She did not look directly at them but she felt that they were eyeing her curiously. Did they really? Or was it because she felt so naked with nothing in her hands? Women seldom go about carrying nothing, she thought. They always have their identities in their hand. Perhaps that's why bag ladies are so attached to their bags. If only I had a bag of some kind, if only a sack. She began to look around for something discarded, something she could carry. A few minutes later she spied a crumpled plastic grocery bag stuck in the shrubbery near an apartment entrance. She retrieved it. A few steps onward she picked up two empty coke cans and put them in the bag. If anyone is watching, she told herself, they will think I am just another bag lady. She added to her collection as she went along—a pint carton in one place, several more soft drink cans in another. At a corner by a mailbox she stopped to organize her findings. Put neatly in order and shielded by a discarded advertising flyer that she picked up off the ground, it looked like a normal small load from the corner grocery. She felt immeasurably better and more confident with something in her hands.

It began to rain as she approached Calvert Street, only a fine May mist but it added to her problems. With neither jacket nor raincoat and no umbrella she was more conspicuous than ever. But the rain gave her an excuse to hurry. She half-ran across the bridge over Rock Creek Park, the empty cans clinking as the bag bumped against her side. She dodged into the first shop doorway she came to and stood there looking back down the street as if for an approaching bus. She drew a deep breath and collected her thoughts. She had to get inside somewhere. The streets were too dangerous. She was too visible. And she had to have money. Without it she couldn't even take a bus or make a phone call. She considered the possibilities that had been half-forming in her mind as she walked.

She could go into a store and say that she was the victim of a purse-snatching. No one would be surprised at that on Connecticut Avenue, this near a Metro stop. It would even explain her torn blouse. But that meant talking to the police. And who could she call from a shop? Sister Margaret Rose? By now they would be watching her. Or worse. Yanni? What name could she give to get by Lars?

No, it would have to be the only other alternative she had thought of. She looked at her watch. She had twenty minutes before the late-morning mass at St. Thomas. It was beginning to rain harder. She would have to go quickly to avoid being soaked. She fished the flyer out of her bag, opened it and held it over her head as she set out briskly toward Connecticut Avenue and the church on the other side of it.

By the time she reached it people, mostly elderly, were straggling inside. A few, younger and more affluent-looking, crossed the street coming from the Sheraton Washington Hotel. In the church vestibule Celia felt a sense of sanctuary. It was like coming home. During their first months in Washington she and Johnny and the children had lived in an apartment at the Wardman Towers, once a very fashionable residence. The Eisenhowers had lived there, as had Mrs. Earl Warren and many other distinguished Washingtonians. While she and Johnny were there, this had been their church. Celia had often stopped in for daily mass on her way to a luncheon in town. She looked at the church clock. Still five minutes—time to see if she could make herself more respectable.

In the restroom downstairs she looked at herself critically. Once she had smoothed down her hair and pressed it close to her head she looked better than she had thought. The light blue blouse and dark blue skirt looked something like a costume, and more "ladylike" than most of her Marguerite outfits—especially when she buttoned the high neck of the blouse. The underarm tear was smaller than she had feared. She took up her sack again and went upstairs, more confident of what she was about to do, but her heart was beginning to beat faster once again.

She felt no guilt. She could hear the clear voice of her sixth-grade teacher in catechism class, "Yes, of course, Celia, it is a sin to steal, but, no, it is not a grave sin—perhaps not even a venial sin—when the person who steals is in great need and steals only what she needs. The example you gave—a woman stealing to feed her children—is a good one."

She had no doubt that her need was as great. Her drive now to escape, to stay alive, was almost animal and she was moving as if by instinct.

The church was half-filled. The worshippers—mostly women—were scattered about. The regulars would have gravitated out of habit to their usual places, Celia knew. The two women in look-alike silk jacket dresses a few pews from the back were her best bet. They had the look of people who had slipped into the first likely places in a strange church. And they were obviously affluent. She knelt in the pew behind them just as the vested priest came out into the sanctuary and began the celebration of the mass.

The mass proceeded rapidly. The scattered congregation rose, sat, knelt, seemingly as they pleased, without any real uniformity. Their responses were muffled, most of them trailing after the decided tones of a few self-appointed leaders up front. Celia tensed as the time for communion neared.

The two women clasped hands in the little ceremony known as "The Kiss of Peace." They turned to share it with Celia. "The Peace of Christ." She smiled mechanically, took their hands one at a time and answered, "The Peace of Christ."

Would the women go to communion? Would they leave their purses in the pew? Theirs was the dilemma of the devout, familiar to Celia. She had felt it so often. Wasn't it crass and materialistic to carry your purse when you went up to take the Sacrament, which made all people of faith one body? To act as if you distrusted those with whom you had affirmed the peace of heart and mind you shared?

The women rose. One, the older of the two, put her bag on the floor, not quite under the pew in front of her. Celia held her breath. The other hesitated, then left hers on the seat. They went into the aisle.

Celia waited until the few people in the back pews joined the communion line. Then she moved quickly. When she herself caught up with the line, the younger woman's wallet was deep in the makeshift grocery bag she had left behind on the bench. Returning from communion, she paused only long enough to pray silently, "O, Lord, let my pain be my prayer. And, O Lord, help me, and keep my children safe." Then she took up the bag and slipped out.

Minutes later she was on the Metro, a new fare card clutched in her hand. Once in her seat she inspected the wallet. Identification, "Constance Turner Owens, Lyme, Connecticut," driver's license, Social Security card, but no credit cards. Its owner was a wise traveler, she thought. A hundred and fifty dollars. Plenty for what she needed now. She folded the bills and thrust them into her bra. She looked around quickly before she let the wallet fall to the floor. Bending, as if to retrieve it, she pushed it under the seat. With luck, given an honest cleaning crew, it would get back to its owner. In any case, replacing its contents would be only a small problem for the lady from Connecticut. And someday she would send back the money.

She set her mind to what she needed if she was to get away. A purse of some kind. Underwear and nightwear. Cosmetics. A blouse. A jacket. New sunglasses. Maybe shoes. It really wasn't very much money after all. The train stopped again and she got off to find her way to the new Hecht's department store.

It was getting late when Celia finished her shopping. Wearing her new clothes and carrying her old ones and her other purchases in a shopping bag, she made her way quickly to the ladies' room and went into the small telephone booth there. She stood thinking. Whom could she call for help? Mindful of Sister Patricia's warnings, she knew she could not count on Frank or even Pat herself if there was danger of exposure.

She went quickly through her list of friends—Polly, Sue, Hannah, all of them. It was no good—she was sure they all believed that she was an addict. She could not be sure they would not call Johnny. Perhaps she could get away by herself—take a bus somewhere. Get a job. She counted the money in her new purse. Only ten dollars left. And she had no credit cards. No checks. Nothing to back up her identity. There was only Yanni, if she could reach him. He would recognize the name Marguerite Bowman. And she must not stay here. Every passing minute made her more sure that searchers would appear. She opened the door cautiously.

There was no one outside at the moment. She went to the mirror, took out her comb, and combed her newly curly hair back severely. She took a scarf from her new shopping bag and tied it around her head turban style. Should she wear the sunglasses? She knew the color of her eyes was too distinctive. But The People had advised sunglasses and would be looking for them. As would McGregor. She put the glasses in her purse. She looked again in the mirror, then fished out her lipstick and widened her mouth. It would have to do. Now to call. There was another telephone near the store entrance.

The phone rang only once and it was Yanni himself who answered.

"It's Marguerite Bowman," she said slowly and significantly.

There was a small pause, then Yanni's voice.

"Oh, yes, Miss Bowman."

"I need help." She spoke cautiously, mindful of the shoppers standing around. "I'm at Hecht's downtown and my—my car has broken down."

"I'll be there in a few minutes," said Yanni. "Which entrance?"

"I'm near the 12th Street entrance. I think it's the best place to be—because, because of the car, you know," said Celia a little desperately. It didn't make sense but she hoped Yanni wouldn't question. "And, Yanni," she added reluctantly, "I'll need some money."

"No problem," came Yanni's cheerful voice. "I still have the cash I took from the till when we closed the shop yesterday. Stay right there."

It was a long fifteen minutes. She took a store sale flyer and pretended to read it as she waited. Finally she heard the slight honk and saw Yanni waving from the window of his sports car. She hurried toward him.

Mindful of Ralph's training, Yanni did not get out to help her in but reached across to open the door. He nodded and smiled his welcome but made no comment until they were well down the street.

"Now tell me," he said.

Drawing a deep breath, Celia did, trying to make her account as clear and coherent as possible. She started with her encounter with Alec McGregor.

"I don't know, Yanni—I think now I should have appealed to him for help. I thought of it. He's such a decent man."

"But that would have got you right back in the hospital!" objected Yanni.

Celia sighed. "That's what I thought then—but now I'm not sure. And this other is worse, I think."

She told him about Sister Margaret Rose's frightened warning that a vaguely defined group aided by Leora was planning to use her as a hostage.

Yanni listened soberly but when she described her struggle with Leora he laughed out loud—and laughed again when she told him about taking the Connecticut woman's wallet.

"Don't panic," said Yanni when she finished, and added apologetically, "That's what that Sister Patricia and her friends who helped us get you out of the hospital were always saying—don't panic—and it sure sounds as if you haven't." He had turned into River Road and was driving steadily away from Wisconsin Avenue as he spoke. "Now listen, I drove all around the block before I drew up to the entrance and I didn't see anything that looked like special police or plainclothesmen or anything. No unusual activity. I think we ought to check with Sister Patricia or somebody—"

"But Yanni, that's just it, I can't. They may be the ones—at least, not Patricia, but the others. And there isn't anyone else," she added. "Just you—and I mustn't lead them to you, either."

"Oh—" Yanni waved a hand, brushing that aside. "Let me think—"

Celia was quiet as he drove on into Bethesda. Finally, when he turned into the exit to the Washington Beltway, she broke the silence. "Yanni, wherever are you going?"

Yanni grinned. "Baltimore, I think. People from Washington never go there, don't you know that? That's where we"—he stopped and amended the sentence—"that's where some of my friends go when they don't want to be seen. We'll find a motel room in one of those places the police never bother and I'll get you some coffee and supplies . . . and," he said triumphantly, "I've thought of somebody who wants to help and who *can* help you, too."

Celia's voice had a note of fresh hope. "Oh, Yanni, who?"

"Mrs. Fraser." He told her of Janie Fraser's call to him. "She never believed that you were addicted. And she's been awfully worried about you. It's been hard not to say anything to relieve her mind. I'll call her about a comb-out or something and tell her to expect a call from you."

"Janie, oh, Janie—I never thought—" Celia's voice was tremulous. "I always liked her so much, Yanni—but diplomatic wives have to be careful . . . so I . . . well, you know, I never even asked her to get involved in Peace Work or anything." She paused, then continued. "Yanni, it's such a good idea. She has diplomatic immunity. Maybe she could get me across the border . . . but you'll have to go there and explain things a little, won't you?"

"I can do that. I'll pretend she sent for me to do a comb-out . . . she'll go along . . . I'll say I have news for her. She's quick on the uptake. I'll go as soon as I get you settled."

"And Yanni, I'll want you to take some kind of message to the others. I'll have to think it out . . . be very careful about what I say. And how you get it to them. You can't be seen with the nuns now. You can't seem to be in touch with Sister Margaret Rose.

# . 22 .

W HEN  MCGREGOR left Secretary Boise that night of their
meeting he was seized with a strong sense of urgency. He was
sure he was on the right track and he felt more strongly than ever that
he must find Celia Mann before she was found by someone else. He was,
he was sure, not far behind her. But three nights later he could report no
progress in his regular call to report to Boise. The secretary sounded as
discouraged as he felt and he hung up, depressed.

But the next morning he thought of his father as he started out in his
car. He wondered how many times he had heard the old man say, "Nothing romantic about detective work, son. And nothing really hard about
running a man down if you want him badly enough. It's just questions,
questions, questions, just slogging along, up and down stairs, in and out
of doors, until you piece it all together. There's always something they
forgot." He would start again at the Adams-Morgan service station
where he had seen the woman who he was sure was Celia Mann. Somebody in the neighborhood *had* to have seen her. Somebody *had* to know
where she might have gone. He had her picture, a publicity photo.

He reached into his pocket for the picture and found himself lingering over it. It was a good likeness of the Celia Mann he had known.
Even the soft white streaks threading her black hair were clear and
distinct.

Hair! Alec McGregor struck the steering wheel with his fist. Somebody had given Celia Mann that mop of red hair he had seen. He knew
who it had to be. He started the car and headed toward Georgetown.

At first Yanni refused to talk about Celia Mann at all.

"I don't discuss my clients, Mr. McGregor," he had said and his face set in lines of Polish stubbornness. "And I don't know anything about Mrs. Mann, anyway. I told the police that. I'm only her hairdresser," he added sullenly.

They sat over coffee in a booth in the corner of the drugstore. It had been immediately apparent to McGregor that Yanni's shop with its confusion of kimono-clad women and attendants was no place to conduct an inquiry.

"We need to talk, Michal," he had said, showing his badge. "Let's get out of here." He had made an effort to sound reassuring and authoritative at the same time. Yanni Michal, although obviously unwilling, followed readily enough.

McGregor studied him. His intuition told him that Michal did know something. How to get at it in time?

Yanni broke the silence. "But I do know this, McGregor. That lady was no druggie, no matter what they said. You should know that yourself—you were with her enough."

So Michal had recognized him. He really is loyal to her, Alec thought. If I can convince him that she is in danger—

He reached across the table and seized Yanni's wrist. "Listen," he said, and began to talk in low steady tones.

"All right, all right," said Yanni at last, drawing a deep breath, "here's what I know, and what we planned."


Janie Fraser was out of her seat at the breakfast table almost before the maid entered the room to announce a telephone call for her. She had been nervously waiting for it ever since she had waked that morning. "She'll call herself to clear the details with you," Yanni had said in his hasty pre-dinner visit the night before, "She's determined to cut any connection to the people who helped her get out of the hospital—to protect us, you see."

Janie had hardly needed Yanni's hurried account of Celia's escape and her present plight. She had been morally sure of Celia's innocence of any addiction from the beginning and, like any Canadian, she was not surprised to learn of corruption and evil machinations at the highest levels of the United States government. Such things were not even unknown in their own. With spontaneous generosity she had offered to get Celia out of the country even before Yanni could frame a tentative request for her help.

Janie came back into the breakfast room looking a little flustered, her husband noticed. He was refilling his plate at the sideboard.

"Who was calling you at this unearthly hour?" he asked.

"Oh, one of the women from that benefit committee," she answered airily. Heaven knows, that was true enough. Angus would expect her to burble on, she thought to herself and went on talking, trying to think behind the screen of her own words. "It was that Mrs. Steinman"—after all, that was the name the houseman had given; Celia must have had a reason for using it—"she's always so drearily serious and methodical. I do wish Celia hadn't insisted on making her the ticket chairman. She wants to consult with me every time she has a new idea." Now, why did I mention Celia? she said to herself. It would've been better not to bring her name up at all. She would have to catch the afternoon plane to Toronto and she would have to invent a good excuse. She could always say her mother wasn't feeling well. Or should she put it on Uncle Archie? Would Angus think it strange if she went off at the drop of a hat for Uncle Archie? Probably not; Angus was awfully fond of him. She would wait 'til he got to the office and call his secretary to tell him that she was going. She would say that she would call him when she got there. Yes, that would be the best way.

Angus Fraser was eating quickly, making his way through the *Washington Post* as he did so. He stood up and folded the newspaper.

"Do you mind?" he asked his wife, pecking at her cheek. "I've got an early meeting and I'll finish this in the office. Do you want the back section?"

Janie shook her head absently. "No," she said, "there's never anything much but food on Thursday morning. You take it. Goodbye, darling. As we Americans say, have a nice day."

She watched him go through the door and felt a little pang of guilt. He was so harassed and busy these days and under so much pressure. She was probably doing a very foolish thing. But how could she say no?

Angus Fraser's secretary gave him his wife's message when he came back from lunch. It was a bit garbled. He could not make out whether it was Janie's mother who was ill or her Uncle Archie. "I'm sorry, Mr. Fraser," the secretary said, "but I took it down just the way she said it and I think that's what she said. But she's going to call you from Toronto tonight. I made the reservations for her," she added conscientiously.

Well, thought Angus resignedly, living with Janie had its little surprises. He would just have to wait for her call. But as he settled down to work, something nagged at the back of his mind. After a while he realized what it was.

"Is today's *Post* still out there?" he asked his secretary over the intercom.

"Yes, I'll bring it right in," she answered.

Yes, there it was on the obituary page. An obviously old photograph of a woman. Her hair was fluffed over her forehead and went up into two wings at the sides in the style of the 1930s. "Hannah Gordon Steinman" read the caption under it. And there was a small headline, WIDOW OF EX-SENATOR DIES IN HER SLEEP. The story began, "Hannah Gordon Steinman, widow of Senator James Steinman of Vermont, died yesterday in her apartment at the Westchester, apparently of a heart attack. Her body was found in the late morning by her maid, Dora Simms. Mrs. Steinman was not known to have a history of heart disease . . ."

Surely Janie had mentioned Mrs. Steinman this morning. It could be another Mrs. Steinman, but he didn't think so. What was Janie up to? He looked at the clock. She would've landed by now. It was no use paging her at the airport. He sat lost in thought. He had to decide what to do. It would be best to follow her up there.

After Celia's call that morning Janie Fraser had gone into a fever of preparation, picking out clothes for Celia and herself, packing, making a list of engagements for Angus's secretary to cancel. When Alec Mc-Gregor appeared at the door and pressed to see her with polite but inflexible insistence she had been furiously impatient.

"Tell him to go away," she said to her flustered maid.

"But he is some sort of policeman, Madame," said Marie in a frightened voice. "He has a badge."

Janie ran down the stairs and confronted Alec, who stood waiting in the hall. "Whatever is this about?" she demanded. "I'm trying to catch a plane—"

"Secret Service, Mrs. Fraser," he said. "Can we talk privately?"

Shaken, she led the way into the little morning room. He shut the door.

"It's about Mrs. Mann. I know you've been in touch," he began, then, seeing her stricken face, he said hastily, "Oh, it's not what you think. I want to help you get her away. It's through Jan Michal that I came here."

When he had explained the extent of the threat to Celia, Janie, in turn, explained her plan. She was going to take Celia with her to Canada—say she was her cousin or something—she hadn't quite figured that out. But she didn't think they would question diplomats at Canadian customs—especially if Angus's aide met them. And Celia would be wearing Canadian clothes. Breathless, Janie paused and looked at Alec expectantly.

He smiled. It was impossible not to like Janie Fraser. Her plan was good except for one thing, he told her—taking Celia Mann to Canada might be taking her into worse danger. "There's a lot of unrest along the border, for one thing, and there are only a few of us on this side who can be thought of as loyal to her at the moment. We couldn't help her in Canada. You don't want to involve your husband's office, do you? If he got wind of it, he'd have no choice but to turn her over."

"Oh," said Janie, "but where then? We've got to take her somewhere."

"I think it's better if I do it," said Alec. "I can protect her physically if it comes to that—not that I think it will," he added hastily, seeing her horrified expression. "And I think it is better to go in another direction. Too many things point to Canada."

"But where?" Janie repeated.

"Somewhere in the resort area. It's that time of year. People are beginning to go. We won't be so noticeable—two people traveling for a Memorial Day holiday. We'll just be getting an early start. They're starting for the beaches already."

Janie's face lit up. "I know. I know!" She seized Alec's arm. "My Uncle Archie Campbell really *is* sick. He'll be in the hospital for months, they say. And he keeps an apartment in one of those grand old places in Maine. He lets any of us use it anytime. I can call and say you're coming. You can be my American cousins—"

Alec considered. It was something. Better than drifting from motel to motel. It might work. "We can try that," he said to Janie Fraser. She was immediately practical.

"Then Celia will have to have different clothes. You know where she is?"

Alec nodded.

"Then wait here. It will only take me fifteen minutes."

Outside the room, she said to the hovering Marie, "That man will take my bags for me. Bring him some tea or coffee or something." The maid went off. Looking after her, Janie thought, I'll still have to take a plane to Canada or she and Angus will get suspicious.

\*   \*   \*

Marcel had taken short leave from his duties at the embassy residence once again and was closeted in the apartment on 13th Street with Frank and Ralph. He was angry.

"It is incredible that she should have gotten away so easily and that there is no trace of her. Your security was very lax."

Frank spoke uneasily, trying to keep to his normal didactic, impersonal tone. "There was no indication that she would be able to act so precipitously—one might even say violently. She is much stronger—that is true—but she was always so docile, almost passive . . ."

Marcel cut him short with an impatient gesture and looked at Ralph. "No sign?"

Ralph shook his head. "With all we got out on the streets looking there's been no lead at all. She's gotten out of the city somehow. With no money she had to get help somewhere."

"Obviously," said Marcel. He paused. "We will have to pursue that step by step. The whole operation is endangered."

"Leora says she was alerted by one of the nuns," offered Frank reluctantly.

"So I hear," said Marcel. He deliberated a moment. "You are their connection. I leave it to you to get two of them to Canada as soon as possible. If they can't help us find her, they can serve as substitutes."

Frank started to demur but Marcel cut him off and turned again to Ralph. "The other connection seems to have been the hairdresser. You take some of the others and get him here tonight. Use whatever means you think best."

Ralph nodded and left the room.


But Leo's men got to him first.

That night Yanni Michal sat in the little office behind the shop preparing his monthly accounts for his tax man to look over. He heard the maid, who had finished sweeping up and putting the shop in order for the morning, go out and firmly close the door behind her. He could hear the faint thump, thump of the dryer tumbling the smocks she had washed.

He tried hard to concentrate on the figures before him. Lars would be there by eight with a dinner picked up from the carry-out across the street and, as always, he would be impatient to get going. Yanni frowned, puzzling as to whether the percentage of income he had ascribed to tips was too little.

"They're beginning to watch that very closely," his accountant had told him. "There's too much cash floating around, going unreported. If I were you, I'd be careful. You don't want them checking your bank deposits." Yanni had smiled to himself. Most of his tips were in cash and his mother in Pittsburgh put them into her bank account and then transferred them to her Senior Citizen's Money Market Fund, where they had been earning a hefty interest for the last few years. She kept meticulous accounts on the backs of envelopes which were stashed away in a kitchen drawer and mailed to Yanni from time to time. But he did not really mind giving the federal government a larger proportion of that income if it kept the tax man happy. But how much? His mind began to wander again.

Yanni, for the past weeks, had been experiencing wild changes of mood. Up to now, he had managed to be content with his life by keeping any seeming contradictions in separate compartments. Bringing things together, "achieving integration," as the people Sister Margaret Rose had introduced him to were urging him to do, might make his life better. But he was not so sure. He didn't really want to make being gay a cause. It was the way he was. He didn't make a big thing of it with his family or with his straight friends and clients. If they wanted to ignore it, okay, they could ignore it. Live and let live—that was the way he saw it.

He thought of what the earnest nun at the Sign Center who edited the gays' newsletter had told him: "But, don't you see, Jan, it's just like being left-handed. Society was intolerant of that, too. And finally people began to see that left-handed people needed to live using that left hand, and that left-handedness is associated with some very rare qualities. It's just the same with gayness. More and more scientists are beginning to believe that it's inherent. And psychiatrists have come to see it. And everyone knows now how many men and women of genius were gay. The task is to get parents to accept their gay children and for everyone to work for the full rights of gays in society. Every person like you, who is established and well known, who speaks out, is helping the cause."

Yanni was not sure that he wanted to help the cause. He felt uneasy with her enthusiasm for it. He could never remember her name, probably because he found her unattractive and he was a little ashamed of that. He himself liked to look nice, and he liked to help women look their best. He did not really understand a woman who let her hips spread in unbecoming slacks and cropped her hair with no regard for line. And all this preachiness was boring.

He sighed and put the problem aside. At any rate, he was glad that he was back in the church. He had never been very religious. He was not sure what he believed. But he knew that it would make his mother happy when he went to mass and received communion with her at Christmastime. And he was glad that he had helped Celia Mann. He only wished he had some news of her.

He heard the front door open and footsteps crossing the reception room. Good Lord, Lars already! And he had brought someone with him. He turned to greet them. But it was not Lars or anyone else he knew in the doorway. Two men in dark suits stood there, one behind the other. They looked very much alike. They had short, bristly haircuts and hard, unsmiling faces. Tax men? The FBI? The maid must have forgotten to lock the door, Yanni thought—then noticed that the first man was still holding a plastic credit card in his hand.

"You Yanni Michal?" the first man asked.

Yanni stood up and nodded.

"You're wanted for questioning, sweetheart," the other said sneeringly. He held out what looked like an official badge for Yanni's inspection, then withdrew it quickly before he could get a good look.

Instinctively, Yanni sparred for time. "Right now?" he said, gesturing toward his desk. "I've got work to finish. It will just take a few minutes and then I'll be with you."

"No, right now," the man answered roughly. "The Man's in a hurry."

The Man? Who was the Man? Like everyone brought up in the '60s and '70s, Yanni was not reassured by the thought that these men might be government agents. Suddenly, he was very much afraid. If only Lars would come—at least then somebody would know where he had gone.

"I'm expecting someone," he said. "I'll just leave a note."

The man seized his arm. "No need for that. Your boyfriend won't need to know where you are"—he was sneering again—"and we're not going to wait for him. Come quietly now. We don't want to get rough."

The other man laughed nastily. "Not here," he said.

They hustled Yanni out the door and into a gray car. A third man, very like them, was sitting at the wheel and the engine was running. As the car pulled off into Georgetown traffic, Yanni Michal, sitting between the two burly men in the back seat, had a feeling that he would not see this street again. He realized, too, that he was not very brave.

\*    \*    \*

Traffic was heavy on the Baltimore-Washington Parkway and it slowed to a crawl as it neared the exit to the airport. Alec McGregor eased his rented Camaro into the right lane. Overhead, planes were thundering toward landing at one-minute intervals. It was that time of late afternoon. The big jets from the West and the South were coming in. The terminal would be swarming for the next few hours. With luck he might get Celia through it unnoticed, although he knew that operatives had it thoroughly covered. They would be at the flight desks and the gates and among the skycaps. His own chance of going unrecognized was slim. He decided that they would have to take a chance on driving even though it was slower.

He found the motel without trouble, drove around to the back and parked. Unit 46. He took his toilet kit and one of the bags packed by Mrs. Fraser and went to the door. He could hear the television tuned to the early news. He knocked once, then three times—according to Jan Michal's instructions. The door opened quickly.

"I'm so glad you're here. I'm starving," said Celia Mann, but her laughing voice changed when she saw who it was. "Oh," she said. Then tonelessly, "Alec." She stepped back into the room and he followed her.

She sank into the chair where she had been sitting. Her shoulders slumped tiredly. "I'm almost glad you found me," she said. "I've been worried ever since I saw you. I was sure you recognized me." She spoke almost absently, her words coming slowly.

"Listen to me, Celia," said Alec McGregor, using her first name consciously to create a bond, a thin strand of trust and connection. "It's not what you think. I haven't come to take you back. I've come to help you get away. We haven't got much time. May I sit down?"

She nodded, finding his courtesy reassuring, as he had intended it to be. He took the only other chair in the cramped, shabby room. Quickly he outlined their situation and told her of Secretary Boise's decision that he must take her away until they could be sure who could be trusted and who could not. He told her of his meeting with Yanni and with Janie Fraser. "It's only the four of us so far," he said, "and I hope we can keep it that way long enough to sort this out."

She listened quietly and smiled a little at the mention of Janie Fraser. He seized on that small sign of acquiescence. "Mrs. Fraser is quite a woman," he told her. "She's practical. There's a bag of clothes in the car—just what you'll need, she said. And hats—maybe a dozen hats."

Celia Mann laughed out loud. "All right, Alec, I believe you. Only Janie would do that. Now tell me what we're going to do."

"The airport is heavily covered, so we'll drive to Atlantic City. We'll take one of the smaller airlines out of there to Boston. From now on we'll have to be Mr. and Mrs. Craig Campbell, Mrs. Fraser's American cousins. I'm Craig. You're Beatrice—Bea for short. For this part of the trip we'd better try to merge into the local scene. People heading for the Memorial Day gambling. We'll have to look as redneck as we can." He looked at her thoughtfully, and then indicated the bag he had brought. "Do you think there might be a pair of slacks in there? And can you frizz up your hair some way?"

Celia laughed again. She was beginning to feel an enormous sense of relief at being once again in Alec McGregor's charge. She rose and rummaged in the bag on the bed.

"It'll just be a few minutes," she said. "I'll do my best," and she disappeared into the bathroom.

When she came out her hair was teased high on her head and she wore the new sunglasses with harlequin frames. She had on a tight black silk shirt, green slacks and high-heeled sandals. She struck a pose and shifted the gum she was chewing.

"Okay, Alec?" she asked.

"Okay," he said. "But it's Craig, remember."

"Okay, Craig," she said, dragging out the vowels in a fair imitation of Polly Haskins's Southern accent.

"You'll do, Bea," he said, smiling. "Now I'll have to make a few changes myself." He took his kit and went into the bathroom. It was spotless, he noted with approval, and all traces of her occupancy had been removed. He took a little plastic pouch from his kit and removed the false mustache he had secured from Yanni. It was sandy, a good match, and its droop changed the contour of his face. He pulled a billed cap from his pocket. He fit it squarely on his head, added a pair of aviator sunglasses, and opened his shirt collar. That should do it.

Celia gasped when she saw him. "You look entirely different," she exclaimed. "I don't think I want to go away with such a strange man."

He welcomed her lightness of mood. It showed that she had the resilience she would need. But he said only, "Now, let's make it fast." Her bag was ready and he took it. She lifted an all-purpose raincoat from the open rack and wiped the dresser with a piece of Kleenex.

"What about the key?" she asked.

"Leave it on the dresser," he said.

They went out into the darkening twilight and he turned the car toward old U.S. 1 and the north. A few miles down the highway he pulled into a Howard Johnson's lot.

"Why are we stopping here?" Celia asked.

"You said you were starving, didn't you?" he answered.

"I like you, Craig Campbell, do you know that?" Celia said. Alec smiled and helped her out of the car. To all appearances a congenial couple, they went into the restaurant and took seats at the counter. I feel as if I'd known him all my life, Celia thought.

They ate slowly and lingered over coffee as long as Alec thought they could. Then they went out and Alec drove the car to the far end of the parking lot. "We should wait until after midnight," he told her. "Nobody has paid attention to us here. If anyone was following we want to let them get as far ahead as possible."

"We'll keep to the back roads," said Alec, when they finally started out. "It's safer."

They fell into close and companionable talk during that late night's ride through the grimier parts of Maryland, Delaware and southern New Jersey. Alec kept the car at a steady pace past the cinderblock buildings and small houses with lean-to sheds on the outskirts of small towns lit by a bulb here or a dim streetlight there.

"There's one thing I want you to know, Alec. I was not a drug user, ever. Alec, I never even took sleeping pills or tranquilizers until Jim prescribed them. They drugged me, Alec. That's what they really did. And somehow—I don't know how—they gave me those headaches. I do hope you can believe me about that."

"I do," he said. "I guess in a way I always did. The stories didn't add up. I interviewed more than fifty people, I guess, in those weeks we lost track of you. Your aunt, your friends, the people who worked for you and"—he hesitated; he could not bring himself to say "your husband"—"the vice-president. Even those who did believe it—or maybe wanted to believe it—couldn't really give any reason or concrete detail. I began to wonder. And something your maid said made me wonder even more."

"What did Juanita say?"

"Let me see. She put it this way. 'The Señora is a woman of *dignidad*.

Maybe she is not happy. Maybe she does not like to be where her husband wants her.' "

"Then she *did* recognize me that day in the post office!" Celia exclaimed. She told Alec a little about her time in the Adams-Morgan
district, but she was steadfast about refusing to name names or give him
addresses.

"I know you want to protect me, Alec," she said. "I believe that. But
you *are* a government official and you *have* taken an oath. Some of the
people who helped can't always be strictly legal—at least, that's what I
think. I don't know. But they took risks for me—I can't betray them."

"But *why* did they? They could have double motives, Celia," he said
soberly.

"Maybe. But I know some of them did it for good reasons. I know
that. So I have to take a chance on the others." She shifted ground.
"Anyway, Alec, I was not conscious when they got me out of that room.
I honestly don't know how that was done. Or who did it."

He did not press her. There would be time. And he needed her full
trust. He could feel that Celia's being in touch first with Yanni, then
himself, had made her more like herself—as if she had, in a sense, come
back once again to her real life. She questioned him about her aunt and
about her children. He told her about Peter's breaking into the conference at the hospital.

"He's a fighter, that boy," he said. "I think he was the one who really
convinced me."

"He did that? He came to see for himself?" Tears and laughter con-
tended in Celia's voice. "Oh, you don't know how good that makes me
feel! I was so afraid he'd believe them. He hasn't been home much, you
see—with camp and school. But he never believed it at all! I'm so
glad."

After a while she said, "Would you like me to drive, Alec? You must
be tired."

"If you'd like to . . ." he said. "We just stick to this road."

They stopped and changed places. She handled the car competently,
finding, after a mile or two, the same steady pace. "I like to drive," she
said, "but I always have trouble getting Johnny to let me when we are
on trips. He doesn't ever want to admit that he is tired. He's almost worn
out when he finally gives in!"

It was her first spontaneous mention of her husband. It was good,
Alec thought, that it was so natural. But he would have felt better if she

hadn't used the present tense. Was it a form of denial? She had to face the danger—all of it—to escape it. He was wondering what he should do about that when he dozed off.

Celia, as she drove, was beginning to work on the same problem in a different way. Alec's comforting presence and his assumption of her protection had begun to lessen her preoccupation with her own plight and the primitive drive to escape and to survive which had held her in its grip. It felt so normal to be on the highway, riding with a man beside her—so like the times during the early campaigns when she had done the same with Johnny—that the realities of the nightmarish world in which she now lived began to recede. She was no longer just a frightened fugitive, as dependent on the mercy of The People as any illegal alien. She was once again the wife of the vice-president, no matter how strange and dangerous the circumstances. She had responsibilities.

True, she could not betray Sister Patricia, Frank and the others. But she could tell Alec what she knew and what she had thought for so long was going to happen. She now had confirmation that a very big, very detailed and very imminent subversive action was under way. She could tell Alec what she knew about that—beginning with the conversation she had overheard in her own home, then telling him what was on the tape, and ending with the confused story Sister Margaret Rose had gotten from Juanita. With that much he could find some way to get word to the president.

When Alec woke and stretched his cramped legs, she said, "Hello there, want to change back?"

"Yes," he said, "but it was a nice break . . ."

When they had changed places, she began.

"Alec, I've been thinking it over. There are some things I can't tell you, but there are others I really should. Just listen and I will begin at the beginning."

"It all begins to add up," said Alec finally when she had finished. "I'll have to be in touch with Boise in the morning."

"It's strange," said Celia to Alec as they drove on. "You know all about me—I know you always study the whole history of anyone you're protecting, don't you?—but I know hardly anything about you, except that you are strong and kind. I don't even know if you're married or not."

"I was, but it was a long time ago. She died. We didn't have any children. Now I have only my parents—they are getting old—and my sister and her family. I was coming from their place on the Patuxent when I saw you."

"Tell me about yourself," she said. "I'd like to know where you were a little boy, and what it was like."

He began to talk randomly, just as the memories came to him, almost as if he were talking to himself. Of the little town in Vermont and his parents' white colonial house on the village green, the tall elms shading the streets. Of the tribe of cousins so close they were like his brothers and sisters . . .

They were still talking as the gray light of predawn began to make patches of the piney woods visible. They were near Atlantic City.

At the airport they separated and changed clothes. When they met again at the counter they looked at each other in mutual approval. She wore a beige linen suit and a smart brimmed hat—one of the two she had selected from Janie Fraser's overgenerous supply. He was hatless, wore a light tweed jacket over a blue oxford cloth shirt and tie, and carried a tennis racquet in a canvas cover.

"Where did *that* come from?" she asked.

"Car trunk," he said, grinning, and turned to the counter.


That same morning, while Celia Mann and Alec McGregor were on their way to Maine, Sister Margaret Rose sat, disconsolate and fearful, at her desk in the social service office at St. Simeon's. She stared glumly at the two notes before her on her desk. One had come in the morning mail. It had been mailed at the main post office and bore no return address. "Dear Pat, dear Frank, dear all of you," it read,

> you must not worry about me. I am safe and I have all the help I
> need. It was time that I took charge of my life. I was only a danger
> to all of you. I can never thank you enough.
>
> M.

The other was unsigned but scrawled in Sister Patricia's familiar cramped handwriting.

Dear M.R.—

Anne Marie and I are off to the border to help Frank with a group of Salvadorans there. They want a Catholic presence of some sort to reassure them before they will take the risk and come across. Anne Marie has cleared her going with Rita at the Center but I haven't told Anna. You know how she feels about my going off on unexplained errands. I leave it to you to explain it to her and to smooth things over. See you.

Sister Margaret Rose did not like the look of things at all. She was afraid that Celia had already endangered her friends by getting away. She wished now that she had told Sister Patricia about warning Celia, about what Juanita had said.

# . 23 .

THE OCEAN VIEW is an island of splendid affluence on the southern coast of Maine. It is a far cry from the modest condominium
blocks, the shabby hostelries and rooming houses for vacationers that
line the main streets of the small coastal towns where the purposefully
simple but big rambling houses of the "old rich" summer people dom-
inate the waterfront.

Half hotel, half exclusive apartments, it has as its center the refur-
bished, traditional, shingled and many-porched inn that gave it its name.
The inn is backed now, however, by two wings of balconied "villas."
There are tennis courts, pools and cabanas, and rustic bridges over the
ocean road to the private beach where the hardy can take their dips in
the frigid ocean waters.

Although it still has a hard core of the summer people who have been
coming there for generations, it is known as a favorite vacation place
for a new aristocracy of corporate executives and media moguls, especially of newly rich Canadians. Part of its attraction is its proximity to
Marbury Downs, the beautiful racetrack and park built in the early
eighties by an international consortium of investors in horseflesh and
racing.

The hotel limousine picked them up at the airport. As they neared
the hotel Alec noted the number of small apartment blocks and inns with
signs bearing a Canadian motif—"The Maple Leaf," "The Montreal,"
"The Canadien." He remarked on it to the driver.

"Oh, sure," said the latter, "lots of them here. We've got quite a few
like Mr. Campbell at the Ocean View. Mr. LaRocque owns two apartments. He has the big racing stables, you know. Million-dollar horses.
He's a good friend of Mr. Campbell. He's at the Ocean View right now.
It's Trans-National race week. The papers say even the Canadian mafia
are flocking in," he added with a cynical chuckle.

What had Mullan, the representative of Fergus from DEA, said about the Canadian mafia? Alec couldn't quite pin it down but the re-membrance made him uneasy. It was a reason for further caution.

Mr. Campbell's apartment was on the top floor of the Ocean View. It was a suite of two rooms and two baths with a long balcony running its length.

"Oh, this *is* nice," exclaimed Celia when the elderly bellman had checked everything, shown them the little pullman kitchen with its stocked cupboards and refrigerator, and left them.

Alec was checking the desk in the sitting room. "Uncle Archie has a box at the Downs, it seems," he said. "It says call the desk for arrange-ments. Would you like to go to the races?" he asked Celia.

"Oh, Alec, could we?" she asked. "I've never been to the races. There just never seemed to be time for things like that."

He was amused. "I don't see why not," he said. "We might as well hide out in style. I'll see to it in the morning. Now," he said, "I'm beat and you must be, too, after last night's drive. I'll sleep here on the sofa. You can lock the door to the bedroom for respectability's sake if you like."

She laughed. "I'll feel safer with it unlocked. You can rescue me if anyone comes. Goodnight, Alec."

When he went down in the morning to arrange for the racetrack he stopped first at the newsstand. A pile of *Washington Posts*, fresh from the airport, lay on the counter. One headline caught his eye. He picked is up, absently laying the coins on the counter, and moved to one side to read it.

This was bad. Really bad. But no one except Mrs. Fraser—not even the hairdresser—knew where they really were. And she had said she was going to Canada. He thought of Celia's expectant face at the breakfast table. Well, it wouldn't hurt to let her have one day—one day of respite and lightheartedness. She had been through so much.

Everything pleased her that day. The Campbell box at the Downs was well forward, out from under the stands. She looked surprisingly pretty in the bright sunlight in a soft white hat and blue-tinted sunglasses she had bought in the hotel shop. ("They hide my eyes better, don't you think, Alec?")

She studied the colorful crowd of standees as they moved to and fro, and exclaimed with pleasure when the famous pair of blue herons, who returned to the Downs year after year, took flight from the pond at the track's center and settled again.

He introduced her to the tout sheets and the racing programs. "The big race is the tenth," he pointed out. She studied the entries.

"I love the names," she said. "Look, here is Pride of Ontario, La Rocque Stables. That must be the man at the Ocean View. We'll bet on him when the time comes. How do you place bets, Alec?"

He explained carefully. "You can bet to win, place or show," he finished, "or you can bet across the board. Clear?"

"No," she said seriously.

"Well, let's place one on the next race and you can learn by practice. Here it is—second race. Who do you like?"

She looked at the list. "Gloucester Lily," she decided.

"How much?"

"I'm cautious, Alec—five dollars across the board."

"Okay. Here I go to make us rich—that poor horse is twenty-five to one right now."

"But with such a nice name!" she called after him.

While he was gone she looked around. Behind her and above were the windows of the Turf Club. People were standing there looking down or studying the racing board through field glasses. Why do they stay inside on such a lovely day? she wondered idly. A face caught her eye— a man who seemed to be looking directly at her. But it couldn't be— Better not to stare. She looked away. When she looked back again the face was gone.

She was thoughtful and frowning when Alec came back.

"Anything wrong?" he asked.

"I don't know. I thought I saw someone I know—a friend of my brother's. But I'm not sure." She brightened. "Anyway there's bound to be someone here who has seen me sometime. They won't notice me because they'd never expect to see me here with a handsome, mustachioed man, would they?"

He acknowledged the compliment with a grin and a bow but persisted. "Where was he?"

"Up there—in one of the windows."

"I thought we'd have lunch up there on Mr. Campbell's membership," he said, "but perhaps we'd better not."

"Oh, Alec, let's do it. I'm sure I'm wrong. And it would be fun to eat up there. That's where all the owners and trainers are, isn't it?"

"What do you know about trainers?" he teased.

"I know they're important. I read Dick Francis."

The headwaiter was pleased to seat the guests of Mr. Campbell. "Up here by the corner window," he said, leading the way. "This is your uncle's favorite place," he added.

"I'm getting to quite like Uncle Archie," said Celia when they were seated. "He does things right. You can see everything from here."

They had just finished ordering when a dark slim man in a red blazer got up from a table near the opposite corner and came over. He bowed to Celia and extended his hand to Alec.

"Paul LaRocque," he said. "They tell me at the hotel that you're guests and relatives of my friend Arch Campbell. I just wanted to say welcome."

Alec stood up. "That's nice of you," he answered. "I'm Craig Campbell and this is my wife, Beatrice."

"I know Arch's lovely niece in Washington," said LaRocque, "but I didn't know he had another just as lovely. He's been keeping you a secret."

"Niece-in-law," said Celia smoothly and sweetly. "It's Craig who is related. We don't see Uncle Archie as much as the others—we're the American branch. Chicago."

"No matter. I'm glad you're here now. I have a horse in the Trans-National tomorrow and I'd be pleased if you would join my party. We'll be taking helicopters over at one o'clock—leaving the hotel about twelve-forty-five. We'll be lunching here, of course. I do hope you can come."

"It sounds wonderful!" said Celia enthusiastically before Alec could stop her. "We'd love it, wouldn't we, Craig?"

When LaRocque had gone back to his table she looked at Alec ruefully. "I can see by your face that you don't think that was wise, Alec. But I couldn't help it. It sound so festive." Her voice was wistful.

He did not want to spoil her enjoyment. "It's all right. I just thought for a moment that it would be better for us to keep to ourselves. But perhaps it's not a bad idea to lose ourselves in the crowds and look as if we're connected." He stopped a minute, then asked, keeping his voice casual, "You didn't see your brother's friend up here, did you?"

"No," said Celia without interest. She was watching the television replay of the last race on the monitor between the windows. "I was imagining things, I guess."


When they got back to the apartment after dinner, McGregor finally faced what he had avoided facing for most of the day. He would not

delay any longer. She had to know how bad things were if only to protect herself. He handed her the *Post* and pointed to the headline:
SOCIETY HAIRDRESSER FOUND DEAD NEAR GAY BAR.

"Oh, no, Yanni—" It was half a question, but Celia knew by the
clutching, cold feeling around her heart that it was true. She took the
paper from Alec's hand and read the story through.

The body of Jan Michal, owner of Mr. Jan's and favorite hairdresser of prominent Washington women, was found in the lot
behind a southwest bar early this morning. Michal was manacled,
apparently the victim of an S-M orgy that got out of hand.

"This has happened before," said Lieutenant Gunderson of the
homicide squad. "They get a little too rough and somebody is seriously injured. In this case, fatally. I guess we will have to do what
they did in San Francisco—hold classes in how to get rough without doing permanent damage."

Michal's body was found by one Joe Bunnell, a self-styled street
person of no fixed address. He was last seen alive by Lars Stedman,
receptionist at his salon, who was bringing him a sandwich from a
carry-out restaurant because Mr. Michal had told him he would be
working late on his accounts. Stedman says he suspects foul play.

"Yanni wasn't like that," he said. "He wasn't into that sado-
masochism stuff." Stedman says that he saw Michal get in a big
car with two men. He thought a third one was driving. He was too
far away, he said, to tell the make of the car.

"At the time I just thought, 'Where is he going? Does he want
me to wait for him?' But now I think he was being pushed into
that car. He was between two men."

Lieutenant Gunderson is inclined to dismiss Stedman's theory.
Stedman, he said, was Michal's apartment mate as well as his
receptionist.

Celia read it through. Then she read it again, feeling increasingly
sick. Finally she looked at Alec.

"I never thought Yanni was like that," she said dully.

"I don't think he was, Celia," said Alec gently. "They dumped him
there to make it look like that. Don't you see?"

It seemed as if her mind wasn't working at all. What could Alec mean?

"They tried to make him talk. And then they killed him. Or maybe
he died under questioning. The important thing now is how much he
told them. They could be closer behind us than I thought."

Celia couldn't accept the idea. Yanni tortured and dead because of her? She felt faint and put her head down on her knees. Alec's voice, going on, came to her in waves of sound.

Late that night Celia lay awake staring into the darkness. During all the long hours since she had learned of Yanni's death, her mind had shied away from what had actually happened. She was like someone trying to snatch something important out of a fire. She snatched and drew back, approached and backed away. She tried not to take hold of what she inevitably had to grasp: Yanni Michal had been tortured to death because of her.

What had they done to him? Her imagination told her what they could have done. Things so agonizing to the nerves, so shocking to the flesh that they had brought on the death of a strong young man. To her, the worst was that he was manacled and helpless. She knew the terrible indignity and humiliation of being helpless at the hands of others. She began to weep. She cried with desperate, hopeless tears.

She cried for loss. Not only for the loss of a friend who had cared enough to put himself at risk for her, but for the loss of those dear to her, her parents who were dead and her children who could not be with her, probably never again. In the terrible grief that washed over her, she knew that she was guilty. She was guilty of Yanni's death. She was even guilty of what Johnny had done. In her failure to see things as they really were, in her stupid clinging to dreams, she had made Johnny into something he was not, and condemned him for what he was. She had carelessly risked Yanni's life with little thought of the consequences because she had not really believed in the evil of the men who killed him. Not really believed . . . After all that had happened she had gone on playing a part like someone in a college play. But it was real. Real. And Yanni was dead. Horribly dead.

In the other room Alec McGregor could hear her hopeless weeping. Finally he could stand it no longer. He stood up, put on his robe and went in. He stood beside her bed.

"Celia," he said desperately, "Celia, don't!" He touched her shoulder tentatively.

"Oh, Alec," she said and reached for him. "Oh, Alec, it's all my fault—" She began to sob again.

He gathered her up like a child and held her, patting her and smoothing her hair. "There now, there now," he said awkwardly. "You mustn't cry, Celia . . . don't cry like that . . . you'll make yourself sick . . . it's not your fault . . . how could it be your fault? If it's anybody's, it's the fault of the people who railroaded you into that hospital . . ."

And that's the God's truth, he thought savagely as he went on soothing her automatically. What gets into these goddamned politicians, anyway—risking everybody and everything . . . ? He burned with a new-felt resentment against John Mann, against the woman determined to be a strong president, against all the manipulators of other people's destinies.

When Celia's crying began to ease and her breathing was normal except for an occasional great shaking hiccup, he put her down gently. He went into the bathroom and came back with a glass of water and a pill. "Yes, it's a tranquilizer," he said. "But you don't need to worry. Your system is clean now. It's mild. Take it. You need it." He put his arm behind her and braced her head and shoulders, holding the glass until she had swallowed the pill and all the water. She lay back. "Don't go, Alec," she said. "Stay here beside me and I won't be so afraid." He smoothed the covers over her, then lay down at her side. After a while he knew that she was asleep. He did not move for fear of waking her.

As his mind drifted lazily from one unfocused picture to another, he began to be increasingly and physically aware of the woman beside him. In her sleep, Celia Mann's hand had fallen trustingly on his. Her body was warm against him. He could smell her skin and her hair. He thought of the ordeal she had been through and the way she had kept trying, responding to whatever help there was. There must be some deep spring of vitality in her, he thought, to keep her going in the face of one betrayal after another. The feel of her hand on his and the sound of her untroubled breathing suddenly filled him with a deep rush of tenderness. And then he knew that his feeling went beyond tenderness. He was aroused by her closeness, the feel of her body against his, and the recognition of the feeling he had for her. He groaned.

He felt her turn and shift. She had been sleeping lightly and she was awake. Her voice came out of the darkness.

"Are you finding it hard to be close to me, Alec?" she asked.

He only nodded. "It's natural, I suppose. I feel it, too," she said softly, "and it's probably our last night before they catch up with me. I hardly care. Oh, Alec."

He felt her face, wet, against his shoulder and then her lips on his cheek. He felt fiercely protective. "They're not going to get you, Celia," he said. "I won't let them." He turned his face to hers. He found her mouth with his own and they kissed, tentatively at first, then hungrily. It was only minutes before they were lost in each other, blotting out the world.

Afterwards he said, "Thank you," and then, after a pause, "I wish—you know that I'm in love with you, don't you? I think it started way back the first time I saw you." His voice sounded surprised even to himself.

"You just think that because of the way things are, Alec," she said quietly. "But even if it isn't so, I'm not sorry. I'm glad I have been with you, Alec. You give me something to believe in."

They lay with their hands clasped, quiet, looking into the darkness, waiting for the day.


While Celia and Alec watched the light appear over the ocean, Sam Drottman, in Washington, was already at the airport boarding the first plane for Lake City. By nine he sat in Adam Mann's office and heard his protest to Leo. The speaker was on and he could hear Leo's replies. Leo's voice was low and menacing to a degree that Sam did not remember ever having heard before.

"I don't like it, Leo," Adam said. "As your lawyer, I have to tell you it's bad business. This violence stuff gets traced, connections get made, the whole thing is blown."

"This ain't lawyer business, Adam. This thing is bad for the organization. How does it look on the street—a dame snatched right from under the noses of our boys. I tell you, the boys are nervous. They better be. They find her or somebody gets burned."

"But it's counterproductive, Leo," Adam protested. "You didn't learn anything from the hairdresser."

"So maybe the boys got in too much of a hurry. They don't like those fruits any more than I do." Leo's accent was growing heavier, an indication of the depth of his feelings. "But one thing we did find out. He was connected. And we put the fear into whoever was connected with him. Somebody will crack. Don't tell old Leo how to do his business, Adam. And tell that Drottman he'd better get moving at his end. We find that dame or it's all over with Johnny. This is no time for arguments."

"All right, Leo. I understand your point of view." Adam Mann knew that the conversation was over. He replaced the receiver and turned to Sam, spread his hands wide and shrugged.

"You see how it is, Sam," he said. "They're never going to give up on Celia and whoever took her and got her away. If the deals they're interested in are blown because of this—if Celia knows and tells—we'd best all look to our own skins."

"Shall we stay here or go away somewhere, Alec?" Celia asked dispiritedly. She was holding her coffee cup in both hands and staring at the ocean. In an effort to lift her mood he had coaxed her out onto the balcony and brought their orange juice and coffee out there. Here and there on other balconies they could see other inhabitants of the Ocean View who were breakfasting in the same way. They were probably newcomers hungry for the sun. Old-line Ocean Viewers, veteran summer people, stayed inside where the wind would not ruffle the morning paper and they could see the network news.

Below them, pool attendants were setting out deck chairs and readying the cabanas. From somewhere behind them came the sounds of tennis racquets and balls connecting in solid thwacks. Beyond the pool area and over the road lay a narrow strip of beach. A few joggers were taking their morning run on the hard sand near the water's edge. It was difficult to look on such a conventional vacation scene and think that it was charged with menace of any kind. Nevertheless, they were menaced and Alec knew it.

He had been considering their options and he honestly didn't know which was best. He only hoped that his judgment wasn't clouded by the conflict of emotions within him. He was achingly aware of Celia as a woman, and despite his worries he was filled with a surging warm sense of happiness. Just before falling into a light troubled sleep, she had turned to him and said, "I can't be sure of anything now, Alec, but I think I love you, too." The closeness he felt to this woman signaled the end of a long loneliness so habitual that he had not realized its pain until it was gone. At the same time he was seized with a fear of loss. The need to protect her was no longer only his duty. It was his deepest need. He could not lose what he had just found. He could not afford any mistakes.

At Celia's question he tried once again to put his thoughts into the clearest and most logical order. He thought they were secure in their disguises for the time being. Chances were good that Jan Michal had not talked. Alec remembered the stolid stubborn face that had confronted him at their meeting and he was inclined to bet on Michal, but even if the hairdresser had talked, he knew only where Celia had been, that she was in touch with Mrs. Fraser, and that Alec, a Secret Service agent, had been on her trail. With luck Janie Fraser was in Canada and, Alec assumed, well protected from any interrogation except, perhaps, her husband's. Alec did not think Celia's danger came from that quarter. He knew Angus Fraser by reputation. One of Canada's best.

On the other hand, the customary procedure for protecting a witness and the best, those in the services had found in recent years, was to keep moving. The safest thing would be to pack up and go right now. But Alec was operating alone. There was no one to cover, no one to see if they were followed, no one to arrange a swap of cars and a safe house. The Ocean View was not the anonymous place Alec had expected when Janie Fraser talked of a condominium. Everyone from bellman to penthouse owner seemed to know one another or, at least, *of* one another. Any sudden unexplained move on their part would cause comment—idle, perhaps, but it would be remembered. The best Alec could do was to arrange with Boise to have them suddenly sent for on some pretext or other. That could take some time. He would have to cast about for people he was sure he could trust.

"It's a flip of the coin, Celia," he said finally, "but I guess we're best off sticking to the original plan, at least for now. We'll attract less attention if we do than if we don't. Anyway, I rather like being Mr. Campbell to your Mrs. Campbell. Let's enjoy it while we can."

She smiled wanly. "It's just that I don't feel up to making small talk with a lot of strangers, Alec, but I guess you're right." She stood up. "Well, here I go, making myself into Mrs. Campbell as fast as I can." She touched his shoulder lightly as she passed, leaving him feeling absurdly pleased.

At twelve-thirty they took the elevator down to the lobby to meet Mr. LaRocque's party. Celia took one last look into the hall mirror before she got in. "This is the very best suit Janie put in," she said. "Don't I look spiffy?" Even to his untutored eye, she did. The suit was soft and silky. The allover print design on the jacket was in the same pale pink as the faint stripes in the skirt. Her hat was the same color and was, he recognized, of that indefinable quality the cognoscenti call smart. "Very spiffy," he said and squeezed her hand before the doors opened. "Here we go."

He was wary. Celia's feeling that she had been recognized at the track the previous day might have been a false alarm, but he intended to keep a sharp eye out. Mr. LaRocque, standing with a knot of people near the lobby doors, advanced to meet them. "Hello, hello," he said heartily. "We are waiting for the cars. Let me introduce you." Once the introductions were over most of the group seemed to lose interest in Celia and Alec, returning to their chatter in a mixture of French and English. LaRocque himself was obviously intent on the chances of his horse in the Trans-National. The "Campbells" stood alone, a little awkwardly, to one side. Only a small dark woman with bird-bright eyes seemed to notice. She moved toward them.

"A nice costume, that," she said, indicating Celia's suit. "I see that you are interested in our Canadian designs."

"Oh, yes—our cousins have introduced me to them. You are Madame Jacqueline, I think Mr. LaRocque said," she added, proud of her quickness. "You are a designer yourself, I think."

"Quite right. I am Jacqueline." She motioned to a dour-looking man who, like them, had been standing a little to one side. "Come, Louis, join us. I was right about Mrs. Campbell. You must ride with us and we can talk clothes. It is interesting to me to talk with Americans about the market. Why don't you get the car now, Louis," she said, "and we can be first at the helicopters." He moved quickly, without a word to either of them. "Louis is my assistant, you see," she rattled on. "He is very talented but he doesn't speak English well and it embarrasses him." She took Celia's arm. "Let us go out and wait for him, *chérie*," she said, moving toward the door. "You will see, it best to get the first helicopter. They make such a wind and disarrange the clothes and the hair." Celia looked back over her shoulder to see if Alec was following. She gave a small shrug to indicate her helplessness under the onslaught of the Canadian woman's determined hospitality.

The car, when Louis arrived with it, proved to be a small Renault. He was jackknifed into the driver's seat, the steering wheel literally between his knees. Mme. Jacqueline, taking advantage of her tininess, wedged into the back, urging Celia into the seat beside the driver as she did so. Alec stood uncertainly on the curb wondering how he was to fit behind Louis on the other side.

From behind came LaRocque's hearty voice. "I see Jacqueline has taken your lady, dear fellow. You must come with me in the limousine— you'll never cram yourself in there—and we'll be right behind them. Go on, go on," he said to Louis. "We'll see you there, at the helicopter park."

It had all happened quickly, but even if Alec had had more time to think, he would not have been able to prevent it. He saw Celia's rueful face turned back toward him as the Renault pulled away. He waved to reassure her before he stepped into LaRocque's big car. He was never sure afterwards whether LaRocque was party to the thing or not. Neither the police that afternoon nor Canadian intelligence later could make a connection. But when they arrived at the helicopter park the first helicopter had already risen and was turning and banking, fading away to the north and west. It never arrived at the racetrack.

# . 24 .

ALEC MCGREGOR took the first plane to Washington. He had scarcely arrived in the secretary's office and recounted what had happened when Angus Fraser, accompanied by Tom Fergus of the DEA, came into the room. The secretary offered them chairs and introduced McGregor to Fraser. As McGregor shook his hand, he noted that Fraser's color was high and that he seemed nervous.

"Fergus is one I've found we can depend on," said Clem Boise to Alec.

Tom Fergus began without preamble. "Minister Fraser here has been working very closely with us on the big cleanup we have talked about. He has just made a quick trip back here from Canada. I think it would be best if I let him tell you about it."

"I'll make it brief," Fraser said. "Ostensibly, as you probably know, I am the political minister, but in my service I am also in charge of certain intelligence operations. This operation is perhaps of much more importance to my government than to yours. The connections which we have discovered must have existed for over ten years. We have very strong evidence that the money flowing from the sale of synthetic drugs and from a counterfeiting operation goes to subversive elements in our country and many others. You probably know, sir," he spoke to the secretary, but turned to McGregor as he did so, "that we in Canada worked out a policy toward terrorism and crisis planning long before you did. We had more reason. But that is beside the point. The point is that I was one of the first to work on the plan and am now in charge of it. Our operation, which we believe is endangered now by the abduction of Mrs. Mann, was leading us to the man who has masterminded the ring over the years. We are sure we know who he is—in a way he almost declares it and dares us to do something about it—but we do not have hard evidence and it is much more important that we break open the whole network than that we take him in. The reason I have come to you now is that aside from Fergus here, I am not sure who in your agencies can be trusted, and something that occurred today makes me quite sure that Mrs. Mann is in Canada or on her way there. It is important for us that you find Mrs. Mann, but I have personal reasons for wanting you to find her alive." He drew a deep breath. "I think Mrs. Mann was in touch with my wife a few days ago. They have been quite close."

"What did your wife tell you?" asked the secretary, showing an uncharacteristic eagerness. Of course, Boise did not yet know about Janie Fraser's part in Celia's flight.

Fraser flushed painfully. "That's just it," he said, "she didn't tell me anything—but I am sure that I am right." In a few sentences he sketched the circumstances surrounding the telephone call Janie had attributed to Mrs. Steinman and Janie's subsequent hurried departure. "But I have seen her since and she told me that McGregor was with Mrs. Mann and was protecting her. Now I have reason to think this is not so—or is no longer so. We received a call today from a terrorist group. They say they have Mrs. Mann. Is that true?"

The secretary simply nodded. "Things add up," he said. "This confirms McGregor's experiences and his conclusion. He's on his way to catch a plane right now."

"If you don't mind, sir," said Angus Fraser, "I'll go with him. He can fill me in on the way. It will be easier for him, and for Janie, if I'm in Canada, too. And I can assure the cooperation of people who will be more useful to you than your usual contacts," he added directly to McGregor.

So you know about all that, thought McGregor, thinking of his work on the border. He was a little irked. Fraser's tone had been a bit patronizing. But he decided against one-upmanship. There were more important things to concentrate on and Fraser was doing his best to help.

When Sam returned from Ohio he knew that the time had come to level with John Mann about Leo. Things were out of hand and he could no longer protect Mann from the facts.

John Mann stared at the door after Sam had left as if he were expecting him to reappear. But he was thinking of something else. Leo was not the only danger, he knew. He was not a man given to introspection, and he found analyzing his own motives difficult. Sam had been his alter ego for so many years that he was not sure why he had not told him what he had known for days now—that the Drug Enforcement Agency had connected some very highly placed Canadians with the profitable trade in synthetic drugs. He himself did not know whether Maurice Chouinard was one of them, but it was very likely that there were among them men whom Maurice had rewarded liberally for his own purposes. They would be the kind of men who would do anything to cut their losses. They would name Maurice without a second thought, or, if Maurice had not dealt with them directly, they would betray the go-between who would lead the authorities to him.

John Mann thought it more likely that Maurice Chouinard would have dealt with them directly. Although he did not understand himself too well, he was, like most successful politicians, astute in his judgments of other men. He had observed in the past that it gave Dr. Maurice Chauinard obscure pleasure to issue directives—veiled directives, to be sure, but directives all the same—to him, the vice-president of the United States. He guessed shrewdly that the French Canadian in Maurice would delight in suborning English and Canadian officials and gaining power over them. He remembered Chouinard's description of drug distribution in the streets of Toronto. And the deep satisfaction with which he spoke.

"They are young kids from the maritime provinces," he had said. "They are poor like dirt, and they have no connections. You have been there, you have seen how they live?" he had asked John and Sam and they both shook their heads.

"It's not much better than the animals. Men speak of the poor French Canadians on the little farms. Well, they are poor in a different way. They try to raise their little gardens so they have enough to eat. But those people—they are the descendants of smugglers. They can raise nothing. They use the canned milk. They drink. The Americans who come up there and buy land, they say how good-hearted they are, how simple, how the families stick together. And that is true enough. Every once in a while when they need more money, young John Neal MacRae or Roy Boy McNeill will bum his way to the big city—sometimes Montreal, but more often Toronto. They like it where there aren't so many Canucks, you see."

Maurice's face had twisted as he gave wry emphasis to the hated appellation. "They become pushers for a while—they all do a little drugs on the side, anyway, just as their parents dealt in what you call moonshine. And then they drift back. Once in a while somebody doesn't get back. He goes to jail or he is killed. It is a small matter. They live with violence, those people. They are always losing their young to drowning or to car accidents on their bad roads along the sea. Oh yes, they are good for distribution. They have no connections and no records."

Thinking of that and the hatred in Maurice Chouinard's voice, John Mann confronted the fact that he wanted to be free of Chouinard himself. He did not care if Chouinard was the key to Canada. There were other leaders there. It would not be a bad thing if Maurice were entrapped. There was no clear connection between Maurice's illegal activities and himself. Elwood Grant? Sam might have to have Leo deal with Elwood Grant, if anything broke. John Mann was tired of Sam's instructions, too, but there was nothing he could do about Sam. Sam and I, he thought gloomily, are like Siamese twins, and Sam was as safe as he could be because they were so inextricably tied together. Yes, this was probably the time to talk to the men at DEA. He reached for the phone on his desk.

President Batchelder received the vice-president standing. She made no explanation for the presence of Secretary Boise and Director Robard, who also stood, one to her left, one to her right. Nor did she make reference to the uniformed marine officer who sat in his accustomed place.

"Mr. Vice-President," she said abruptly, "how do you explain this?" She gestured toward the marine. He pushed a button. Murat's voice filled the room. Then his own.

His first thought was that Murat—the son of a bitch—had made his own recording and turned it over to the White House.

His second was that the president hadn't known. Had never known.

The agency had used him. For its own purposes. Goddamn them. He had been sold a bill of goods. But why? His anger fought with fear and confusion. His mind scrambled furiously.

"The explanation is right there, Madam President, if that thing hasn't been doctored," he said. He fought to keep the anger out of his voice and was careful to match her formality with his own. "I thought I was carrying out an operation you had approved . . ." The shock effect was wearing off. He wasn't finished yet. The agency could not make him the goat . . . "After all, it isn't the first time the agency has done what a president wanted without involving the highest office . . . Diem, Allende, Nicaragua . . ." He was feeling more confident as he ticked them off.

"You thought *I* wanted to overturn the democratically elected governments of Mexico and Canada? By force of arms?" Lily Batchelder's voice was incredulous.

Put like that—here in this room—it did sound unbelievable. But somehow, in Murat's suave voice, in his careful elliptical phrasing, it had seemed quite reasonable. John Mann knew that he was no fool and he *had* thought the story plausible.

But John Mann's voice was less certain. "That's what I believed, Madam President. I had no reason not to believe it."

"And maybe you wanted to believe," grated the old secretary, breaking the president's stunned silence. "Maybe you were thinking of your arms-dealer friends and your family's and associates' investments." The old man was very angry. This wrong one—this flawed pup who should have been eliminated from the litter—was not going to get away with it anymore. The glibness, the charm, the false sincerity weren't going to work this time. He had seen to that. Lily would hear it all. He nodded at Robard, who took the cue.

"If you believed that the president had such a plan," he said in his dry, precise voice, "why did you suggest the investigation of Maurice Chouinard to DEA? Why cripple the operation, if you thought the president wanted it?"

Boise did not give Mann time to answer.

"I think you should know, too, Mr. Vice-President"—his use of the title was mocking—"that we have pretty good evidence that you were involved in the drugging of your wife—obviously to keep her quiet . . ."

John Mann stood looking from one to the other like a bull harassed by picadors.

President Batchelder had had enough. She cut them off. She was the president. She would handle this.

"We can deal with all this later," she said crisply. "Just now I must see to controlling the damage." She looked at Mann. "I would like you to wait in your office until I send for you again."

He started to protest but she raised her hand sharply. "Not now!" Grudgingly he turned to comply. Two Secret Service men were waiting behind him. Had they been there all the time? They moved smartly to join him, one on either side. The marine officer rose and moved in behind. Guards, not protectors. Lily had phrased it as a request but it was an order. Detained! He was being detained right here in the White House. He went out quietly. He had no choice.

When he had gone she turned to the others.

"Thank you, gentlemen. I owe you an apology. I didn't think it possible—I thought it a forgery or a hoax of some kind." She looked at the director. "You still won't tell me where you got the tape?"

The director shook his head. "I can't, ma'am. Not even if it costs me my job at the bureau. I can ease your mind, perhaps, by telling you that I am the only one there who knows about it." He had promised young Mann and he meant to keep his promise.

The president smiled bleakly. "Very well. Now I have things to do. Would you care to sit on the sofa there?" She moved behind the desk and sat down. She pressed the intercom.

"Get me the chief of staff."

In less than a minute they heard the mechanical growl of the chief's response.

"General," said the president, "listen carefully. The country is in a state of emergency. I want you to put the Air Force at all our Southern bases on alert and all Army ground troops in a state of readiness. Have Admiral Bennington find out what Navy has in the Caribbean and near our West Coast. Whatever it is—carriers, destroyers, submarines—start them moving toward the coast of Mexico. If they're very near have them stay there just outside the twelve-mile limit." Boise and Robard could not hear the words but there was a startled and questioning tone to the answer of the politic army veteran, who had maneuvered himself to the very top of the nation's military, and who probably thought the president of the United States had taken leave of her senses.

"Those are my orders, General Hayden," snapped Lily Batchelder, "and I *am* the commander-in-chief!"

They could hear the words this time.

"Yes, ma'am! I'll get on it."

"And when you've done that come here to my office. I'll fill you in." She pressed the button on the telephone console, which cut him off, and buzzed the intercom again.

"Now, the secretary of state."

When the secretary was on the line she repeated her statement about the national emergency, then continued, "Inform the Mexican ambassador *and* his deputy chief of mission that they are to meet with you in your office at twelve o'clock sharp."

The reply evidently annoyed her. Her voice was sharp.

"Mr. Secretary, I know very well that it is not the accepted protocol to have the ambassador and the minister together, but today that is what I want you to do. And, Mr. Secretary, do whatever is necessary to have a deportation order ready for Minister Hernández-Mateo and two of your security men ready to escort him to the border. Yes, to the *border*—not just to the plane." Her voice was acid now. "When you have complied, Mr. Secretary, come to my office and I will fill you in. You will have to assist the ambassador with a rather complicated communiqué for his president. We will offer him help if he needs it."

Again she pressed the intercom button.

"Get me Prime Minister Baxter, please."

In an amazingly short time the prime minister of Canada was on the line. A modicum of Lily's charm crept back into her voice as she greeted him. "Good morning, Mr. Prime Minister, how are you? . . . Well, not so fine this morning, Mr. Prime Minister. We have received some very disturbing information here. Your ambassador will have the full details for you shortly. But first, Mr. Prime Minister, there is something I need to know. I understand that your agency in cooperation with our Drug Enforcement Agency has launched an investigation of a rather prominent man in your government circles. I assume that you are fully informed on that . . . Yes, that's the one. . . . I see—you are letting him run, as you say, until your men can gauge the extent of the network and uncover as many connections as possible. Very sensible . . . Thank you, Mr. Prime Minister. That helps me with a decision I have to make."

She put down the telephone and turned to Robard and Boise.

"I think, gentlemen, that I will do nothing final about the vice-president just yet. I will not ask for his resignation." Had he snowed her after all? thought Secretary Boise. But her next words allayed his momentary concern.

"I will suspend his official duties, but we will let him run, as the prime minister puts it." She turned to Robard, "Will you convey that to Vice-President Mann? He is free to return to his Capitol office— with appropriate escort. And now," said the president when Robard had nodded and gone out, "I'll have the press secretary in."

As was fitting, President Batchelder's press secretary was a woman.

After her election, the president had exerted every wile she possessed to lure the toughened popular AP reporter who was dean of the Washington press corps to the White House. To the surprise of almost everyone, she had succeeded. Clare Manning's standing with the press had a great deal to do with the president's good relations with them. Manning came into the office now looking very old-shoe in her practical, rather rumpled suit and flat-heeled shoes. She had notebook in hand.

"Yes, Madam President?" she said, and nodded to Boise on the sofa.

"Clare, I want a press release put out as soon as possible. An announcement. Vice-President Mann is being relieved of his official duties to concentrate on the search for Mrs. Mann. The investigation is at a crucial stage and he must give it his full attention. That sort of thing. You know the right words. Not too much. Just enough for a story."

Clare Manning raised her eyebrows but showed no other sign of surprise or curiosity.

"Will do, Madam President." She went out again.

# . 25 .

CELIA MANN climbed painfully out of the tiny aircraft, very conscious of how rumpled the suit she wore had become. She remembered Jacqueline's scornful words as she had left her and boarded the waiting Lear Jet. "To think that Madame had so little interest that she did not know she wore one of my finest creations—made especially for her friend!" Celia herself had been transferred from plane to plane three times, each plane smaller than the one before. This time a car was waiting. It must be the end of the journey.

Marcel was in the car. Frank put Celia Mann in the back and got in beside her. Marcel drove down the street and around the nearest corner. Frank kept looking back. "Yes," he said to Marcel, "their man was out there. I think he checked the plates." Marcel gave an expressive shrug.

"No matter," he said. "They will be changed as soon as we stop."

Frank settled back and looked at Celia.

"You look very nice in those clothes, Marguerite," he said. She felt a surge of irritation. Why did he keep calling her Marguerite? And what difference did her clothes make now? But Frank had merely needed an introductory remark of some kind to lead up to what he had to say.

"I think you should know before we get there," he continued. "We have been called in by the leader of The People. He has"—he paused, feeling for a word—"he has a need for you now."

"Need?" echoed Celia Mann. "What sort of need would he have for me?"

Frank cleared his throat. He was obviously uncomfortable, but he answered directly. "They—he needs to use you as a hostage. We owe him a great deal, and we need his help for our work. You must understand, Marguerite. We could make no other choice. And, to tell the truth, he did not leave us a choice. We will be hostages, too." He continued, "When you left Washington you put us in a bad position, although I know you meant it well."

He speaks as if I were a student or his child, Celia thought. Maybe the reason he keeps calling me Marguerite is that he thinks of me as Marguerite, his creation. He does not seem to realize what he is talking about. But she really did not care.

Celia felt drained and basically incurious. She had only begun to struggle and she had already lost. She thought bleakly of Alec. She had lost him, too. They turned into a narrow passageway, turned again and drew up behind a dark building, where only a dim light glowed. She realized that it was the kind of light that sometimes illuminates door buzzers in apartment buildings. Underneath it was a small brass plate. "Jacqueline Chouinard, Haute Couture." Chouinard! So that was it. Marcel got out, motioned them to go ahead, and then reached around them to press the buzzer. The door slid open and he urged them into the small hallway. There was a tiny, bronze-grilled lift. He opened it for them and said, "They wait on the second floor. I wait here. There are the plates to change and other things."

As the grille closed behind them and the small lift rose, Celia felt raw fear for the first time since she had been taken away from the hospital. I'm afraid now because I was beginning to hope again, she thought. And they caught me so easily.

The room into which they emerged seemed large for such a small building and very brightly lit.

Maurice Chouinard advanced to greet her. He bent over her hand and said with satisfaction, "Madame, we meet again. My sister welcomes you to her home. Unfortunately, it has to be for a very short time. You two have met, I believe."

Jacqueline Chouinard was seated in an elaborately carved Victorian chair. She wore a silken at-home costume and looked, indeed, as if she had not been hundreds of miles away only hours ago. She rose courteously at her brother's mention but said nothing. Pat sat awkwardly in another of the elegant chairs looking out of place. She did not look at Celia. Why, thought Celia, I do believe she has been crying. She was oddly touched. Crying for me? She has not been so toughened by her life after all. A man was standing awkwardly by the mantel. He looked angry and upset. He does not belong here, either, thought Celia. Then she saw the slight pale girl sitting in the half-shadow behind him. Sister Anne Marie! Although she had not seen the novice since that day in the Senate dining room, she recognized her at once. It was for the young and idealistic girl Pat had wept, she knew instinctively, not for Celia after all.

"Sit down, do, please," said Maurice smoothly to Frank and Celia, indicating a small loveseat. "You have not eaten, I understand, and you will have a long night and a journey tomorrow. And you will want to change into something more suitable. My sister will take care of that. There is not much time for a dinner, but Jacqueline has arranged for you to have some of our hearty French-Canadian peasant soup. You will find it nourishing." As if on signal, his sister began clearing the marble-topped coffee table in front of Frank and Celia and drawing a little table up near Pat. Silently, she indicated the armchair beside the mantel to the man standing there and drew up a table for him, too.

A maid came through a swinging door carrying a tray of glasses and a decanter, which she placed beside Maurice.

"But first, an aperitif while I explain things," he said and busied himself with the glasses.

Celia took hers numbly, without thinking. The shock—the terrible dropping feeling inside her—that she had felt upon seeing Maurice was subsiding. But she felt weak and perspiration had broken out on her forehead. She was glad of the drink, whatever it was. She tasted it, glad that her hand shook only a little as she raised it. It was a vermouth, sweet but good. She raised her glass ironically to Maurice.

He smiled. "I am glad that Madame retains her aplomb," he said, "and I am sorry to inconvenience her."

He is playing with us, Celia thought. I will not give him the satisfaction of showing fear. She hoped her voice would be steady as she spoke. "I understand that I have you and The People to thank for my life, Dr. Chouinard."

"We cannot afford to be sentimental, we who work for the oppressed of the world. Let us just say that when I heard of the good sisters' project, it seemed to me that you were worth a good deal more alive, so I thought it best to help. I hope you do not mind if I say that your husband's *confrères* sometimes act a little hastily, without sufficient thought. In the matter of the hairdresser, for example."

Cold and cruel. He was worse than she had thought him. But Celia simply nodded. "I also understand that you hoped to use me as a hostage. I'm afraid"—her voice wavered just a little—"that no one will be willing to risk very much for me. Of course, you may not want very much."

"I think you underestimate your value in the eyes of the world, Madame. Your disappearance has been a blow to the prestige of your great country. It does not look well if they cannot protect the families of high officials at the very gates of your White House, does it? Of a certainty, Madame, your president will risk a great deal to have you back. And, as to what we want in exchange, we want your husband." His voice was icy. "The vice-president allowed himself the folly of thinking that he could betray me—me, Maurice Chouinard, leader of The People—and that I would not know! What foolishness! Did he think I would not have eyes and ears in the Canadian delegation and in agencies of your government as well? It was time for us to make a demonstration of the power of The People in any case. Your long-awaited arrival gives us that occasion."

He looked around the room. "But now we must eat. We have a journey and some of you will have work to do tonight. Our official friend, here," he nodded toward the man near the fireplace, "will have messages to bear and arrangements to make before morning. Oh, yes, he will be very busy."

So that is somebody from the Canadian government, Celia thought. A civil servant. The maid came in bearing steaming cups of soup. Celia Mann was surprised to discover that she was very hungry indeed and that her appetite had not disappeared.

At what he called his office, a modest unnamed suite on one of the top floors in one of the older buildings in downtown Toronto, Angus Fraser busied himself with phone calls and low-voiced conversations with a series of aides who came and went, summoned mysteriously by a means Alec could only guess at. It was clear that Fraser was indeed a man of importance.

Finally, he called Alec in. "It's even worse than I thought," he said. "All indications are that they are planning something big. Perhaps they planned on the arrival of Celia Mann from the beginning, perhaps they only decided recently, but her turning up here now is a signal of some sort. One of our men disappeared today. On his way to meet me at the airport. If we're lucky, he'll turn up with instructions. That's what they've done before in other places. Or, he may turn up dead with the instructions pinned to him. A warning. Frankly, the thing that worries me most is the clout their having Mrs. Mann gives them in your country. We have pretty clear-cut rules here about how far we'll go in responding to terrorism. I regret to say that you do not." He looked at Alec apologetically.

Alec felt a surge of anger. This was Celia Mann he was talking about—Celia in the hands of cold, methodical madmen. And the man talked of how far it was wise to go to get her back! He saw her face as he had last seen it when she got into the car at Ocean View, rueful, forlorn, looking back at him for reassurance. His heart contracted. Careful, he said to himself, careful. Everything depends on being calm, professional, letting them find her so I can help her. Fraser's next words appeased him a little. "If I'd only listened more carefully that morning!" he said, "I might have guessed that Janie had heard from Mrs. Mann. And I could have forestalled all this—saved Mrs. Mann from this."

"We all think things like that," McGregor said. "If I'd had sense enough to realize that Chouinard might turn up in Maine, we wouldn't be in this mess now, either. Maybe we'll catch up before it's too late. I gather there's been no sign of the car sighted at the airport?"

"None."

"Well, I'll have to be in touch with the secretary, as you know. I'll be getting over to the consulate now, if you don't mind. And I'll check back here later to see if there's anything I can do to help."

"Do that," Fraser said absently. "It looks as if I'll be here all night. I can send John over with you if you like."

"No need for that," McGregor said. "You may need him. I'll get a taxi."

Afterward he realized that he should have found it strange that the taxi was so easily available. He was barely out the door when it slid up to the curb and he saw the smiling black face and heard the cheerful "Taxi, sir?" Still thinking of what Fraser had told him and what he was going to say to Secretary Boise, he got in automatically. He gave the address of the consulate.

"Yes, sir, right away, sir," said the driver, "just got to look at my map here. I'm new at this. I just got my license this morning." His cheerfulness was warming. The accent was musical—one of the islands, McGregor thought to himself, a former British possession, no doubt, where citizenship made entry into Canada easy. He waited patiently

while the driver studied the map, then started up. After a few minutes,
McGregor realized that they had left downtown Toronto. They seemed
to be in a warehouse district.

"Look here," he leaned forward and said to the driver, "are you
sure you're not lost? This isn't near the address I gave you."

"Not lost, boss." The driver's voice was still cheerful. "Just got to
stop at my garage."

"Good God, man," McGregor exploded, "I don't have time for that.
Let me out. I'll get another cab." The man's a fool, he thought. He's got
to get back to the garage to find out where he's supposed to go.

But the driver did not stop. "No taxi here, boss," he said. And, peer-
ing out, McGregor could see that he was right. He settled back, fum-
ing to himself.

They came to a building with a few gas pumps outside and a yawning
garage door. The driver turned smartly in and stopped. McGregor
heard the door slam shut behind them.

"What is this?" he asked angrily and got out. The light was dim,
the garage cavernous and shadowy. But he could see the black Mercedes
clearly enough and that people were transferring from it to a van,
which was parked beside it. A stocky, well-dressed man with carefully brushed gray hair moved away from the two vehicles and came
toward him.

"Welcome, Mr. McGregor," he said, "you are just in time. I am
Maurice Chouinard, leader of The People." The tall slender woman
just about to step into the van turned toward him.

"Alec! It's you," exclaimed Celia. She ran toward him. "Oh, Alec,
Alec, I'm so glad. I was so afraid of what they might have done to
you. I thought the same people took you—there in Maine." Her voice
broke. "Such awful men . . . they laughed about killing . . ."

"A touching scene"—Maurice Chouinard's suave voice cut in—"but
Madame should know that we of The People do not kill without purpose. My men, naturally, are of a somewhat coarse nature and will
make their jests. But I fear I must part you once again. I have need
for the services of Mr. McGregor. I think he can ensure that your
president will measure the seriousness of my intentions. Things could
be extremely unpleasant for Madame and the other ladies if he does
not."

Alec cursed silently. He knows how I feel, he thought. He looked
at Chouinard. So this was the spider. A deceptively mild-seeming man

with none of the outward marks of the megalomania that could lead an anonymous unknown to challenge the might of the United States through its president. And yet Alec, hearing the echo of that chillingly matter-of-fact announcement—"I am Maurice Chouinard, leader of The People"—had no doubt that this was exactly what Chouinard intended.

"And now, Madame, it is back to the van," said Chouinard. "If your, ah"—he paused meaningfully and pronounced the next word with a touch of sarcasm—"your *friend* performs his task well, you need have no fear for your life, or his. If not—well, as I have said, my men are somewhat coarse and take a certain pleasure in rendering the justice of The People."

At his nod one of the men near the van advanced and took Celia by the arm. McGregor saw her pale and flinch. He felt unmanned by his own helplessness. How many times had he said it to the recruits in training for just this eventuality—"Never be a hero and endanger others. Never give the creeps an excuse for violence. Remember—they're waiting for one." Now he found himself shaking from his own effort at self-control.

The bombings began in the morning. They spread across the country, meticulously timed, one after the other, so that whole school buildings were blasted and fragmented just before the first children began to arrive. Atlanta. Louisville. St. Louis. Denver. San Diego. Those they called the early birds, some dropped off by their working mothers, and then all the others, crowding from the nearby streets, alighting from the buses, arrived to stand staring into gaping, smoking holes. Boston. Chicago. Minneapolis. Great Falls. Seattle. Then precisely at the same time in each city, identical tapes appeared at the news desks of selected television stations.

In Washington, one appeared in the guard booth at the east gate of the White House. It must have been carried by someone being shuffled through in one of the misnamed VIP tour groups, but no one had seen it dropped or placed. Another was delivered to Joe McClelland of WTEC in the sack of doughnuts and coffee brought to him every morning from the cafeteria across the street. He was trying to work the news of the bombings into the fewest possible words for the upcoming news break and he merely glanced at it as the "gofer" fished it out, but when he saw the almost sedate label in bright red letters "concerning the bomb-ing," he rushed into the recording room with it, motioning frantically to Jim Pullman, the producer, and to Donna Chase, his co-anchor, as he did so. Inured as they were to tragedy and disaster, they were aghast at what they heard. They looked at each other in horror and disbelief.

"Shall we break in now and go with it, Jim?" asked Joe McClelland.

The producer shook his head. "No, this has to go higher up. Play it again. I want to get it exactly clear before I go upstairs."

Reversed and started again, the tape unwound its deadly message spelled out in a toneless impersonal voice.

To the people of America, greetings! This morning begins the Year of The People. To show you that we are powerful, we are everywhere, and we mean to restore the world and its goods to the oppressed everywhere, we are beginning our takeover by blood-less means. But we are prepared to shed blood, if it is necessary. This morning's bombings were of buildings where your children would have been sitting within another hour. Tomorrow, there will be bombings that take lives to show that we are indeed in earnest. It is permissible to sacrifice a few for the many. We are holding five Americans hostage to demonstrate that not only your children but the powerful of your nation are not beyond our reach. We will release them in exchange for Vice-President John Mann. Begin-ning at noon tomorrow, we will kill them, one by one, in very pain-ful ways, unless and until we know that he will be delivered to us. Your president has received our instructions.

"Good Lord!" said the producer, again dumbfounded at what he heard. He turned to the others.

"Who got the tape? Joe? Get Sheila and get to the White House. Donna, you start digging on the hostages—who are they, who knows them? What do their relatives say? You know how it goes."

"Get things started to go with the tape," he said over his shoulder as he started off. "I have a hunch upstairs is going to say go with it at once."

At the White House, the president, Secretary Boise and their advisers had been in conference since six o'clock that morning. Admiral Bickson, head of the National Security Agency, was there. FBI director Robard was there. The head of the National Security Council had taken his place at the table. Only Vice-President Mann was missing. Angus Fraser was with them. They had been warned of the bombings, but had been helpless to prevent them. Angus had been told what was to happen during the night by the Canadian agent, who, according to his expectations, had been released as a courier.

He had not, however, been expecting Alec McGregor, who had arrived with the agent and whose mission was to spell out the situation involving Celia and the other hostages, and to deliver Maurice's instructions for handing over John Mann at the Boston airport. Although Fraser had pointed out that his usefulness to the terrorists was over and that he would be at risk, McGregor had insisted on going back, saying that it was his duty to protect Celia Mann if he could. "He felt very strongly about it," said Fraser. "We had to let him go and honor the order not to follow him."

Fraser had been in immediate touch with Washington and had flown into Andrews Air Force Base in an unmarked plane just before dawn.

They sat around the long table listening to the tape for the third time. The news of the bombings had been like hammer blows. It left them numb. The tape had clicked off and the silence deepened.

Finally, the president lifted her head and looked around at them. Her fine, aristocratic features seemed to have lost definition, and her face sagged with inexpressible weariness.

"Well, gentlemen, what do we do?" she asked, spreading her hands in resignation, "None of your agencies predicted this, none of you seemed to have known of its scope. None of you tried to prevent it. The United States of America is at the mercy of madmen."

No one answered her. Angus Fraser looked around the table. The other men there were either looking down at their hands or staring absently into space. He cleared his throat and addressed the president.

"If I may speak, Madam President?"

The president turned to him with a kind of dull surprise, "Yes, Mr. Fraser?"

Angus leaned forward, "I do not think that the situation is quite as bad as you think, Madam President. It is bad enough and it will get worse before it gets better. But I think we can ride it out. We in Canada have been studying this man for some time. It is true that he is a genius of sorts and the organization he has managed to put together is superior to any terrorist group so far—any terrorist group of the last twenty years, that is. But there have been others like it. The Irgun, for example. Its world support grew because there was a basic justice in its demands and because injustice against the Jews had grown so monstrous. Maurice Chouinard and The People started with a basic wrong and their wide support has grown as the abuse of human rights has grown so monstrous. He has been very clever in his understanding of this and his use of it. He has even been right in some of the things he has done. But he stepped over the line into conscienceless criminality long ago, and his genius has grown into a kind of madness."

Angus paused and looked around the table. His reasoned, careful voice had had its effect. They were looking at him now and there was a sign of hope on some of their faces. He continued, "Every terrorist movement, every guerrilla force, depends on the support of the people around them who are sympathetic but not fully engaged. There are never very many in the hard core, never very many militants. They depend upon a mystique, on convincing people that they are number-less. Every such movement runs the risk of going beyond its support, of moving too soon, of losing the ability of its members to disappear into the populace—'to swim like fish in the sea' as they put it. Clearly, Choui-nard has gone beyond that. He has lost touch with the fact that the people who want to hire cheap undocumented workers, or make their private piles in drug dealing, or the petty officials willing to pad their pockets with bribes, do not really want to kill little children, or innocent adults for that matter. His support will fall away. There will be informers and people seeking to break clear, and my men in Canada will be wait-ing. Your men will be ready here. You, Madam President," he said to Lily Batchelder, "have the great task of maintaining order and calm until that happens."

The president had changed as Fraser was speaking. Her eyes had brightened. Color had returned to her cheeks and her small proud head had lifted as if to a challenge.

Now she said—and the Southern drawl was back in all its mellow-ness—"We thank you, Mr. Fraser. I blame myself. We should not have needed you to tell us that. What you are saying is that we need to buy time."

Secretary Boise stood up, looking very stooped and old. He said heavily, and his words fell with a thud, "And it's up to John Mann to buy it for us, isn't it?"

They had been so close to finding her. And he had been doing what he had always done best—using a crisis to straighten out what needed straightening, shaking things up, getting rid of the rotten wood, finding fine new timber like McGregor—and all for nothing!

I am too old, thought the secretary, too old for this new and terrible world.

The clamor in the press room was deafening. Vice-President John Mann's press conference had been announced for twelve o'clock. For almost an hour, what seemed like the whole of the Washington press corps had been fighting to get into the room. The men and women of the print media were fighting for space in front of the television cameras and shouting insults and cursing the camera and sound men as they did so. The television lights already made the room unbearably hot. Outside, reporters and photographers who had not been able to get into the room lined the corridor, continually breaking through the ranks. White House security guards were threatening to clear them out.

John Mann sat in his hideaway in the Capitol, staring at the statement he had written. And he knew that when he got up from that desk and went out of this room, he would not be coming back. The tape had talked of an exchange of hostages.

It was Sam who brought Secretary Boise's sober message. "The way they said it, it sounds as if they want to hold you until they get the political concessions they want," said Sam. "And the FBI hostage team will be there." The words of the message had been stark: "The president leaves the decision to the vice-president." Johnny Mann smiled grimly. He knew that the president was buying time. He knew that he was expendable. He also knew that there was nothing else the president could do. It made it easier for her—for all of them—that Maurice had talked of his being a hostage. John Mann knew that Maurice was clever enough to have anticipated that. But Maurice did not want a hostage. He wanted revenge. He wanted the men who served him in his own government to get the message that he could not be betrayed, not even by a vice-president of the United States of America.

Sam was talking, trying to fill the terrible silence between them. "That one woman hostage they wouldn't identify—the newsboys think it must be Celia. It sounds like Celia, doesn't it? That's one thing we figured wrong—I never thought it could be Maurice who took Celia."

John Mann nodded. It was Celia; Celia was Maurice's final insurance. If he, John Mann, were to let Celia die . . . There was a certain rough justice in that. It probably appealed to Maurice's sense of humor. It was like Maurice's image of himself, the courtly gentleman forced to extreme measures, to respect Celia's need for anonymity. Maurice knew what his allies were made of and he had Adam's measure, as well as that of Johnny Mann.

Sam spoke again uneasily. "We're going to be a little late and they're howling over there." As John Mann got up and took his statement from the desk, Sam added hesitantly, "What are you going to tell them, Johnny?"

"That I'll make the meet, and the exchange," said John Mann.

"I'll go with you," Sam offered.

John Mann shook his head. "You and I got beyond that sometime back, Sam," he said and went out the door without looking around. Joe Manfuso and the other agents assigned to guard and protect him fell in behind, symbols of a government now become a helpless giant.

They jolted along in the cold van huddled together for warmth, each lost in her own thoughts. They were alone because Alec had been sent away with the Canadian and Frank had gone off with Chouinard. Celia spoke first. "They killed Yanni . . . I suppose you know. In a horrible way."

After a minute, Pat's voice came out of the darkness, "It's terrible, but not as terrible as you think. When it gets too bad, your mind goes away out of your body."

Celia spoke out of her new fear and despair.

"Can you pray, Pat?" Celia asked. "I can't. It seems to me that God has gone away. That Jesus is an illusion."

"Oh, Celia," said Sister Anne Marie. Celia knew that she was crying quietly.

There was a long silence. Then Sister Patricia answered, "Yes, I guess I pray. Not to the Jesus hanging on the cross whose suffering they used to try to work us up about. But to the Jesus I saw there in South America. Jesus in his little ones.

"I was supposed to teach the catechism to them, you know—the men they worked like brutes on the hillsides of the coffee plantations, men who knew no other way of bringing the crop to market but walking barefoot on rocky paths, bent double under baskets loaded with twice their weight.

"And there were the women, half-starved, up before dawn feeding the

children what little they had and scratching hopelessly at the little patch
of garden, then walking miles, one child under their belt and another at
their breast, to work all day picking under the sun and walk back again
as the darkness came—if they were lucky, with a peso or two to turn
over to their men and maybe a sack of beans to boil and mash for the
children's supper. And no rest in the night—at night their men fell on
them to prove their manhood and the hungry babies cried, and the next
morning it started all over again."

Her voice went on, tonelessly. "They were the Jesus I know. After
they had pulled out my fingernails and I was spreadeagled on the bare
springs of the cot in the cell and they came at me with the cattle prods, I
thought of them and what would happen to them if I betrayed the people
trying to help them."

Celia felt her shift restlessly on the hard seat. Then her voice came as
if from a distance. "Who knows, maybe that was sharing in the suffering
of Jesus as we were taught. He did say, 'Whatsoever you have done for
the least of these, you have done for me.' Maybe the reason he only
talked about giving them food and drink was because he knew we could
not stand knowing what else we would have to do on their behalf. Or
maybe even *he* could not imagine what man would do to man . . . and
do . . . and do . . . over and over . . ."

"I see what you mean," said Celia, "I guess I do. Christ lives in His
people. But the people trying to help the poor and the desperate . . . if
you mean people like these . . . like Maurice Chouinard and these men
here . . . if they're The People, they seem as bad or even worse than the
others. Did you know they were like that? That they helped us only to
make us hostages? Why Pat, I think they're going to start a war! Hundreds, thousands, maybe millions will be killed. How could our God
want that?"

Another silence. They seemed to rock back and forth jarringly through
an endless night. Finally Pat answered.

"I have been thinking about that a lot lately. In South America I knew
good men and women who loved their people and were willing to give
up their lives for them. These—The People—aren't like the good ones
there. These only seem to want power. I see that. But it is true, too, what
you say—even there many of the little people died. Their villages destroyed. Their young men taken. And the people fighting for them
seemed to get as cruel as the people who would not let them grow and
change and help themselves . . . I don't know what to think anymore . . ."

She said this quite tonelessly. Her voice trailed off. Incredible as it was, she seemed to have fallen asleep. Celia could hear her even breathing. On her other side, she heard Sister Anne Marie.

"Celia, I don't understand French, but I know the driver talked about taking us somewhere. Where do you think we're going?"

"Toward Montreal, I think," said Celia.

"What do you think they're going to do?"

"You heard them, Anne Marie, they're going to exchange me—us— for Johnny somehow—or try to . . ." She was seized with sudden resolve. "But I'm not going to let them. I won't go. They'll have to kill me first." But even as she said it the faces rose up . . . Susie . . . Peter . . . and Alec . . . oh, Alec, Alec . . . it was not so simple.

"They will try to rescue us, Celia. I know they will. They know more about that now—how to save hostages, I mean. Maybe no one will have to die . . ." Sister Anne Marie's voice trailed away into uncertainty.

Celia felt a faint hope rising. It was possible. Alec would try to bring the nightmare to a halt. He would try. Sister Anne Marie took her hand.

"Celia," she said, her young voice scarcely more than a whisper, "Celia, pray with me." She began, her voice rising and falling in the familiar cadences of the rosary. At first Celia did not respond, but after a while she joined in.

"Hail Mary . . . blessed art thou and blessed is the fruit of thy womb, Jesus.

"Holy Mary . . . pray for us now and in the hour of our death."

Sometimes prayers were answered, Celia thought. Sometimes. She held to the thought. "Our Father, who art in heaven," she prayed, "deliver us from evil . . ."

But when they finally reached the lonely airstrip carved out of the fir and birch somewhere north of Montreal, Frank and Maurice were waiting and Alec was also there. He had returned and was a hostage, too, like themselves. He brought news of the bombings and of the hapless threatened with annihilation by The People. The children. The sick in the hospitals. There could be no question of resistance. No refusal to go. Not now.

They boarded the plane together in the first gray light.


The old secretary had come up in the plane with the vice-president. There was one hope left and he clung to it. It came within the realm of his responsibility. Fraser had found a defector during the night. Under interrogation the man had revealed that there was a plan for "The

Boston Operation" at "headquarters"—a plan and a map. For hours Fraser's men had been searching for it.

"We've set up a communications room in the control tower," said the mayor when he met them. "All channels from there are cleared, of course. Our men are waiting for you right now. Mr. Higgins here will escort you while I go on to the rendezvous point with Vice-President Mann."

The mayor was flushed and nervous. "You understand, don't you," he said, as they walked toward the terminal, "that it's a very slim chance. We don't have the demolition men to work simultaneously on multiple locations. Even with the bomb squads you sent in last night. And even if we get the locations it will be touch-and-go. All sites will have to be cleared for blocks around. And we'll have to get the sick children and old people out—and the people in whatever other locations the bastards have targeted. Frankly, I don't think we have a Chinaman's chance of doing it."

The communications chief at Logan was frankly admiring when the FBI equipment was in place.

"State-of-the-art, state-of-the-art," he kept saying, repeating the current phrase like a shibboleth. "And so small!"

Even the taciturn FBI man could not resist agreeing. He was proud of his equipment. "Triple split screen," he said. "Patched into the president's office, our decoders, and the prime minister's."

"There's a signal now," said his assistant excitedly.

His chief tapped out the requisite password. With what seemed agonizing slowness to the secretary, names began to ribbon out in the green glow of the center screen.

"It's the list, it's the list—they've got the locations!" shouted the assistant.

"All right," said the Boston police officer at the phone bank. "Call 'em out. I'm relaying."

# THE EXCHANGE

I T WAS A fine, clear, bright May afternoon at Logan Airport. The
farthest runways shimmered in the morning sun. There was an unusual stillness. All air traffic had been halted. The only movement was
that of the sails of a few boats moving slowly along the edge of the landing area. Logan literally sat on the sea, thought John Mann. Those boats
must be crewed by members of the hostage team. All others would have
been warned away. He did not find the thought consoling. It had been
fifteen minutes now since the last word from the tower. He had no hope.

They could hear the plane from Montreal before they could see it,
and when it touched down lightly, handled skillfully by the unknown
pilot, they did not speak as they watched it taxi slowly toward them. It
stopped with a final scream of the jets, still far off, but directly opposite
the entrance where they were clustered. Only then did the small knot of
people move out slowly from the doorway. The plane door had swung
open. They were stopped by the amplified voice, metallic, echoing and
disembodied, which seemed to emanate from a dimly discerned figure in
the darkness beyond.

"Stop! So far. No farther. We will let you see your hostages first."

A chain ladder clattered from the door and hung swaying. One by
one they clambered down—two men, three women. They stood as they
had clearly been ordered to do, facing the airport, seeming to shrink
from the brightness of the day.

The voice boomed out again.

"Listen. Listen carefully. I speak once and once only. We want in
exchange only one man. You know who he is. When he has come close
enough, we release the hostages. You will make no tricks. Our friends
in your city have planted twenty bombs in your institutions. One trick

**319**

and they go off, one by one, and hundreds die. Now I give the word. I count to ten. One, two, three . . ."

Behind him the mayor groaned. "They mean it—that school this morning . . . just to show us . . . three children dead. We don't have time . . ." With a shrug John Mann threw his jacket over his shoulder and stepped clear of the others.

He walked steadily and slowly. He had known from the clipped accent that the voice was that of Maurice Chouinard. It was only a matter of time now. The account would be settled here on the tarmac or there in the plane. He thought the sky more blue than he had ever seen it and tried to think only of that.

There must have been a signal. The hostages were coming toward him. Their pace quickened as they passed him—the solid, tall man, a young woman weeping inconsolably, a small, thin woman with curly gray hair, oddly ducking her head. But the tall woman, French-looking in chic black, the sun glinting on her red hair, kept to a walk. And behind her, Alec McGregor. They neared each other at the same measured pace, their steps on the tarmac almost in time.

He could see her blue eyes now, steady and watchful. Watchful. Why not? he thought. She had no reason for trust. John Mann did not pause or turn his head as he passed her.

He heard her footsteps falter. "Oh, Johnny . . ." It was half a sob.

He looked straight ahead but spoke into the air. "Don't be sorry. It was all over anyway."

He heard her smothered cry. Then he heard her footsteps quicken. Her voice lingered in his ears as he went on—the last trace of love, the last of human sounds, he thought.

He heard rather than saw Alec McGregor stop dead in his tracks and, almost at the same time, the shout from behind him, "They're clear! They're clear! Everybody's out!" He caught a glimpse of men and vehicles rushing toward the plane from the bay side.

He saw bursts of smoke cloud around the plane as the smoke bombs rained around it, and the tail explode as a small rocket hit. He heard Alec's heels hit the tarmac and felt the bruising impact of his tackle. The last thing he saw was Maurice with the lifted submachine gun wreathed in smoke but clear and distinct in the plane doorway.

The watchers saw them hit the ground. Alec McGregor was on top of Mann for a moment but jerked and rolled aside as the first burst hit. The second raked John Mann's body. They saw Maurice crumple and fall as one of the snipers finally got the range. Then it was very quiet. Alec McGregor and John Mann lay side by side in the sunlight.

"You have no choice," McGregor had said to her on the plane. "You are not alone. There are the others. We do what we have to do."

"But"—she had whispered it to him weakly because she did want to live, more than ever—"He did say, 'Greater love no man hath . . .'"

"Give your husband that then"—Alec's voice was sober as he took her hand in his—"give him that, if you have to. It may be all there is left."

# EPILOGUE

"**D**AY IS DONE . . ."

The notes of the bugle rose—mellow, piercing, mournful—high into the reaches of the Capitol Rotunda.

"Gone the sun . . ."

She stood next to the flag-draped coffin with Peter and Susan on either side. Susan gripped her hand tightly as if she would never let go. Behind her stood Bill Cratte at attention and her Aunt Susan Raley. She had wanted no one else. Behind them in serried rows crowded the members of the House and Senate and their wives.

"From the lakes, from the hills, from the sky . . ."

Across from her stood the president, head erect, hand on her heart as was correct, and Secretary Boise, looking old and stricken. So she herself had stood yesterday at the end of the simple ceremony at Arlington.

She had faced Alec's mother and father. They supported each other, one as frail and elderly as the other, but dry-eyed and proud. She had seen his sister, weeping softly—with the same fresh-cheeked, Scots face. Her husband held her arm tenderly, and the two boys looked sober and very sad. The younger one looked absurdly like his uncle . . .

"All is well. Safely rest . . ."

The tears streamed unchecked down her cheeks. Peter put his arm around her and pulled her to him. He was so tall now, like his father.

"He did the right thing in the end, didn't he?" he said in a choked voice.

"He did the right thing in the end," she said.

But she was not thinking of his father.

As the wives of United States senators and presidential candidates, ABIGAIL MCCARTHY and JANE GRAY MUSKIE have both been intimately involved with the Washington political scene and with national election campaigns.

Abigail McCarthy is the author of two other books: *Circles*, a best-selling novel, and *Private Faces, Public Places*, a memoir. She is a frequent contributor to newspapers and magazines ranging from the *New York Times* "Hers" column to *Commonweal*.